Maybe it's not the worl~~~

adjustment or two it's what the world might be.

—Thomas Pynchon, *Against the Day*

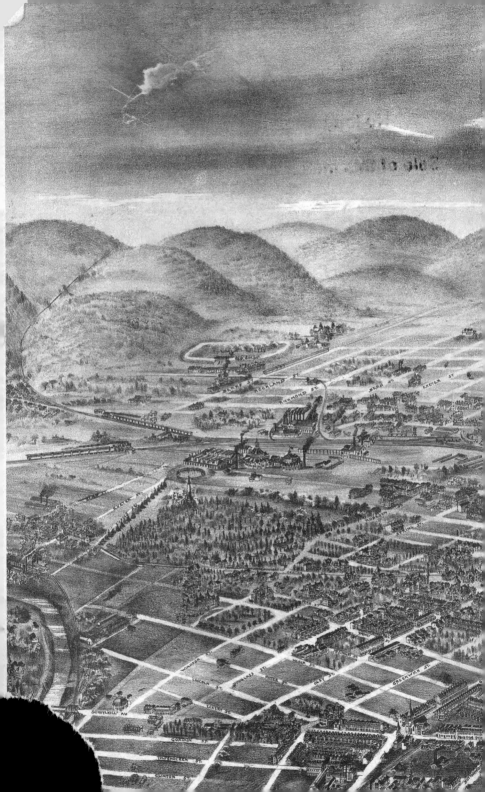

The Pennsylvania Coalfields
June 16—June 18, 1877

Chapter One

he three men were moving fast, in single file, dashing across the patches of stark moonlight and into the safety of the shadows like night creatures with an owl at their backs.

"Jasus, Mary and Joseph!" grunted the tail-ender, a fire-plug of a man clutching a sawed-off shotgun. "If I stub me toe on one more rock I'll blow the bastard thing to smithereens!"

"Shut yer gob, Bertie," hissed the man in the middle, "and mind McCool's satchel or it's us ye'll be blowing to smithereens."

The man in front paused for a moment, shifting a heavy carpetbag from one hand to the other before he turned to look at them. Despite a bushy walrus moustache and a black slouch hat pulled down nearly to his eyebrows, his face looked disarmingly boyish, but the other two seemed to know better. They fell silent instantly, trading uneasy looks.

"You'd best save the gassing for Maloney's," he whispered, so softly he could barely be heard over the rustle of the breeze in the trees and the busy hum of the cicadas. "Remember, there's supposed to be a new watchman and he may not be a rumdum like Timmy was." He motioned to them to follow and slipped away into the darkness.

1

Meanwhile, in a brightly gaslit parlor on the other side of town a pair of onetime lovers stood glaring daggers at each other, teetering on the edge of violence.

"I told you before," the woman hissed, "you and me are *through*. You have a hell of a nerve sneaking up the back stairs in the night like a dog in heat. If it's deaf you are now, I'll say it again louder: I don't *want* you here no more!"

The big man gave her what he hoped was a winsome smile: "You know you don't really mean that, angel cakes, you always say things you're sorry for later when you get mad."

Mad *hell*, she thought, she was just getting warmed up. She caught his eyes fixing on her breasts where they showed in the V of her negligée and pulled the gown together with a disgusted growl. There had been a time when she'd found that little-kid grin of his endearing, just like that touch of an accent that he'd never quite managed to lose. Now either one was enough to make her want to twist his nose.

The big man could see her expression hardening and he felt his own anger breaking through despite his determination to sweet-talk her.

"I expect you'd rather be billing and cooing with your pretty little boyfriend, is that it?" He sneered, biting the words off and spitting them at her: "You and him all lovey-dovey, and no more thought of *our* good times than the man in the moon!"

She rolled her eyes scornfully: "Pretty? That pretty little boy could cut your gizzard out as soon as look at you, and don't you forget it!"

The big man felt the blood rising in his face; he knew he was skating too close to the edge, but he couldn't keep back his hand as it flew up to strike her.

2

"Go on," she screamed, "hit a woman like the big ugly coward you are. But you'd best kill me when you do or you'll rue the day!"

He froze, stopping himself by a tremendous effort of the will and letting his hand fall back slowly to his side. "Damn it, woman, I've always loved you," he said thickly. "You know that."

She folded her arms on her chest and gave him a flat stare. "You love sticking your peter in me, that's what I know," she said in a voice cold enough to crack granite. "The only *person* in this world you love is the one whose nasty mug you shave every morning, and I gave up hoping I could change that a long time ago."

His thoughts felt heavy and sluggish with rage: should he have one last go at loving her up and bringing her around, or should he just say to hell with it and give her the beating she had coming? He rolled his shoulders ominously, lowered his head and moved towards her . . .

○━┰

The man with the carpetbag held up his hand for the other two to stop. For some minutes they had been moving along a white picket fence that bordered the road until finally they came in sight of a large, rambling Victorian house set back from the fence by a hundred yards or so of flower-bordered flagstone path.

The moonlight bathed the white shingles of the house so that it glowed like an apparition, but the windows of the upper stories showed a murky gloom that made all three men uneasy. To make it worse, a long verandah ran along the front of the house, its roof interrupting the moonlight so that it cast everything below it into inky darkness and made it seem as if the whole house was settling slowly into a black sinkhole.

"There's niver a copper up there," quavered the man with the shotgun, "the useless shite's ta home in . . ."

The leader turned on him angrily and cut him off with a hand over his mouth. He waited a second to make sure the message had been received, then he squatted down and opened his bag, taking out three calico flour sacks with holes cut for their eyes. He tugged his over his head, handed out the other two, then bent over the bag again and took out three bundles of dynamite, each with a long spool of wire attached to it. Finally he took a blasting machine out of the bag, attached the wires from all three bundles to it, and set it down carefully at the bottom of a drainage ditch that ran along the fence.

Now he beckoned to the other two, handing each of them a bundle of dynamite and a spool of wire. He bent towards the one with the shotgun and put his mouth directly to his ear as he whispered:

"Be a good lad and leave the blunderbuss here, will you, Bertie? And don't be stubbing your toe and falling down on that dynamite or we'll be meeting next in Hell."

The other man frowned sulkily and laid his shotgun against the carpetbag. The leader picked up his own bundle of dynamite and started towards the front door, unspooling the wire as he went. The other two were fanning out to either side, following a plan they had rehearsed till they could do it in their sleep. Even so they walked on tiptoe, sticking to the grass for silence and jumping at every little nighttime noise.

For a few moments, everything went as smooth as butter. Then, someone stepped on a windfallen branch that broke the hush with a crack like a pistol shot. The three men froze, staring towards the darkness at the front of the house like mice watching for a cat. One heartbeat, another . . . then there was a sharp, ringing metallic CLICK! and a pair of glowing red eyes pierced the gloom and swiveled slowly towards the noise of the snapping branch, whirring loudly as they moved.

"Aw, shite!" wailed Bertie. "A fookin' *Acme!*"

4

The leader's voice snapped at them like a whip: "Bertie, Fergus, don't budge—those things follow *movement!*"

"To hell with that and you too, Liam McCool," yelled Fergus, "I'm *hooking* it!"

Throwing down his bundle of dynamite, he took off wildly across the lawn, his arms pumping like pistons, and as he did heavy footsteps slammed across the verandah until a hulking figure appeared at the top of the stairs.

Seven feet tall, unnaturally precise in its movements, dressed in the blue serge uniform of the Coal and Iron Police and bald as an egg, the creature's glowing red eyes stared out of a shiny pink porcelain face as expressionless as a chunk of pig iron. Slowly its head swiveled to follow the hysterically fleeing man and its eyes glowed an even more intense red as it whirred and clicked into a crouching position.

"Aw, hell!" muttered McCool, reaching for his pocket.

In the same moment, the creature sprang upwards, leaping through the air for a good fifty feet and landing with an appalling thud not far behind his prey:

"*HEEEEEEEEEEELP!*" screeched Fergus.

McCool pulled a Colt Peacemaker out of his pocket, aimed it carefully and fired towards the "Acme." The heavy slug struck it square in the back and it stopped running abruptly and turned its glowing eyes towards McCool as Fergus, momentarily reprieved, disappeared into the night howling like a banshee.

"Fook me!" groaned Bertie through chattering teeth, "I ain't stickin' around for no . . ."

"Yes you are," said McCool flatly. "I need you. Give me your dynamite and don't move an inch or I'll put the next bullet between your deadlights."

The creature started stalking back towards McCool, picking up speed with each step as Bertie moaned with terror.

"Shut up," McCool said. "I'm going to run towards the house and get the thing to follow me. As soon as you see I've got its attention you get down in that ditch with the blasting machine and when I sing out 'NOW!' you push that plunger home! Got it?"

"Aw, shite!" Bertie sobbed.

"Good," McCool said and took off at a run towards the house, pistol in hand and both bundles of dynamite stuffed in his jacket pockets.

For a moment, the "Acme" came to a full stop, its head swiveling and whirring as it looked back and forth between the two men; then it turned and loped after McCool in great, thudding bounds.

"Jesus, Mary and Joseph!" muttered Bertie as he crossed himself. Then he turned and sprinted like a racehorse for the drainage ditch . . .

"You remember?" the big man asked hoarsely. "You remember how it was with us?"

He was holding her close, his hands under her gown, running up and down her back and cupping her buttocks as he buried his face in her breasts. Thinking at the same moment: *By God, she knows how crazy I am about her, how could she let herself be bedded by that young whelp? I swear I'll kill the both of them before I let him have her again . . .*

At the same time she was thinking: *I remember how it was, all right, in another second I'll be lying down on the floor for him, right here on my own carpet in my own sitting room. I was stupid to let him put his hands on me, he can fire me up as easy as starting coals with a bellows . . .*

"There, now," he muttered through the thickness in his throat, "there now, little girl . . ." He pulled her gown up around her waist and then let go for a moment to fumble for his buttons. But it was a fatal delay, just long enough to let her self-control flood back. She pushed him away sharply:

6

"Get away from me, I mean it!"

He stood there stunned. "What the hell are you saying, woman?"

"I'm saying I'm not handing over my diary and you're not getting anything *else* either," she rasped. "Now sling your hook and get to hell on out of here. My true sweetheart treats me like I'm *somebody*, and if you studied on it from here to the Last Trump you wouldn't have no idea what that means."

"You're *somebody* are you, you brainless cow?," he roared, grabbing her and pulling her close again. This time, though, she had crossed from passion into fury and she punched him in the ear hard enough to make him howl with pain and let her go. In an instant she was across the room at her desk, jerking open a drawer and pulling out a stubby, nickel-plated revolver.

"Get out," she shrieked, "get out before I shoot you right in your dirty bollocks!"

He moved heavily towards her, barely registering her words, not even caring about the shiny little gun as the fury rose in his head and flooded his brain. . . .

○—ェ

McCool leapt up the front steps two at a time, trying to stay calm as the thudding steps of the "Acme" got close enough to shake the ground under his feet. God knows how much those things weighed, but he had just seen that their steel skins were thick enough to stop a slug from a .45 Colt. As for their power . . . he tried not to shudder, remembering an "Acme" he'd run into one night on a Wall Street bank job. He'd tied up a horse and buggy in a back alley for his getaway but before he'd gone a hundred yards the filthy thing had caught up with them and torn the screaming horse to pieces like you'd unjoint a chicken.

McCool spun around on one foot and drove the other into the front door, so hard that it came off its hinges, flew into the vestibule and slid across the floor. Without a pause, he followed it inside and dropped his bundles of dynamite into an elephant's-foot umbrella stand as he tore on through the house to the kitchen and out the back door. A moment later, he heard the crashing footsteps of the "Acme" as it followed him inside.

Continuing his mad dash, around the house now and back towards where he'd left Bertie, Liam crossed his fingers mentally. Henry Royce was a first-rate mechanic and his Manchester factory had made the Acme line the top automatons on the market for durability and effectiveness; Liam just had to hope the limey still hadn't figured out how to make them *smart*.

He cleared the house and started back down the lawn towards the road, where he could just make out the top of Bertie's hat sticking up out of the ditch. The sounds of wood smashing and glass breaking from the inside of the house seemed to point to the thing being convinced that Liam was still in there with him, but on the other hand why push it?

"NOW, BERTIE!" he bellowed, simultaneously belly-flopping on the grass and covering his head with his hands. An instant later there was a stupefying thunderclap and a flash as bright as day as the explosion picked Liam up and blew him across the road like a dry leaf . . .

The woman in the negligée was badly frightened now. She had known the big man back in the city before ever she came here, longer than any of the people in Henderson's Patch had known him, and she had never seen him like this. Sure, he was excitable; maybe all the more so because he made such a fetish of being strong and steady and hard to rile. And all the while it made the pressure build, like a steam boiler with no relief valve, so when he finally blew he made one hell of a big noise. But not like this. This time he looked *crazy*.

"All right, then," she said, angry that she couldn't keep a tremor of fear out of her voice. "There's no need for us to be enemies, why don't we just have a glass of whiskey and talk things over . . ."

He grinned at that, but the look of his eyes made her blood run cold. Then he started towards her—calmly, purposefully, still grinning a little as he tore off his shirt, then the cotton singlet he wore under it. The thought flashed through her mind that he was going to rape her, and instinctively she pulled back the hammer of the little pistol. The big man paid no attention. As he threw his singlet to the floor he leapt towards her, grabbing for her gun hand and wrenching her arm aside.

For a moment she fought him hard, harder than any man had ever fought him, raking her nails across his chest till she drew blood, and then trying to force her arm around so that she could shoot him. But at the last moment, when she was within a hand's breadth of putting the muzzle of the pistol into his armpit, his bulk and strength overcame her and a moment later there was a muffled thud as her eyes flew wide open and a strangled cry escaped her. Then her body went completely slack and the big man pushed her away from him in a spasm of horror and nausea.

"Ohmygod," he muttered in near hysteria, "*Ohmygod, ohmygod!*"

As if in answer a stupendous explosion split the night, shaking the house like an earthquake, smashing the windows and knocking books and pictures to the floor. For a moment the big man just stood there with his jaw hanging open, struck to stone. Then he flew into action, the craziness melting away like wisps of smoke as his mind was seized by a single, burning thought: *"escape!"*

o—⌐

For a few moments Liam lay in the middle of a dense patch of bushes, stunned and deafened as bits of board, brick,

9

upholstery and God knows what all rained down around him. Then he forced himself to his feet and looked for his men: there was Bertie, the eejit, cowering in the ditch like Judgment Day had come, while Fergus was God alone knew where—probably in Philadelphia by now.

"Stir your stumps, dammit!" Liam yelled, "five minutes and the coppers will be swarming us like flies!"

He ran back across the road, retrieved his satchel and opened it, beckoning to Bertie to join him as he pulled out a folded bed-sheet, a box of carpet tacks and a hammer. Then he crossed to the gate, reached up with one hem of the sheet and tacked it to the crosspost overhead, handed one of the dangling sides to Bertie and tacked it to an upright while he held it, drove a couple of tacks into the remaining side and stepped back to admire his handiwork.

The designs at the top were plain as day in the moonlight: a crudely drawn obvious coffin next to an equally simple revolver. Below the symbols, in six-inch-tall letters, were painted the words:

"NOW, MR. BLACK LEG HINDERSON WE WARRANTED YE BEFORE AND WE WILLNT WARIND YOU NO MORE. CLEAR OUT OF THE COALFIELDS RITE NOW OR NEXT TIME WE COME CALLING WHEN YER TA HOME.—M. M. 16 OF JUNE 1877."

With a little nod of satisfaction, Liam stuck the hammer, the tacks, the loose wire and the blasting machine back into the satchel, then dusted off his hands and turned to Bertie:

"All right, then, me old son," he said with a grin, "we've had our Fourth of July, now we'd best get home and get our beauty sleep."

He slapped Bertie on the shoulder, grabbed his bag and melted way into the night.

Chapter Two

iam McCool trotted briskly along the forest path listening to the monotonous screeching of the katydids, watching the yellow streaks of the thumb-sized lightning bugs that flitted here and there, smelling that cloying flowery smell that always seemed to come out at night here in the sticks and thinking that Central Park was all the Nature anybody really needed. Plenty of leaves, birds, noisy bugs like those pests sawing away in the bushes there—just the thing if you were in the mood for it.

Liam cursed as one of the big lightning bugs zipped past his ear. Back in the city everything was a decent, normal size, or at least it had been when he left. Not like those lightning bugs and the rest of the freakish creatures he'd started seeing around here a while back. He dodged another grotesque bug and shuddered in spite of himself.

People were saying the bizarre fauna had started after Stanton strung up the leaders of the Iroquois uprising, that it was all down to Indian "medicine." Crazy? A really bad thought, anyway—there were a lot of damned mad Indians around since Stanton picked up where Andrew Jackson's Indian Expulsion had left off . . .

Liam jacked up the pace of his jog, desperate to leave Nature behind and get indoors, where he could at least *imagine* city life. True, he did have a pal or two back home who insisted on dragging him out to the Park to make him play Walden, but when they finally got fed up with the bugs and greenery, he could escape back out to Fifth Avenue, see crowds of people, read a newspaper with today's news (here in Henderson's Patch a week old was a new paper), buy himself a beer and a sausage and generally live in 1877 instead of the Middle Ages. Liam had grown up in Five Points, in a Mulberry Bend tenement, and they had all the Nature you could use there only mostly the human kind and enough of that to keep m. de Balzac busy scribbling novels till his hand fell off.

Liam chuckled. He was really sick of Henderson's Patch and pleased as Punch to be leaving. He might as well have been on the moon during these past months as an unwilling snoop for the Pilkington Agency. The only links to the outside had been the private wire at Boylan's saloon and the line that Henderson's Anthracite leased on the Government Wire, so he'd had to go twenty miles to Pottsville if he wanted to send a telegram back to the city. Not that there was much point in it most of the time, since Secretary Stanton's Eyes read everything on all the wires everywhere and you couldn't say "boo!" on one of them without expecting a knock on your door later on.

A series of thunderous hoots sounded in the distance— the steam whistle at Henderson Anthracite's pit-head calling out the volunteer fire department. Liam smiled wryly. There'd be hell to pay over blowing up Henderson's house, by tomorrow the town would be crawling with Coal & Iron bluecoats like when you kick an anthill. And if the coppers got their hooks into him they'd never believe he'd nearly talked himself blue in the face to keep the Lodge from blowing up Henderson himself along with his house. He'd had to work his jaw like Moody and Sankey preaching hellfire before Boylan agreed to play it smart instead, to warn Henderson that the Mollies had his measure instead of killing him.

And then there was that damned Acme. Liam rolled his eyes just thinking about that miserable hunk of boiler plate. He had seen at a glance it was one of the special calorium-fuelled ones with all the works inside instead of the standard model with the firebox on its back. The new ones could go forever without being refuelled, all you had to do was give them water for steam every eight hours. The trouble was, no matter how desperately everybody else tried to discover it, only the Brits had hit on the secret for refining calorium from pitchblende—which meant that Royce could charge what he liked for his "Imperial" Acmes. So far only the Government in Washington was allowed to buy calorium, which meant he'd just blown up one of the Department of Public Safety's most expensive toys and they'd be way madder about that than if he'd murdered somebody.

There was a sudden racket of something big thudding through the woods nearby and Liam skidded to a halt like a Steamer with its brakes jammed, dropping to his knees and listening with taut concentration. There'd been a lot of talk lately—hushed talk, looking-over-your-shoulder talk—about strange animals roaming at night, stuff right out of the Delaware Indian legends. Like he'd heard the other day from Paddy Delahanty, a miner whose wife went batty after seeing an owl with a thirty-foot wingspan carrying off a bleating sheep. And truth to tell, the lightning bugs and those pesky katytids were just as bad as the big critters—he'd seen a katydid in the bushes at Maggie's the other day damn near as big as a nickel stogie, not to mention which, Maggie's lodger Kreutzer had said they'd taken to *stinging* now. Who ever heard of stinging grasshoppers?

Damn this place, anyhow! At night in the city you might run into a pack of boozed-up Hudson Dusters looking for trouble, or a hold-up man with a twitchy finger, or maybe even a couple of Eyes trolling the saloons for seditious talk—all bad enough, sure, but he'd rather take his chances with them any day than with some ridiculous yokel nightmare of giant birds and bugs. And ye gods, what was that *smell?* Liam wrinkled his nose and fought down the urge to vomit. Whatever was making all that noise gave off a stink like the cells in the Tombs: puke and slop buckets, plus something worse—like a whiff of the ripe dead bodies lying under the sun at Gettysburg.

He flattened himself out on the ground, peering into the dark shadows until he caught a glimpse of a big indistinct shape pushing its way through the brush. A moment later it emerged into a dappled patch of moonlight and Liam's breath caught in his throat: a wolf, but like no wolf he'd ever seen— the size of a brewery horse, panting and looking around as if for him, *personally*, its eyes glowing like coals, its tongue lolling out and enough teeth for a whole pack of ordinary wolves glinting in the moonlight.

"Blessed Mother!" he murmured involuntarily and the thing looked sharply in the direction of his hiding place. Slowly, gingerly, Liam reached for his Colt (thinking simultaneously that he might as well throw acorns at the beast), when suddenly another sound swelled through the night and seized the attention of man and wolf-thing alike:

From somewhere overhead, growing steadily until it made Liam's very bones thrum in sympathy, came the sound of a titanic, angry bee. Liam closed his eyes and shook his head: this was clearly a night he should have stayed home in bed, reading Count Tolstoy's new book. Somewhere not far away, and coming fast, was one of the Secret Service's Black Deltas—huge, rigid, delta-shaped hydrogen balloons powered by six aerial screws, or propellers, each one driven by its own, silenced Corliss aerial steam engine.

Liam had heard that the Secret Service now had special telescopes for seeing at night, and that worried him even more, since he happened to know that each of the Black Deltas had gun ports for six steam-driven Gatling guns, capable of firing 1,100 rounds of .45-70 ammo per minute. Liam had fired one of the old hand-cranked ones back in the War and had been appalled to see it chop through a 300-year-old oak tree like a knife through a hunk of cheese. He squinched his eyes as tight shut as he could and put his hands over his head, praying. The wolf-thing, on the other hand, spooked suddenly and ran off in another direction, crashing through the brush like a herd of cattle.

Suddenly there was a sparking zzzzzt! from somewhere overhead and the forest lit up as bright as day as a monstrous carbon-arc lamp started playing back and forth across the tops of the trees and a stentorian military voice shouted through a megaphone:

"You, there, below! Halt where you are! I say again, HALT OR WE'LL SHOOT!"

Instantly, without waiting for a response, the Black Delta cut loose with a deafening stream of bullets, glowing incendiary rounds that created a sort of hellish umbilical cord between the Delta and the ground below. Liam prayed without pausing, every prayer he could remember from Sunday grace through the Lord's Prayer to the Rosary and back again. Finally, after what seemed like days, the firing ceased, the illuminated squares of the gun ports closed—making the Delta invisible again—and then with a throbbing hum the airship veered off to the east and disappeared.

They must have called that thing in from the Secret Service station in Pottsville, Liam thought inconsequentially. He raised himself to a sitting position very gingerly, as if he were made of glass and might break if he moved too fast. The moonlight was glinting off a carpet of little golden tubes on the forest floor around him, and Liam leaned forward to pick one up: a .45-70 cartridge case, they must have fired thousands of them. Somehow that little piece of reality brought Liam to his feet.

"Bad 'cess to ye, Mr. Stanton, and to all your dirty thugs," Liam muttered, looking skywards. Then he took off loping again towards Maggie's house. It wasn't far now, and—winded and mind-blasted as he was—he couldn't help smiling as he thought of her. If his Ma had still been alive he didn't know if he could have taken Maggie home to meet her, but then his Ma—who'd been governess to a milord's kiddies—wouldn't have been too happy with what he'd made of himself either. *Liam McCool, King of the Silk-Stocking Cracksmen?* No, he didn't think so, even though in his day he'd been the best of the best, and he was still a lot prouder of that than of what they'd turned him into by forcing him onto the right side of the law.

Almost to Maggie's now. Liam slowed to a walk, reaching into his pocket for a comb that he ran through the bushy moustache he'd been affecting since he started this job, that and the long hair he wore tied into a pigtail with a strip of rawhide. Maggie had never seen him any other way and he couldn't wait till they got to Philly and a barber shop where he could lose the lip-shrubbery and shorten his hair enough so his pals wouldn't give him the horselaugh when they saw him.

Elbowing his way through the thick underbrush that screened Maggie's backyard from prying eyes, he suddenly came to a halt. Something was very wrong. By this point he should have been seeing light through the bushes; on this night of all nights Maggie should have had every light in her private quarters lit to welcome him. A sense of foreboding knotted his stomach as he stepped forward into the yard: there was plenty of moonlight, but the house itself was as dark and silent as a tomb.

Liam pushed out into the yard and ran across it and up the back stairs, hoping against hope that Maggie was just asleep, worn out by all the preparations for their trip. He knocked, hoping to hear her joyous welcome from somewhere inside, but instead the door swung inwards. Liam shook his head slowly, trying to deny the evidence of his eyes—Maggie always kept her doors locked tight, ever since a break-in months ago.

He forced himself to push the door the rest of the way open and entered, his steps dragging. The hallway outside Maggie's quarters was as dark as the inside of a coal scuttle, and he had to fumble back and forth on the wall before he could find the gas jet and strike a match to see where he was going.

There. At the end of the hall the door between Maggie's quarters and her boarders' part of the house was locked tight as always and doubly secured by a heavy bolt. But it was the door on his left, the one that led into Maggie's parlor, that made Liam's heart drop into his shoes: on the jamb and on the doorknob next to it were smears of blood, and on the hall floor there was half a bloody footprint, its sole in the hallway and the heel-print concealed behind the closed door.

Chapter Three

rudgingly, almost against his will, Liam turned to see what the gaslight had revealed in the hall behind him: the bloody footprint coming out of Maggie's parlor was joined by a string of others, less and less clearly marked, heading towards the outdoors.

Automatically he began his "photography" routine, a retentive brain and a safe-cracker's eye for useful details recording everything he saw. The prints had been made by a man with small feet, hurrying in pointy-toed dress shoes and moving fast enough to leave scuff marks. Maggie's house was well off the beaten path and on a Saturday night her lodgers would be in town, so what was he running from? Only one way to find out: Liam gritted his teeth and opened the door, recoiling as the hall filled with the reek of burnt gunpowder and death.

The room was dark and Liam hesitated to turn on the light. *You'll not be bringing her back to life by standing here sucking your thumb*, he told himself. Fumbling for another Lucifer, he scratched it on the doorjamb and held it out to the gas jet . . .

It was as if that little *pop!* of igniting gas had turned on the sun, making everything in the room unnaturally stark and brilliant as it revealed Maggie lying on her back with her dead eyes staring up at the ceiling, her negligée (the blue one she'd loved so much, the one he'd bought her at the Expo in Philly) pulled down to her waist exposing her breasts, and up to her stomach, exposing her white thighs and the dark patch between them. In the middle of her chest, just under her breasts, was a small, bloody hole in a black halo of burnt powder, a great pool of darkening blood spreading from beneath her across her favorite Turkey carpet.

Liam collapsed to his knees next to her and grabbed her stiffening corpse, holding her tight and rocking back and forth as he ground his teeth and growled deep in his throat with pain. Tears poured down his face, the first he'd shed in a lot of years, since the winter of 1863 before the Draft Riots when he'd seen his mother's body on a trolley in Bellevue.

"I swear, Maggie," he grated out, "I swear to you I'll make whoever did this pay."

He held her for another moment, willing the tears to stop, then laid her back down gently, tugging at her negligée until it covered her the way she would have wanted it. Then he got to his feet, moving stiffly as though he'd aged a lifetime.

"Who did this?" he muttered as he looked around for clues, making sure that he'd forget nothing he saw when he remembered it later. He'd been a brilliant safe-cracker in his day, and only partly because of little tricks like using the doctor's stethoscope he'd pinched from Bellevue to listen to the tick of the box's heart as he moved the dial. The main reason he'd never been caught, until that disastrous favor he'd done for Mike's Uncle Tolya, was the way he could photograph a room in his mind, visiting the target on some pretext ahead of time and committing it to memory so it would become as familiar as his own bedroom.

"It had to be somebody you knew, didn't it Mags?" he murmured, looking around for any sign of who her caller had been.

Not Maggie's boarders, surely. Mousy Arthur Morrison, the head accountant at Henderson Anthracite, would have been swilling whiskey at Maloney's, getting up the courage to sweet-talk one of Boylan's waitresses. And Hiram Kreutzer, Henderson's holy Joe chief engineer, would still be at Mrs. Clark's restaurant reading one of the Reverend Beecher's sermons as he ate his pot roast and nipped at the bottle of blue ruin she kept in the cupboard for him.

And Lukas? He was a mystery man sure enough, known only by that one name. But earlier in the day Maggie had said something about him leaving for New York to do research on his book about the coalfields. If it hadn't been for that, Liam would have been on his scent like a bloodhound. His very appearance made him seem a bit suspicious, like some eccentric out of a play: built like a bull gorilla and ugly as a prize-fighter but always dressed in the height of fashion whether he was bending his elbow at Maloney's or going down the mines "to see the lads at work first hand."

But even if you had judged the book by its cover and picked Lukas for a Five Points plug-ugly disguised as one of his betters, you knew different the minute he opened his mouth: he had the mellifluous voice of some famous professor, someone used to being listened to attentively.

And Lukas wasn't just some rough diamond polished smooth, either. Liam had been pals with "Little Adam" Worth, a celebrity among thieves and con men who could pass as a gentleman at the Harvard Club. But to someone with Liam's uncanny ear for languages, even the Prince of Thieves had an echo of his hard-luck origins behind the Harvard cadences. Not Lukas, though. Liam could tell the man was a swell born and bred. The mystery was where? Liam could catch the foreign ring to some of his vowels but even he couldn't be sure of Lukas' native tongue.

Liam shook his head: it didn't matter—none of the boarders made sense to him as a murderer. Not without enough hard facts to build a story, anyhow. First, the bullet. It must have gone all the way through Maggie, blowing out a spray of blood as it went—Liam could see the traces on the floor and the furniture behind her and it looked like she had fallen backwards right on the spot. He knelt down again and pulled her up by her left shoulder, far enough to see the size of the hole in her back. Big enough to put his fist in.

He shook his head again and stood up, looking towards Maggie's bookshelves to see if that was where the slug had ended up. There. Maggie had loved the spunky suffragist writing in Victoria Woodhull's "Weekly," and one of her treasured bound volumes had a ragged hole in the spine right in line with where she'd been standing.

Liam crossed to the shelf, pulled out the volume and flipped it open: at the end of a channel with accordioned paper bunched up ahead of it was a big lump of lead. Liam turned it over, seeing from the way it had mushroomed that the head of the bullet had been notched, and from the base—which was still intact—that it had to be a .44 or .45. He put the slug back in the book for whatever bluecoat would show up to investigate; then, with a sick feeling of foreknowledge, he walked over to Maggie's desk and pulled out the drawer. Sure enough, the pistol was gone, just a few spots of gun oil where it had lain on some papers.

Months ago, when some drunk from Maloney's had tried to climb into her window, Liam had bought her a pistol to ease her mind. It was short-barreled and easy to handle, nickel-plated to make it look more lady-like but with enough punch to knock down a buffalo—a Webley British Bulldog in .45 caliber which he'd made even more lethal by cutting crosses into the slugs. Liam didn't even have to check his mental photograph to know it wasn't lying around anywhere, the killer must have pocketed it.

Clearly the man had been in a hurry—there had been a perfunctory effort at cleaning up but it was easy to reconstruct what had happened: Maggie struggling with her attacker, breaking away, grabbing the pistol, then wrestling with him till he shot her. Maggie was a fighter, she wouldn't have gone easily . . .

Liam went back to her body and knelt next to it again, fighting his emotions until he could examine her coolly. Her right hand was balled into a fist, and there was a glint of gold between the fingers. Liam pried them open carefully against the resistance of the deepening rigor mortis, noting as he did that Maggie's carefully tended fingernails were broken and that she had shreds of bloody flesh under them—whoever it was hadn't gotten away scot-free, she had definitely left her marks on him.

Then, as her hand opened the rest of the way, Liam saw what she'd been clutching in her fist: a gold souvenir medal from the 1876 Philadelphia Centennial Exposition. The killer must have been wearing it around his neck on a chain, and Maggie had gotten the medal and a scrap of chain in the struggle without his noticing it. Probably so fired up by then he wouldn't have noticed if his nose was missing. Then a painful twinge as Liam noticed the inscription on the other side: "Love from Mags." She must have torn it from around the killer's neck. It took him a moment or two to get his mind cold again; after all, they'd both had plenty of other lovers before they met, and they'd both known it and not cared a damn.

He shook his head hard, clearing it: *don't be a hypocrite, McCool* . . . Then he closed his eyes to check his memory picture again . . . something was out of place, something he missed the first time around . . . He turned and headed unerringly for a corner of the carpet at the other end of the room, rucked up slightly as if somebody had kicked it passing by.

Liam grabbed it and jerked it the rest of the way, already certain what he'd see: *Yes, damn it to hell!* Once they had decided to make their break for San Francisco Liam had

22

asked Maggie to be their banker and she had kept their nest egg under a doctored floorboard—a half-dozen big Mason jars filled with silver dollars, a substantial number of gold eagles and some bits of jewelry, all the spending money they would have blown on foolishness in the days before they threw in together.

All gone. Just the empty jars and a couple of forlorn silver dollars that attested to the killer's hurry. Liam sat down hard on the floor next to the cache, thinking it was a good thing he'd kept aside a money belt full of gold eagles as a secret reserve against bad luck but having to work hard to keep from yelling with anger at the thought of their vanished nest egg. All that work building it up all those months, all the fun they'd shared as they squirreled away a tidy grubstake, the money to buy the restaurant that Maggie planned to make California's finest, the money that Liam had meant to use to let him buy a nice little house for his Gran not far from him and Maggie and start a bookstore that would someday put Brentano's to shame. All those happy dreams stolen. Stolen by the same low-life son of a bitch who'd stolen Maggie's life.

He shook his head briskly. It wouldn't do to carry this black rage around inside. If he was to honor Maggie and their dreams he'd have to clear his mind and start over, to be as cool and determined as he'd ever been until he managed to get back to the city where he could see Mike and the boys. Once he was back they could pull a few jobs to help him rebuild his grubstake and give him time enough put his hands on Maggie's killer. Then and only then he'd get out from under that old bastard Pilkington, collect Gran like he'd planned to do with Maggie and vanish like a puff of smoke, leaving the Eyes and the coppers scratching their heads. *Up and at 'em, Liam me boy!*

He got to his feet, walked over to Maggie, knelt down and kissed her gently, then stood again and walked over to the door.

"Good night, darlin'," he said to Maggie. Then he turned the gas off and left.

○━

Outside, the prints of the pointy-toed shoes were clear in the moonlight, sharply indented in ground that was still a little soft from the day before's rain and still showing the murderer's haste: heavy at front and light at back as he ran, with a distance between them that made Liam re-assess his guess at a small man. Small feet, but longer legs than he'd thought. And something else, what the hell was that? A furrow cut by something catching, skipping over the ground until it caught deeply again, cutting at an angle to the footprints and going on around the side of the house where it looked for sure like it would intersect with the running footprints . . .

Liam picked up his own pace until he turned the corner of the house and came to a sudden, disgusted stop as he reached a clearing there where Maggie had planned to build a garden shed. Fresh marks of torn bark showed white on a string of trees, right up to one that had a deeper gouge and the prints of a chain pressed into it.

The murderer had come here from who knew where, in a Stanley Flyer, a neat little two-seat airship with a super-quiet engine and a handy steam winch you could use to drag your anchor until you hooked a tree like a fish. Then all you had to do was hit the winch to pull you slowly and quietly down to the ground, where your Flyer would wait patiently till you were ready to jump aboard and soar off into the night.

He stood there for a moment, stewing. Then he was snapped out of it by a new series of hoots from Henderson's emergency whistle, along with the distant clangs of the volunteer fire wagon. By now, everybody in town from the drunks in Maloney's to the few peaceful and sober citizens to be found in Henderson's Patch on a Saturday night would have turned

24

out to watch the fire and read the "Coffin Notice" that he and the others had left on Henderson's front gate.

Slipping back into the darkness of the woods and crossing himself against the return of the wolf-thing, he took off at a steady jog. By this time tomorrow, he would be in New York—as for the rest of it, he'd just have to take it one day at a time . . .

Chapter Four

hat one trip down Henderson's mine had been enough to last him a lifetime. He hadn't *had* to, it wasn't any part of the job Pilkington had set him, but he'd been drinking with the lads after one of the Mollies' Lodge meetings, arm-wrestling and showing off and playing the fool one way and another, until finally someone challenged him to work a shift down there like the rest of them.

His heart had clutched right up like a fist and the sweat had started running down his armpits; he'd been deep underground once before, in 1872 when they were digging the caissons for the Brooklyn Bridge, and it had nearly done for him. A sandhog who was a cousin to one of his pals in the Butcher Boys had needed help talking to a foreman about some back wages and three or four of the boys had gone down together to make sure the man saw reason, Liam not knowing then how bad he'd be hit by his fear of being closed in. He had learned fast enough and he'd only gotten out with Mike Vysotsky carrying him on his back.

But, like a fool, there he'd been five years later in Pennsylvania on a job he hated going down a hole again like it was a stroll in Washington Square. And no, he hadn't healed miraculously in the years between and he'd only ended his suffocating panic by pretending to trip on a rock and knock himself cold against an ore car so they'd have to send him back up. You'd think he'd learn, but Micks have hard heads.

Now, that little experiment had made two times down a hole and he was pretty sure he wouldn't survive a third, so just *what* in blue blazes was he doing in a mine a *third* time, way to hell and gone away from anywhere at all, not a soul to be seen, not a spark of light, and nothing but a THUMP! THUMP! THUMP! and a giant throbbing in his skull like he'd been dropped all the way down the shaft and landed on his conk? If he didn't get out of here *soon*, if that damned *thumping* didn't stop, if he could only ... open ... his ... *eyes* ...

o—┰

"WHAT?" Liam bellowed, stumbling out of bed and nearly going head-first into the wall as he scrabbled at the latch-key with sausage fingers. What miserable, pea-brained lowlife had such important business they couldn't wait till he woke up and washed his face?

Finally he managed to tear the door open, throwing it wide and cocking his fist to pound whoever it was to a jelly. But instead of the expected drunken miner or lodge brother from the Mollies, someone he could cheerfully pop in the beezer, his tormentor was a sort of plump, smiling Mr. Pickwick— the most innocent-looking of callers, a cheerful, clean-shaven middle-aged man with red cheeks, a fringe of graying sandy hair, a big nose and very sharp brown eyes behind wire-rimmed spectacles, his brown checked suit and waistcoat adorned with a pewter watch chain and a gold badge that said he was a Chief Inspector in the Coal & Iron Police.

"Mighty sorry to raise such a ruckus," the newcomer said with a foxy-grandpa smile. "I knocked just as nice as could be for a bit there, but I guess you must have made quite a night of it." He pulled a big turnip watch out of his waistcoat pocket and looked at it with feigned astonishment: "Land o' Goshen, it's a quarter past noon already!"

"Mmf," Liam grunted. He was as naked as a jaybird and he felt like his head had been filled with boiling oatmeal. Grabbing the sheet off the mattress to make himself a toga, he saw that the bottle of rye he'd bought to hold his private wake with had just about a finger left. He picked it up by the neck and held it out to his caller.

Pickwick smiled apologetically: "Not before lunch."

Not bad, Liam thought. The old boy could manage a tone of mild reproof as nicely as a parson, not something you'd expect from your run-of-the-mill flat foot. He definitely remembered this Pickwick bird from somewhere, and if the fog in his brain would just clear for a moment . . . ah, there it was! He nodded and smiled a little, which made his visitor narrow his eyes suspiciously.

It had been back in Five Points, Liam recalled: the new Police Headquarters building at 300 Mulberry Street, not long before the Draft Riots. Liam's Pa had dragged him there by the ear to complain he'd stolen his watchchain, only the drunken shite-pot had been so far gone that Liam had already palmed the chain back into his waistcoat pocket before they went inside.

Then, as soon as Liam had seen he had the coppers' attention, he out-hammed John Wilkes Booth playing the heartbroken little tyke and making a fool of his blowhard Pa. And Pickwick? He'd been one of the coppers looking on and tsk-tsking over the sorry spectacle. Liam stifled the beginning of a grin, keeping the memory to himself for a tactical advantage.

"What can I do for you, Inspector . . . ?"

"Barlow," the man said with an avuncular chuckle, "Amos Barlow, and pleased to make your acquaintance, Mr. McCool."

This one could be dangerous, Liam thought, returning the Inspector's smile with one of equally false bonhomie and raising him a jolly wink and a handshake.

"If you don't mind . . . ?" he said, gesturing to his toga.

"Of course, of course," Barlow said good-humoredly, "in fact, I was about to suggest we take a little walk so I expect you'll be wanting your shoes and pants."

He turned politely and made a point of examining the few small shelves of Liam's library while Liam scrubbed his face at the washstand and put on some fresh clothes. He had bought three cheap dark suits before he left New York, but the open window was telling him it was already hot out and he decided on a pair of corduroys and a cambric shirt. Let Barlow sweat in his nice thick brown suit and waistcoat!

"My, my!" the Inspector was saying with a look of amiable astonishment, "seems you do have the gift of tongues, eh Mr. McCool? Here's Goethe and *Les Misérables* alongside Mr. Twain and Mr. Dickens, and . . . Heavens above, what's *this?*"

Liam had a talent for languages, all right, and an even better one for reading tones of voice: what was that odd little shading at the bottom of Barlow's wouldn't-hurt-a-fly geniality? Something sharp and avid, like the yip of a hound tracking an escaped convict . . .

Sending the sweetness and light right back at him, Liam raised his eyebrows innocently and said: "Why, that's Russian, Inspector Barlow, Mr. Tolstoy's last book 'War and Peace.'"

And my pal Mike Vysotsky stole it for me from some dimwit Grand Duke in the Fifth Avenue Hotel who never even cut the pages, he added mentally, unable to keep a satirical smile from popping to the surface.

Either the tone or the smile piqued Barlow's attention and he threw Liam a sharp look:

"*Rooskie*, eh, fancy that! I expect you can speak the lingo with our Little Russia neighbors on the other side of the Mississippi, then. The ones that keep sending us their crazy anarchist bomb-throwers . . ." Then, a nicely-timed

29

moment later, with an air of sudden inspiration: "Say, I don't suppose you'd be related to *Francis* McCool, now, would you, Mr. McCool? The famous Fenian agitator?"

That was more like it, thought Liam, the copper's needle-jab. "I would," he said cheerfully, "and I hope the Devil has set a whole army of bluecoat imps to thumping him sober with their billies. But if you're aiming to put me in the frame as a spy for New Petersburg you can think again—I've no more use for their brand of baloney than I do for the Fenians."

"Ah," said Barlow with a frankly appraising look, "your old man put you off politics, did he?"

"You could say so," Liam said. "Of course, thirteen years of drunken beatings and blather about Free Ireland may have helped with that, not to mention him putting my Ma in Bellevue with two black eyes and a handful of broken ribs just before she died. Whoever it was that put a bullet in him saved me being a murderer someday."

"I didn't much care for him myself," Barlow said, "though I wouldn't have shot him over it." He put on a look of doleful sympathy: "There were a lot of bullets flying in the Draft Riots, I don't expect I have to tell you, it could have been anybody pulled that trigger."

Liam shrugged. "If you meet the fella that did, tell him I'll buy him a drink. Otherwise, let's stop fooling around—are you here about Henderson's house or Maggie's murder?"

Barlow nodded and chuckled: "I like a man that isn't afraid to take the bull by the horns."

Liam shrugged. "If there's any bull around here it isn't me throwing it."

Inspector Barlow smiled a little, nodding absently as he weighed that.

"What do you say we have our little stroll now, Mr. McCool? I took a quick look at Miss O'Shea's place before I sent for the Coroner, but I need to give it a good going-over before too many people tromp across it. If you'd really like to help catch the fellow who did it you might as well come along and keep me company."

Liam opened the door to the hallway and gestured: "After you, Inspector." And to himself: *Mind how you go, Liam-me-lad, this dog bites!*

0—r

Outside Mrs. Finnegan's Boarding House, a beautiful Spring morning was giving the lie to gloomy visions of dynamite and murder. To Liam's tenderized senses the explosion of birdsong, glaring sunshine and shouting kids was just about the limit, and Barlow smiled as he watched him out of the corner of his eye.

"They tell me you and Miss O'Shea were sweethearts."

Liam grunted, trying to squint his eyes enough to shut out most of the sun without letting himself trip over something.

"Don't use the hard stuff much, do you?" Barlow sounded amused.

Liam looked like he was fighting the urge to throw up. "My idea of drinking is a stein or two of Ruppert's while I'm watching the Punch and Judy at Harry Hill's."

"Can't say as I blame you pining for the big city, not after six months in this one-horse burg."

Liam threw him a sharp glance, then nodded to himself; whatever was going through his mind, it gave him a sardonic little half-smile.

They walked in silence for a bit, each of them throwing an occasional covert glance at the other. After a few blocks Barlow started showing a slight limp and Liam couldn't resist a jab:

"Sprain your ankle chasing the Molly Magees, Inspector?"

Barlow frowned. "That's a poor sort of joke, young McCool. Fact is, I was chasing rebs at Gettysburg and caught a Minié ball instead."

Liam heard the tone of mild reproof again and he grinned: "You do that Parson Brown turn just about perfect, Inspector. Yessir, you could have been a daisy of a confidence man—I'd say you missed your calling."

Barlow smiled sourly. "I wouldn't be making jokes about the Mollies if I were you. Maybe they didn't do all the murders and destruction the prosecution said at the trials, but somebody must have done *something* or they wouldn't be hanging ten of them in Pottsville next week."

Liam looked solemn. "Words of wisdom, Brother Barlow. Shall I lead the hymn now?"

That one finally got through the grizzled copper's guard and a choleric flush ran up his plump neck and into his jowls; Liam moved to cut off an angry retort:

"I tell you what, Inspector—you quit trying to catch me off balance and treat me like somebody that's been around the block a few times, I'll return the favor, OK? And be a sport, don't wave the bloody shirt at me over Gettysburg, I had my fourteenth birthday on Little Round Top, chasing Rebs with the 20th Maine."

This time it was Barlow that gave Liam a sharp look. "You were at Gettysburg?"

Liam laughed. "How about that? Imagine not knowing a simple thing like that, and you one of Stanton's Eyes."

That one jarred the Inspector to a standstill. He turned and stared at Liam as if he didn't believe his ears. "Just *what* are you trying to . . . ?"

"Come on, Barlow," Liam said impatiently, "Like you said, I've been down here in the coalfields for six months, and I never saw a C & I that came within a mile of you for brainpower. Those boys are all local hayseeds happy to take Mr. Gowen's two bits for thumping miners with their billies and cadging free drinks from Boyo Boylan. *Anyway,* I happen to know that once upon a time you were a New York harness bull and never mind how."

"You do, do you?" Barlow bit off the words with a snap, glowering.

"Uh huh. Didn't I say I'd been around the block once or twice? It was never *me* that told you I'd been down here six months, and none of these C & I dimwits knows if I've been here a day or a year. Nope, you were reading my file somewhere in a Secret Service office before you came down here to play the homespun old bluecoat. And anyway, '*Inspector*,' I'm sorry to have to reveal this deep trade secret to an opponent, but you've got the Stanton *smell* on you—there isn't the lowliest dollar-a-day dip back in the big city that couldn't spot you coming a mile away."

Exasperated by Liam's facetious wink, the Inspector turned his attention to their surroundings, sweeping them slowly with the policeman's habitual scan for suspicious movement. As he turned, curtains fell closed at his look and the scattered strollers along Main Street's board sidewalks dropped their eyes or pretended they'd been looking somewhere else.

"They shut the diggings down this morning," Barlow said in a conversational tone, "and it looks like they'll stay that way till we collar the boys that dynamited Henderson's house."

"Going to starve them into submission, are you?" Liam shook his head in mock admiration. "I guess old Stanton could teach a thing or two to those serf owners over in Little Russia. Say, have you ever heard of a *nagaika*? That's a whip the Cossacks use on Sioux Indians and bullheaded Russian peasants, strip a man's skin right off his bones. You tell Secretary Stanton about that trick, I expect he'll give you a shiny new silver dollar."

"That smart mouth is going to get you in big trouble one day, sonny. The orders to close down the diggings came from Mr. Gowen, and I'd say him owning the Reading Railroad and the Philadelphia and Reading Coal & Iron Company gives him about all the pull he needs to make Henderson or anybody else close their diggings, wouldn't you?"

He leaned forward and stabbed Liam's chest with his forefinger: "As for Secretary Stanton, he *likes* smartmouths like you. He'll take all of you he can get, there's such a heap of rocks need breaking up down at Andersonville Prison."

Satisfied with his riposte, Barlow started down the street again. Liam followed along at his side, looking amused.

"No need to get your dander up, old man, I like Secretary Stanton right back. As my dear old dad used to say about Boss Tweed—'sure and he's a *darlin'* man.' Of course, there's those that think Stanton's a little too *much* of a good thing, you know? Secretary of War was one thing, but the war's been over a dozen years, and here's Stanton still at the helm, running some new-fangled Department of Public Safety and Lincoln still President under the Emergency Act, and nobody's seen hide nor hair of a voting box since '61."

He grinned satirically at Barlow, whose head had sunk down between his shoulders so far that he looked like a sort of angry turtle.

"Not that I'm complaining, mind you," Liam added in an innocent tone, "I wouldn't dream of it! Every night when I go to sleep I kneel by my bed and and thank the Lord for Mom and Dad and my little dog Spot and Secretary Stanton, who protects us from the evil Russians across the Mississippi and the wicked Brits across the ocean and the dastardly French Communists in Mexico and . . . and . . ." Liam pretended to reel and clutch his forehead in desperation: "Why it fair boggles the mind how many terrible evils that kind old man Stanton is defending us from!"

"All right, McCool," growled the Inspector, "either shut up or I'll break your head with my stick."

They were just approaching the corner of Maggie's street and Liam could hear a hubbub of strange voices coming from the direction of her house. His face darkened as he registered the sounds and he felt his cheerful mood melting away.

"Ah, to hell with Stanton and with you and your phony playacting too—in fact, all you Department of Public Safety shysters can go piss up a rope as far as I'm concerned. You're just down here sucking up to Mister Franklin B. Gowen for his great patriotic feat railroading ten Mollies into rope neckties— you don't care a plugged nickel for my girl Maggie or justice for whoever killed her either, she wasn't *rich* enough for that."

Barlow gave Liam a long, searching look; then he nodded slowly as he reached some private conclusion. A few hundred yards ahead of them Maggie's house sat just at the end of the dirt road where the street petered out into the woods. The house itself was painted a sparkling white with light blue trim, the picket fence an equally pristine white barrier between the dirt of the road and a thick green lawn. It was easy to see that Maggie had put a lot of love and elbow grease into making it pretty, and somehow that made it twice as sad to see the herd of policemen tramping it into a sea of mud.

"You're dead wrong, boy," the Inspector said, "about why I'm here, anyway. Secretary Stanton takes it mighty seriously when something happens to any of his people, and though I'm pretty sure now that you didn't know it, Maggie O'Shea was one of ours."

For once, Liam was totally speechless. He shook his head, stunned.

"That's right," Barlow continued. "She wasn't a sworn agent, but she was working as an auxiliary. Your Maggie was one of Secretary Stanton's Eyes."

Chapter Five

he Schuylkill County Coroner's wagon was sitting in front of Maggie's gate and as they approached— Liam with his face as black as thunder, his hands stuffed in his pockets and his chin sunk on his chest, Barlow appraising him out of the corner of his eye. Before they reached him, the driver flicked his horses' flanks with his reins and the wagon moved towards them, clanking and squeaking.

Liam couldn't bear watching it go. Instead, he squeezed his eyes shut as hard as he could and after a moment a couple of tears ran down his cheeks as the wagon moved past. Abruptly, he opened his eyes wide and turned on Barlow in a fury:

"What the hell do you *mean*, Maggie was an Eye?"

Inspector Barlow took Liam by the shoulder and gave him a little shake.

"Easy, lad," he said in a kindly voice. "Back in the city you may be the King of the Silk-Stocking Cracksmen and the flyest bird in Mulberry Bend but down here in Henderson's Patch, after six months out of the swim, you're about as fly as a great big lump of coal."

"You can skip the poetry," Liam grated. "Just answer my question."

"Let's start with this," Barlow said, "like it or not you're an Eye yourself."

For a moment it looked like the Inspector might have gone too far—Liam's face turned absolutely white, then red as a beet, then Liam growled low in his throat and moved towards Barlow with a look that made the older man raise both hands like a copper stopping traffic:

"Whoa there, Sonny Jim," Barlow said sharply, "put your brain back in charge!" Liam halted, still mad but listening, and Barlow continued: "You're down here working as an agent for Mr. Pilkington, aren't you?"

Liam had figured that Barlow knew all about him, but hearing it said out loud was like a faceful of cold water; he looked around sharply, but thank God nobody was near enough to have heard it. Barlow shook his head exasperatedly:

"Don't be a jackass, McCool! You think I'd give you away to the Mollies and see six months' good work wasted and you with a bullet in your brain? I'm just trying to give you some idea which end is up, and I mean why working for the Old Man, for Mr. P., is no different from working for Stanton himself!"

Despite Liam's ominous glare Barlow moved closer and lowered his voice: "I know you were nabbed trying to break into the safe at the Union Square office of Pilkington's International Detective Agency. Doing a favor for a pal, sez you, but still Breaking & Entering any way you slice it. And I know you were sent to Sing Sing to do a five spot for B & E, from where Mr. Pilkington got you out on his own personal say-so, so's you could join the Mollies and blow the gaff if they tried to stop the hangings. The only thing I don't know is just why he picked on you out of all the fly birds that's stuffed in the Big House . . ."

Barlow raised his eyebrows expectantly, letting Liam know it was his turn to tell what he knew. After a moment Liam shrugged and made a wry face:

"You can put that down to your Boss, old-timer—and I mean dear old Eddie Stanton as runs the Federal Department of Public Safety, not some hick that runs the Coal and Iron coppers. Last I heard, old Mr. Pilkington's boy Willie was the big cheese in the DPS's Secret Service."

"So they say," Barlow said, looking thoughtful. "Don't stop now, you've got my attention."

"Well, the thing is, Willie Pilkington and me happen to go back a long ways." Liam laughed without much humor: "Back in '63 I had a sudden urgent need to leave the city, and anyway—I was going to be fourteen pretty soon and like the fella says, I wanted to See The Elephant. Willie on the other hand, didn't much care to do his Army service, thank you—as I recall, his exact words were: 'I have other priorities.' So I took his $300 and ended up on Little Round Top charging the 15th Alabama with nothing but my pig-sticker."

The 20th Maine's bayonet charge was famous enough to send both men into a moment of remembrance. Then Barlow shook his head:

"I guess you Saw The Elephant."

"Yep. And the India Rubber Man and the Fat Lady into the bargain."

"Funny thing, though," Barlow said. "I heard that at the time, Willie Pilkington was all broken up and tragical because the doctors had told him he had a heart murmur that would keep him from serving in the war."

"Is that so?" Liam said. "Well, *I* heard there's a Tooth Fairy that comes to good little children at night and puts a penny under their pillows."

Barlow nodded slowly, thinking it over. "You're a smart lad, McCool, so I expect I don't have to beat this dead horse too hard. You know that Daddy Pilkington, Old Mr. P., ran the spy service against the Confederacy when Stanton was Secretary of War. So when Mr. P. needed an ancient moss-back that looked like a C & I inspector to see how his operation was doing down here, he just got on the voicewire to his pal Eddie in Washington and borrowed me from the Secret Service."

He cocked his head for a moment and grinned sardonically at Liam. "And likewise, when Franklin Gowen called the Old Man to say he'd heard rumors the Mollies were going to make sure the hangings never happened, Mr. P. decided he needed someone dependable who looked like a right young thug to go undercover with the other young thugs so he got on the voicewire to Son Willie, who obligingly came up with his old comrade-in-arms Liam McCool."

Liam folded his arms on his chest and gave Barlow a long-suffering look: "Are we through yet, Inspector?"

Barlow just grinned and shook his head. "I'm not sure the penny's dropped yet, young McCool, not to where you really get it that you're working for Secretary Stanon just like me. That little bulletin from Frank Gowen set Eddie Stanton to thinking. What if all this worker unrest and the hangings of the Iroquois seditionists and the Molly Magees and all the rest of it has put a dent in the Public Safety? So just to be safe, Secretary Stanton took the hint and put all his Eyes on alert in case the Little Russians decided to take advantage and send their airships across the Mississippi, or the Communist Frenchies in Mexico took a notion to visit their comrades in Florida with troops and gunboats. It's all wheels within wheels, young fella, wheels within wheels within wheels . . ." he paused dramatically, "and these are dangerous times and *anybody* that's called on is going to end up doing their duty with the Department of Public Safety, like it or not."

Liam made a face. "OK, that's what you say makes me an Eye. But how about Maggie?"

"She had a little trouble once, too," Barlow said, "something she needed to make amends for. It was back in her New York days, something to do with the labor unions. Now, you know the DPS doesn't have a very high opinion of unions . . ." he spread his hands and left Liam to fill in the blanks.

Liam shook his head tiredly and pulled open the gate into Maggie's front yard.

"Let's go," he said. "That's about all of that I can stomach right now."

o——┳

The Coal & Iron bluecoat standing at Maggie's front door threw Inspector Barlow a salute as he approached and stepped aside as Barlow and Liam climbed the front steps.

"Everything OK?" Barlow asked. "No snoops? No gawkers?"

The man grinned. "Some, sir, 'specially when the Coroner's van showed up. But I just mentioned as how there was lots of Spring vacancies in the Pottsville clink and they cleared out spry-like."

"Well done, Billy. You keep a weather eye out, now, and I'll see to it somebody relieves you for lunch."

The guard touched the peak of his uniform cap and opened the door for them. Liam made a face as he saw the chaos of muddy footprints in the hallway:

"Maggie would have killed you if she saw that mess."

He looked down the hallway that ran past the front parlor to the dividing door, the one that Maggie had always kept firmly locked. It was cracked open now, an inch or two of light showing in the gap.

"Did they run that stampede through the back, too?"

They walked down the hall with Barlow in front. As he reached the door to Maggie's quarters he halted for a moment with his hand on the knob and gave Liam another reproving look:

"Billy's no thinking-machine, but he got here in time to keep everybody away from Miss O'Shea's personal quarters till I arrived. Except the Coroner, of course."

He opened the door the rest of the way and went on into Maggie's parlor, Liam following with his feet dragging.

The curtains had were wide open now and the room was flooded with light, brighter than he had ever seen it—somehow it put a distance between Liam and what had happened here, and he felt a welcome sense of relief.

Barlow gestured towards the spreading patch of blood on the carpet, dried black now.

"You all right to talk about it?"

"Depends. What is it you want to talk about?"

"Miss O'Shea came aboard as an auxiliary back in '73 but we hadn't asked her to do much until the Mollies started terrorizing the coalfields. That was when we decided to ask Mr. P. to put McPherson in as a spy with Boylan's lodge and we sent Miss O'Shea down to Henderson's Patch to open this boarding house and give McPherson a safe place to use as a post office. Once he broke the case and we rounded up the terrorists his life wasn't worth a plugged nickel around here so we pulled him out—but we left Miss O'Shea behind to keep an eye on things."

Liam squeezed his eyes shut and rubbed his forehead hard with his fingertips. It seemed like Barlow had driven every word in through the top of his head with a sledgehammer and Liam was beginning to feel dangerously like knocking the old man down and kicking him till he shut up. Barlow nodded sympathetically:

"I know all that is making you pretty sore, but nobody knows better than you that the DPS and our helpers like Mr. Pilkington don't offer any *choices* about where we send you and what we need you to do. On the bright side, though, we don't usually interfere with an auxiliary's private life and we didn't with Miss O'Shea's either. Of course we kept a bit of an Eye on her . . ." Barlow smiled blandly. "No pun intended."

"Get . . . to . . . the . . . *point*," Liam said through gritted teeth.

"I'm just saying that once I had a good look around the scene of the crime I was pretty sure the murder didn't have anything to do with politics. That's why I wanted to take a good look at you since you were Miss O'Shea's current sweetheart.

Now I'm just as sure it was somebody else, someone she'd thrown aside but who was still sweet on her."

Liam examined the Inspector thoughtfully; maybe he wouldn't kick the old bastard's slats in after all:

"How do you figure it?"

"I noticed when I turned her over that the way the blood had stained her gown the fabric must have been pushed up from below and pulled down at the top after she was shot and the blood was pooling. Was it you that straightened it out? I like to know these things if I can find them out."

Liam gave him a wry smile. "Why don't you just ask me right out, was I here? Yes I was here, dammit, I came calling and found Maggie like that." He hung up for a moment on the memory, then pushed it away and continued: "I don't know what the lousy rat was up to, doing that with her gown; maybe just making her look like a bad woman, somebody that was asking to be violated. But Maggie . . . Maggie would have really hated having any stranger see her like that."

Barlow nodded. "I'm thinking the murderer had a real grudge against her." He gestured towards the bloody footprints leading back through the door to the hall. "I followed those out to the backyard, and I'd be willing to bet the second set I saw going around next to them was yours." A small smile: "Do I need to have you stand in them so I can make sure?"

Liam shook his head: he hadn't been wrong, the old boy was sharp.

"I pondered on the footprints all the way through half a bottle of bad rye, I expect even Billy could have put it together sooner or later. It had to be somebody dressed up for a visit, somebody that knew Maggie well enough to know you had to come in through the back if you were calling on her because the front way was for boarders, and somebody that surely didn't want anybody seeing him coming or going. And he either had a copy of the key, or she let him in once he said who he was." He screwed up his face as if the words had tasted bad.

"Which you figured because . . . ?"

Liam shrugged. "She kept the place locked up tight, ever since some drunks bothered her a while back."

"I guess she must have let him in," Barlow said carefully, his eyes drifting towards a tabouret behind the desk. On it sat a bottle of French brandy with a few fingers out of it and two empty glasses. Liam made a face.

"Yeah," he said, "I saw that last night. I hate hard liquor and Maggie never took more than a sip of anything. Must have been some she used to keep for the rat that killed her." His voice hardened. "But get this, Barlow, I don't give a *damn* about any of that, what she did with some other bird 'once upon a time.' Both of us had been around plenty on our own, but once the two of us got together we started a whole new page."

Barlow let it drop. "You've got a mighty sharp eye for details, Mr. McCool. Better than most coppers."

Liam shrugged. "Comes in handy sometimes."

"I expect," Barlow said drily. He looked around the room. "Well, young McCool, tell me what else your cracksman's eye caught, maybe you can help me lay my hands on this villain."

Liam looked slowly around the room, registering the changes.

"I see you found the bullet. I might as well tell you it was me that gave Maggie the gun it was fired out of, a nickel-plated Webley Bulldog in .45 caliber."

"Was it you notched the bullets?"

"You don't suppose *she* knew how, do you? I expect she went for the gun when he tried to go further than she wanted him to. Then he managed to turn it around on her when they wrestled for it. The bastard probably took a shine to that nice nickel finish and just dropped it in his pocket. But I'll tell you one thing—he had to be plenty strong to beat Maggie wrestling. When she was mad she could coldcock a mule if she took a notion to."

Barlow nodded. "I was figuring he had some weight on him from the depth of his footprints. Small feet, wearing those pointy-toed opera shoes, but going by the average height to-distance-between-footprints ratio he shouldn't be any shorter than you. For a man of normal height to make that deep a print he must be carrying some heft around on those little tootsies. You notice anything else?"

Liam hesitated: "You'd find it sooner or later, but you might as well know about it now."

He walked over to where he'd looked under the carpet the night before, knelt down and turned the rug back again. Then he took up the floorboard and gestured to the empty Mason Jars.

"When the Panic started in '73 Maggie lost every penny she had in the Fourth National crash—that's probably why she ended up working for you people. Anyway, this is how she did her banking after that."

Barlow squatted down next to Liam and examined the cache minutely. "Looks like our friend made a withdrawal before he left. Practical fellow, this murderer—waste not, want not."

Liam gave him a hard little smile: "I'm just hoping he hung onto something that I'll recognize when I run into him; I expect he did—somebody that greedy probably still has his first dime." He stood up, dusted off his knees and looked around the room. "That's about it as far as I know," he added. "Except maybe the tickets, I didn't check that before."

He went over to Maggie's desk and pulled open the middle drawer. He searched carefully, examining envelopes and papers tied up with lengths of ribbon, finally running out of patience and turning the contents out onto the desktop so he could rummage freely. At last he came up with a brown paper envelope that had "R. R./Frisco" written across it in bold letters. Its ribbon had been removed and stuffed inside, but otherwise it was empty.

"Damnation," Liam muttered. "Besides my pistol and our savings that thieving skunk took the tickets Maggie got us for the Trans-Little Russia Railroad to San Francisco. First class, I guess that'll be a pretty penny when he asks for a refund."

"Anything else?" Barlow was peering at him expectantly, as if he were waiting for Liam to notice something he'd missed.

"Wait a minute . . ." Liam pulled out one drawer after another and searched through them feverishly, irritated that he'd forgotten something that important. Finally he gave up and slammed the drawers back into the desk, glaring at Barlow as if all this misery were his fault.

"Her diary," Liam said. "Maggie wouldn't even let me touch it, but she'd always say that one day it might be the saving of us. Now what in the name of the Devil himself did that murdering swine want with Maggie's *diary*?"

Shaking his head angrily Liam turned and headed for the door.

"Hang on a minute," Barlow called after him.

"*What*?" Liam was tired of being careful with the old pest. "I haven't got time to stand around holding hands, I need to get my life moving again."

"I just wanted to ask what you know about Miss O'Shea's boarders. Bound to be more than I do."

Liam rolled his eyes but turned back. He pointed overhead. "Directly upstairs, that's Arthur Morrison, the accountant at Henderson Anthracite. He's a milksop, wouldn't say boo to a goose, let alone do murder. The front rooms on this floor, that's the chief engineer at Henderson's, Hiram Kreutzer. He's waiting for his wife to bring the kiddies so they can buy a house. In between times he's practicing for sainthood except for the occasional snort of gin, so I'd count him out. The upstairs front now, that's Lukas—looks like the Missing Link, talks like a professor and dresses like a fashion

45

plate. But if you want hard facts . . ." Liam shrugged: "People know about as much about Lukas as they do about the Grand Cham of Tartary. Last thing Maggie said about him was he was off to New York . . . I think she said he was interviewing somebody for some big book he's writing. As far as I know, he was supposed to be back next week . . ." He spread his hands: "That's all."

Barlow was plunged into thought, eyes narrowed and lips working as if he were chewing on a persimmon. Finally he nodded.

"What would you say if I told you it looks like this Lukas is gone for good?"

"What do you mean, gone?"

"I mean scrammed, cleared out, absquatulated."

Liam was taken aback. "He took everything with him?"

"I haven't had time yet to go through it with a fine-tooth comb, but if he left anything behind the mice must have carried it off."

"That's too many for me," Liam said, "I'm pretty sure Maggie didn't know anything about him leaving."

Barlow shrugged. "No telling just when it happened, but it had to be either him or somebody else that got his stuff together, so it must have been when Miss O'Shea wasn't around."

"She goes . . . she went around every morning with the cook, shopping for stuff for dinner and the next day's breakfast, I guess it could have been then—Morrison and Kreutzer would both be out of the house at work. But why would Lukas have cleared out like that unless . . . ?"

Barlow nodded. " . . . it was him that killed her. It's a possibility."

Liam's impatience had vanished, replaced by a kind of hungry, predatory focus intense enough to make Barlow glad he wasn't the prey.

"OK if I have a look?"

"Why not? Come on, I'll keep you company."

The door to Lukas' suite was standing open and Liam could see from the hall that the place had been stripped. Still, you never knew. He and Barlow entered and started turning the place upside-down: mattress picked up, pictures lifted off their hooks, sofa pillows thrown on the floor, rugs rolled up and the floorboards tapped for hiding places, closets opened and scoured, wardrobes pulled away from the wall; Barlow even stuck his arm up the chimney and got nothing more for his pains than a sleeve-full of soot.

Liam stood there looking around the room for a moment, then saw where Barlow had pulled all the drawers out of a big bureau and grinned:

"You'd make a poor sort of thief," he said, pulling the drawers out the rest of the way, turning them upside down and stacking them on the floor. Then, as he started the right-hand set of drawers, he hit pay-dirt:

"Well, well, well," he muttered. A big white envelope was held against the bottom of the drawer with sticking-plaster and Liam ripped it free impatiently. The first thing he came up with made him sit down on the bed as if the wind had been knocked out of him. It was a photograph taken at the Centennial Exposition in Philly, a picture of Maggie and Lukas all lovey-dovey and grinning at the camera like a couple of idiots. Liam stared at it with such a stricken expression that Barlow left him alone for a moment or two.

Finally he pulled himself together, handed the picture to Barlow and turned the envelope upside down so that the contents fell out onto the mattress. Some of them seemed to be love letters from Maggie to Lukas, and these Liam pushed away to one side. The only remaining item was a pamphlet with a pink cover printed in Cyrillic letters: Динамит—Лекарство от Капитализма [*Dinamit—Lekarstvo ot Kapitalizma*]. Underneath the Cyrillic words were English ones: "Tipografia of The People's Will. Springfield, Illinois *Guberniia*, 1876." Barlow peered at it over Liam's shoulder:

"Looks like Russian," he said. "Can you read that?"

Liam nodded and started to answer, then caught himself and stared at Barlow with a quirky little smile.

"Whoa, old man, not so fast!"

Barlow frowned: "What's your game, McCool?"

"No game, just time for a little quid pro quo."

"Uh huh. And what would that be?"

"You tell me everything Pilkington said when he briefed you on coming down to Henderson's Patch, and I mean *everything*. Treat me square and I'll tell you what the pamphlet's about. Otherwise you can wait till you get back to Washington and give it to one of the DPS bright boys."

Barlow pursed his lips and stared at Liam as he chewed on that; after several long moments Liam fancied he could about hear the gears grinding in the old boy's bean.

Liam finally had to laugh. "I knew a fellow once could hypnotize chickens putting his finger on their beak," he said. "They looked just about like you do now when he got finished with them."

Barlow snorted irritably. "Sure I'll tell you. It's no big secret—he said your job's done here now. Thanks to you we're ready to put the collar on the lads that mean to blow up the prison yard Monday. Your orders are to check in with McPherson in Pottsville and then report back to Pilkington HQ on Union Square. And that's supposed to happen toot sweet, no dilly-dallying."

"That's it? That's *everything*?" Liam's look was as black as a thundercloud. "I'm supposed to '*report to headquarters*'?"

Barlow seemed a bit taken aback. "What's the problem with that? That's what he said."

"I'll tell you what the problem is! Old Pilkington told me at the beginning that when this job was done, we were *quits*. He'd tell the New York cops to tear up their papers on me and I was free as a bird."

Barlow spread his hands. "I don't know anything about that. All I know is what he told me: you check in with McPherson, then you report back to HQ."

"And what about my Gran? Pilkington sicced the coppers on her for running a policy bank, then he said they'd hold up the arrest warrant till I had done this one little job for him. If I did it right, he said, he'd make sure the court voided it. What about *that* then, are they still hanging a sword over my grandma's head?"

Barlow shook his head helplessly. "Like I said, all I know is what he told me."

"*Damn* that old twister anyway! We had a deal."

Liam turned away abruptly and headed for the door.

"Hold on!" Barlow said sharply. "We had a deal too, and I did my part."

Liam made a face, picked up the pamphlet and read aloud: "'*Dynamite—The Cure for Capitalism.*'"

Barlow was riveted. "You don't say?"

Liam flipped the booklet open at random and translated out loud: "Death to the bourgeois! Always, wherever he may be, he will be overtaken by an anarchist's bomb or bullet." He snorted and threw the pamphlet aside, on top of the love letters. "What a pack of morons! Sounds like Stanton's sermonizing about national security turned inside out, you people and these evil crackpots deserve each other."

He threw the pamphlet back on the bed, spun on his heel and headed out the door.

"Hey!" yelled Barlow. "Where do you think you're going?"

His only answer was the sound of Liam's heels clattering down the stairs.

Chapter Six

s he stepped outside and closed Maggie's front door behind him Liam stopped short, struck by the finality of the moment. For weeks he had been tying himself into knots trying to figure out how to get free of the mess he was tangled in thanks to Pilkington holding his Gran hostage—the whole "big-city-cracksman-on-the-run" charade he'd been performing to keep the Molly Magees sweet; the dynamitings; the constant, sickening danger of being forced to commit murder in spite of himself; the stewing misery of his companions, angry men stuffed down a mine like sardines in a can; the endlessly interlocking consequences of each lie he was forced to tell, with each bit of violence spreading its ripples into infinity until he felt himself drowning in it all, a maelstrom greedy enough to swallow Manhattan.

And now life had simply turned the page.

He stood for a moment soaking up the late afternoon sunshine, closing his eyes and spreading his arms as if to pull the warmth deep into his bones. Then, whistling absentmindedly, he set out along the dusty road back to the main street of Henderson's Patch, running through the information he had gathered on his own and with Barlow's help. He smiled wryly at the thought of the grizzled copper with his big beak and his little-old-man specs—not so much Pickwick, after all, maybe the Ghost of Christmas Yet to Come. If that was how Barlow figured in Liam's story, some kind of Herald, then Providence hadn't lost its irritating sense of humor.

He turned the corner onto the main drag and picked up his step a little, eager now to get to Maloney's and settle things with Boylan. It was good he'd had his moment of meditation back there, because once he sat down across the table from the Grand Chieftan of the Shamrocks' local lodge and looked into his cruel little pig eyes, he would have to work hard to keep his wits about him.

"Ahoy, McCool!"

The shout broke into Liam's reverie and he stopped short: it was Fergus Dineen, his companion from last night's adventure, coming towards him at a brisk trot, his thin, sharp-featured face crinkled with anxiety.

"Ah, Liam, I'm that glad to see you!"

Liam grinned ironically. "Well now, will wonders never cease? I would have sworn you'd legged it to Outer Mongolia by now." And then, relenting at Fergus' crestfallen look: "What's up then, is it trouble?"

Fergus grinned uneasily, shifting back and forth like a banty rooster on a hot rock. "Sure, I'm sorry Liam, but it's them fookin' Acmes as turns me blood to water. I've fought the Limey landlords' bullyboys with naught but a spade and a shillelagh and held me own. But them metal things ain't natural and I'm thinking it's the Devil himself as put them here to spite us!" He shuddered at the memory and then forced himself back to the moment. "As for trouble, there'll be plenty if we don't get down to Maloney's sharpish—himself's raising hell wondering where you've got to."

"That's a laugh," Liam said with an answering grin, "seeing as how I'd bet it was Himself sicced the C & I Inspector on me. Come on, then, I wouldn't want Boylan to piss himself fretting."

He started walking again, briskly, Fergus half trotting to keep up.

"I wouldn't be tweaking his nose if I was you," Fergus said, "the hangings are only five days away now, and he's wound tight as a fiddle string. I know he'll be wanting a report on how the work in Pottsville is going."

"Then he shall have it," Liam said with a bland smile.

"And another thing," Fergus said, his voice plunging to a conspiratorial whisper despite the fact that the nearest listeners were a couple of kids rolling a hoop with a stick a block away, "he's heard a rumor that McPherson's in Pottsville!"

Liam threw him a sharp look. "What? The Pilkington detective?"

Fergus spat angrily into the road: "Pilkington stool pigeon, more like. I knew that shite-pot when he was the Boss' fair-haired boy."

Nobody in Henderson's Patch had spoken openly about the Great Detective throughout the time he'd been here, and Liam was having to struggle to keep from showing his interest:

"You don't say, now? You knew him right up to the end?"

"Right to the bitter end, trials and all." He dropped his voice again, looking around to make sure nobody could hear: "And who was it then, was saying to the Boss from the very first that Mr. Music-Hall Irish was all blather and blarney and blindfolding the Devil?"

Liam gave that a small grin. "I don't imagine Mr. Boylan welcomed your advice."

"He did, like hell." Fergus snorted disgustedly: "McPherson sucked up to him from the word go, and it must be said our Grand Chieftain likes to hear a flattering word. So there's the Great Sleuth McPherson leading us out on raids and punishments with the Boss' blessings, making the Mollie Magees the terror of the coalfields, and all the time narking to the owners." He shook his head bitterly. "There's no villain so low as an informer, and no informer so vile as one that narks on fellow Irishmen to Mr. Franklin B. Gowen—that whey-faced son of a bitch isn't just a bloodsucking slave-driver, he's a damned Ulsterman born and bred!"

Liam just shook his head and looked pained, for once at a loss for words. Words other than "informer," anyhow, that one twisting in his guts like a poisoned dagger. Fergus, happy to have the stage, continued with furious sarcasm:

"You wasn't here then, but that narking piece of shite actually climbed up on the stand and *testified* against us at the trials, stood there smirking like a good little boy while they sentenced one after the other of us to death. I tell you this: when they go to hang the first ten next Thursday, every single snapped neck and weeping mother will be down to Pilking-ton's hoor, Mr. Seamus McStoolie."

The story seemed to be getting to Liam. He cleared his throat hard and said: "That's a heavy burden . . ."

But Fergus was off again: "And the hell of it is, McPherson wasn't even worth two cents as a mate. I've read all them eejit tales in the papers as how he was always standing the rounds in Maloneys, singing songs and dancing a jig at the drop of a hat, but the truth is that son of a bitch was a skinflint and a tightwad that could squeeze a penny till it shit ha'penny stamps! And God forbid you might be wanting a kind word and a pat on the shoulder and come asking *that* swine to be a comrade. Most like he'd spit on your shoes—that young fel-la's eye was always on the main chance, and his greatest and tenderest care was for one thing and one thing only: onwards and upwards for darling Seamus McPherson. And would you believe it?" He bent closer to Liam, whispering again: "Word's come to the Boss from the Chapter in Pottsville: somebody's actually seen the dirty squealer there, not ten miles from where we're standing!"

That jolted Liam: "Jasus, Dineen! Someone actually saw him?"

"Hard to believe," Fergus said solemnly, "but whoever told the Boss swears it's true! Still," he said with a gesture towards a big, open-fronted saloon in the next block, "I expect it's himself will be telling you about it."

Deep in thought, Liam just nodded as they approached the broad wooden steps leading up to Maloney's. Fergus was silent too, looking anxious again as Liam pushed open the batwing doors and stepped inside.

Liam felt his spirits sink the moment he crossed the threshold. It was always the middle of the night in here: the shutters closed tight and the heavy curtains drawn, a permanent miasma of spilled beer and dense tobacco smoke killing the freshness of the outdoors and dimming even the artificial daylight of the only electrical system in Henderson's Patch.

More than once Liam had wondered where the money came from—Boylan could only charge the miners so much for cheap Pennsylvania whiskey and local draft beer, and paying for a fine new Tesla steam generator and a constellation of those fancy Tesla "Helios" light globes would have called for an army division of off-shift miners drinking day and night for a century. Not to mention the steam pianola tinkling away in the background, that Boylan had brought home from the Exposition in Philly for a sum that would pay ten miners' wages for a year.

Thudding footsteps approached Liam and Fergus from behind, making the plank floor tremble, and both men turned to deposit their weapons in a basket shoved towards them by one of Boylan's bouncers. Six feet tall, dressed in a good broadcloth suit with crisp white linen and a polka-dot bow tie, the thing had the stolid look of most automatons, although its rubber skin looked much more natural and human than the painted-porcelain mugs of Royce's Acmes. And no wonder, Liam thought. Produced in Samuel Colt's Hartford factory, with a miniaturized Stanley steam turbine, Colt's precision engineering giving it lifelike smoothness of motion and Ada

Lovelace's latest "Predictive Engine" giving it a distant semblance of human brain power, a brand-new Lovelace-Colt "Columbia" (which this one appeared to be) cost more than all the miners in town could make in a lifetime, maybe two lifetimes.

As the thing clomped away, bearing Liam's pistol and Fergus' Case knife to the checkroom, Fergus shivered and spat on the floor.

"Sure, McCool, if I live to be a hundred years old I'll never get used to them tin soldiers. God help us if the buggers start talking, it'll be time to go live in a cave."

Liam grinned and nodded towards the back of the room: "We'd better hustle, the Boss is giving us the evil eye."

Seated in state at a round, polished-mahogany table near the exit was the Cerberus of Maloney's, Grand Chieftan of the local lodge of the Order of the Shamrock Daniel Xavier ("Boyo," if you dared) Boylan. Glowering like a thundercloud, his big shiny red face with its shiny black cap of brilliantined hair and glossy black handlebar moustache shimmering with displeasure, Boylan abruptly hoisted his 6-foot-7-inch, 300-plus pounds of muscle and hard fat out of his chair and folded his arms on his chest as he snarled at the approaching pair:

"And just where the hell do you think you've been, McCool?"

Liam smiled affably, sat down at the table and poured himself a drink from a half-empty bottle of Jameson's.

"*Sláinte!*" he toasted, and then: "Come to that, Boss, I've been wasting my morning answering questions for a Coal & Iron copper that thought I just might have killed Maggie. It wasn't you as steered him my way, was it?"

The big man dropped back into his chair with a thump, grabbed the bottle of Jameson's and poured himself a drink twice the size of Liam's, then downed it in a gulp and wiped his mouth on his shirtsleeve. He gave Liam a withering look:

"If mouth was money you could buy out Carnegie himself."

Liam gave him a placating grin, picked up the bottle and poured Boylan another big slug without refreshing his own. *Mind your eye, McCool,* he said to himself. Today wasn't the day to be ruffling the Grand Master's feathers—if he wanted to get out of Henderson's Patch without stirring any dangerous suspicions about his motives he'd have to play this meek and mild and make sure Boylan believed his excuses whether he liked them or not. The last thing he wanted was to give that weaseling old humbug Pilkington any excuse to say he hadn't held up his end of their deal.

"Sure and no offense was meant, Boss." Liam said in his most disarming manner. "The truth be told, I was just on my way here when I ran into Fergus looking for me. What can I do for you?"

"You can give me your report on the Pottsville tunnel, and none of your lip." He glared at Liam, but he was mollified enough that his tone was more bark than bite.

Liam nodded reassuringly: "Everything's looking lovely," he said, "the boys figure they'll be crossing under the prison wall by tonight, and that leaves plenty of time to get everything ready."

"How far beyond the wall do you mean to dig?"

"Another six feet will put us right under the middle of the seats they're putting out for the nobs. With all the fireworks the boys are hauling in there, you'll be able to hear the bang in Pittsburgh."

Boylan nodded grimly. "Maybe when the dust settles they'll realize the Mollie Magees still have all their teeth. And how many invites have they given out?"

"Our pet screw reckons it's near on three hundred—every one of them some big-cheese pal of Gowen's or the Governor's or the Warden's or some other good Christian that's slobbering for the sight of Mollies dancing on a rope and pissing their pants."

Boylan gave Liam a grudging little smile: "For all you're a whopping great pain in the arse, McCool, you've done a grand job organizing the Attack Section."

"I'm glad you think so, Boss, for I'm about to ask you a favor."

"Are you, now?" Boylan's eyes narrowed with suspicion. "Well, don't be shy, man, spit it out!"

"I need some time off," Liam said. "Just a couple of weeks," he added apologetically, "so if you'd be agreeable I'd like to ask Fergus to take over as foreman till I get back."

Boylan's face had turned a deep reddish-purple, bulging so furiously that for a moment Liam thought his head might explode: "*Two weeks!?*" Boylan roared. "Have ye gone bughouse, McCool? Right now we need every man we've got to be at his *post*, not off lollygagging."

"Come on, Boss," Liam pleaded earnestly, "I've done everything I can to set this job on the rails and it doesn't really need me anymore. The tunnel's so near the end a tame badger could finish the digging. And Fergus can shepherd it to the end without a hitch, he's a good lad and he knows the job backwards. As for me, I won't rest till I can start tracking down the rat that killed Maggie."

Boylan's fury seemed to evaporate all of a sudden and he sat for several moments sunk in thought as he stared appraisingly at Liam. Finally he said:

"I'm thinking it'll take you a lot longer than two weeks to find him."

He picked up the bottle of Jameson's and poured two more shots. Liam knocked back his in one gulp and waited. Boylan watched him with a sour little quirk to his lips before he continued:

"What makes you think you know where to start?"

There was a touch of sarcasm in Boylan's voice that Liam didn't like.

"Are you trying to tell me something, Boss?"

"Sure, if I were it'd be the labors of Hercules to make you hear me, wouldn't it, McCool? And you as ready to listen to good counsel as a cigar-store Indian!"

Boylan's anger was coming to the surface again and he leaned forward to grab Liam by the upper arm. He continued in a low growl, his eyes blazing:

"Maggie O'Shea was here in Henderson's Patch a good two years before you showed up. If you're as fly as you're made out to be I won't have to tell you she was no shrinking violet. She had sweethearts whenever the mood took her and she made no bones about it. Hell, that's how she came here—Henderson doesn't let anybody set up for business in this patch without paying for the privilege, and Maggie had something he liked better than money. Come to that, she was my sweetheart too, for a while, and it like to broke my heart when she gave me my walking papers. So what makes you think you know which one of Maggie's lovers would be the one that did it?"

Liam wasn't happy with Boylan's hand on his arm, but he kept his voice carefully neutral:

"Just this: there was only *one* of you cleared out of town in the last twenty-four hours without leaving so much as a collar button behind."

Boylan flinched so hard that he almost dug his fingers through Liam's bicep.

"What the hell . . . ?"

Finally running out of patience, Liam took hold of Boylan's wrist by one of the pressure points he'd learned from Harry the Jap and pressed it slightly; Boylan howled with pain and jerked his arm back, baring his teeth like a dog about to attack.

"It'll feel better in a few minutes," Liam said tersely. "Meanwhile, you can tell me what you know about where Lukas went. Was it you that cleared out his rooms?"

Boylan just stared, black fury in his eyes.

"Because if it was, you missed a couple of things—like a picture of him with Maggie at the Expo in Philly."

"Pah!" Boylan scoffed. "Maggie loved that place, she'd go there with anybody that'd buy a couple tickets for the boat from Pottsville. You took her there yourself, more than once."

"Uh huh," Liam said. "But that wasn't all I found. There was a bunch of love letters, too, billy-doos from Maggie to Lukas."

This time Boylan looked surprised: "Where . . . ?"

"Never mind where I found them," Liam said. "Just give me an idea where Lukas was headed when he left."

Boylan's jaw set hard and Liam could see he wasn't going to say another word.

"I know it was somewhere in New York," Liam said, "because he told Maggie a few days ago he was going there to do some of those interviews for that book of his. What happened, did he come back for something and get into an argument with her? Sure, he probably tried to get her to give him one last roll in the hay and then he lost his temper when she told her no."

He stared at Boylan abstractedly for a moment, visualizing the scene as Boylan stared back at him stonily.

"That had to be how it went," Liam said, nodding to himself more than Boylan. "Then he left here in a panic thinking somebody heard the shot and came by Maloney's by the back way to tell you to clear his stuff out before the C & I's came around investigating."

Boylan spoke again now, his voice flat and hard. "You've got some imagination, McCool. So why don't you imagine this: if Lukas can order Daniel Xavier Boylan around like a plantation nigger, then just *maybe* he's somebody that a smart lad like you should steer well clear of."

Liam nodded slowly. "Thanks for the whiskey, Boss. And when you're next in touch with Lukas, warn him he'd better keep a weather eye out. New York is my city, and when I get back I'll be looking up my old pals and asking them to help me search for Lukas. I don't know if you've heard of the Butcher Boys, but every man Jack of us grew up on those streets, and if I ask them to find me one particular *flea* out of New York's ten trillion vermin, they'll have it in a pill box before you can say boo."

Touching his forehead in a mock salute, Liam turned and headed back towards the saloon's entrance. Boyle stared after him, his eyes narrowed with thought, then beckoned to Fergus:

"Dineen, you're the new tunnel foreman. And meanwhile go tell Collum I want to send a telegram and make sure my Flyer's steamed up and ready to go."

As Fergus took off, Boylan got to his feet and looked towards the front, just in time to see Liam retrieve his pistol, push through the batwing doors and disappear into the street.

"All right, then, *Mister* McCool," Boylan muttered, "let's see just how sharp you are."

Chapter Seven

utdoors again, the spring sunshine warm on his face and the fresh breeze blowing away the last stale fumes of beer and tobacco smoke, Liam resolved to stay away from saloons until he could do an hour of jiu-jitsu practice with his sparring partner Harry the Jap and not even break a sweat. Age was starting to creep up on him—he'd be thirty in a couple of years—and he had no intention of ending up in Potter's Field like the legions of penniless Micks waiting there for him to join them. He meant to die old, rich and surrounded by good books, which meant he'd better get busy. Step one: pack his stuff, hire a ride to Pottsville and catch a train for Philly and points North.

By this point in his musings Liam was ready to sprint the last half mile to his boarding house, but before he could break into a run he saw something that made him stop short. Not a hundred yards away and moving towards him with a worried, abstracted expression, his thoughts plainly miles away from Henderson's Patch, was that fussy old maid Arthur Morrison—now the sole upstairs occupant of Maggie's house.

Something clicked in Liam's mind and it must have sent out a thought-wave because Morrison halted abruptly, turned towards Liam with a look of pure panic on his face and started to back away, holding his hands out in front of him as if he were warding off some grisly specter. Then, a moment later, he turned on his heel and took off in the opposite direction, running.

"Hey!" shouted Liam. "Hold on a minute!"

But Morrison just ran faster, his elbows flapping out to the side as if he were some ungainly flightless bird trying to escape a hungry cat. Liam made a face and poured on the speed, closing the gap so swiftly that he came level with Morrison in moments. He reached out and grabbed the little man's shoulder, bringing a startled "Eep!" from his prey. Morrison jolted to a stop and faced Liam with a look at once terrified and abject, the sweat pouring down his face, wilting his stiff collar and soaking the underarms of his heavy black suit.

"What's your big hurry?" Liam inquired mildly.

"I . . . er . . . it's, it's . . ." Morrison stuttered.

"Take it easy, Morrison, I don't bite. Why are you running away from me?"

The accountant pulled a neatly folded linen handkerchief out of his breast pocket and mopped his face before answering in a plaintive, reedy voice:

"No offense intended, I assure you, Mr. McCool. It's just . . . it's just . . . well, everybody knows you're one of the Mollies, and then there was the explosion at Mr. Henderson's house, and the coffin notice from the Mollies, and . . . and . . ."

He really looked as if he were about to burst into tears and Liam patted him on the shoulder:

"No one's going to blow you up, Arthur, don't worry. But I have to talk to you about what happened to Maggie last night."

At that, every last drop of blood seemed to disappear from Morrison's face, leaving it an alarming shade of gray. The little man jerked his head around as if he were trying to find some avenue of escape, and Liam decided he'd better take a firmer hand.

"Come on," he said, "let's go across the street to Mrs. Clark's place, I'll buy you a drink and a ham sandwich."

"No," said Morrison desperately, shaking his head so hard it looked in danger of coming loose. "No, no, I . . . er . . ."

Liam took hold of his arm: "It isn't a request. Let's go."

As the opening door rang the little bell suspended above it, Mrs. Clark—a plump, white-haired lady in a blue gingham dress and a pink apron—looked up from a well-worn issue of *Godey's Lady's Book* and gave Liam and Morrison a grandmotherly smile:

"Well, now! What can I bring you boys?"

Liam returned the smile as he pushed Morrison ahead of him to a table in the furthest corner of the room:

"How about a bottle of bourbon and a couple of glasses, Mrs. Clark? And a couple of nice thick ham sandwiches?"

"Right away, Mr. McCool," she said.

As Mrs. Clark bustled cheerfully in the background, Liam leaned forward across the table and gave Morrison the gimlet eye:

"OK," he said, "talk to me. I know you never go to Maloney's till after eight, that means you must have seen or heard *something* downstairs before you went out."

The panicked look had come back into Morrison's eyes and he kept opening and closing his mouth like a fish out of water.

"I . . . I can't . . ."

He got a momentary reprieve as Mrs. Clark brought them a tray with the whiskey and sandwiches and a big glass pitcher of water, but a moment later she went back to the counter and her interrupted *Godey's*, leaving Morrison on the hook.

"By Heaven," Liam muttered, "I'm beginning to wonder if maybe you're the one that killed her!"

"*No!*" Morrison whispered hoarsely. "You're *crazy*, I worshipped Miss O'Shea!"

63

Liam shook his head disgustedly and poured Morrison half a tumbler of bourbon.

"Drink that!" he ordered.

"I don't . . . I don't really . . ."

"Damn you, Morrison," Liam said in a low voice. "You drink that up and get a grip on yourself, or I swear I'll haul you outside and drag you up and down the street till you wish you had."

Despairingly, Morrison grabbed the whiskey and gulped it down. Liam watched with his arms folded impatiently until at last a bit of color came back into the accountant's cheeks.

Liam leaned forward and poked Morrison hard in the middle of the chest: "Now cut the shilly-shallying and tell me straight out. What do you know about the murder?"

Morrison squinched his eyes shut and grimaced as if Liam were pulling out his fingernails.

"For the love of God, McCool," he said hoarsely, "it's as much as my life is worth."

Liam examined him for a moment, then leaned forward and lowered his voice again:

"What if you had enough money to get out of Henderson's Patch and go wherever you wanted?"

Morrison's eyes popped open and he peered at Liam inquisitively.

"I don't know what Henderson pays you," Liam continued, "but I don't expect it amounts to a hill of beans. What if I give you five hundred dollars in gold, would that loosen your tongue?"

"Are you *serious?*"

Morrison shook his head as if he were a little dazed.

"I've dreamed for years of traveling to the Orient," he continued, "of sailing from San Francisco to the Hawaiian Islands and China. I've lived like an anchorite, denied myself everything, scrimped and saved till I had just about enough.

And then that dirty swindler Jay Cooke went under in '73 and took my savings with him, every blessed penny. If I could get my hands on five hundred in gold . . . "

Morrison's voice trailed off and his attention drifted away from Liam into visions of sugar plums. Liam left him alone for a few moments, giving the hook time to set.

"You come over to Mrs. Finnegan's with me and I'll give you the money right now. But first you'll have to tell me what you know about Maggie's killer."

Morrison blew out a heavy sigh, grudging the return to reality. "I won't deny I'm tempted," he said cautiously, "but I can't just jump on it, there's something I have to look into first."

Liam stifled his impatience, knowing better than to spook Morrison before he gave up the information.

"How long will that take?"

Morrison pondered that, his forehead creased into a washboard of worried wrinkles. Finally he said: "Are you willing to swear to that five hundred?"

Liam fought with an urge to tweak the little man's nose. "I said it, I mean it," he snapped. "Twenty-five nice shiny double eagles."

"Very well," Morrison said, nodding as if to convince himself. He took the damp handkerchief back out of his breast pocket, wrapped it carefully around his ham sandwich and stowed it away in the pocket of his jacket.

"I believe you board at Mrs. Finnegan's . . ."

"Top floor, on the street side."

"One way or another I'll come over there tonight after it gets dark," Morrison said with slightly tremulous resolve. "Say around nine o'clock, would that be satisfactory?"

"That would be just fine," Liam said. "I'll have the money ready, but you don't get a penny unless you're ready to talk."

Morrison nodded again, turned on his heel and hurried away, opening and closing the front door so fast it barely jingled the bell. Liam stared after him abstractedly, then picked up his own sandwich and started munching; he hadn't had anything but whiskey in his stomach since supper time yesterday, and suddenly he was ravenous enough to eat a bear.

"Could you bring me some lemonade, Mrs. Clark?"

She smiled. All the single lads were substitute sons to her, and she was happy to see Liam pass up the whiskey; Mr. Clark had been from County Mayo, and sadly he had never passed up the whiskey.

"Of course, dear."

As she was getting out the lemons the front door opened again, revealing Inspector Barlow and a strikingly good-looking young woman wearing a light gray suit of cashmere and brocade silk and a jaunty Milan straw hat trimmed with velvet perched on top of a coil of lustrous chestnut hair. As Barlow stood behind her holding the door open she entered and looked around, taking in every detail with lively, wide-set eyes of such a startling deep blue that Liam felt something lurch alarmingly inside him.

"Good morning, ma'am," she said cheerfully, "you must be Mrs. Clark."

As if in spite of himself, Liam noted that her voice was a musical alto, with just a touch of a well-bred New York accent—the sort of voice that could soothe a mad dog and make it lie down and roll over. Mrs. Clark, however, stood with her jaw hanging open, as stunned as if she'd been struck by lightning. A moment later, she managed to gulp out a question of her own:

"Miss Fox? *Becky* Fox?"

"The same," the young woman said with a grin, "and pleased to make your acquaintance."

But Mrs. Clark wasn't standing on formality. Instead, she rushed out from behind the counter and threw her arms around Miss Fox with such energy that the young woman started laughing.

"Gracious!," she said after a moment, "what have I done to deserve all this?"

66

Mrs. Clark pushed her away to arms' length, inspecting her with a kind of worshipful affection.

"What have you *done*?" Mrs. Clark echoed. "You only got my baby sister released from that horrible Tombs, that's what you've done! If I live to be a thousand years old, I could never repay you for that, you sweet, wonderful woman!"

Becky Fox blushed as deep a crimson as Liam had ever seen and made embarrassed noises as Mrs. Clark hugged her again and kissed her on both cheeks.

Liam, meanwhile, was finally putting the live woman together with the engraved portraits he'd been seeing in newspapers and magazines for the past few years. *Becky Fox.* One of the most famous women in America, maybe the world. Mrs. Clark's sister must have been one of those hard-luck babies in the Women's Prison on Leonard Street that Miss Fox wrote about in *Harper's Weekly*.

Becky Fox had pulled a stunt that took more nerve than Liam could believe, dressing as a streetwalker, pouring gin on herself and then smacking some dumb harness bull and screaming at him till she got thrown in the can. *"Two Weeks in the Black Hole of New York,"* the story in *Harper's Weekly* had been called, and what she'd seen going on in Leonard Street's fifty rat-infested cells were things nobody who hadn't been locked up on the men's side could believe.

Liam got up from behind his table and approached the others so he could bow to the newcomer.

"Miss Fox," Liam said, "I've been a prisoner in the Tombs myself, and there isn't a one of us that doesn't admire your courage."

If anything, she looked even more discomfited this time, and Barlow's eyes narrowed with sly curiosity as he caught the spark that jumped between Becky and Liam.

"Now, folks," he said in his best Parson Brown tones, "you're making this poor young lady just as embarrassed as if she'd won all the blue ribbons at the Sunday School picnic.

And here I've been carrying on all morning promising her a slice of the best apple pie and a cup of the best coffee this side of Delmonico's Restaurant!"

Instantly, Mrs. Clark bustled away to fetch a whole pie and the ham she'd cut into for Liam's and Morrison's sandwiches and whatever else she could think of to make a fitting feast for Becky Fox. Barlow took the occasion to introduce Liam to the reporter:

"This is Liam McCool, Miss Fox, the fellow I was telling you about."

As she registered what Barlow said, her remarkable eyes teared with such genuine compassion that Liam almost teared up himself.

"You poor man," she said, taking both of Liam's hands in hers, "I am so *terribly* sorry to hear about what happened to Miss O'Shea."

"Thanks, Miss Fox, I . . ." Liam cleared his throat loudly, unnerved by the effect her sympathy was having on him. " . . . I expect she'd be happy to know you mourned her passing. She was a great admirer of yours, in fact I think she read just about every word you've written. You and Victoria Woodhull were her ideals."

He turned and gestured to the table he'd just vacated. "Won't you and Inspector Barlow come and join me at my table? I'd be honored."

She gave Liam a radiant smile and he found himself making one of his mental photographs: forehead—high and serene, just fringed by a bang of auburn hair; eyebrows and lashes—thick and her own, free of any kind of warpaint; eyes – a blue deep as a mountain lake, steady, fearless, ready for anything; nose—straight, strong, no cute little upturn; mouth – wide, half-smiling even in repose, the lips pink and full without a hint of rouge; chin—firm, forthright, determined . . .

Finally, not quite keeping the chuckle out of his voice, Barlow spoke: "Miss Fox is young and strong and she could probably stand here all day while you stare at her but us old fellows need to sit down . . ."

Liam woke up at that, as embarrassed as Miss Fox had been earlier. Fortunately, this was the moment when Mrs. Clark came bustling towards them holding a tray laden with food and a big china pitcher of lemonade.

"Shoo!" she said, driving them ahead of her. "Sit down, for pity's sake!"

Saved by the bell, Liam thought, and for a while everybody concentrated on a banquet of ham and fried potatoes and chicken fricassee and green beans and pickled gherkins and so much other stuff that Liam finally ran out of space and had to quit. Then he wiped his mouth with his napkin and gave himself up to staring unashamedly at Miss Fox, who just smiled and kept on eating. He liked the way she ate—no Miss Goody Two-Shoes pretense of eating like a bird, this baby could pack it in like a stevedore. He grinned at her:

"What brings you to Henderson's Patch, Miss Fox? Was it Mrs. Clark's cooking?"

"Nothing quite so pleasant, I'm afraid." She gave him a level, serious look and he felt that odd lurch again. "Did you know that Miss O'Shea had promised me a story?"

The question rocked Liam back on his heels—as often as he'd heard Maggie mention Becky Fox, he'd never heard her say a word about being in touch with the reporter. He shook his head uncertainly:

"I did not, Miss Fox. Can you say what it was about?"

Becky Fox gave him a regretful smile: "I wish I could, but the note she sent me at *Harper's* said it was too important for anything but a face-to-face meeting and that it needed to be soon, as she was planning a trip. So one of my reasons for coming here was certainly to talk to her."

As much as he tried to sound casual, Inspector Barlow was plainly hanging on Becky's every word:

"May we ask what the other was?"

"Of course," she said matter-of-factly. "I mean to write about the hangings."

The Inspector sat back in his chair, his expression as strained as if she'd just stamped on his toe but he was too polite to let on that it hurt.

"You're in luck, Miss Fox," Barlow said after a momentary pause. "Mr. McCool's as thick as thieves with the Mollies."

Barlow was watching them both now, as vigilantly as an angler who has flicked a nice new Royal Coachman into the middle of a promising pool, but Liam was too distracted to be cautious:

"Don't you ever get tired of playing your copper games, Barlow?" Putting the lid on his irritation he turned to Becky: "The Grand Chieftan of the local Lodge is Boyo Boylan and you can find him at the big saloon down the street—if I know Boyo, he'll blather on till your ears fall off. But just why you would want to dignify this dirty farce by writing about it, I can't fathom. No offense intended, Miss Fox."

"I'm hard to offend," she said with a smile. "Though I would like to know what you mean by 'dirty farce.'"

Liam shrugged. "A few of the prisoners deserve hanging—I'm no friend of people who shoot unarmed men or blow up the innocent with the guilty. But most of these lads are just being made examples of. I'm sure you know the trials were rigged, what with Gowen being both the Public Prosecutor and the owner of the Philly & Reading Coal and Iron Co., so I'd say that makes the hangings themselves nothing more than Lynch's Law."

Barlow threw an uneasy glance towards Becky: "Now, just you hang on a minute, McCool."

"I don't think so, old man," Liam said with steel in his voice. "I'm hoping *somebody* in America will finally tell the truth about the hangings." He turned back to Becky: "Pennsylvania law says executions have to be public, but they're keeping ordinary folks outside the walls and handing out front-row tickets like party favors to all of Mr. Gowen's rich pals. That ought to make a pretty picture for your readers, the fat cats watching the mice get their necks snapped."

Becky was watching him intently. "Thank you," she said. "If what you say is true I promise you I'll write it. But to be honest, it's only one part of my story. The main story is the mess America's in less than a year after all the Centennial hoopla. The last few months I've been traveling everywhere the railroads will take me, and from what I've seen the whole county is sitting squarely on top of a powder keg. I don't know yet quite what it will take to light the fuse, but these hangings could strike the spark."

Barlow looked flustered and mad, like a father who has just discovered his daughter smoking cigarettes.

"I surely do hate to argue with a lady, Miss Fox," Barlow said in an aggrieved tone, "but I just can't believe things are that bad. I've traveled some myself, and I haven't been hearing that kind of talk."

Becky laughed. "Forgive me, Inspector," she said, "but I'm guessing you have that 'Police' look whether you're in uniform or not, so these days nobody would be likely to speak their minds around you. Not when Secretary Stanton and his people make no distinction between honest discontent and sedition."

Barlow's face was dark with unhappiness: "I just can't abide the thought of you giving your readers such a one-sided . . ."

Becky laid a hand on his arm and interrupted him gently:

"I'm afraid you've been away from the city too long— you won't find a single New York paper that doesn't echo what I say. Do you have any idea how many tens of thousands of penniless New Yorkers are sleeping in Central Park or asking the police to give them their night's lodging in a jail cell?"

Barlow just stared at her glumly. She waited for a moment for him to reply, then she shrugged and went on.

71

"There was an editorial in the *Sun* just before I left which said flat out that Washington was in the hands of the Money Power and that it made no difference who was the President or what the parties in Congress called themselves, they were all the dummies of the banks and the industrialists. And the *Sun* is a *conservative* paper." She smiled wryly: "I imagine I needn't tell you that Secretary Stanton decided the editor must be insane and arranged for him to have a nice long rest in the locked ward at Bellevue."

Barlow frowned ominously. "Well, now, Miss Fox, I'd say you ought to be sensible and keep that thought in mind while you're writing on your piece for *Harper's.*"

Becky shook her head with a regretful smile and turned to Liam: "The Inspector tells me you were at Gettysburg with the 20th Maine."

Liam just nodded, ready to listen to her talk for the rest of the afternoon. She nodded and went on:

"What would you say if I told you the war against slavery was about to be fought all over again?"

This time Barlow blew up: "What in Sam Hill do you think you're talking about, young lady? If there's anything we don't need right now it's loose talk about war!"

She smiled sadly. "And I expect this time it will be fought even more bitterly and cruelly than it was in '61–'65. We're the only modern nation except for the French Commune that isn't based on some form of slavery. The British Empire has Industrial Feudalism, with its factory serfs. The European empires and kingdoms all copy Britain feverishly, hoping to catch up with her, and right across the Mississippi from us Little Russia has its mixture of red Indian slaves and Russian peasant serfs. When they look around and see those armies of docile workers our industrialists are absolutely livid at having to pay wages and deal with the specter of unions. They're telling their pet Congressmen that they can't compete with the other Great Powers if slavery isn't restored. It's a matter of national honor, you see."

Barlow had lapsed into sullen silence, but Liam was riveted: "I don't get it, Miss Fox. Who's going to declare war on whom?"

Becky gave him a cryptic smile. "It's going to be a lot more complicated than last time, Mr. McCool, you can count on that. And the stakes will be even higher."

Liam nodded thoughtfully. He knew Becky Fox's reputation as a journalist and now that he'd met her he was as sure as could be that she knew what she was talking about. That wasn't a happy thought.

"I've had about all the fighting I can stand for one lifetime," he said with a somber look. "I'll bet you've had a finger in the wind for a while now—when do you expect the war to break out?"

"Sooner rather than later. Coming down here I talked to people on the Pennsy—that's our biggest railroad, they have almost 200,000 workers. And the owners keep cutting their wages without cutting dividends to the Pennsy's shareholders. Some of the men I talked to have had their wages cut to 75 cents a day—they can't live on that themselves, let alone keep a family." She made a wry face and shook her head. "I think there'll be a strike on the railroads before the month is out, and when that happens it's anybody's guess what happens next."

"I guess I'd better get moving while I can, then," Liam said. "I'd have quite a job getting to New York on foot."

"You're absolutely right, Mr. McCool," she said. "And I think *I* had better get after Mr. Boylan now and get on with my article."

As she got to her feet, the men got to theirs as well and Liam gave her a little bow. "It was a real pleasure meeting you Miss Fox, and I'd be happy to accompany you to Maloney's if you'd like an escort."

She gave him her radiant smile again and held out her hand for a forthright shake. "I hope we may talk again,

Mr. McCool," she said. "But I think I'd better have an escort of Coal & Iron Police if I'm to go into the lion's den."

Liam stayed standing and watched as Becky and a somewhat subdued Inspector Barlow left, stopping on their way for one more effusive exchange with Mrs. Clark. She had stirred him up but good, Liam thought, and he was a little irked with himself for being so susceptible so soon after losing Maggie. Then, suddenly picturing Maggie wagging her finger at him and reading him the riot act, he burst out laughing. If Maggie's spirit were looking on right now she was probably telling him to stop giving himself airs. There would be snow-drifts in Hell the day Becky Fox paid any mind to the likes of Liam McCool!

Chapter Eight

as it Australia or was it more like Staten Island? It had appeared there during the endless April rains, when Liam had spent so much time staring at the ceiling that he had seriously considered going outside and running around in the mud yelling and throwing things. At first the water stain had been just a kind of formless blotch but then it started filling out and spreading into map-like shapes until it took only a little imagination to see himself trekking through the Outback looking for gold. Or maybe strolling along the South Beach Boardwalk looking for a beer garden where he could get a stein of Ruppert's and pick up a girl over from Brooklyn for an evening's jollification.

"*Aaargh!*"

He'd had enough waiting. He slid off the bed and stood up to stretch, listening to his joints pop as he reached for the ceiling. Then he pulled out his watch (a nice Waltham railroad chronometer that he'd hooked from Brooks Brothers during his first weekend home after Gettysburg) and saw that the hands had barely moved since he looked at it last. At this rate it would be sometime next year when the blasted thing finally said nine o'clock.

He threw himself onto the bed again, wincing at the screech of the spavined springs, and reached towards the bedside table for the nice new *Leaves of Grass* that he'd bought at Brentano's before beginning his exile in the coalfields. He had just started thumbing through it in search of the "Song of the Open Road" when he heard a strange whirring noise approaching from the distance—like a colossal hummingbird with a screechy overtone like chalk on a blackboard. It took just a split second for the penny to drop before Liam leaped off the bed:

"Damn it, *no!*"

He grabbed his Colt off the dresser and clattered away down the stairs to the street.

○━┳

There was still a hint of light in the sky with the Summer Soltice so close, and Liam looked around feverishly for the source of the whirring . . . There! Just discernible against the night sky, not too high yet, maybe a hundred yards or so above the town and climbing, was a black Stanley Flyer with its engine heavily silenced. Liam didn't think twice before raising his pistol, aiming well above the escaping machine and firing three shots after it. A total waste of time, but . . . damnation! Return fire winked towards him and a moment later the sound of shots and a nearby ricochet followed, prompting Liam to throw himself into a roll away from the spot where he'd been standing into the shelter of an ancient chestnut in Mrs. Finnegan's front yard.

For a moment or two, Liam just lay there catching his breath and listening to the sound of the Flyer fading into the distance. Then, a sudden flare of orange caught his peripheral vision and he jumped to his feet, looking for the source.

There! Now he could see the flames plainly—it had to be Maggie's house, there wasn't anything else in that direction. It had jumped into his mind the moment he heard the distinctive thick whirring of a silenced Stanley Flyer: *Morrison, something's happened to Morrison!* Liam shoved the Colt into his waistband and tore off down the street in the direction of the steadily growing fire.

Why had he been chump enough to buy Morrison's song-and-dance about having to "look into something"? If he really had seen Maggie's killer—and the little man's muck sweat had made that seem a good bet—then Liam should have wrung it out of him then and there! As it was all he had was hunches and scraps of evidence, not enough to collar Lukas and see him hanged for it which was what he'd set his heart on . . .

"McCool! McCool, slow down!" Barlow's shout and the thunder of hoofs behind him made Liam stop short and turn back to look: the Inspector was coming towards him at a gallop in a two-seater buggy, and with a sharp jerk on the reins he slowed it just enough for Liam to jump aboard.

"Looks like it must be Miss O'Shea's place," Barlow said grimly.

"Didn't you leave a guard on it?"

Barlow made a face. "Talk sense, McCool. The poor girl was already dead, what was the point of wasting a man watching her house?"

"It isn't Maggie I was thinking of. It was Morrison—I was going to give him five hundred dollars in gold for the name of the man he saw last night."

"Damnation!" Barlow shook his head, exasperated. "He must have seen him through the peephole."

"Peephole?"

"I went back to Miss O'Shea's this afternoon, I wanted to talk to Morrison myself. But Kreutzer said he'd gone off somewhere in Oliver Finnegan's steam jitney so I decided to have a look around his rooms without him." He snorted disgustedly. "Turned out the little degenerate had drilled a peephole in his floor so he could spy on Miss O'Shea, and that means he must have seen the murder and recognized the murderer. The way

I figure it, certain people . . ." he raised an eyebrow at Liam ". . . scared the murderer off by blowing up Henderson's house with enough dynamite to flatten Grand Central, and as soon as the killer ran off Morrison grabbed his hat and headed for Maloney's and a nice big double whiskey to soothe his nerves."

Liam groaned. "Can't you make that nag *move* a little?"

Barlow snapped the reins sharply and a few moments later they careened around the corner onto Maggie's street so fast they almost galloped into the volunteer fire department's pumper.

"Whoa!" shouted Barlow, tugging on the reins, but Liam was already out of the buggy and running.

As he pushed his way through a chaotic mob of gawkers, Coal & Iron bluecoats and volunteer firemen, Liam scanned the upper floor anxiously. Was there a chance of getting in to see if Morrison was still there, dead *or* alive? The moment the thought went through his mind there was a crackle of splintering glass and the windows of the upper floor burst open as billows of flame gushed out.

"If he's there, he's done for," Barlow said.

"I'm going in."

"Are you *crazy?*"

But Liam was already gone, tearing up the front steps and through the front door into the burning house.

Squinting to keep the smoke from blinding him, Liam grabbed Maggie's cloak off a hook in the hall and wound it around his head to keep his hair from catching fire as he took the stairs two at a time. The door to Lukas' suite was open, and Liam noted even as he ran towards Morrison's rooms that the fire seemed so far to be burning upwards rather than outwards—it had burnt through the wall shared by the two upstairs lodgers, but it had only burnt through to Lukas' sitting room in a couple of places. Morrison didn't smoke, so it didn't take a genius to figure it for arson—Liam just hoped there was still something left to examine for clues.

He grabbed the knob of Morrison's door, cursed as it blistered his hand, then backed up and kicked the panel square in the middle. As if that was all it had been waiting for, the door burst out into the hallway and another billow of flames engulfed Liam.

Thanks to Maggie's cloak the worst of it seemed to be a thoroughly singed moustache, but one glance into the room was enough to make Liam drop flat to the floor. There was an inferno raging around the edges of the room—walls, curtains and furniture—and there was an empty red coal-oil can on the floor which gave Liam the picture in an instant: the killer had doused the perimeter of the room to make sure it would turn into a crematorium, saving the last few drops for Morrison, whose corpse lay in the middle of the floor with a gash up its middle that had poured his guts onto the floor.

It would have taken more than a splash of coal oil to make that mess burn, but by the time the room had burned and taken the rest of the house with it, the incineration would have been complete. Throwing caution to the winds, Liam threw aside Maggie's cloak, grabbed the corpse's ankles and scuttled out into the hallway, staying as low as he could and dragging the grisly mess behind him.

"Great God in Heaven!" shouted Barlow as Liam appeared in the doorway, smoking like a barbecued ham and dragging the burnt and bloody corpse behind him. The Inspector snatched a full bucket of water from one of the C & I bucket brigade and poured it over Liam's head, and a moment later, spluttering and gasping, Liam was on his knees next to the corpse going through its pockets.

"How did that bastard know Morrison was going to *talk?*" Liam croaked hoarsely.

Barlow grimaced. "I'll give odds that's where Morrison went this afternoon, he probably wanted to test whether he might get more than your five hundred from the killer."

"What's this?" Liam exclaimed. Folded over twice and concealed in a buttoned pocket inside Morrison's waistcoat was a thick sheaf of printed papers. Liam wiped the blood off on the grass and spread them out on the ground next to the corpse.

"Our tickets for San Francisco." Liam's voice was thick with bitter grief.

Barlow bent over for a closer look: "Yours for sure?"

"Look there," Liam said, pointing, "Maggie wrote 'M's' on hers and 'L's' on mine." He wiped the blood off his hands and stood up, leaving the tickets on the ground. Then, with a furious snarl, he kicked the corpse hard enough to turn it over on its face.

"Easy, lad," Barlow said gently, "that won't do you any good."

Liam growled an inarticulate retort. Then he grabbed another bucket of water from one of the C & I's, rolled up his sleeves and washed the blood off his hands and forearms as well as he could, ending by scooping double handfuls of water onto his face and rubbing until most of the soot was gone and he felt a little better.

"He must have watched through that peephole while the killer stole our money and Maggie's diary," he said to Barlow. "Then as soon as he left, Morrison scurried downstairs and looked for anything else that wasn't tacked down. Once he found the tickets, all he needed was enough money—mine or the murderer's, whichever one of us was paying top dollar—to go off and have his Great Adventure. Greedy little coward." His lips quirked into the semblance of a grin: "Sorry I kicked him, it was just me thinking about him sitting there drinking my whiskey and sniveling about the Orient, and all the while him with our train tickets tucked up snug in his waistcoat."

Barlow laid his hand on Liam's shoulder and gave him a shake. "Come on," he said, "let's have a look around and see if we can find anything that points us towards the murderer."

Barlow took a coal-oil lantern from a bluecoat, turned the wick up as far as it would go without smoking and then led the way towards the back as both of them scanned the ground intently.

"It must have been one of Boylan's people this time," Liam said, thinking out loud. "I'm sure as can be that Lukas is off in New York scheming his next move and he'll have told Boyo to keep a weather eye and clean up all the traces." A flash of enlightenment hit him: "Right! Morrison spent most of his evenings at Maloney's—he would have seen Boylan and Lukas with their heads together. So he goes to Boyo today and tells him it's all up with his boss if he doesn't come up with a better offer than five hundred."

Barlow shook his head. "If that's how it happened, why did Morrison use Finnegan's steamer to go gallivanting? He could have walked to Maloney's in five minutes." Then, seeing Liam frown with concentration as he looked for an answer, Barlow held up a hand to stop him: "Anyway, the fact is our friend Boylan is probably half-way to New York himself, by now. When Miss Fox and I went looking for him at Maloney's we were told he was 'away.' It took a little persuasion to get the rest of it, but it turned out that's where he was away to—he told his lads he'd be back in three or four days."

"I can see fresh marks from the Flyer's anchor on the ground and the trees," Liam muttered distractedly, "but I don't see any new footprints. There was a good heavy shower a couple of hours ago—you'd think if the killer walked this way to the house . . ." He broke off abruptly and pointed towards the edge of the circle of light cast by Barlow's lantern. "Look over there, see what I see?"

As they moved closer with the light, it revealed a series of indistinct impressions in the mud, spaced like footprints and going from a tree with fresh chain cuts in its bark to the back steps.

Barlow shook his head disgustedly. "Tie a couple of burlap sacks around your feet and you're in business. If this was one of Boylan's little helpers, he'll have been told to leave no trace this time and threatened with hanging by his thumbs if he does." He frowned as something occurred to him and then shook his head, looking irritated: "The only problem is, you said the Flyer was black. Boyo knows as well as anybody that painting a Flyer black is a Federal offense—only the Department of Public Safety is permitted to use black Flyers."

"That settles it," Liam said. His jaw was set hard and his eyes glittered with angry resolve. "There's nothing more to be done in this two-bit burg, I'm going back to the city."

Barlow examined him for a moment and then nodded. "Just remember, you're to see McPherson in Pottsville before you leave. And when you hit New York, don't let the grass grow before you report in to Mr. Pilkington."

"He'd better not have anything more to tell me than, 'Thanks for a job well done and you can stop worrying about your grandma,'" Liam said. "If he tries to go back on his word I'll make him rue the day, and I don't give a tinker's damn if his darling Willie runs the DPS' Secret Service or the Department of Heaven itself, God included!"

With that, he turned on his heel and headed off into the smoky darkness. Barlow nodded, and said more or less to himself:

"Good luck, young McCool."

Chapter Nine

ne thing Mr. P. harped on when his operatives were working undercover was staying in character. Liam had long ago lost track of the number of times he had sat through tutorials on "personation skills" at the Pilkington Agency headquarters on Union Square, the Old Man expansive in his overstuffed armchair, his stout frame clad in black broadcloth and starched linen, his rosy cheeks framed with fluffy white mutton-chop whiskers, pontificating about detective work while Liam sat like a naughty boy in his straightbacked wooden chair looking out the window towards Tiffany's jewelry store and thinking what a treat it would be to slip in there some morning around 2:00 a.m. to fill his pockets with sparklers.

Just about then, of course, he'd remember how the warders in the Tombs liked to punctuate *their* lessons with a billy to the kidneys and his attention would snap back to the Old Man's disquisition on sleuthing:

" . . . and just tell me how in Tophet the brainless ninny could have expected to get away with personating a conductor on the Pennsy if he couldn't name the stops between Philadelphia and Harrisburg? I assure you, my boy, when it comes to entering into a role and living it with every fiber of your being, Edwin Booth himself can't hold a candle to a seasoned Pilkington operative at the top of his form!"

Over and over, Mr. P. had reminded Liam that once he was in the Mollies' territory he could no longer think like the free-spending King of the Silk-Stocking Cracksmen; instead, he must remind himself that he was a flat-broke fugitive, pressed for every penny. Which had boiled down in practice to endless irksome details like not spending good money on transportation for his regular excursions from Henderson's Patch to Pottsville.

Liam had really loathed this ordeal. As far as Boylan and the others were concerned, when he took those weekly trips to town he was going to Pottsville to oversee the progress of their tunnel from the basement of a house near the prison to a spot directly under the spectator's seats in the prison yard. In reality, though, he was in Pottsville to report to Seamus McPherson, the star of Pilkington's International Detective Agency, now deeply incognito as a hypochondriac clergyman on the third floor of Pottsville's Excelsior Hotel and as welcome to Liam as bagful of snakes.

Today, thank God, he had finally been able to shuck off the hitching-a-ride routine and instead of sitting amongst a wagonload of muddy piglets he had dipped into the money belt that had once held his reserve for the journey West with Maggie and used it instead for the first leg of his trip East to find her killer, making the journey on the front seat of Oliver Finnegan's steam jitney, clean and presentable in one of his cheap dark suits and glorying in the thought that everything he saw out the window he was seeing for the last time.

If there was one pesky fly in Liam's ointment, it was Ollie's answer to his quizzing about Morrison's last trip. It turned out that after his encounter with Liam the mousy accountant had hired Ollie to take him to Pottsville "to send some telegrams and pay a call or two." Now that he could translate that as "to visit the scum who'd killed Maggie and blackmail him," Liam had a momentary fantasy of telling Ollie to drive straight to the murderer's lair and settling his hash then and there. Unfortunately Morrison had been sharp enough to ditch Ollie the minute they got to town, arranging to meet him at the train station a couple of hours later, and there was precious little likelihood of the killer's having hung around this dump any longer than he had to.

Where had that miserable little pill Morrison *gone* while he'd been in Pottsville? Chances were that Liam would never know, but that didn't stop him from racking his brains over the question for the rest of the drive.

Finally, after an hour or so of jouncing over rutted dirt roads, Oliver putt-putted onto the smooth paving stones of Pottsville's main street and Liam pointed towards a red-white-and blue-striped pole and a sign announcing "Orsini's Barber Shop."

"Right over there, Ollie me lad!"

Pressing a shiny new gold eagle on the delighted boy, Liam jumped out and strode off down the pavement, whistling.

Inside Orsini's, a foppishly dressed young man with luxuriant Dundreary whiskers and a gold watch chain that could have anchored a small yacht was holding forth in an irritable tenor, his voice occasionally breaking with emotion:

"And I'll tell *you* that I can think of no more *striking* illustration of the terrible power for evil of an organization bound by secret oaths and controlled by murderers and assassins than the Molly Magees and all their works!"

"Controlled by poppycock and balderdash!" shouted his opponent, a red-faced middle-aged man with wire-rimmed spectacles and a neat Vandyke beard, whose more modest silver watch chain was ornamented with a Masonic seal. "These 'bloodthirsty murderers' of yours are nothing more than simple workingmen who have been *railroaded* by Mr. Franklin Benjamin Gowen!"

A sunburnt, white-haired oldtimer in faded blue-jean coveralls broke into wheezing cackles at that one, finally managing to say between gasps:

"Railroaded! By jiminy *that's* a good one, seeing as how Frank Gowen is President of the Philadelphia and Reading!"

Liam cleared his throat loudly and the barber started as if he'd been stuck with a pin:

"*Madonna mia!*" A plump, cheerful-looking man with slicked-down black hair and a handlebar moustache turned towards Liam with an embarrassed look and gestured him towards the empty barber's chair.

"Sorry, sir, I'm afraid us Pottsville folk have got our brains pretty well addled with waiting for Black Thursday. Nobody in these parts ever heard of ten men all getting hanged at once."

"Can't say I blame you," Liam said, "I'm from New York, and I never heard of it either. Matter of fact," he added with a gentle emphasis on business, "I'm on my way back there and I'd like to get rid of the lip spinach and the Colonel Custer hair."

"*Subito, signore!*" the barber said, swirling his striped hair cloth like a bullfighter's cape and wrapping Liam from neck to knees. As the snipping commenced, the red-faced man went back to his attack:

"I'll tell you who *I'd* like to see dancing on air come Thursday . . ."

"For pity's sake give it a rest, Maclean!" The foppish young man raised his eyebrows and rolled his eyes in an elaborate show of long-suffering. "The next thing we know you'll be telling us you're a secret Molly Magee!"

"You mind your tongue, Freddie Swanson," the red-faced man said sharply. "You know as well as I do that I'm a true-bred Ulster Scot! I've no more patience with Fenian plots than you do, but for my money Seamus McPherson belongs on the gallows with the rest of them. He led them in their villainy and then he turned around and betrayed them to their enemies! And I expect he's done a lot better out of it than twelve pieces of silver."

The barber had just finished shaving one half of Liam's lip but he couldn't resist turning back to the others and waving his razor for emphasis:

"I tell you how we deal with such a *porco* as that one in Sicily—"

Turning the razor over he swept the dull side across his throat: "*Zzzzt!*" he hissed dramatically, "and *tutto finito!*"

Liam smiled weakly as the barber returned to his shaving. *Think pure thoughts, Liam me lad,* he admonished himself, *or this* bandito *will have your head in his basin . . .*

The red-faced man resumed his attack: "And I'll tell you another thing, young Mr. Swanson! All this misery over hanging the Mollies is going to drag the country even deeper into Secretary Stanton's quagmire!"

Swanson looked around nervously. "For mercy's sake, Mac, mind what you say in public. We haven't had the DPS arresting anybody in Pottsville yet, but there's always a first time!"

Maclean blew out an exasperated sigh. "Listen to yourself. Are we free men in the United States of America, or we some kind of damned serfs in Little Roosia? I'll tell you here and now, that's not why your Papa and I fought at Chancellorsville and Vicksburg. And not so the City Council could vote for a curfew neither, nor spend $3,000 of our hard-earned money on one those evil Acme police things to shoot any poor soul that's abroad after dark! I've never been much of a believer, but if those things aren't the work of the Antichrist what is? Not to mention all the damned giant bugs and animals?" He lowered his voice nervously: "I heard tell there was a *werewolf* out the other night, tore one of Olson's dairy herd into mincemeat and didn't eat a bite of it! " He wagged his finger at Swanson: "You heed my words, Freddie, this country's on a downhill run to Hell and hanging ten men at once is just going to give us an extra push!"

As Swanson glowered sulkily the white-haired old-timer nodded his agreement: "You've pegged it, Mac. Where's Lincoln, anyway? Nobody's seen hide nor hair of him for the last six months, and all we hear from Washington is Mister Secretary Stanton and his damned Latin slogans. *"Per Aspera ad Securitas."* What's that when it's at home, anyway?"

Liam had just had a final dusting of talcum on his freshly bay-rummed cheeks, and as he got up out of the chair and pressed a gold piece into Orsini's hand he turned his newly boyish face towards the disputants and grinned: "It means 'Through Hardships to Security' and I've heard tell they'll be printing it on all the greenbacks next."

Suddenly reminded of the stranger in their midst the other men turned stricken faces towards Liam as he nodded cordially and headed out the door.

Coming out of Hartley's Department Store an hour later, Liam stopped to admire himself in the store window. After all these months disguised under a bushel of surplus hair, he felt light enough to float down the street. Part of that was just the prospect of shucking off his hated spy masquerade and going home, but he reckoned he might be forgiven a moment of vanity at the sight of the old Liam McCool in the window: clean-shaven, with curly auburn hair cut short enough to look like a city swell instead of a Hottentot and topped by a crisp new derby, smoked glasses to screen the candid hazel eyes that always seemed to provoke a song and dance about how young he was, and a lightweight gray suit with all the trimmings, silk shirt and tie and socks and shiny boots, all off the rack but classy enough to set him back four of his carefully hoarded double eagles.

Setting off towards the Excelsior at a jaunty pace, Liam looked around Pottsville with the friendly, charitable eye that went with being simply a tourist on his way home. It was a pretty enough little town, framed by green, rolling hills and just far enough from the mines to keep the neat white shingles and picket fences of its imposing three-story houses from turning gray with soot.

The Schuylkill River sparkled in the mid-day June sunshine, and as a small steam launch chugged past on its way downriver, Liam couldn't help a twinge of nostalgia for the times he and Maggie had taken the excursion boat to Philly just ninety miles away. The poor kid had dreamt of exciting journeys, and that was the best she could do in this neck of the woods, from here to the Centennial Exhibition and home again. He could never grudge her the times she'd gone with other sweethearts before him, but it broke his heart to think she'd never have the chance now to ride the Trans-Little Russia Railroad to the *guberniia* of California.

The street was beginning to fill up with prosperous-looking shoppers and folks just out for a stroll in the pleasant spring weather. As a passing gent tipped his hat politely Liam returned the salute with a smile, thinking how little it took to make the difference between a bum and a gentleman in most people's eyes.

Some, of course, would never see Liam as anything but an outcast and he was on his way to see one of them right now. At least there would be some entertainment in the encounter—Liam grinned at the thought of Seamus McPherson's face when he saw him in his new turnout. In fact, that would probably be the only good moment in an occasion that promised to rank right down there with some of the real blue-ribbon nadirs. He and McPherson liked each other about as well as your average mongoose and cobra, and that had been the way of it from the first moment they set eyes on each other.

He couldn't be sure just what it was the Great Detective objected to about him, but he suspected it was a combination of him being ten years younger and the fact that Mr. P. had taken Liam under his wing after he sprang him from the Tombs to be trained for undercover work.

Liam knew perfectly well that the whole ridiculous business had originated with the popularity of that damned Frenchman Gaboriau's stories about the crook-turned-copper Lecoq. Though the Old Man had grown up rough in the slums of Leeds and should have known better, this Lecoq foolishness seemed to have taken root in some buried romantic streak, resisting even the vitriol of his General Superintendent George Bingham, who had declared furiously that Mr. P. making Liam into a detective was as likely to succeed as training a timber wolf to fetch the morning paper.

Great Detective McPherson's reaction was even simpler: fuming green jealousy at the thought that anybody dared challenge his position as Teacher's Pet. He had spent his childhood slaving in an English landlord's fields in County Kerry and his adolescence knocking about the mines and foundries of Britain's Tyneside before he took ship for New York, and the thing that impressed him most about his new homeland was the fact that all it took to leap from the gutter to the top rung was plenty of money.

That was all Seamus McPherson needed to know—getting rich became his polestar, and no job was too small to move him closer to his goal. For a few checkered years he worked at everything from slaughtering pigs to driving a hack until finally he landed a job with Pilkington as a "spotter" on the elevated railways, watching for crooked conductors who pocketed the transport company's money. Here was work to McPherson's taste! He loved working under cover, and he had an almost feral hunting instinct. His success in sweeping the

El's trains clean was so great that he started moving from one Pilkington client to another, rising steadily in rank until he became the supervisor of spotters for the Philadelphia and Reading. The line was owned by Franklin B. Gowen and the rest became history.

It was the Panic of 1873 that did the trick. When the banks started failing, the big companies stopped spending and they were the ones who had been paying Pilkington's bills. Racking his brains for a way to stop the hemorrhage of money, Mr. P. came across a report from the Superintendent of his Philadelphia office that quoted McPherson on the Molly Magees' threat to Gowen's coal empire. Always secret, always ready to use violence against oppressors, the Mollies had sprung up more than once among Ireland's peasants and once again among Pennsylvania's Irish miners. Seamus McPherson had known them in County Kerry and now that he'd seen them here he knew they meant business—so why shouldn't the Agency go after them and save some money for Mr. Gowen?

Pilkington recognized a winner when he heard it and so did Gowen, who realized that Molly terrorism gave him the perfect stick for beating the struggling miners' union into submission. All they needed, the two men decided, was a super spy to infiltrate the Mollies: an Irish Catholic, a single man who wouldn't leave behind troublesome and expensive survivors, a man tough enough, shrewd enough and gregarious enough to mine coal, drink with the "bhoys," and pass muster as a Molly. *Ecce* Seamus, mused Liam.

A furious racket of barking broke into Liam's reverie and he stopped and looked around for the source. Across the street and half a block or so behind him, a matronly looking woman in a plum-colored walking costume with a huge bustle, her head almost lost beneath an outlandishly showy hat topped with what looked like artificial fruits, was walking an over-sized French poodle with its coat trimmed into pom-poms and puffballs. The dog had frozen suddenly in its tracks, transfixed with terror and fury as it barked at an approaching Acme, its china doll's face smiling vapidly under a peaked blue cap and its body costumed in a Pottsville police uniform. Liam noticed with uneasy curiosity that its right arm terminated in some unfamiliar machinery that looked a lot like a small Gatling gun.

"Stop it, Fifi!" the woman shouted, a hysterical note edging her voice. "Stop it at once, you stupid dog!"

By now the poor creature was in an ecstasy of fear, crouched down nearly to the pavement, its mouth drawn back in a ferocious snarl. The Acme, unsurprisingly, paid no attention to the dog and clanked stolidly forward, but before the little drama could come to a climax, the crowd around Liam broke into screams and yells as they pointed up into the sky.

As Liam followed their pointing fingers he instinctively dropped into a crouch and covered his head with his hands as the biggest bird he had ever seen—a bald eagle with a wing span at least thirty feet from tip to tip—dove towards them with a harsh scream that turned Liam's blood to ice.

The speed of the plummeting bird's attack was astonishing—it seemed to Liam that he barely had time to blink before the eagle had sunk its extended claws into the hapless dog like grappling hooks and swept back up with its howling prey, climbing so fast it would have been out of sight in seconds if the police Acme hadn't chosen that moment to raise its right arm and unleash a torrent of bullets at the escaping bird. It sounded to Liam like the cartridges were no bigger than .22 caliber, but they were plenty big enough to shred the poodle. It screamed horribly and then fell silent, which seemed to infuriate the eagle; it dropped the lifeless carcass, executed a kind of aerial loop and dived again, shrieking its unnerving war cry, directly towards the Acme.

The automaton—still wearing its vapid china smile—raised its arm further and continued to fire a deafening stream of bullets at the eagle. To no apparent effect, however, for in a second the bird had taken hold of the Acme by its head, and with a mighty beat of its wings surged upwards again. This time, when it had reached an altitude about equal to twice the height of the surrounding buildings, it abruptly let go of its prey. The Acme, cartwheeling wildly as it tried to right itself, landed in the street with a thunderous crash that tore off the Gatling-gun arm. For a few moments it lay there feebly trying to sit up and leaking steam from every aperture. Then, with an earsplitting roar it blew up, sending its arms and legs and still-smiling head smashing through various store windows. For another moment or two all was silence except for the tinkle and crash of glass.

"Sweet Christ," Liam murmured. It had been a sendoff he wouldn't forget in a hurry. Somehow the big bugs and that buffalo-sized wolf had seemed semi-acceptable in a back-water like Henderson's Patch. Out in the deep sticks you could believe in all kinds of primitive rubbish, ghosts and hoodoos and whatever. But Pottsville was a *city*, for pity's sake! If this really did have something to do with Indian "medicine" they were all in for a bad time of it, there probably wasn't a square inch of land in the U.S. that hadn't been settled by Indians one time or another.

Crossing himself instinctively, Liam stood up and dusted himself off. Then, as the street slowly came back to life and Pottsville police and spectators started pouring onto the scene, Liam picked up his pace smartly and headed off down the street.

Chapter Ten

cPherson's room was on the top floor of the Excelsior at the end of a long corridor and the hike (elevators not having made it out to the sticks quite yet) would have given Liam plenty of time to rehearse his approach to McPherson if it had seemed worth the bother. But he knew that even if he walked Broadway from Union Square to Central Park he still couldn't come up with a way to dodge the Great Detective's bullying and bellyaching. As long as McPherson was Pilkington's proxy here in the coalfields, he could do what he liked, serenely confident that his boss held the whip hand over Liam.

Liam gritted his teeth and knocked.

"Who's there?" a voice yelled from inside.

Liam grimaced at having to give the ridiculous password: "Mr. P.'s favorite nephew!"

The knob turned and the door started to open, just far enough for Liam to make out a broad, shiny red face framed by slicked-back sandy hair and a bush of sandy whiskers that didn't quite cover the clerical collar. But before he could open his mouth to say hello, McPherson's expression switched from narrow-eyed suspicion to terror and he started to slam the door shut again. Liam barely managed to wedge his foot into it:

"What the blazes are you playing at? Let me in!"

But McPherson, balked from closing the door, stepped back sharply and started to pull a pistol out of his jacket pocket. Not pausing to think about it, Liam threw the door open and lunged forward, clamping a vice-like hold on McPherson's gun arm and simultaneously pulling him off balance so that he was standing on one foot and bending backwards.

"For the love of Mike," Liam snapped, "it's just me with a haircut, get a grip on yourself."

For a second or two McPherson snarled and strained to stand upright, his eyes wild and blind with fear, but as Liam tightened his grip and pushed him further off balance, the fury slowly drained out of his face and gave way to a sullen glare as he realized who his caller was:

"All right, damn you, let go of me!"

Liam pulled McPherson forward onto both feet and started to relax his grip, but just as he was about to let go he did a double-take on the pistol and grabbed onto McPherson's arm again, bending it painfully back against the elbow joint and jerking the pistol upwards so that McPherson ended up jamming the muzzle into the soft flesh under his own chin.

"Ah, Jasus!" McPherson shrieked. "Yer breaking my arm!"

"I'll blow your goddamned head off if you don't tell me where you got the pistol," Liam grated.

McPherson's expression changed abruptly from agony to a kind of shifty panic: "Pistol?"

"Yeah, that's right," Liam said between his teeth, "the nice new nickel-plated Webley Bulldog that I gave Maggie to keep her safe. Speak up now or your brains are going to go flying right out the top of your head!"

A kaleidoscope of expressions chased across McPherson's face and settled quickly on injured rage as he found his voice again:

"I don't have to explain myself to you, you miserable little shite, you're the one who'd best explain himself to *me* or answer for it to Mr. Pilkington!"

That just made Liam bare his teeth crazily as he clicked the hammer back to full cock and and jammed the pistol barrel deep into the tender flesh under McPherson's chin. McPherson shrieked louder, his eyes rolling with terror:

"I'll see you rot in the Tombs, you son of a bitch, she was already *dead!*" Liam's face was pale as paper and set in a frozen snarl as he pushed the gun harder and deeper into his enemy's throat, so that McPherson could barely move his tongue as he choked out:

"I went there on Mr. P.'s orders!"

Liam's anger deflated abruptly; he twisted the pistol out of McPherson's fingers, let the hammer back down and dropped it into his own pocket.

"The Old Man gave you orders to visit Maggie." Liam's voice was as flat as a gravestone.

McPherson had to massage his throat before he could answer. "Not that it's any of your damn business," McPherson croaked, "but yeah. She was an Eye, didn't you know?" He sneered as he said it but thanks to Barlow Liam did know, and McPherson's gibe fell flat. "She reported to me on a regular schedule. It was her as collected all the doings of the Mollies for me after I left, and once you got here Old Pilkington kept her at it so we'd have a double-check on *you.*"

"Never mind they've already got ten Mollies heading for the gallows next week." Liam snorted in disgust. "Once you put the collar on the lads in the dynamite tunnel there's no more harm left in the Mollie Magees than there is in a handful of Shriners."

"There's more to national security than stopping dynamiters." The venom dripped from McPherson's words: "Mr. P. heard as how your darling Maggie was about to spill her guts to that hoor scribbler Becky Fox and the DPS wanted her put on warning. Not dead," he added hastily, *"warned."*

Liam looked at him for several long seconds, his eyes boring like gimlets. Finally he nodded and shrugged. "I don't have to paint you a picture of what'll happen if I learn you've more to do with it than that."

The older man flushed darkly and started to raise a hand as if to punch Liam, but an instant later he overcame the impulse and lowered his hand.

"I ought to loosen a few teeth for you, McCool, but I don't expect a tarted-up gutter rat like you to fight fair and square so let's get down to business. The old man sent me a telegram about you wanting to go on leave, so go ahead and speak your piece. Then get out of here so I can open the windows and fumigate the place."

Liam was only half listening, wondering instead just what Mr. P. had said in his telegram to McPherson that he hadn't written to Inspector Barlow earlier. Had he mentioned the information Liam had given Barlow about Boylan's people spotting the Great Detective at large in Pottville? Maybe he'd just hang onto that morsel as a hole card . . .

"I guess the Old Man must have told you the same thing he told Barlow," Liam said. "I'm getting ready to head for New York, but I'm supposed to clear it with you first."

McPherson gave Liam a sour little smile. "Well, that makes it easy then, because I'm not clearing it—you're needed here."

"I know you don't want me around for my company, so where's the problem?"

"I'll tell you the problem," McPherson grated out. "I don't like to see jail birds walking around free amidst decent people. I promise you, McCool, I mean to see you back in the Tombs if it's the last thing I ever do."

Liam forced himself to keep a level tone: "As far as I know, whether or not I end up back in choky depends strictly on the Old Man, so if you won't tell him it's all right for me to leave I guess I'll just have to go talk to him myself. But I'm not going to spend another day in the coalfields if the moving finger of God Himself writes the order on that wall over there."

The Great Detective's face had been flushing darker and darker until it looked like he was on the verge of apoplexy.

"Who the Devil do you think you are?" he roared. "You little dog-puke, it's not up to you to be telling me what you will do and what you won't do, I'm in charge here and I'm telling you I need you to take over Schuylkill County for the Agency as soon as the hangings are done."

He moved closer to Liam, getting right up in front of him the way coppers do when they're about to give someone the collar. He poked Liam in the chest as he continued:

"Mr. P. needs me in Chicago to run the operation there. I'm only here until this Mollies business is cleaned up, and then I'm heading west on the next express."

Liam smiled. So *that* was the story. The Chicago office was second only to New York, and Bill Henkel—who'd been sent out there by the Old Man to pull things together after the Great Fire in '71—had been ailing for the past few months while every senior operative in the Agency waited in the wings for a chance to pounce on this plum assignment.

"So Henkel finally croaked, did he?"

"*Mister* Henkel to you, trash."

"Whatever you say, *Mister* McPherson, but I'm not going to sit here in Pottsville holding your coat while you go do battle with all the other big bugs for a chance to land in Henkel's chair. Ask the old man to send down some other stooge from the Union Square office, I'll apologize to him in person when I get to town."

McPherson closed his eyes for a moment, then blew out a big, pent-up breath and shook his head disgustedly. Turning away from Liam, he walked across the room with a heavy step until he reached the curtained windows, where he parted the drapes just enough to peer down into the street.

"Three months I've been sitting in this dump," he muttered, "just waiting to see if there's any way I can help strengthen the case against the Mollies. Once they sentenced

them to death you'd think they'd let me out of here, bu
suddenly they're afraid the gang will stage a raid and sp
the lot of them. So I ask them for someone on the spot to k
an eye on Boylan, and sure enough, you show up like You
Lochinvar and discover the great tunnel conspiracy. OK, I se
that's covered, can I go now? But no again, they want me to
supervise you."

He turned back towards Liam and his voice went up an
angry notch:

"Does Mr. P. offer me any extra pay for sitting here
like the Man in the Iron Mask? No, of course he doesn't,
he's so damn tight he'd make an Ulster Scotsman look like a
drunken sailor. So I have to sit here counting my pennies while
Mr. Gowen pours money into the Agency's coffers, and every
last one of those dollars is on *me*, McCool. If it wasn't for the
memo I wrote about the Molly Magees, Mr. P.'s outfit would
have bust like an empty pot once the banks started going
under. The reason there *is* a Pilkington's office in Chicago
now is because of me, and you can tell the Old Man I said so!"

With that, he dropped into an armchair like a marionette with its strings cut and stared dejectedly at the ceiling.
After a moment he added in a sarcastic tone:

"Is there anything else I can do for you, McCool? If not,
get out before I decide to shoot you after all."

Liam hesitated, tempted to let the Great Detective find
out the hard way. Then he shrugged the thought aside. All
that old bastard Pilkington would need to justify breaking
his word was for anything to happen to McPherson that Liam
should have warned him about.

"As a matter of fact, there is something else: I had it
from Boylan himself that you've been spotted in Pottsville and
it probably won't be long till they figure out where you've been
holed up. Sounds to me like you've let your cover slip."

The big beefy map of Boylan's face abruptly went from
a boiled pink to a fish-belly white. He licked his lips a couple

mes as if he couldn't swallow, then waved his hand sharply
1am:

"Get out!"

Liam nodded, started to answer and then thought
etter of it; he didn't actually wish McPherson any harm, but
he for damned sure didn't wish him well, either.

"Good luck," he said in an ambiguous tone.

Then he opened the door, checked the hallway in both
directions, and left.

Chapter Eleven

eading down the hall towards the central stairway Liam felt relief surge through him like a tumbler of whiskey on an empty stomach. He knew it was foolish, in fact he was pretty sure McPherson meant him real harm and that they'd be locking horns again soon. The Great Detective was known to colleagues and crooks alike as a vindictive enemy who clung to his grudges like a barnacle and savored the prospect of revenge like a Sicilian.

But Liam wasn't in the mood for dark thoughts. Tomorrow could look after itself and right now he felt like Sinbad the Sailor after he'd got the Old Man of the Sea off his back. All he had to do was kill an hour or so until the Pennsy's New York Express steamed in and then he'd be on his way to the promised land.

Lost in a pleasant daydream of the places he'd visit on his first day back home, Liam was snapped out of it instantly by the sight of a gorgeous redhead marching down the hall towards him like she was trampling out the Grapes of Wrath plus anything else that might get in her way. She was wearing a light Spring frock that did nothing much to hide ample curves rivaling Maggie's and she had that same translucent redhead's pallor. The face was different—more of an Irish country girl than Maggie had been—but she surely had that same go-to-hell look. As she drew level with him he tipped his hat appreciatively:

"Morning, Miss."

She threw her head back as she passed and gave him an angry "hmph!" for his pains, which tickled him so much that he had to turn around and watch her as she strode away.

He heard a chuckle behind him: "I wouldn't bother, sir."

He turned to see one of the Excelsior's liveried bellmen, a plump middle-aged man with a red face and a redder nose, grinning at him widely.

"She's a corker, all right, but just now I think she's taken."

Liam returned the smile, adding a touch of male complicity. "Too bad. Who's the lucky fellow?"

"Would you believe it, sir? He's some kind of preacher!" With an ironic snort he pointed down the hall and Liam turned just in time to catch the redhead rapping smartly on the door he had just exited from.

"Come out of there this instant!" she yelled, "I know yer in there, ye lying blarney-monger!"

Her accent was fresh off the boat, and her voice was so loud and shrill that McPherson—clearly hoping to shut her up—opened the door quickly and dragged her inside.

The bellman shook his head disapprovingly. "What's the world coming to, sir, I ask you? First we get that fancy-pants Reverend Beecher that was tried for adultery last year, him preaching the Holy Writ on Sundays and diddling the chippies on weekdays, and now here's another randy old goat chasing the young quim—probably doesn't even take off his backwards collar when he climbs aboard!"

"He's got more than one girl, then, does he?"

"Why, bless you sir, he's built up a regular harem! He goes out most nights after it's dark drinking and tom-catting around, but he has his special sweeties. Eileen, there, she's one of Mrs. Olliphant's girls and pretty much his favorite. But I think he's taken to sparking somebody else on the side—Miss Eileen flounced in yesterday fuming and fussing and asking where he'd been keeping himself the last few days."

There was the secret of the Great Detective's broken cover right there, Liam mused. He wasn't the only skirt-chaser in town who resorted to Mrs. Olliphant's girls; in fact, it was even money that Mrs. Olliphant's was where Morrison had first seen McPherson. Liam smiled wryly and shook his head in pretended wonderment. He couldn't help thinking of the little book that Mr. P. made every new operative memorize from cover to cover: *Fundamental Tenets of Pilkington's International Detective Agency.*

The old hypocrite had figured from the beginning that his business would never grow if people thought of the Agency the way they did of the regular police, which was pretty much: "set a thief to catch a thief." There wasn't a city in the U.S. where coppers were paid enough to live on, so they made up the difference any way they could and only greenhorns believed the police were honest. Mr. P.'s answer was to insist that *his* operatives set shining examples of honesty, sobriety, and probity—that way the big-money customers he liked best would feel easy in their minds about putting their problems in the hands of a Pilkington operative. Poor Mr. P.! If he knew that his precious Great Detective "improved the shining hour" by boozing and lifting petticoats he'd have a seizure.

"Well," Liam said aloud, "let's hope the parson mends his wicked ways before someone tells his Bishop about it." He gave the bellman a wink, tipped his hat, and headed off down the stairs.

Once he was back on the street Liam could scarcely restrain himself from breaking into song. A beautiful day, his hated Mollies disguise consigned to the trash bin, McPherson done with for now and the gold for a ticket to New York in his money belt. Filling his lungs with the insipid country air, he grinned as he thought how good it would be to be back in the city, breathing in the familiar fug of steam engines, horse droppings, factory smoke, and the dank vapors of two rivers and an ocean.

"You seem awfully cheerful, Mr. McCool."

Liam almost jumped out of his skin as the musical voice came from behind him.

"Sorry! Did I startle you?"

Becky Fox's merry grin gave the lie to her apology as she cocked her head and examined the new (and somewhat flustered) Liam.

"You could give a fellow a heart attack, Miss Fox."

Her grin widened: "I should have thought you were much too young and healthy for that, Mr. McCool. Unless—like Samson—your haircut has enfeebled you."

Liam returned the grin and decided to stop complaining. He crooked his elbow, inviting Becky to put her arm through his:

"May I accompany you to your destination, Miss Fox?"

She took his arm and moved close to his side, which he found a lot more disturbing than he had expected.

"I would be delighted," she said. "As a matter of fact I believe we're bound for the same place."

He gave her quizzical look: "I'm not going back to Henderson's Patch, you know?"

"Neither am I. That's why I thought we might travel together." She gave him a sidelong look, enjoying his mystification.

"That's too many for me," Liam said with a hint of exasperation. "I don't know where you're going, but you do know where I'm going. Are you a psychic too?"

Unable to restrain herself, she burst into a peal of laughter. "I am so sorry," she said at last, "but you really are such fun to tease—even better than my brother, and I had thought he was very nearly perfect."

Becky Fox was certainly full of surprises, Liam thought, not the least of which was how fresh and girlish she looked for a woman who had been locked up in the Leonard Street prison and chased across Mexico by a pack of moustached *bandidos*. Not to mention traveling on foot to Omsk with a convoy of Siberian prisoners and riding camelback across the deserts of Arabia with a band of Bedouins.

"As a matter of fact," she added with a small touch of contrition, "Inspector Barlow knew I was leaving today so he sought me out this morning and asked me to bring you a message."

Liam nodded slowly, wishing for a moment that he *was* a mentalist—could Barlow possibly have told her about his undercover work for Pilkington's?

"Don't worry, Mr. McCool, your secret is safe with me." Liam struggled to suppress a wince and Becky pretended not to notice it. "Miss O'Shea and I had been corresponding before I came here and she had already told me a good deal about the Pilkington Agency's involvement with the Mollies. That's why I came here, hoping to interview her more fully and of course . . ." she spread her hands ruefully, "you know the rest."

This was a lot more than Liam had been prepared for. He grasped at the nearest straw: "So what was Barlow's message?"

"Apparently he'd had a telegram from Mr. Pilkington in New York saying that there had been 'developments' in the investigation of the mysterious Lukas, and that he wanted you there as fast as the railroad might bring you."

Well, thought Liam, that's torn it. Pilkington sucks me into his business by wrapping it up with mine—at this rate I'll never be free of the old bastard.

"Also," Becky continued, "he said you would want to know that when the firemen finally put out the blaze he found *footprints* in Mr. Morrison's room."

Instantly Liam's brain was racing: "Did he, now? Did he describe them?

She reached into her reticule: "He did better, he made a tracing."

She handed Liam a strip of butcher's paper on which the prints of a pair of small men's shoes had been traced with a heavy pencil. Not the pointy-toed opera style this time, normal walking boots . . . but the size looked about the same to Liam.

"Inspector Barlow said that it looked like the killer had stepped in Morrison's blood but hadn't troubled to clean up the prints, probably expecting them to burn up along with everything else."

Liam nodded. Then it couldn't have been Lukas that actually pulled the trigger after all, nor Boylan either—as far as he knew they had both left town by the time of Morrison's murder. Not that any of that was graven in stone: he was sure that it had been Morrison's killer he'd shot at on the Stanley Flyer, and anybody with the money to keep one of those handy could have transferred to a big delta-wing somewhere outside of town and been in New York lickety-split.

Liam folded the paper carefully and stowed it away inside his jacket: when he had enough other evidence to be dead certain who the killer was he could fool around checking footprints. Till then they were just one more clue, and at this point he didn't want more clues, he just wanted to get his hands on Lukas.

"My most sincere thanks, Miss Fox." He laughed. "You've just helped Barlow make the whole business even more complicated."

"That's a woman's mission, is it not, Mr. McCool?" She gave him a solemn look. "Now," she said, tugging his arm in the direction of the hotel's cab rank, "while we drive to the station you can explain to me how it is that you managed to learn Russian and French while becoming the King of New York's Silk-Stocking Cracksmen."

Liam rolled his eyes. This was going to be an interesting trip.

New York
June 19–June 27, 1877

Chapter Twelve

Blast those people! Adolf Hochstein was the goose that laid our golden eggs!"

"That he was," Boylan said gloomily. "Vysotsky's boys took a carpetbag full of perfect five-dollar notes off him, and worst of all, they got his plates. Not to mention the press and the inks and tools and paper and every other bloody thing save the clothes on his back! I just barely caught hold of him at the Grand Central Depot—sweating buckets, he was, and looking like he had a flock of banshees on his tail. To hear him tell it, Vysotsky swore if he dared come back to New York he'd serve him his bollocks in a plate of borscht."

Lukas nodded pensively, staring at his comically distorted reflection on the side of the silver coffee pot as he drifted away to some mental refuge where Boylan and the luxurious sitting room and the money problems and all the rest of it faded like smoke.

Boylan watched him patiently, having learned long ago that interrupting one of the Boss' brown studies was a risky thing to do. Lukas was a rare bird, no two ways about it, and Boylan found himself wondering again just where he hailed from. The first time he'd seen him the Boss had been boxing bare knuckle in a Hell's Kitchen basement, and it hadn't been a pretty fight. The other fellow had been a big, muscled-up dago from Five Points, and Lukas had pounded him to a jelly in nothing flat without getting winded or raising a sweat, just smiling like he enjoyed the exercise. So when he was introduced to Lukas later on, Boylan—who fancied himself a fair-enough mauler but no fool—had made a great point of acting meek as a lamb.

Which reminded him, he'd just that morning heard the butler—a foreigner with some queer sort of accent—calling Lukas "Your Highness." Your *Highness?* And here the man's dearest dreams were of nothing more nor less than putting a carload of dynamite under every King and President on the face of the planet, or so he said. To hell with it, Boylan decided, he'd be better off concentrating on breakfast.

As if at a signal, Lukas returned to the present with a chuckle and a boarding-house grab for the giant chafing dish of sausages and bacon and smoked herring that sat between them on the dining table:

"I should be ashamed of myself, letting Vysotsky's antics interfere with my breakfast—it's a capital mistake to worry about trifles on an empty stomach."

Boylan tugged unhappily at his moustache: "Begging your pardon, sir, but it won't seem such a trifle when the lads from Pittsburgh and Baltimore come and ask for their dosh. How are they to get things done with no money?"

"My dear Boylan," said Lukas through a mouthful of toast and sausage, "would you teach your grandmama how to suck eggs? I know that revolutions take money—how the Devil else can you *fight* money?"

He snorted indignantly and speared sausage and smoked herring onto his fork till the enormous wad of food made Boylan a bit queasy. Stuffing the lot into his mouth in one effortless bite, Lukas continued:

"Still, one mustn't be put off a great goal by minor disappointments—the key to success is unwavering determinantion,

112

so if one path is foreclosed by ill fortune we must simply open another."

He picked up a crisp linen napkin and wiped off his beard and moustache before continuing with an expansive wave:

"Shoving the queer was fine as long as we had plenty of Hochstein's splendid fakes to work with, but you must agree it was a little slow as a source of funds. I've been thinking for a while now that it was high time we went over to direct expropriations."

Boylan raised a quizzical eyebrow: "Sir?"

Lukas grinned widely, his nimble imagination already seeing the job done and his problems solved:

"Banks, my friend, banks! They grow fat on the money of corporations that suck the blood of working men and women. It's no crime to take their money for the Revolution— it's simply *expropriation*, like the Government seizing a right of way for the public good."

In spite of his misgivings Boylan couldn't help chuckling at the thought: "Sure and it's a crime to let them *keep* the money when you look at it that way. Would you be having any special bank in mind, then?"

Lukas got to his feet, dusted the crumbs off his hands, and strolled over to an enormous pier glass in a gilded frame replete with carved cherubim and bunches of grapes. Then, with all the finicky precision of a scientist adjusting some complex and priceless machinery, he set about grooming his beard and moustache with a tiny silver comb, tugging at his cravat and his collar points, and brushing invisible bits of lint off his embroidered waistcoat and his gray cashmere morning suit. A final glance to make sure his shoes had retained their mirror finish and then he smiled at Boylan in the mirror, pleased to see that his lieutenant had finally learned not to show the least hint of impatience during this important ritual.

"Of course I have, Boylan."

He crossed to the dining room windows and pulled the heavy red velvet curtains open all the way, letting in a flood of spring sunshine. Beyond the windows, Washington Square Park spread southwards towards West 4th Street, its decorous expanse of foot-paths and flower gardens sprinkled with nannies and prams from the surrounding townhouses, gentlemen sitting on benches enjoying the June weather and their morning papers, and kids from the neighborhoods beyond the townhouses chasing pigeons, yelling happily and playing games. Lukas smiled indulgently: after all, even a dynamiter could enjoy a June day in New York. Then he pointed east across the Park and looked back at Boylan:

"Just a half-dozen blocks from where I'm standing— The Gotham Savings Institution on the corner of Bleecker and Broadway."

Boylan's cheerful expression darkened in an instant and a groan escaped him.

"Aw, Jasus, Boss!"

He was caught in a cleft stick. On the one hand, Lukas liked naysaying about as well as the Pope liked Lutherans. On the other, Gotham Savings was smack in the middle of Butcher Boys territory, and in that neck of the woods it was as much as your life was worth to steal an apple off a pushcart without asking them pretty please first.

Most of the old-school New York gangs like the Hudson Dusters and the Dead Rabbits were something like neighborhood clubs for drinking and mayhem, but the Butcher Boys were serious professional criminals, high-class operators who made the city's coppers look like hayseeds. Their head man Mike Vysotsky, known far and wide as the Mad Russian, was bad enough. But him and that shite-poke McCool had been tight as twins, and now that McCool was on his way home from Henderson's Patch Boylan would rather sit bare-arsed on a nest of hornets than mess with the Butcher Boys.

"You seem distressed, *cher collègue.*"

114

Mother of God. When the Boss started speaking in tongues, thunder and lightning weren't far away . . .

"Aw, nivver a bit, yer Honor!" Boylan said hastily, an extra touch of brogue jarred loose by his anxiety. "It's just the surprise of it, a big bank job."

"Excellent, excellent," said Lukas with an urbane smile, "otherwise I'd have been forced to conclude that you were anxious about that mountebank Vysotsky and his ragtag and bobtail of pickpockets and sneak thieves."

He strolled back and settled in an armchair across from Boylan, crossing his legs and tugging at his trousers to keep from spoiling the creases.

"Now, then. The delegates from the Pittsburgh and Baltimore Attack Sections will be here tonight to make their reports and collect their funds. We'll just have to put them to work helping us with the bank—then when they go back to their comrades they can have a bit of extra money to spread around."

Boylan tried to keep the skepticism out of his voice as he asked: "That's just the four of us, then? The Gotham is one of the few banks that's come through the Panic with money to spare, and I know for a fact they keep four armed Pilkingtons aboard day and night. Not to mention, the dicks have a direct wire to tbe Pilkington Agency headquarters on Union Square. That's not a dozen blocks from the Bank, sir, the guards will have it swarming with law before you can say 'Bugger!'"

Lukas grinned cheerfully: "They may have a wire to headquarters, but I have these!'" He reached over to his desk, pulled open the top drawer and brought out a stout pair of wire-cutters. "Don't worry, my friend, I have everything worked out to a nicety. Remember, the Trainmen's Union is planning a General Strike for June 27th —that's this coming Wednesday, Boylan, we haven't time to fool about. And whether the strike takes place or is put down by the police it'll be war—workers and bosses at daggers drawn. So we must be *ready* to seize the moment and help it to move in the right direction, chances like this don't come along more than once in a lifetime."

You had to give it to the Boss—when it came to the old fire and brimstone he could out-palaver Moody and Sankey, hymns and all. Boylan set his jaw resolutely:

"Just tell me what you need and when you need it!"

Lukas nodded and smiled. "We'll do it Sunday night. This part of town is dead as a doornail on Sundays, so the 'when' for preparing is right away. *What* we need is dynamite, but with all the digging and tunneling on Manhattan Island, that should be easy enough to scoop up. Now, then. Is there anything else on your slate before you get busy with the fireworks?"

Boylan hesitated for a moment. "I know you don't reckon it for a problem, but I'm still that bit bothered about McCool setting himself at your heels. When I saw him last in Henderson's Patch he was bound and determined he'd have you for killing Maggie O'Shea."

Lukas got that distant look again, the tight set of his mouth hinting that he might be finding the threat more serious than Boylan suggested.

"The shame of it is," he muttered, "that the man was a first-rate organizer—we could have used him here if he hadn't given himself up to a vendetta." Finally he shrugged and turned back to Boylan: "I expect if he'd stayed with the job in Pottsville the Governor and Gowan and the rest of those swine would be shoveling coals in Hell today. However, it's an ill wind that blows no good. The fact is that yesterday's hangings have lit a fire under other workingmen that won't be easily put out." His expression hardened as he looked into some private distance: "Ten corpses swinging in the wind, Boylan. It's a picture that will keep on reminding their brothers and sisters of what awaits them if they let the owners win!"

He got to his feet abruptly and strode across to the windows. This time he just stood staring out across Washington

Square Park, a belligerent grin on his face and his hands jammed into his pockets as if he were spoiling for a fight . . .

"Don't worry, Boylan—just keep up the good work and you'll soon find yourself on the ride of a lifetime!"

"Ride, sir?"

Lukas turned back from the window and chuckled as he pounded a massive fist into his palm.

"What would you say, Boylan, if I were to tell you that in just a few weeks from now you'll no longer be the right-hand man of Lukas the Mysterious Foreigner, but aide-de-camp to Prince Nikolai Aleksandrovich Yurevskii, *the new Viceroy of Little Russia?*"

○—┰

Outside, strolling casually along a path in the Park that gave him a good view of Lukas' house, swinging a heavy walking stick and whistling "Oh! Susanna," was Liam McCool.

His pal Mike—who had kept in touch with innocuous, DPS-proof letters while Liam was in exile—had boasted of buying one of the pricey new Tesla voicewire machines and Liam had promised Becky to use it to call her at *Harper's* and let her know when he was setting out to see his grandma. Once Liam got used to the tinny sound of the thing he could tell she was excited when he told her his boys had a solid line on Lukas; he had agreed to meet Becky here, outside Lukas' house, and then to go on from Washington Square Park to Five Points by steam jitney.

Liam pulled out his watch and looked at it again, the fifth time in as many minutes. Where was she? He wouldn't have expected her to run this late unless there was a problem, and the thought made him uneasy.

Besides (and he grinned sheepishly as he realized it) he was eager to show himself off to her in full Big-City feather. Now that he'd had time to visit his flat on Bleecker Street Liam was dressed like a young swell—a four-button cutaway suit of lightweight brown-and-gray checked cashmere, a stiff white collar, red paisley cravat and handkerchief, and brilliantly polished brown boots. The one fashionable item that Liam had rejected was a derby hat—he hated hats and told anybody who wanted to know that he had given his to a Five Points rag-and-bone man for his mule.

The stick, on the other hand, was something special. The body was highly polished ebony, and it had been invisibly fitted together by Harry the Jap (who was the Butcher Boys' artificer as well as Liam's pal and jiujitsu partner), after he hollowed it out to form a perfect sheath for a 15th-century *katana*, a super-sharp and flexible samurai sword that had been forged of five layers of steel, folded and hammered sixteen times by some forgotten Muromachi swordsman and finally stolen and broken off at the hilt by some dumb Swede sailor who sold the pieces to a junk shop in Frisco.

It was the kind of challenge Harry loved: turning a gaijin's trash into a unique and beautiful object. A gifted craftsman to begin with, Harry had put extra care into this job—a labor of love intended for Liam, who had saved Harry's life in a pitched battle with the Whyos. Once he had finished the work and presented it to Liam, Harry instructed him painstakingly in its use: like a true katana, it had an extra-long grip to permit a two-handed hold, and once the catch was released, its stick-sheath—regularly lubricated with *goji* oil—would simply fall away, permitting the samurai trick of drawing the sword and striking your opponent in one lightning-fast move.

By the time Liam was through training, he could lose the sheath and cut a sheep's carcass in half with a move so fast that it made even the taciturn Harry smile. Not that Liam wanted to use it on anyone—he didn't really like hurting people. At the same time, he had to admit that he didn't want anybody trying to hurt him either and the katana stick was a useful weapon if the need for one arose unexpectedly.

He shook his head grimly: like it or not, the need for weapons had been suggested to him more and more forcefully during the last few days, most recently by the colossal Norway rat he'd run into coming out of an alley on Houston Street just a half hour ago. The thing had been nearly the size of a bulldog and it had faced off with Liam, hissing and squeaking furiously until he'd taken a swipe at it with the katana and forced it to pelt away down the street. Whatever else was going on, Nature was seriously out of joint and not just back in the sticks; despite his normally happy temperament, the mystery of where it was all heading filled Liam with foreboding.

Liam watched Lukas watching him through the sitting-room window and wondered just who it was that had been dogging his steps since he and Miss Fox pulled into the Exchange Place Terminal in Jersey City. Was it Lukas, or somebody who worked for him? Whoever it was, they were really good—as alert as Liam was, he hadn't caught so much as a glimmer of a face or figure, just the constant awareness of someone there behind him wherever he went, watching and waiting for . . .

"*Mr. McCool!*"

Liam started, then shook his head and smiled as he realized the voice was Becky Fox's. He turned to find her standing behind him, looking wonderfully slim and spring-like in a simple green silk day dress without a bustle and a token hat of the same material. He grinned and gave her a little half-bow:

"Well, Miss Fox, I reckon you could give lessons in silent stalking to old Sitting Bull himself."

She smiled back—a little anxiously, it seemed to Liam.

"Is everything all right?"

"Not really," she said, "but I'm dreadfully sorry I asked you to wait just so that I might go with you. I shouldn't have kept you—I know you must be fretting terribly about your grandmother."

"She's waited six months now to see me again, I expect an extra couple of hours won't make any difference. Please—" he gestured towards the bench "—let's sit down for a minute while you tell me what's troubling you. We can catch a cab when you've caught your breath."

She hesitated for a moment and then gave in gratefully and sat down. "As I said on the voicewire I meant to stop at home on the way here, just to let my family know I was back. But when I got to Gramercy Park . . ." She turned those bottomless blue eyes full on Liam and he had to fight a sudden urge to pull her close and comfort her: " . . . my Mother told me that Secretary Stanton had issued a personal rescript confining Papa to our home until further notice."

Liam frowned with bafflement. "Why? I thought your father was a big judge. And what the Devil does 'further notice' mean?"

"Stanton doesn't care if you're a judge or a washerwoman,' she said bitterly, "he won't brook the least hint of criticism. My father and some of his friends—other judges and some lawyers and journalists—have formed a study circle to plan an official inquiry into DPS high-handedness in New York. All quite legal and by-the-book, nothing remotely secretive. But Stanton's screed called it a criminal conspiracy, and he means to punish them and make an example of them."

She closed her eyes and grimaced painfully. *Maggie, girl,* Liam thought prayerfully, *help me out here . . .* And then, with a quirky little half-smile: *Right, then, damn the torpedoes! . . .* He took hold of Becky's hands and held them tight until she opened her eyes and smiled a little.

"Whatever you need," Liam said, "just ask me. If there's anything at all that I can do to help you, you can count on me."

"Papa will have the best lawyers and the whole judicial establishment of New York on his side, but Stanton has the powers of a Torquemada. If he decides to mount an Inquisition I fear for all of us."

"I don't get it," Liam said in frustration. "What about the Constitution? What about the 'rights of free men' and all that Fourth of July stuff a half a million Yanks died for? Even Stanton can't just wave his hand and make that go away."

"He doesn't have to. He'll just *suspend* the normal standards and procedures." Becky shook her head and smiled a little. "'Until further notice.' Whatever Inspector Barlow might think to the contrary, there will be war soon, and once it breaks out the cry of the day will be 'public safety,' 'the security of the nation,' or whatever they choose to call it. Why do you suppose we still have a 'State of Emergency' a dozen years after the failed attempt on President Lincoln's life?"

Liam still had hold of Becky's hands and he suddenly realized she'd made no attempt to pull away; the thought made an odd little tingle run up the back of his neck and he was sure he could feel the tops of his ears turning red.

"All that's as may be," he said in dead earnest, "but if I'm not much good on the *legal* side, I'm a whizbang when it comes to the other one. If there's anything useful to your cause that's being kept under lock and key anywhere, just point me and I'll go get it for you."

She cocked her head and examined Liam penetratingly, the moment stretching out long enough that Liam started to get uneasy. But before he could say anything further, she nodded as if she'd just come to a important conclusion and got to her feet, pulling Liam with her.

"Come on," she said, "let's go find a cab and pay a call on your grandmother. We can talk some more as we're driving."

Liam turned to look towards the north side of the Park, where Fifth Avenue ended and the downtown flow of traffic usually deposited a shifting delta of horse-drawn carriages and steam jitneys. Today, though, the traffic was being kept away from the Park by a row of improvised barriers, and one of the imposing Colt-Lovelace automata in full NYPD uniform stood squarely at the intersection of 5th and Waverly Place, its arms folded warningly on its chest. Liam turned to Becky with a puzzled frown:

"What's all that about? And why use an Acme instead of live coppers?"

"It's the DPS again. The Trainmen's Union has called a General Strike for Wednesday, and the DPS has city police and reserve troops and its own people in plain clothes covering every park in town to prevent public gatherings. They're covering mostly the big areas like Central Park and Union Square. That leaves automata for the little parks. Look there!"

She pointed across the Park towards MacDougal Street, and after a moment Liam was able to pick out another Acme standing in a narrow alley between two buildings.

"There's another one over on the University Place side, and a couple more on the south end between . . . What on earth?"

Liam saw it too—a steam jitney was approaching the barriers at top speed, showing no sign of slowing down; a moment later it crashed through them, scattering bits of lumber in every direction as the vehicle screeched to a stop a foot away from the Acme, which flung its arms wide in a pantomime of alarm. In the same instant a man wearing a black hood that covered his whole head jumped out of the passenger side of the jitney, took two steps towards the Acme and clamped a large brown paper package against the automaton's chest with a distinct metallic clank. Surprisingly, the package stayed in place, emitting a faint wisp of smoke as the man jumped back into the cab and it tore away into the distance.

"Get down!" shouted Liam, grabbing Becky and pulling her with him as he fell flat to the path and covered her as well as he could with his own body. Simultaneously, there was an ear-splitting explosion and bits and pieces of the shattered automaton flew in every direction, followed by five more explosions as close to each other as the fire from a battery of

Parrott guns. More chunks of metal flew overhead, shrieking and whistling before the fragments smashed into buildings and crashed through windows.

"Good God," muttered Liam dazedly, still firmly on top of Becky.

"I don't want to seem ungrateful, Mr. McCool, but ..." she said in a somewhat muffled voice. Instantly Liam leapt to his feet, blushing a bright scarlet as he pulled Becky to her feet.

"I'm very sorry, Miss Fox," Liam said awkwardly, "I just ..."

"Don't even dream of apologizing," she said firmly, "just look at *that!*"

She pointed to the bench they'd been standing by, and now Liam saw that half of the backrest had been torn away by shrapnel. He shook his head grimly, for once at a total loss for words.

"It's the Whyos," Becky said in a slightly shaky voice. "They declared war on the automata a few days ago when Danny Lyons was seized by one of the 'curfew Acmes' and hauled away to the Tombs."

"They got Danny?" Liam raised his eyebrows. "I wouldn't want to be an Acme just now. That was quite an operation, there must have been a half dozen jitneys all timing their attacks to the second."

"The thing I don't understand is what made the paper packet stick to the thing."

"That at least is easy," Liam said with a small smile. "Did you catch the clank as he jammed it against the Acme? There would have been some big, powerful magnets around the dynamite."

Becky put her arm through Liam's and guided him eastwards, towards the Broadway side of the Park. "It'll make quite a story," she said with a wry echo of Liam's smile. "That is, if I can find anybody who's willing to print it."

Chapter Thirteen

as the neighborhood changed much since you were a boy?" Becky looked around curiously, as if she were trying to imagine growing up where Liam had.

"Not a whit. It may not be pretty, but it's still got more get up and go than all the rest of New York put together."

They had let their steamer go at the corner of Canal and Mulberry, choosing to walk the few blocks to his grandmother's flat so they could enjoy the spring sunshine. As they passed the corner of Bayard and Mulberry a shrill whistle split the air and Liam and Becky looked up to see a pretty, dark-haired woman about Liam's age leaning out of a second-story window on the other side, waving and showing a generous amount of cleavage. Liam waved back, grinning appreciatively:

"Hallo, Rosie darlin'!" he called back. "Mind you don't catch cold!"

The young woman grinned, stuck her tongue out at Liam and disappeared back inside. Becky gave him an arch look:

"I see you're something of a celebrity."

Liam spread his hands innocently: "Well, I've been to prison, haven't I? Not to mention cracking enough rich cribs to buy a fancy place uptown."

Becky acknowledged the riposte with a smile and they walked for a few minutes in silence, enjoying the tumult of street life boiling around them: sidewalk beer halls with oompah bands picking up the overflow from the Atlantic Gardens a couple of blocks to the east, musicians playing bagpipes and fiddles and squeezeboxes, tumblers and jugglers throwing somersaults, spinning plates and eating live coals, street singers, Punch and Judy shows, an Italian organ grinder with a monkey and a dog that walked on its hind legs, a Hindu sword swallower, and a Gypsy with a cross-looking bear on a chain and a placard advertising "Fortunes, Magic Potions and Curses."

And everywhere a full-throated Babel of English, German, Yiddish, Russian, Italian, and every kind of unidentifiable gibberish as buyers and sellers haggled over old clothes, new knives and cutlery, books, pistols, broken-down chairs, anything someone with a few dollars or a handful of pennies might want to take home with them, as well as a stupefying variety of foods being hawked by pushcart vendors—oysters, hot yams, fresh-roasted peanuts and corn on the cob, knishes, Sicilian sausages, hotcakes and coffee, and sweet baked pears waiting to be lifted by their stems from syrup-filled pans.

"By Heaven," Liam said feelingly, "I can't tell you how much I missed all this down in the coalfields—I'd sooner spend six months on Devil's Island."

Becky looked at him thoughtfully. "If it's not too personal," she said, "I'd like to know how you found yourself in a position to get shanghaied by Pilkington's Agency and shipped off to Henderson's Patch."

"My *position*," Liam said with a wry grimace, "was flat on my back on a rope bed in the Tombs, watching a cockroach cross the ceiling and betting how long it would take him to reach the other side. How I got into that *particular* position is a long story."

"I don't mind if it's long," Becky said, "I'm a good listener."

Liam laughed. "All right, then. It all started with me doing a favor for my pal Mike Vysotsky. Something I swore I would never take a chance on and Mike knew it, too. Only he wasn't asking for himself, he was asking for his Uncle Alyosha."

"Good storytelling," Becky said. "Lead off with a mystery."

"Well, there's no mystery about me and Mike—we grew up together, right here in Mulberry Bend. My Gran still lives in the flat I was born in, and Mike and his family lived right next door. You may have read about Aleksandr Vysotsky, that was Mike's dad."

"The *anarchist?* The one who tried to blow up Boss Tweed?"

"That's him. Of course, when I was a kid he was just the crazy man next door, always walking up and down the floor of his sitting room making speeches to nobody while Mike's ma worked in a book bindery and Mike ran the streets with me. *My* dad, now . . ." Liam shook his head. "He and Vysotsky were like peas in a pod. There's a novel for you when you've time to write it: *'The Anarchist and the Fenian, A Tale of Old New York.'* It was like they'd entered on a pact to save the proletariat by swallowing all the drink in town before it could reach the workers and bring them to harm."

They stopped for a moment to watch a juggler twirling a plate with each hand while he balanced another on his nose.

"Didn't you say on the train that it was your father who started you on languages?" Her tone was one of mild reproof, as if she didn't approve of slanted reporting.

"It's true enough," he said grudgingly. "He'd been a schoolmaster back in Dublin, Greek and Latin and a fair bit of a scholar with it—he drilled me like a Tartar on the Classics till I was old enough to escape. And my Ma had been a governess to an English Duke's kids, that's another long story . . ." Liam drifted away for a moment, then shrugged it off and came back to Mulberry Street. "You're right, though,

126

the poor man could never understand why he wasn't a grand success here in the Land of the Free and he tended to take it personally. Of course," Liam laughed without much humor, "when he got off the boat there were signs everywhere he went saying 'No Irish Need Apply.'"

"Did you teach yourself Russian, then?"

This time the humor was back in Liam's laughter: "Not much! When he was little Mike couldn't speak English worth a rip, so we taught each other, starting with all the curse words we knew. By the time I was through I could make a Russian sailor's hair stand on end, and poor Mike got the short end of that stick—Russian cursing is like epic poetry, but English hasn't got enough boring cuss-words to fill a thimble." He grinned reminiscently. "That's how the Butcher Boys came about, one by one all the odds and sods in Five Points drifted together with me and Mike—a Jap kid, a Frenchie from up North in Acadia, a Hunkie from Budapest, a whole omnium-gatherum of international misfits and not one of us older than twelve."

He put out his elbow for Becky to put her arm through and they started walking again. "Some of your uptown colleagues seem to think poor kids start gangs out of wickedness, but I expect you know better." He looked at her questioningly.

"Of course," Becky said. "It's the same everywhere I've been—kids are weak and numbers give them something to face the world with."

Liam nodded. "Trouble was, everybody wanted a piece of us—especially the big boys in the Dusters and the Whyos and the Dead Rabbits and all the rest. Fly little kids are precious—you can train them as dips, you can send them down chimneys, just like Fagin. We weren't having any, so we set up on our own."

They walked in silence for a moment, enjoying each other's closeness without quite knowing what to make of it. Finally, Liam resumed briskly, as if being matter-of-fact would help him steer clear of risky emotions:

"And that's about it, really, each of us would go the limit for any of the others, and that's why Mike turned to me when his Uncle Alyosha got pinched for heisting a painting from Astor's mansion."

"The Rembrandt? *Mike's uncle* was the one who did it?"

"None other. Naturally Astor had Pilkingtons all over the place when he brought the canvas home, and Alyosha winkled it right out from under their noses the first night. It made them look so bad they had to say it was a gang of art thieves—they put it about that it was Max Shinburn and Adam Worth working together. But it was all down to Alyosha, he did it on contract for a rival of Astor's and nobody would have been the wiser if the flaming eejit hadn't started drinking vodka with some pals and shot his mouth off. The Pilkingtons pinched him later and beat him till he gave them a signed confession. That's what Mike wanted me to get for him, out of the big strongroom in Pilkington HQ—Alyosha's confession."

He fell silent for a few moments and Becky finally poked him in the ribs: "For pity's sake, Mr. McCool, a little less suspense if you please!"

"Ah, it still makes me mad to think of it. I never try a job like that without going in and having a look first. Maybe two looks, maybe three—you don't want to hurry a thing like that. But they wanted to put Alyosha on trial and lock him up fast, so I had to go in cold—the confession was all they had, and their case would have collapsed if I had gotten it." He snorted irritably. "But they got me instead. And a couple of weeks later old Mr. P. himself showed up in the Tombs and pulled a reverse Fagin on me."

"I see," Becky murmured.

"Not quite, you don't," Liam said. "I was counting on them sending me to Sing Sing after I went to trial, and I could have escaped from *there*." He grinned at Becky's surprised look: "Little Adam Worth and I got to be quite chummy a while back when we found out we'd both been in the War, and one night he told he how me busted out of Sing Sing back in '65. Nothing to it if you know what you're doing. But old Mr. P. was too slick for me."

Becky looked pained: "He used your grandmother to make you agree."

"Good call, Miss Fox. My Gran was all the family I had after Pa was shot in the Draft Riots, but she'd really been the one that raised me as far back as I can remember. My poor Ma had a big heart and she loved me the best she could, but most of the time she had her hands full with my old man. Whenever the Punch and Judy show started up again, Gran would grab her hat and her purse with one hand and me with the other, and off we'd go on our travels."

Liam paused for a moment, remembering, then laughed and went on: "She'd drag me wherever the fancy took her, up in the Central Park for a picnic or out to Staten Island for fish and chips or to the Metropolitan to see the paintings, or off to Harry Hill's concert saloon to hear Harry himself read out his awful poems, and her all the time cracking jokes and telling tall tales and chatting up every stranger we ran into. There's nobody quite like the old girl, and that's a fact."

"Surely Pilkington hasn't threatened to harm her?"

Liam made a face. "My Gran's no angel, Miss Fox. These last few years she kept food on our table by running a policy bank for one of the Italian gangs. Old Pilkington sewed her up tight on that rap and he put it to me plain and simple. Either I played his game or I stayed in the Tombs until I forgot the look of daylight and Gran got locked up in Leonard Street. Nobody knows better than you how bad that would be. When I was still planning to head for San Francisco with Maggie I got in touch with my pal Mike and fixed it for him to get Gran out of New York under Pilkington's nose and bring her to meet us in St. Jo, But when Maggie was murdered I decided it was time to call Pilkington on his promise to let her go after I finished my work with the Mollies." He made a face and shrugged: "You can see how that worked out."

Becky's face flushed angrily. "What a vicious old reprobate."

"He is that, Miss Fox. But Pilkington and I made a deal," he added grimly, "and I mean to make him keep to it since there's nothing left to do with the Mollies but round them up and clap them in choky." He stopped and pointed to the building ahead of them. "Here we are then. Are you game to meet a fierce old lady from County Galway?"

Becky smiled. "Lead on, McCool!"

The contrast between the festive atmosphere outside and the Stygian gloom inside was overwhelming. Uptown, Secretary Tesla's electrification policy had resulted in bright-as-day carbon-arc lighting on parts of Fifth Avenue and the Central Park, as well as softer indoor electrics in every building that could afford to install the new Tesla Steam Generators.

Here in Liam's old tenement building, he and Becky were making their way upstairs with the aid of a single gas bracket on the third-floor landing, and the steps themselves were dark enough to make their climb painstaking. Add to that a thick palimpsest of smells, from today's cabbage and onions through last week's drunken piss, plus the pandemonium of yelling, tears, arguments and knockdown fights swirling through the hallways around them, and the sense of dislocation was sharp.

Liam put his foot through a broken step and bit back a curse. "Mind this step," he cautioned. "I don't think anything's been mended here in fifty years."

"I've seen worse," she said. "I think perhaps it was in Bombay," she added, laughing.

"You're probably wondering how I could leave my Gran in a dump like this when I've got a nice empty flat on Bleecker Street."

"Well, I *was* a little curious about that."

"Wait till you meet Gran," he said. "She didn't want to leave all her old friends here in the Points and there was no budging her even though I argued till I was blue in the face. That old lady could will a charging rhinoceros to stop dead in its tracks."

"Unlike her meek and docile grandson," Becky said with a grin Liam could hear even if he couldn't see it.

"I'll tell you one thing, she's moving back with me now, if I have to throw her over my shoulder and carry her off. I've got to get her out of Stanton's reach as fast as I can."

"I'm afraid you'll have to go a long way to achieve that."

"That's what's got me worried," he said. "I'm thinking I'll have the lads in the Butcher Boys mount guard on her day and night till I can figure out how to get us out of the country."

"Where were you thinking of going?" she asked. Liam thought he heard a touch of disappointment in her voice.

"Maybe France. The Commune's *Sûreté* is as bad as the DPS in some ways, but if you're a foreigner and you aren't political they don't really care. Or maybe we can catch the Trans-Little Russian railway to the Free City of Los Angeles, every fugitive in the Western Hemisphere is holed up there and the Volunteer Police make things plenty hot for spies and stooges, never mind *who* they belong to."

They had finally reached the third floor and Liam gestured down the hall towards their right:

"That's where Mike and I grew up," he said.

As he spoke the door nearest them flew open and an old man wearing trousers with suspenders over a ragged suit of Long Johns burst into the hall looking frantic.

"Ah, Liam, 'tis you at last," he cried in a heavy brogue. "I'm that glad see you, only I'm afraid you're too late!"

Liam froze for a moment, his face falling: "What the Devil do you mean, man? Surely she's not dead!"

"Not that," the old man said miserably, "not that at all, Liam dear, but she's been *taken*. Two ugly bruisers from the DPS came for her this morning, and took her away in the clothes she was standing in!"

Liam was stunned, his expression so sick that Becky reached out and took hold of his arm.

"I'll kill Pilkington," he said at last, his voice choked. "I'll tear the heart out of his body and feed it to the rats."

He turned and started back down the stairs, moving so fast that Becky had to run to keep up.

Outside on the street Liam stood stock-still for a moment, looking around with such a crazy expression that Becky grabbed him by the arms and shook him.

"*Liam McCool!*" she said sharply. "Don't you move a *muscle* till I can see you've come to your senses!"

After a moment Liam snapped out of it and let go of a long, shuddering breath. "I'm sorry, Miss Fox," he said. "I think I must have been dreading that for months without admitting it. The only way I had of staying in touch from that Godforsaken Henderson's Patch was by mail, and right up till we returned to the city Mike was checking on her and telling me she was fine. But I've never really trusted Pilkington to keep his word." He took a deep breath and let it out very slowly, then did it again and grinned. "There. My pal Harry says when in doubt, take a deep breath. I promise you I won't do anything rash, but Mr. Pilkington and I must have a reckoning. Right now."

Becky assessed him thoughtfully and finally nodded. "Very well," she said, "only you must promise to me meet for dinner at Delmonico's to tell me how the meeting went and if you're to do that you'll have to stay out of jail. My father's troubles are enough for me right now, I don't need to be worrying about my friends."

She took his arm and propelled him down the street towards Park and the nearest cab stand, as Liam reflected that it felt surprisingly nice for Becky Fox to describe him as a friend. Becky was thinking about what she'd just said herself and smiling a little as she followed it in various directions, so that neither of them was quite alert enough to be forewarned when a couple of heavy-set thugs in full Bowery Boys regalia suddenly stepped out of the alley just ahead of them and barred their way.

The two were dressed identically, each wearing a black silk hat square on top of his head, red cravats with their shirt collars turned over them, fancy silk vests with embroidered flowers, black frock coats and pants and heavy boots. Their faces were red and shiny with booze, and each had a half-smoked cigar stuck into the corner of a sneering grin.

"Well, well," said Liam evenly. "If it isn't Tweedledum and Tweedledee."

"You'd best shut your face, McCool," the First Thug snarled, "before I put me boot in it."

"They told us he'd likely be rude," said the Second Thug in a chiding tone. "But they didn't say we couldn't teach him some manners before we brought him in." He looked at Becky and frowned. "What about her, then? They didn't mention *her*."

The First Thug grinned lazily as he pulled a heavy revolver out of his pocket. "I'm thinking we should take her back in the alley and get acquainted. Once we've hogtied Mr. McCool, that is."

"Cracking fine idea, Kev," grinned the Second Thug, as he reached out and grabbed Becky by the arm, pulling her towards him.

In the same instant, and before Becky's indignant gasp had left her throat, Liam had whipped the *katana* free of its sheath, then whirled around as he swung the blade down through the First Thug's wrist and on around through one of the Second Thug's ankles.

To Becky it seemed as if life had frozen solid for a split second, like one of Mr. Brady's photographs. Then, in the next split second, the First Thug's gun fell to the ground with his hand still clutching it and he began screaming shrilly as a fountain of blood gushed from his wrist and he stood and stared at it, paralyzed. Now the Second Thug's jaw dropped with shock as he let go of Becky, tottered for a moment and toppled over, screaming still louder, his severed foot remaining planted on the ground in half of its boot as the ankle parted from it, gushing a second fountain of blood.

Faster than Becky could follow, Liam had wiped his blade on the First Thug's jacket, slipped it back inside the stick and taken her arm.

"Time to go!" he said urgently and pulled her along with him as he strode rapidly towards Park, leaving the two thugs howling on the pavement behind them.

Three minutes later, they were seated inside a cab, steaming briskly uptown as Liam examined Becky anxiously. She had a few spots of blood on her skirt, but otherwise she seemed unharmed.

"I'm sorry about the blood," he said.

"That's quite all right," she said in a somewhat shaky voice. "But I do hope life around you isn't always this exciting."

A little shaky himself now that he thought about it, Liam gave her what he hoped was a reassuring grin. Then he took her hand firmly in his and leaned back against the seat.

Chapter Fourteen

nd I say by God, it isn't *fair!*"

"Mr. McPherson!" Pilkington frowned disapprovingly and wagged his finger. "I won't have you or anyone else around me taking the Lord's name in vain!"

The Great Detective and his boss were sitting in Pilkington's Union Square office with the windows raised to let in the fine spring weather; a fitful breeze had set the curtains to undulating gently and pigeons could be heard cooing in the eaves.

Across the Square, the building which had once been the headquarters of Tiffany's was now (Tiffany's having bowed to force majeure) the New York headquarters of the Department of Public Safety, on the roof of which a giant billboard had been erected displaying the motto *"Per Aspera ad Securitas"* in golden letters twenty feet tall. Towering above the motto, and picked out day and night with colossal carbon-arc searchlights, was a stark, black-and-white representation of the All-Seeing Eye—a staring eye surrounded by rays of light and enclosed by a triangle.

McPherson, whose broad pink face shone with perspiration from a combination of his dark, heavy suit, three large whiskeys and a good solid head of injured feelings, tried to look contrite without much success.

"But you as much as promised me, sir! You said as soon as Bill Henkel was gone I was the obvious choice to take over the Chicago office, and Bill turned up his toes two weeks ago!"

Pilkington laced his fingers across his ample stomach and beamed reassuringly at McPherson, his twinkling eyes, his rosy cheeks and his fluffy white hair and whiskers combining to make him the perfect archetype of Dear Old Granddad.

"There, now, my boy," he murmured comfortingly, "you know perfectly well I'll see you right in the end. But just at the moment everybody in the firm is going to have to make some short-term sacrifices and accept a few temporary inconveniences in order for us to meet the challenges ahead of us."

McPherson ground his teeth. "Yes, sir," he said. "It would help a lot if I had any idea what you're talking about. The last I heard from you, you were telling me how vital it was for me to keep a steady hand on the helm down there in Pottsville. Then all of a sudden I get urgent orders to report to Union Square. I was sure it was going to be about Chicago, but instead you're telling me about sacrifices and challenges and I'm damned . . ." he bared his teeth and scrunched up his face as he fought to control his tongue, then grated out: " . . . *switched* if know what's going on."

Pilkington looked at him thoughtfully for a few moments, then nodded: "Very well, Agent McPherson, I think it's time for me to take you into my confidence."

He gestured out the window towards the DPS building. "Why do you think Tiffany's has moved and the DPS has suddenly filled every office in that building with researchers and Secret Service operatives? It's the threat of *war*, McPherson. War with Little Russia, and according to Secretary Stanton it's a threat we may not be able to avert. From now on you and I and every other man and woman in the Agency will be devoting ourselves day and night to warding off this nightmare, but if we fail we'll be at war before the summer's over."

McPherson turned pale and sat back in his chair. "*War? Why?* . . . How . . ."

Pilkington held up a hand to stop him. "There will be changes you can't possibly imagine and about which you don't yet need to know. But New York is going to be a hive of activity, the *fons et origo* of a new and vastly more powerful United States, and as always when it comes to security, Secretary Stanton's will be the directing hand." He paused ruminatively, his face clouding a bit as he stared up at the ceiling. After a moment he shook the mood off and continued briskly:

"I must admit that just like you I spent some time dreaming of a great preferment while Secretary Stanton searched for a man to run his Secret Service; after all, hadn't I worked hand in glove with him throughout the War? But as he told me himself when his final choice fell upon Willie: youth must be served and age must stand by to lend support with its greater wisdom." He bent forward in his chair, fixing his guileless blue eyes on McPherson:

"And needless to say, Secretary Stanton will be relying on the Pilkington International Detective Agency for confidential services no one else can be entrusted with, so if you fulfill your assignments to the utmost of your ability, there will be no *limit* to your future. Do you take my meaning, Agent McPherson?"

For a moment McPherson looked a little dazed, his mind racing through the possibilities the Old Man had opened up. Then he smiled slowly and nodded his agreement:

"You can count on me, Mr. P., you know that. Just tell me what you want me to do."

"Good. And please note that this assignment is *strictly* confidential, *no one* else is to know." His eyes bored into the Great Detective's until he seemed satisfied that his message had gotten through. Then he continued, with heavy emphasis on every word: "Your primary task until I tell you otherwise will be stick to Lukas like glue and make sure I am informed at all times of his movements and, if possible, his plans. Secretary Tesla has come up with a clever adaptation of his voicewire machine that will let us listen day and night to what transpires inside Lukas' house. The device is much smaller than a voicewire box, but it will require clever work on your part to conceal it and put it in action. It's up to you to figure out how to get Lukas and his servants out of the way for the hour or so it will take you to accomplish that."

"I don't get it, Mr. P. I know Lukas is some kind of anarchist and the brains behind the dynamite plot in Pottsville, but for us to invest this much effort in keeping an eye on him?"

Pilkington got up abruptly and walked to the bank of windows, staring towards the DPS building. He peered towards it for a few moments as if he were hoping to see right through it, then he shook his head exasperatedly and turned back towards McPherson.

"Believe it or not, Lukas is working for Secretary Stanton."

"What?"

Looking thoroughly disgruntled, Pilkington returned to his desk and dropped into his chair to a protesting creak of springs.

"It's a policy I've never totally approved of, nor do I believe that I've been told all that I should know about it. But Secretary Stanton has told me enough to let me say with assurance that Lukas' talents will make him inestimably valuable to the future of our republic. At the same time, however, I can't help saying that he is one of the most false and duplicitous individuals I have ever met, a crook to the very marrow of his bones, and I mean to know as far as is humanly possible just what he's up to at all times. Can you carry out this assignment for me in total secrecy?"

McPherson sat up straighter: "You can count on me, Mr. P. Through thick and thin."

Pilkington relaxed enough to produce his grandfatherly smile: "I am delighted to hear it, my boy. Now, before I let you go, do you have any other questions?"

"Just one, sir. I'd like to ask why you've brought McCool back to HQ? If you want to talk about false and duplicitous, that sneaky little blatherskite is the . . ."

But Pilkington was shaking his head firmly. "Believe me, McPherson, I regard him with the utmost possible wariness. But Secretary Stanton has entrusted me with a task that can only be pulled off by an experienced undercover who's completely at ease in the Russian language and I've got a handle on McCool that makes me willing to take a chance on him . . ."

He spread his arms in a gesture of resignation and McPherson nodded unhappily and stood up. "Just let me say, sir, that anytime you decide you want to see young Liam brought to heel I'm just the man for you. In fact, I would pay for the privilege!"

Pilkington smiled slowly, thinking that over. "I'll remember, Agent McPherson. And now if you'll . . ."

He was interrupted by the sound of a commotion in the outer office—the clatter of furniture punctuated by the shrill voice of Pilkington's secretary:

"You can't go in there until I check with Mr. Pilkington! Are you crazy? Do you want me to call a guard?"

Pilkington reached under his desk and pressed a button; instantly a section of bookcase behind his desk slid open to reveal a stairway. Pilkington gestured towards it:

"That will take you out in the direction of 16th Street. From now on I want you to report to me twice a day by voice-wire; if I'm not here leave a message with my secretary."

McPherson looked doubtfully towards the outer office and the continuing commotion: "Are you sure you don't want me to . . ."

"I can take care of myself, Agent McPherson." He smiled slightly as he took a Frontier Colt out of a holster under his desk and laid it on the desktop. "Now get out there and get busy."

"Yes, sir."

McPherson hastened into the secret passage and Pilkington pressed the button to close it, but before it fully closed the door to the outer office burst open and Liam strode in, his face flushed with anger. Half-turning for a moment to register the movement of the bookcase, he turned back and strode forward again as the secretary stepped into the open doorway behind him, her hands fluttering as if she were trying desperately to take wing:

"I'm *so* sorry Mr. Pilkington, he simply wouldn't be . . ."

"It's all right, Annie, I'll see Mr. McCool."

She pursed her lips disapprovingly and backed out, shutting the door after her. The minute the lock clicked, Liam leapt forward and leaned across the desk so that his face was no more than six inches away from Pilkington's as he bit out the words:

"You slimy, double-dealing old son of a bitch, where . . . is . . . my . . . *grandmother*?"

Pilkington pulled back in his chair but his voice was calm as he answered: "Now, now, Mr. McCool, we have many things to talk about, and your attitude isn't going to help us at all."

Liam's voice went up a notch: "We only have *one* thing to discuss, and that's your promise to free my grandmother from surveillance the moment my job in Pottsville was done. She'd best be free and unharmed right now or I will make you the sorriest old man in these United States!"

In spite of himself, Pilkington's eyes dropped towards the six-shooter on the desk in front of him, but with the speed of a striking snake Liam snatched it up and jammed it into his belt.

"Oh, no you don't." he grated. "I want your answer *now*."

Pilkington's answer was to reach under the desk and press another button, ringing a bell that could be heard clanging loudly somewhere behind the bookcases, which abruptly swung wide on the other side of Pilkington's desk as two burly agents carrying drawn pistols rushed into the room towards Liam.

"Hold it right there . . . !" was all that one of them succeeded in saying before Liam spun around on one foot, kicking the pistol out of his hand as the movement carried his foot through an arc that ended with his heel slamming against the other agent's chin hard enough to knock him cold.

As the second agent crumpled to the ground, the first—badly frightened—took up a bareknuckle boxing stance and sent a badly aimed punch at Liam, who knocked it aside with an exasperated frown.

"Don't be stupid," he muttered, reaching out and jamming a knuckle into the side of the man's neck. The first agent's eyes rolled up into his head so that only the whites showed and he folded to the ground with a thud.

Without missing a beat, Liam whipped the six-shooter out of his belt, leaned back across the astounded old man's desk and jammed the muzzle into his forehead hard enough to *thunk!* audibly against his skull and rock him back in his chair.

"Now," said Liam. "Talk! Let's start with you sending your bullyboys after me down in Five Points."

Pilkington looked genuinely taken aback. "I didn't send anybody after you, why should I? I expected you to come here under your own steam."

Liam cocked the hammer with an ominous *click-clack!* For the first time, Pilkington's eyes flickered with a hint of fear. "You would, wouldn't you?" he said.

Liam didn't bother answering. After a moment Pilkington let out a ragged breath.

"All right, Mr. McCool. You have the upper hand. But I have your grandmother, so you'd best sit down and listen to what I have to say. "

For a moment, Liam seemed to be weighing the pros and cons of blowing off the old man's head just for the hell of it, and Pilkington's face turned a dirty pinkish-gray. Then Liam grunted, let the hammer back down and took the muzzle away from Pilkington's forehead. He stood in front of the desk with his arms folded, the pistol still firmly gripped in his fist.

"Speak," he said.

Pilkington took the handkerchief from his breast pocket and wiped his face a little tremulously.

"Your grandmother is quite safe," he said with a touch of acid. "For the moment."

"What the Devil do you mean by that?"

"I mean," Pilkington continued with a touch of asperity, "that Agent McPherson's reports from Pottsville had already made it clear to me that you are what nautical men call a 'loose cannon' and that I must exercise the most finical care in dealing with you. When I heard from Agent McPherson that you had gone so far as to threaten his life during your final meeting with him, I thought I had better take some precautions."

Liam shook his head incredulously. "I may be a thief, but my word is as good as gold. What is your word worth, you scabrous old dog-puke?"

Pilkington's expression hardened: "I haven't time for such fripperies. The security of the United States of America is in my hands and the hands of a few other knowledgeable and dedicated men, and promises have no meaning whatever as long as we are facing the threat of an internecine war with Little Russia. As to your grandmother, suffice it to say she is in a safe place and in the most perfect health—though I am told she is no more amenable to the dictates of prudence and common decency than is her grandson."

"When do you mean to set her free?" Liam's voice was menacing, and Pilkington's eyes narrowed warily.

"I have a mission for you that is of absolutely crucial importance. Believe me when I say I wouldn't dream of sending you forth on it without some guarantee of your good behavior, and your grandmother's remaining in our care for the time being should do very nicely for that purpose. If you fulfill your assigned duties as well as you did at Little Round Top you may have your private life back again when it's all over."

Liam was having a hard time resisting the urge to kill Pilkington and have done with it. He spoke in an unsteady, harsh tone that made Pilkington look longingly towards the buttons under his desk:

"Tell me about this mission of yours and don't waste words. And stay away from your alarm switches."

Pilkington licked his lips and dabbed his forehead with his handkerchief. "We need a seasoned undercover who speaks Russian to go to Little Petersburg and find out what happened to one of our agents in the Little Russian Ministry of War, it's as simple as that."

"I'm sure it isn't. What are you leaving out?"

"His name was Lt. Col. Vasilii Chuikov—he had prepared a report on Little Russia's war plans and he was supposed to use the excuse of a fishing trip on Lake Superior—what they call Lake Petersburg now—to escape and take the report to our HQ in Chicago. We've heard rumors of improvements in the Little Russian Aerial Navy that could be disastrous for us if they're true . . ." he hesitated and his eyes shifted away towards one side. "In any event, we've had no word from Chuikov and we *must* have the information."

"Spit it out, Pilkington," Liam said furiously, "what don't you want to tell me about?"

Pilkington glared at Liam. "Very well. But you reveal this to another soul at the peril of your grandmother's life. We've also heard rumors of the discovery of vast pitchblende deposits in the southwestern territories of Little Russia, in the mountains where the Apache Indian people live. Chuikov was supposed to find out if the rumors were true and confirm the location. I doubt you know it, but pitchblende is the ore from which . . ."

But Liam was already making connections: " . . . calorium is extracted. I'm willing to bet you've got your hands on someone who knows the secret of refining calorium and that this whole dirty scheme is about seizing Little Russia's pitchblende and using it to beat out the British industrialists."

Pilkington's lips quirked as if he had just bitten into a very sour lemon. He stared at Liam for several long, sullen moments. Finally, he shrugged.

"I insist that you sit down while I give you your instructions, I'm tired of straining my neck. And listen to me *very* carefully. Just remember . . ." he leaned forward and gave Liam a nasty smile . . . "if you don't get hold of this information and bring it back to me in this office *no later than July 3rd*, you will never see your dear old grandmother again."

Chapter Fifteen

his town is going crazy, Lyovushka, and I'm not just talking about giant rats and cockroaches, I'm talking about everything everywhere is nuts and nobody knows what's next. This morning, it's your Gran gone. A couple of hours ago, it was all of the boys—and I mean *all* of them, even Harry the Jap couldn't manage to pull a fade in time. And all kinds of other people I'm hearing about, too, people like us and uptown nobs both, from all over the city—there's a knock on the door and the next thing you know you got Eyes coming out of the cracks in the wall. The only reason they didn't get me was that Harry called on the voicewire while they were busting his door down, and I went and dragged Abe Hummel down here with a mountain of legal papers before the Eyes even started up my staircase."

It was late in the afternoon and the shadows were already lengthening along MacDougal Street as Liam and Mike Vysotsky strolled and confabbed. Vysotsky, a sturdy, bouncy young man whose normal style was a bottomless mix of nervous energy and laughter, was a study in gloom and uneasiness, looking around as if he expected more Eyes to pop out of the nearest coal chute. He ran his palm over his pale, cropped hair and tugged on his broken nose as if he was trying to straighten it.

"Did Pilkington say anything about them sweeping people up?"

Liam shook his head. "He said we were going to be at war with Little Russia pretty soon and the way I got it was that was going to be an excuse for just about anything Stanton & Co. feel like pulling from here on in. I'm surprised they even paid any attention to Hummel's writs."

"Howe and Hummel are just as crooked as those bums, and they know it. Why do you think Mother Mandelbaum has them on a five grand annual retainer? Those two shysters know all the dirt on all the big cheeses in this city—and Washington, too. As long as the politicos want to pretend they're playing by the book—all fair, square and above board—we're going to need Abe and Billy holding our hands."

"Where are they taking the people they're putting the collar on? Is there any word on the grapevine?"

Vysotsky made a face. "Rumors. Rumors about rumors. I give them that much—they got things sewn up tight, nobody's daring to open their yap. The one whisper I'm hearing the most is they're going to be used for something. Put to work, maybe."

He looked around urgently and then leaned closer to Liam, speaking right into his ear: "I tell you this for free, *bratushka*, if we're going to be taking on the DPS we're going to need a real war chest—we need to crack a bank, and we need to do it fast."

Liam nodded. "Fast is right. Pilkington expects me to get to New Petersburg, do his dirty work and bring home the bacon by a week from Wednesday. That means you'll have to find out where he's taken Gran and the boys while I'm gone and have a plan ready for how we can go spring them before that old rat pulls any more tricks."

"First things first. What do you say we make a withdrawal from the Gotham Savings Institution? Tomorrow night when it's nice and quiet?"

"Suits me," Liam said. "I cased the one on the corner of Bleecker and Broadway a few months ago, before Henderson's Patch."

Vysotsky grinned. "Who ever said great minds don't think alike?"

Just ahead of them a cheerful light spilled into the deepening shadows from a plate glass window with ornate gold lettering: *The Kettle of Fish—Saloon—Free Lunch*. Vysotsky gestured towards it:

"Come on, let's see if Jimmy can give us a table in the back."

Meanwhile, in the drawing room of a fine old brownstone on Gramercy Park West, Becky Fox was biting her tongue as she submitted to an unctuous exhortation by Horatio Willard ("Willie") Pilkington, Chief of the Department of Public Safety's Secret Service. and (no less important to him) uneasy victor in the long struggle to escape his father's tutelage.

"Nobody in America knows better than you do, Becky dear, what perilous times we're living through." He smiled anxiously, the movement making his smooth, plump pink cheeks look even more like a baby's bottom. "Dynamiters and trade unionists are doing their utmost to tear the social fabric to shreds. Jealous foreign rivals eye our markets like hungry jackals, waiting to pounce on our customers and carry them away to their lairs. Anarchists and communists and free-love harpies fill the pages of our newspapers and journals with their poisons . . ." His voice quavered a little, the touch of revivalist anguish made popular by Moody and Sankey.

"I was only asking," Becky said with deceptive mildness, "why your office refused to acknowledge a writ of Habeas Corpus for the release of my father and his colleagues."

A fleeting look of exasperation flickered behind Willie's watery blue eyes before he got a fresh grip on his unctuous mood.

"There are times when even the Great Writ must give ground to the needs of a threatened public, Becky dear. *Vox populi vox dei*, as the proverb has it, and nowhere more so than in the preservation of our precious democracy. Of course the Department of Public Safety would never dream of denying the right of prisoners to challenge the legality of their arrest, but under our Emergency Regulations the use of Habeas Corpus must be *temporarily* suspended, for the general good."

"Very well, then," she said in her flattest no-nonsense tone. "I was warned to expect this by David Dudley Field, who I'm sure you know has undertaken to represent my father's interests. And I'm sure you also know that Mr. Field has the ear of many powerful men in Congress, all the more so since his recent service in the House of Representatives. Since you refuse to acknowledge the writ, I must warn you that I have asked Mr. Field to pursue every possible legal remedy against your Secret Service and the DPS and Secretary Stanton into the bargain."

Pilkington's expression hardened and the bogus air of stump-preacher entreaty dropped away as the muscles at the corners of his jaws worked angrily.

"I had heard you were keeping company with a dangerous criminal and Fenian agitator," he said coldly, "and I can see that he has had a less than beneficent effect on your views."

In spite of herself, Becky broke into a peal of laughter. "Honestly, Willie Pilkington, you are as big a humbug as you were when you were a little boy in short pants. If after all these years you could believe for an instant that I need *anybody's* help to form my opinions then you're a lamentable advertisement for the skills of Pilkington's International Detective Agency."

Not trusting himself to answer, Pilkington abruptly got to his feet and strode to the windows, where he stood for a moment staring out at the pleasant green vista of Gramercy Park while he struggled to master his irritation.

Becky studied Willie's stout form, expensively clad in bespoke tailoring that couldn't quite hide the results of his love of good port and extra desserts, and reproached herself for forgetting the adage about never poking a bear with a stick. Willie had a very tender *amour propre*, as any alert woman could easily read in the care with which he slicked his thinning brown hair over a palm-sized bald spot.

Tch! she said to herself. *Be nice!* Out loud, and in her most contrite tone, she said: "I *am* sorry, Willie, I didn't mean to upset you."

Accepting the olive branch, Pilkington returned to his seat and dropped into it with a put-upon sigh.

"Becky, dear, you know how deeply I care for you and how much you worry me with your Quixotic sallies against the powers that be. And I know you're all too aware of the dangers that face America today, your travels and your contacts with the public make you uniquely well-informed. So I hope you'll excuse my importunity in returning once more to my plea that you give serious thought to my proposal of marriage. If only we were man and wife it would be so much easier for me to protect you . . ." he paused briefly but significantly ". . . and your family."

Becky could feel the angry flush spreading up her neck and into her cheeks: *"The impudence of him,"* she thought furiously, *"to drag Papa's fate into this!"*

As used as she was to keeping a neutral tone with the people she interviewed, she couldn't keep a quaver of emotion out of her voice as she answered him: "I suppose, as before, you would insist that I must give up my writing career."

"Well of course . . ." he spread his hands in a gesture of appeal, "you would have new responsibilities, new duties . . ."

Becky bit her tongue again, but she didn't need to speak in order for Pilkington to read the mixture of affront and iron resolve in her expression. He shook his head disgustedly and stood up again.

"I might have guessed you'd be pig-headed as ever. But out of consideration for our years as neighbors and school-mates I must give you fair warning: I'm very well aware of your travels and your interviews in regards to a projected series on the trade unions and their threat of a general strike."

Becky felt a chill run along her spine. "Indeed?" she said carefully.

"Yes," he said, "Indeed. And we have informed George Curtis at *Harper's Weekly* that even if he calls in all the IOU's he holds from members of Congress and of the City and State Governments, they will not be enough to protect him and *Harper's* from the most draconian response if he dares to pub-lish your articles."

Becky got to her feet, clearly signaling the end of their tête à tête. Pilkington nodded and moved towards the front door, but before he opened it he added:

"Please think before you make any final decision, Becky. I don't want you to make yourself our enemy."

She moved around him and held the front door open: "I'm not your enemy, Willie. But until you can respect my rights as a citizen and a woman I can't be your friend either."

Pilkington stared at her for a moment, his jaws working; then he gave her a curt nod and headed down the front steps, tight-lipped and furious.

Chapter Sixteen

Liam said, "I hear they're having a hard time raising the money to put up the whole statue."

He and Becky had been ambling along the Fifth Avenue side of Madison Square Park on their way to the Delmonico's at 26th, enjoying the mild June evening and each other's company, when they were stopped short by the sight of a gargantuan bronze arm gripping a flaming bronze torch in its fist. A platform big enough for the entire New York Philharmonic had been erected for it in the middle of the Park, and curious strollers were walking around peering at the disembodied limb with awed and slightly mistrustful expressions, like Lilliputians stumbling across a chunk of Gulliver while out for a promenade.

"I'm afraid Secretary Stanton's security measures have put something of a damper on the fund drive," Becky said with a hint of irony, "especially since the finished statue is meant to show 'Liberty Enlightening the World.'"

"Hmmm," said Liam, transferring his gaze from the slightly creepy bit of statuary to the much more rewarding vision of Becky Fox dressed for the evening in a forest-green silk gown accented by a simple necklace of emeralds and opals. Madison Square had been one of Secretary Tesla's most recent experiments with electricity broadcast wirelessly from a colossal tower in the wilds of the Bronx and though Liam missed the soft glow of the old gaslights, the new incandescents gave the evening a holiday sparkle that matched his mood: no question about it, Becky made him want to smile even when he had little reason to.

"As usual," he quipped, "you have the *mot juste*. Plus a few extra for good measure."

She shrugged modestly and returned the smile: "Words *are* my trade, after all."

They resumed their stroll, in no particular hurry to go indoors out of the rare perfection of the spring evening. A faint mist had risen from the East River with the cooling of the day and mixed with the smoke of the city's countless steam engines to give the air a tang that made Liam think of the Long Island shore in October.

They had plenty of company tonight, too—as if the city had turned out for a breather after a week of unseasonable heat. Usually Madison Square was frequented by the well-to-do of the city, drawn by expensive shops and fine restaurants, but tonight there was a good-natured hubbub of swells and working folk alike, not to mention dips and boosters of every description. As one of these jostled Liam casually, Liam grabbed his hand with a grip like a bear trap, halting it on its journey out of his pocket.

"Lose something, did you?" Liam asked the dip in a mild tone. The man turned pale, let go of Liam's wallet and shook his head frenziedly, taking off like a scalded cat the moment Liam freed his wrist.

"Might be wise to keep a firm grip on your reticule," Liam said to Becky with a grin, "the Brotherhood's out in force tonight."

"Speaking of crime," she said, "have you learned anything new about Lukas?"

"My pal Mike has been keeping an eye on him. Not just for my benefit—it seems Lukas has been raiding Butcher Boy territory."

"Just what *is* Butcher Boy territory, or aren't you allowed to say?"

"It's no secret. Not from the law or the competition, anyway—we lay claim to Greenwich Village, everything north from West Houston to 14th Street and everything east from the Hudson to Broadway. We aren't like the Whyos or the Dead Rabbits or the Hudson Dusters—we don't get drunk in public, we don't fight in the streets, and we never bother a Square John. High-end stealing is our business, and we like to think the main difference between us and Jay Gould or Rockefeller is that we go to prison if we get caught."

Becky looked puzzled. "And Lukas is trying to stick his finger into this pie?"

"That's what Mike says. All I can tell you is that Lukas was partnered up with the best engraver in the funny money game, a Swiss named Hochstein, and Lukas' boys started shoving the queer all over town. When they tried shoving it on businesses in our part of the city, Mike gave Hochstein a chance to repent his wicked ways and he vamoosed for points West. Now we hear that Lukas has been making moves that look like he means to to try cracking a bank, maybe one in the Butcher Boys' neighborhood. What *we* can't figure is why a fellow with a butler and a nice house on Washington Square needs to take the bread out of the mouths of honest crooks."

Becky was nodding to herself with a pleased little smile, as if she'd just found a missing puzzle piece. "I think I can help you with that. According to my sources Lukas has been pouring money into the agitation behind the strike movement. Not that the railroad workers wouldn't be just as mad without his help, but they'd probably be a lot more peaceful if it were just their own union egging them on. As it is, Lukas is pouring coal oil on the sparks and hoping for an explosion." She glanced around quickly and then lowered her voice: "I have a source in the Imperial Russian consulate who says Lukas was a brain surgeon and a Professor of Medicine at the Imperial University of St. Petersburg. Not only that, the Paris office of the *Okhrana* says that even though Lukas is a member of the Royal Family, he was the one behind the bombers who blew up Grand Duke Vladimir Aleksandrovich, the Tsar's favorite son and heir apparent. The big question is who's behind *Lukas?* There are rumors that he's a Little Russian spy, that he's hand in glove with Secretary Stanton, that he's in league with the Antichrist and Heaven knows what other outlandish skullduggery."

Liam walked along in silence for a few moments, his chin sunk on his chest as he kicked a stone along the pavement and pondered on what Becky had said. Finally he looked up and nodded briskly:

"I can see that my personal business with Lukas is going to have to stand in line for a bit. But that's all right— justice for Maggie will be just as sweet if it has to wait till I've gotten Gran free of Pilkington and his thugs. Anyway that old villain has put me on a schedule that barely leaves me time to breathe, and him with Gran tight in his clutches till I deliver."

Becky could hear the stress in Liam's voice but she couldn't resist trying: "I'd don't suppose you'd like to share the details with me, would you?"

He stopped and gave her a level look: "There's little in this world I wouldn't be ready and willing to share with you, Miss Fox. But I haven't quite decided myself just what I should do."

She returned his look just as levelly and the two of them stood locked in a moment of wordless communion until the thread was snapped by the sound of drums and trumpets approaching on 26th from the direction of Broadway. In spite of themselves they both turned towards the music, a rousing Sousa march.

"Just look at them, will you?" Liam said. "That's the full brass band from the Marine Barracks at the Brooklyn Navy Yard, they only turn out for big occasions."

As they watched, the Marine bandsmen—resplendent in their dress blues and led by a color guard bearing the American flag and the Marine Corps flag—marched up 26th Street and executed a smart right turn down the center of the Park, where they finally halted in time with the end of the music. For a moment or two the silence was broken only by the murmurs of the crowed, then the band struck up "Hail to the Chief" and a bright light flashed from the top of a building onto a blank, canvas-draped wall at the south end of the Park.

A cry of "Magic lantern! Magic lantern!" went up from the crowd, only to fall silent abruptly as the mournful, sympathetic face of President Lincoln appeared on the canvas, accompanied by a message in ten-foot-tall black letters that scrolled slowly across the screen under the portrait:

"MY DEAR COUNTRYMEN! JUST TWELVE YEARS AGO THIS WEEK, THE LAST SHOT WAS FIRED IN THE TRAGIC CONFLICT THAT COST THE LIVES OF MORE THAN HALF A MILLION OF YOUR FELLOW CITIZENS. SO IT GRIEVES ME DEEPLY TO COME BEFORE YOU NOW AND SAY WE MUST BE PREPARED FOR THE POSSIBILITY OF A NEW WAR, AGAINST A CRUEL AND DETERMINED ENEMY. BUT DO NOT BE AFRAID, FOR THE BONDS OF OUR BROTHER-HOOD HAVE BEEN TEMPERED IN THE FURNACE OF OUR PAST TRAVAIL. ABOVE ALL, MY FRIENDS, WE MUST STAND UNITED AND FIGHT AS ONE NATION, SO THAT RIGHT AND JUSTICE MAY TRIUMPH ONCE FOR ALL!"

As the last word scrolled past and disappeared, the Marine Band struck up "The Star-Spangled Banner" and sky rockets went up from the 23rd Street end of the Park. Liam shook his head grimly:

"I doubt there's many of us from the last time around who'll be overjoyed at the sound of that." He held out his arm and pulled Becky's through it.

"I don't know about you, Miss Fox, but a glass of wine and some dinner sound mighty fine to me just now."

"Amen," she said. As they turned and walked pensively towards Delmonico's the Marines segued smoothly into "My Country, 'Tis of Thee," but they hadn't played more than a few bars before there was a crackle of gunfire from the rooftops on the Fourth Avenue side of the Square. Liam ducked involuntarily, pulling Becky with him, and as the crowd began shouting and screaming they turned back to look.

Flashes of gunfire could be seen on the rooftop from which the magic lantern was beaming, and a moment later a body was flung off the roof into the midst of the onlookers, who scattered as if it had been a bomb.

"What in Heaven's name . . ." Becky began, but her voice trailed off as the picture of Lincoln disappeared from the canvas-draped wall, leaving a glaring white rectangle that was replaced moments later by a crude but powerful drawing of Secretary Stanton with an axe buried in the top of his head and his features hideously distorted. Underneath the portrait in huge red letters were the words: "KILL THE BEAST STANTON AND ALL HIS MURDERING THUGS!"

There was a moment of stunned silence and then an inarticulate babble swept through the crowd, swelling slowly and peaking with a roar like a tidal wave as a dozen or so Police Acmes spotted around the perimeter of the Square let loose all at once with a terrifying screech of high-pressure steam whistles. Then, their whistles still screaming full blast, the Acmes started running crazily through the crowd towards the building from which the body had been flung, their great metal feet smashing and clanking on the pavement as they simultaneously unleashed a ripsaw din of mini-Gatling gunfire towards the building's roof.

"Let's get out of here!" Liam shouted, taking Becky by the arm and pulling her in the direction of Delmonico's.

"Absolutely not!" she shouted back, grinning excitedly and pulling hard in the opposite direction. For a brief moment they were locked in a tug of war, but Liam saw in a flash that the only way he would have a chance to keep her safe would be to stick by her side.

"Come on," she yelled, "help me get through the crowd!"

She was pulling him in the direction of the giant statue's arm and most of the panicked crowed seemed to be pushing in the opposite direction, stampeding west towards Fifth Avenue. Gamely, Liam moved up ahead of Becky and cleared a path for them, pushing and punching through the maddened herd until they were able finally to break out onto the grass in front of the platform supporting the titanic arm.

"I want to get up there where I can see what's happening," Becky yelled, "but it looks like we need to find a vantage point down near the torch. Give me a hand up, will you?"

Liam rolled his eyes, jumped up on the platform and then reached down to pull Becky up; a moment later she was standing beside him in the lee of the thing's enormous bicep, which seemed to be a good twelve feet thick. Becky was flushed and excited, grinning happily as she pulled a small leather-bound notebook and a pencil out of her reticule.

"You certainly do know how to show a girl reporter a good time," she laughed, leaning forward impulsively and giving Liam a kiss on the cheek; then she turned and ran down the platform towards the torch, leaving Liam momentarily flummoxed.

Becky had picked out a fairly sheltered observation post behind the statue's wrist, and as Liam caught up to her a chorus of "oohs" and screams went up from the crowd as a half-dozen sparking bundles arced from the rooftop towards the attacking Acmes.

"Dynamite!" shouted Liam, pulling Becky down as a series of bone-rattling blasts went off one after another, filling the air with fragments of pavement and metal that whistled and moaned through the air in tones that instantly threw Liam back to Gettysburg. For a long, stretched beat there was silence, and in the wake of the explosions the air around them seemed to reverberate like a giant gong. Then, crazily, a skirl of bagpipes sounded nearby, accompanied by shouts and the thump of a big marching drum.

Becky jumped to her feet, looking around in every direction. "Look," she cried, pointing westwards. "It's the railroaders!"

Marching towards the square along 26th Street came a phalanx of railroad men in working dress, from the striped overalls and red neckerchiefs of the engineers to the crisp blue uniforms and brass buttons of the conductors, the seemingly endless column led by a coal-blackened fireman playing "The Wearing of the Green" on the pipes and flanked by laborers holding aloft a giant banner that read "Support the General Strike!"

As the marchers started across Broadway towards the northern edge of the Park, a stentorian voice roared out from behind Becky and Liam:

"Bandsmen! Down instruments!"

The drum major, a gargantuan, barrel-chested Master Sergeant whose stiffly waxed moustache-tips jutted skywards like bayonets, watched the marching workers grimly as his men set their instruments down on the grass, his face growing redder by the moment as he smacked the palm of his left hand with the globe of his baton.

"Oh, oh," muttered Liam. He turned to Becky: "More trouble!"

As if in agreement, the Master Sergeant drew himself up to his full height, drew in a breath that expanded his chest enough to strain the gold buttons on his tunic and roared:

"All right, men, let's throw those bums in the East River!"

With an answering roar of approval, the Marines tore off across the grass towards the marchers and a moment later the neat column of railroaders dissolved into a swirling, bellowing battle royal.

Becky, who had been scribbling furiously in her notebook, looking up every few seconds to scan the square again and unconsciously push back the wisps of hair that had come loose in the heat of the moment, froze abruptly and cocked her head, listening.

"Do you hear that?" she asked, catching her lower lip with her teeth as she strained to hear something in the distance.

Liam laughed. "You mean the sound of cracking noggins?"

Becky shook her head impatiently: "Listen!"

A moment later he caught it: the clamor of fire bells and steam whistles approaching Madison Square at top speed. Liam shook his head uneasily and laid a warning hand on Becky's arm:

"This is beginning to feel a whole lot like the Draft Riots," Liam said, "do you think I could talk you into making up the rest of your story?"

Becky grinned. "Where's your sense of adventure, Mr. McCool? And anyway, how could I make up characters as piquant as *those*?"

She pointed southeast in the direction of Fourth Avenue and 25th, where a phalanx of duded-up young toughs was pouring into the Square and making their way towards the fighting. At the forefront, dressed in the obligatory heavy boots, black suits with flowered waistcoats and derby hats with eight-inch-high crowns, were a couple of big and surpassingly mean-looking thugs chewing cigars and swinging knobby shillelaghs.

"Unless I'm mistaken," Becky said with the relish of a birdwatcher spotting an elusive sort of nuthatch, "those are the two Dannys, messrs. Lyons and Driscoll fresh out of the Tombs."

Liam nodded glumly: "And all the darling little Whyos tagging along for the party."

At that, the sound of the fire bells suddenly grew much louder and a hook and ladder screeched into the Square from Broadway and 24th, followed by another and then another, all three of them swarming with firemen and what looked like hastily uniformed soldiers. The lead fire engine turned left and tore towards the fighting, steam whistles hooting and bells clanging, and as they came closer the soldiers raised their rifles over their heads and yelled like Banshees.

"Well, there's the last straw for you," said Liam, "unless I miss my bet those are the anointed champions of the Swell Set, New York's own 195th Light Infantry."

Becky shot him a look. "Run into them before, have you?"

"Oh, yes," Liam said with a mirthless grin. "My commander at Little Round top sent me to ask them to lend us some men and ammunition, but I couldn't find them till I slogged all the way back from our position to Meade's headquarters. Then their boss said I should find someone closer to our position."

"Ah," said Becky. "Well, it's not for nothing they call them the Kid Glove Regiment."

The arrival of the soldiers and the Whyos at almost the same moment seemed to drive the battle into a frenzy that quickly turned lethal—as the 195th's commanding officer ordered his men to fire, the Whyos started shooting back, and a few moments later a bundle of dynamite flew from the midst of the gangsters and arced through the air towards the soldiers, its fuse twinkling merrily in the evening gloom. The Light Infantry tried desperately to get out of the path of the explosives, stumbling and shoving and emitting unsoldierly shrieks. But not fast enough—with a stunning explosion the dynamite went off in their midst, blowing pieces of men and equipment in every direction.

Liam took Becky firmly by the arm. "That's torn it," he said, "you'll definitely have to make the rest of it up, your poor pa has troubles enough without you being blown up on the way to Delmonico's."

"Yes, Liam," said Becky mildly, and as Liam jumped to the ground on the safe side of the huge bronze arm, she slid down the curved surface to Liam's waiting arms. Without really meaning to he held her for an extra second or so, thinking involuntarily about her unaccustomedly meek tone and her calling him Liam, before she grinned again and tugged on his sleeve:

"Come along then, if we don't hurry they'll give someone else our reservation." She sprinted away so briskly that Liam had to pour on the speed to catch up with her. Fortunately the distance from their observation post to the block of buildings on 26th and Fifth that housed Delmonico's was less than a hundred yards, and Liam was relieved to see that Becky was heading towards an alleyway that seemed to run between the restaurant and a building that housed a *modiste* and a bookstore.

"In there!" Becky called out, pointing, and a moment later they were safely—if a little too fragrantly—sequestered in the narrow lane behind Delmonico's kitchens, standing between a row of heaped-high garbage bins and the roaring, steam-driven blades of the kitchen's exhaust fans. Both of them stood panting for a moment, listening in spite of themselves to the racket of gunfire, dynamite explosions and screams, then Becky signed to Liam to follow and headed down the alleyway towards 27th Street, where a narrow band of light shone between the buildings.

Before they reached it, Becky stopped before an anonymous-looking doorway illuminated by a single gaslight and knocked loudly: three raps, a pause, then three again. After a moment a spy-hole opened and emitted a gleam of light from inside, which dimmed as someone leaned forward to look out. Then the door opened cautiously to reveal a middle-aged waiter in Delmonico's livery, his bald, wrinkled brow furrowed even deeper by anxiety as he looked around to either side of Becky.

"It's all right, Joseph," she said in a gentle, reassuring tone. "We're both expected."

"Yes, Miss Fox," he said, still looking anxious. But he stepped aside and gestured for them to enter,

By now Liam's curiosity had been stoked to a fever pitch, but once again Becky was hurrying ahead, this time up a short flight of stairs. At the top, a row of closed doors stretched away down a corridor into a dimly gaslit distance, but Becky stopped at the first one and repeated her cryptic knock. This time it opened immediately to reveal a figure that made Liam want to rub his eyes and look again: a compact, medium-sized man in a rumpled white suit and floppy black bowtie, with a bushy head of graying curls and a drooping walrus moustache that quirked upwards into a welcoming grin. He held out his hand to Liam, who took it disbelievingly:

"Mr. Twain?" he gulped.

"Just call me Sam," the man said in a cheerful drawl, "and I'll call you Liam."

Chapter Seventeen

s Twain drew Liam into the interior of the sumptuously furnished chamber (one of Delmonico's private dining rooms, as it turned out), two more strangers got to their feet: the first an impressive, dignified black man with a mass of long, wiry white hair, his big aquiline nose and fierce brow belied by a radiant smile, and the other an elegant and aristocratic old lady whose high, smooth forehead and unlined face were set off by blue eyes that sparkled with humor and intelligence.

Liam didn't need any more introduction to them than he had to Mark Twain—or Sam Clemens, as he seemed to prefer—both had been pictured in New York's journals and newspapers more often than Liam could count. The man was Frederic Douglass—a former slave, now a world-famous reformer, writer and statesman—and the woman was the Honorable Augusta Ada Byron, Countess of Lovelace and daughter of Liam's beloved Lord Byron, not to mention her own eminence as a mathematical theorist and the inventor of the Lovelace "predictive engine." Douglass stepped forward and Liam offered his hand:

"It's an honor to meet you, sir."

Douglass shook Liam's hand warmly: "It's my pleasure, Mr. McCool, it's we who will be honored if you consent to join us in our undertaking."

A tiny alarm went off in Liam's brain, but it wasn't enough to keep him from bowing to the daughter of the great poet:

"And a very great pleasure and honor to meet you, Countess."

She burst into a peal of merry laughter and reached out to take Liam by the hand: "For goodness' sake, Mr. McCool, I've been an American for a good many years now, and plain Ada Lovelace will suit me nicely!"

Becky smiled as she noted a rare blush climbing Liam's cheeks. "I'm afraid you won't turn yourself into plain Ada quite that easily for Mr. McCool, Ada dear, he's a fervent devotée of your father's poetry."

Miss Lovelace chuckled and put her arm around Becky's shoulders: "Your father's a man of no mean fame himself, Becky, so you'll know just what I mean when I say that every woman must struggle to step out of the shadows of the men in her life, but it's even harder for those of us whose fathers cast particularly long shadows."

She shook Liam's hand warmly and he could feel the blush climbing the rest of the way into the roots of his hair as he returned her grip. Surely, he thought, it would take a downright monster of sang froid to shrug off falling in with such luminaries as these. Still, it wouldn't hurt to stay on his toes—whatever they were all here for it looked like they wanted him to take a goodly piece of it and he didn't want to end up buying a pig in a poke.

As Douglass and Ada Lovelace sat back down at the table, Twain pulled out two more chairs for Becky and Liam:

"All right, folks, everybody take a pew and let's call this meeting to order! Miss Fox, Liam, what can I give you to drink?"

Becky had been eyeing a big silver bucket on the sideboard filled with ice and bottles of wine and beer.

"I'm sure the solemnity of the moment calls for champagne but I'd just as soon have one of those Ballantine's," she grinned and nodded towards the beer.

"I'll drink to that," Liam said, "and then maybe someone will let me in on this 'undertaking' that Mr. Douglass mentioned."

Twain nodded thoughtfully as he poured drinks for Liam and Becky and opened another for himself. He took an appreciative sip and then leaned forward across the table and fixed Liam with his eye as he spoke:

"Well, young man, have you heard anything about the Freedom Party?

Wondering just what he'd gotten himself into, Liam shook his head.

"It probably sounds a deal grander than it is," Twain continued, "but we expect we'll be picking up more members every day as dear old Father Stanton cranks up the heat." He grinned slyly: "and we'll be needing all the help we can get if we're to keep him from plunging us all back into the days of the thumbscrew and the *bastinado*."

Liam smiled a little. "I haven't got anything good to say about Stanton and his people, as Miss Fox may have told you. But do you really think they mean to start an Inquisition?"

It was Douglass who answered, his rich orator's voice stirring even across a table: "Mr. McCool, what do you know about the present condition of our freed slaves?"

"Not much beyond what I read in the papers, sir. But even that little tells me that in the southern states the Reconstruction has turned their 'freedom' into a bad joke. As for those who've made their way north . . ." he made a wry face— "times are hard and jobs are scarce, and newcomers aren't too welcome whether they're from Alabama or Sicily."

Douglass nodded grimly. "A fair summary," he said. "So what do you suppose will happen if the moment we declare war on Little Russia we see the following . . ." He held up his hand and counted off the points on his fingers: "(1) martial law is also declared throughout the United States, (2) all the white workers excepting a few who will be kept on as job instructors are sent into the Army to fight Little Russia, and (3) all the northern blacks are impressed into the factories as a Labor Army while all their southern brethren are put back to work in the fields?"

Liam was stunned. "It doesn't bear thinking about," he muttered. He turned to Becky: "This is what you were talking about with me and Barlow back in Henderson's Patch, isn't it?"

She nodded unhappily. "And according to what we've learned it's only the first stage."

"There's more?" Liam shook his head incredulously.

Becky turned to Miss Lovelace: "Ada, would you mind telling Mr. McCool what you learned when you met with Col. Colt at his Hartford gun works?"

The great mathematician winced as if she'd been struck by a migraine. "Poor Samuel was almost beside himself. It seems Stanton has been working hand in glove with our big industrialists to put them literally on top of the world. When the projected measures have been completed our factories will have a labor force that makes American industry the envy of investors world-wide: a perpetual supply of workers who are tireless, cheap and completely docile. Stanton himself came to Hartford to tell Samuel of the new ordinances and to make it clear that henceforth every factory floor would have an overseer from the Department of Public Security as well as the one placed there by the factory's owner."

Liam could feel his patience starting to give way. "How in the name of all that's holy is Stanton going to pull off a stunt like that when every day he swears up and down to anybody that cares to read a newspaper that all these emergency measures and restrictions and regulations of his are only in force until it's plain that the danger's past?"

166

Twain snorted. "Well, young man, if Edwin McMasters Stanton is not the most blackhearted liar in all Creation he has missed it only by the skin of his teeth."

Liam stared at the others for a long moment, feeling an oppression as heavy as an anvil sitting on top of his head. Finally he turned to Douglass: "What's the 'second stage' to be then, sir?"

Douglass smiled without much mirth and gestured to Ada Lovelace: "That's a question that can best be answered by our scientific advisor . . ."

"In a sense, the second stage has already begun," she said in a professorial tone, "though the public may not actually see its operation for a couple of years yet." Catching Liam's baffled frown she smiled apologetically: "I'm sorry, Mr. McCool, I'm afraid my tutors gave me the bad habit of starting with a puzzle to catch my listeners' attention. The explanation is simple enough—the second stage will based on the application of technology which is still far from perfect, though the questions involved are being worked on day and night by Prof. Babbage and Henry Royce in England, by me and Samuel Colt here in America, and no doubt by many other mathematical/industrial teams throughout Europe and Asia."

"Automatons," Liam said with a groan. "The perfect workers." Then, as a thought hit him, he added: "Except for one thing, Miss Lovelace. They're *stupid*. Workers may demand wages, they may need food, they may even call strikes, but they have *brains*."

"Ah," she said with a bittersweet little smile, "that's the problem in a nutshell. I've been working for some years now on a mathematical model for how the brain gives rise to thoughts and the nerves to feelings, what you might call a sort of calculus of the nervous system. And I'm confident that I'm close to a solution that will improve my current predictive engine beyond all recognition with the use of storage batteries and a complex electrical network. But of course I wouldn't help Stanton if they held my feet over a fire." She turned to Becky:

"Becky, dear, would you please tell Mr. McCool what you've learned about Secretary Stanton's plans in the event that one of the many bright sparks laboring over the problem of intelligent automata offers him a solution? What will he do with it?"

Becky sighed and shook her head: "The black Labor Army will be sent West at once to work under the supervision of our white soldiers, taming the wilderness and carrying out construction work, while their places in the factories will be taken by specialized automatons."

"Wait a minute," Liam said. "Won't Little Russia have a thing or two to say about that?"

Becky smiled bleakly. "That's why Stanton is in a hurry to have his war right now. The Empire of Tsar Aleksandr II is completely preoccupied at home with massive uprisings of Central Asian tribes who want to bring back the glorious days of Tamerlane and revive the Mongol Empire. If Stanton waits till Aleksandr's army and aerial navy are free to support Little Russia he hasn't a prayer of success. But he can't just attack Little Russia without provocation, either. If he does, Great Britain and Germany have treaties with Russia that will have them sending their armies and aerial navies to attack us at once—and believe me, they'd be thrilled to have an excuse for it. So Stanton needs to send our Army and Aerial Navy in as soon as he has a decent pretext for it, and then follow up with the rest of stage one the minute he declares martial law here at home."

"And meanwhile," Ada Lovelace added in a tone tart enough to curdle milk, "Stanton will seize the Colt/Lovelace Automaton Works and open the door for your old acquaintance *Lukas.*"

"*What?!*"

Liam had been so taken aback that he had almost shouted the question, and Ada Lovelace chuckled in spite of herself.

"Becky and I had rather thought that would catch your attention. As it happens, "Lukas" was once known as Prince Nikolai Aleksandrovich Yurevskii, son of Tsar Aleksandr II by his morganatic marriage to Princess Yurevskaia, not to mention the most brilliant brain surgeon in the history of the Imperial University."

"Don't tell me," Liam said, shaking his head disgustedly, "Lukas has figured out how to put artificial brains into automatons."

"Oh, no," Miss Lovelace said, "he has figured out how to use *real* brains."

For what seemed like a long time Liam simply stared at Miss Lovelace. Finally he cleared his throat and said:

"Real brains."

She nodded tiredly. "From the little information I have been able to glean, it seems that Lukas has identified the areas of the brain that control various important bodily functions and figured out how to wire them directly to an electrical system similar to the one I have envisioned for my predictive engine. How he will be able to maintain a living brain inside an automaton, I have no idea. But I have learned of one other horrifying innovation: he has managed to wipe all traces of personality out of the subject brains, and all traces of individual volition, so that they will be perfectly trouble-free instruments for receiving and storing information and executing instructions. When you take this together with the rumors that identify him as the only man in the world apart from a team of research chemists at Cambridge who knows how to refine calorium from pitchblende, the mind fairly quails at the prospect."

"If only I had killed him the moment I met him," Liam muttered in frustration. "I hate to think where he and his playmates mean to get the brains they need." He turned to Becky: "What about Lincoln? Where is *he* in the midst of all this madness?"

She smiled and shrugged. "As you might imagine I have pushed and prodded every source I have in Washington in the hope of learning that. But all anyone will admit is that ever since John Wilkes Booth's *attentat* on the President's life, Mr. Lincoln has become increasingly reclusive. The last public address he gave was nearly a year ago, and he looked unwell then." She quirked her lips wryly—"There are even those who whisper that Stanton has the President tucked away somewhere, like the Man in the Iron Mask."

Liam's chin sank onto his chest and he stared unseeingly at the tabletop for several minutes. Finally he looked up and took a ragged breath:

"All right then, friends, somebody tell me where and how I come into all this."

It was Becky who answered, reaching out and laying her hand on Liam's arm as if she were trying to inspire him by some sort of Mesmerism.

"You said not long ago that if there were anything useful to my cause that's being kept under lock and key you would be ready to go and get it for me."

Liam nodded slowly, thinking that there was probably nothing under the sun he wouldn't try if she asked him to, but that he definitely didn't want her to know it. Not yet, anyway.

"And what might that be?" he asked in a cautious tone.

"It's an indian relic," she said. "In a locked case in the Smithsonian Museum."

He stared at her, his features immobile.

"In Washington, D.C.," she said. Unable to stop himself, Liam rolled his eyes.

"And it's not just my cause it's useful to," she added hastily, "though it will be, it's your cause too, and your grandmother's, and all the rest of us who aren't Stanton's myrmidons."

Liam nodded, thinking about Government guards and alarm systems and how far from New York Washington was.

"And one last thing," Becky added a bit desperately, clearly unsure of Liam's response: "We must leave tonight. You and I, together."

Liam broke into helpless laughter. "Are you sure that's all?"

Becky looked so worried that Liam relented at once and put his free hand on top of Becky's:

"I'll do my best," he said. "I can't promise more, since I've already promised to help Mike with something tonight, and you know he's a brother to me."

Becky bit her lip and nodded. "I'll be waiting at home, as long as I can. I must leave no later than midnight."

"Agreed, then," Liam said, "and I'd better get going." He stood up and turned to the others:

"I must admit," he said with a grin, "that was absolutely the most interesting bottle of beer I've ever drunk." He bowed to the company, squeezed Becky's hand and left before he could think twice about it.

Chapter Eighteen

iam stopped to wipe his face with a hand towel he'd brought in his jacket pocket, cursing the diabolical excellence of the two little locks. Gotham Savings had always been more than a little puffed-up about its "impregnable" security, and though Liam's presence in their strongroom had stuck a pin in that boast, it was true they hadn't stinted themselves on lockwork. The locks on this safe deposit box, for instance, one for the bank and one for the customer, had been made by Chubb in England and both confirmed Liam's feeling that the Limeys were spiteful, conniving, overbearing shite-pots and no friends to the Irish.

Gritting his teeth, he pulled his little carbide pocket lamp closer, changed his picks for a springier pair and went back to work. Any other time he might have made short work of the locks with a few drops of "soup" and a jimmy. But Mike had said that they didn't want the Gotham crowd to have the least suspicion that anybody'd been inside their precious strongroom, that way it would be at least a couple of months till the job was discovered since Mike's source had put the box's owner on vacation in London and Nice till September.

The sweat was starting to sting Liam's eyes, so he wiped his forehead again and then pulled out his watch. 10:04. If he could just get this moving a little faster, he'd have the job done, his exit made, and the swag handed over to Mike in plenty of time to cover the dozen or so blocks uptown to Becky's home on Gramercy Park South . . .

Hah! With a silvery little whisper the bank's lock gave up the ghost. Almost there. Inside were the personal skimmings of a junior partner in one of the firms that supplied Tiffany's—according to Mike's source, more than a million dollars' worth of AAA grade rubies and emeralds, plus a healthy selection of perfect diamonds. Once all the payoffs were taken care of that would give them enough of a war chest to fight Stanton and his plug-uglies forever, and the beauty of it was that the gems would fit nicely into his money belt, whereas printed money could be devalued or declared worthless any time the Government took a notion to play games with it, and it would take a small army to move a million dollars' worth of gold.

Hah, *hah!* There went lock number two! Liam had been thinking about the next step so intently that it took him less than a minute to have the box open, scoop out the little envelopes of jewels and get everything closed up again. Another minute to give his working area the eagle eye and make sure he'd left no signs, and another couple to stow the gems away in the dozen pockets of his traveler's money belt, re-button his shirt, slip on his jacket, pick up the grate to the air duct, turn out his lamp and pocket it, and then shin up the rope that dangled into the strongroom from the open maw of the ventilator.

Well enough pleased to have to stifle the urge to hum, Liam put his finger-tips through the hole in the grate and drew it back towards its frame, into which it suddenly *thunked*, pulled tight by the heavy-duty magnets fixed there by Adam Worth a couple of years ago. Little Adam had been keeping a safe-deposit box in the Gotham for a while now, and once it had occurred to him that a way of entering the strong-room at night might come in handy, it had taken the game's greatest con man no effort at all to send his bank "shadow" off on an errand for long enough to let him loosen the four screws in the corners of the grate, set the magnets in place, replace the screws with dummy screw-heads and glue, put it all back spick and span and return to examine the collection of stolen cameos he was about to deposit. Mike had agreed that they owed Little Adam a diamond of the first water for this one, it was like having the keys to a candy store.

It took Liam a bit more effort to crawl painstakingly through the bends of the duct till he reached the point where it came out in the Gas Company's tunnel, then a repeat of the grate routine and Liam was standing on the floor of the tunnel brushing himself off and pulling out his watch, thankful for the gaslights that studded the brick walls every hundred yards or so in both directions. 10:18. Still running to schedule, thank Heavens. Coiling up the rope and stuffing it into his pocket with the feeling of a job well done, Liam headed off in the direction of Mike's place.

O——⚷

He hadn't gone a dozen steps when he heard noises in the tunnel behind him: the sound of steel hammering on steel, then a cascade of falling bricks, then a yelp of pain and a volley of muttered curses. He froze in place, wondering uneasily who was making the noise, then he turned and started cautiously back in the direction he'd come from. It was almost impossible to guess what he might find ahead. There were by now several hundred miles of tunnel under Manhattan: some the Water Company's, more belonging to the Gas Company, and lately miles and miles of new tunnels belonging to the various underground railways.

A few years ago Liam had stolen the latest maps from the City Planning department, and since then he and the Butcher Boys had worked out the routes underground from their headquarters to most of the desirable addresses in town. But one of the things they had found when they first started exploring was the fact that they weren't the only New Yorkers who could pry up a manhole cover. Apart from legitimate workers there were plenty of other thieves with the same idea, not to mention a mob of outcasts of every kind, some of whom made you glad you were going armed. Suiting the action to the thought, Liam slowly drew his Colt .45 and held it at the ready, but before he could reach the source of the continuing noises, a sharp voice rang out from behind him:

"Hold it right where you are! And put the pistol down on the ground!"

Liam's heart sank into his boots. He recognized the voice, though he couldn't quite place it. After setting the pistol carefully on the sandy floor, he stood up again and turned towards the sound of the voice, but before he could even complete the turn, a brilliant light flared from an electric lantern and shone directly into his face, blinding him.

"Well, well," the voice continued from behind the light in mocking tones, "if it isn't Liam McCool, the King of the Cracksmen himself. I can see you've been casing the job, as you people say, and very commendable, too. Alas, Mr. McCool, we have actually come to *do* the job, so I'm afraid all your hard work will prove to have been in vain."

He had the voice now, Liam thought bitterly. None other than the arch-villain himself. Lukas.

"Good evening, Prince Yurevskii," Liam said in Russian, "since you were kind enough to use my title I must certainly use yours."

"Goodness," said Lukas mildly, "where did you learn to speak such excellent Russian?" Then, his voice suddenly hardening, he added: "Boylan! Search him and make sure he's disarmed. And Mr. McCool, raise your hands above your head as far as they will reach—please believe me, if I see them drop by so much as a centimeter I will be forced to shoot you, and that would be a pity."

At that, Boylan stepped out from behind the blaze of light, grinning nastily. "None of your monkeyshines, McCool, the Boss is a Jim-dandy shot and as far as he's concerned you're pretty much surplus to requirements."

Liam gave them both his flattest stare, thinking that he was only going to get one move and he had better be dead sure it was the right one before he made it. Boylan patted him down with professional speed and quickness, then swooped down and grabbed the Colt off the ground, holding it steadily on Liam as he backed away to re-join his boss. As Boylan drew level with him Lukas turned off the torch and dropped his pistol into the jacket pocket of his immaculately tailored country squire tweeds.

"It's certainly true I've no need of you," Lukas said in a pleasant enough tone, "but I'm not a brute and I wouldn't dream of harming you unless you become a nuisance. Now, then. I assume you're here because of Gotham Savings?"

Liam shrugged. "I've been trying to think of another good reason for being down here, but so far I'm stumped."

"Quite. Well, I doubt there will be much left in the vault after my men are through—I was fortunate enough to secure the builder's plans and I'm confident that my analysis of the structure has identified the vault's weakest point. A few sticks of dynamite and we should be able to empty all the reserves of currency and gold coinage before the police have time to yawn and rub their eyes."

They must have brought hand trucks with them, Liam thought, *though I still doubt their score will beat ours . . . still, I'd better pretend to be upset.* He smiled sourly:

"Not bad for amateurs, though my pals in the Butcher Boys won't be at all happy about it."

Lukas raised his eyebrows humorously: "Dear me! I must make sure to be troubled by that thought when I've the time, but just now we have an uprising to finance and I'm in rather a hurry. My associates and I are creating a new world, Mr. McCool, and that doesn't allow much time for idle pursuits."

"'The passion for destruction is a creative passion,' isn't that what Bakunin says?"

Lukas gave Liam a coolly appraising look and then smiled a little. "A well-read cracksman, upon my word. I'm no anarchist, Mr. McCool, but Misha Bakunin made a valid point there. When the old order has petrified and its dead weight is stifling the life out of society, it must be swept away. But don't misunderstand me. The destruction is just incidental, everything I do is for the betterment and the happiness of mankind, a fact—if I may say so—which was my main appeal to our mutual sweetheart Maggie, who had a solid background in the Lady Printers' Union and whom I would no more have harmed than I would my own sister, believe it or not as you please."

He reached into an inside pocket, pulled out an ornate gold watch and flipped open the lid. "The evening moves on apace," he said, "so if you will forgive me, I must tear myself away from this fascinating conversation and hurry to my next appointment." He turned to Boylan: "I don't want him killed, but I don't want him leaving here to summon his friends either, not for a while in any event. Immobilize him however you like and then go help the others."

Without another word, Lukas spun on his heel and took off down the tunnel. Boylan grinned wolfishly and thumbed back the hammer on the Colt: "I'm not to kill you but I'm to slow you down. Sure and leaves many a lovely choice for yours truly, wouldn't you say so, Mr. McCool?"

Becky frowned at the dignified old Seth Thomas ticking away sedately on the mantel and ground her teeth as she paced from one end of the sitting room to the other. 10:52! She had been sure that Liam would be here by now so that she'd have time to explain the details of their mission in Washington and answer any questions he might have about it. Certainly once they were airborne the thrumming vibrations of the silenced Flyer would overwhelm any communication short of putting her mouth against Liam's ear and yelling into it.

She paused for a moment, stopped in her tracks by the train of thoughts that followed that picture of putting her mouth to Liam's ear. She stayed with it for another moment or two, reluctant to tear herself away, then shook her head irritably to dissipate her daydreams.

"*Rebecca Susannah Fox,*" she upbraided herself, "*you are a silly goose and a ridiculous poseuse! Fancy you pretending to be Becky Fox, the intrepid lady reporter from* Harper's! *Would Becky Fox be swept off her feet by some charming scapegrace with clever green eyes and . . .*"

"*Ahem!*" came the familiar exclamation from behind her.

Becky turned a bit guiltily, glad that her father wasn't given to mind-reading. She hurried to his side and gave him a hug. She couldn't help noticing his gaunt cheeks and his unhealthy pallor—whether it was from his involuntary confinement in the house or the anxiety that gnawed at him every day, she couldn't bear witnessing the loss of his ruddy complexion and his usual beaming good cheer.

"How are you, Papa?" she asked, trying to keep the worry out of her voice.

Judge Fox smiled wryly. "Not half so well as I shall be when Stanton's carried away in manacles to Andersonville but quite cheerful nonetheless, Becky dear. I am a bit concerned though, about your friend Mr. McCool. If he arrives too late a great many interlocking bits of our machinery will be unable to function properly."

"I know it, Papa," she said with a frown. "I'm as sure as can be that he is doing everything in his power to get here in time, but you know what can happen with this much unrest in the streets."

Becky was watching her father's face closely, reading between the lines for any sign of unwellness, and she could tell that something was still troubling him.

"What is it, Papa? I can tell that something's still troubling you."

Judge Fox waved his hand exasperatedly. "I'm not even sure if it's worth mentioning, but President Lincoln hasn't been far from my thoughts since this evening's announcement of the impending war. You know how closely I've worked with the man over the years, ever since that first long-ago campaign. I feel it in my bones—there's something deeply wrong about the present situation and I know I'm not the only one having nightmares about the Man in the Iron Mask. If there's any way that you can find it in your power to learn what's become of him while you're in Washington, for pity's sake don't hesitate—I feel certain that the pro-war party want to see the nation mobilizing within days, and the only thing that might turn back their greedy passions would be for Abraham Lincoln himself to stand before the people and speak against this great evil."

Becky hugged her father close, trying not to let him see the tears in her eyes. "I promise, Papa, if the answer can be found I shall find it and bring it back to you."

Before he could answer a powerful, muted throbbing became audible above them, increasing rapidly in intensity as it descended towards the Fox residence and then cutting off abruptly.

"Capt. Ubaldo has arrived," Becky said tensely, "I hope all the uproar in the streets has kept our neighbors from taking any special note of it. Come, Papa, let's go let him in."

They hurried down the hall to the back of the house, arriving at the door of the darkened kitchen almost simultaneously with a sharp rapping at the window.

"Welcome, Captain," Becky said breathlessly as she opened the door and a heavily scarved and fur-clad figure hastened in, bowing to each of them in turn before he unwrapped some of the scarves from his head to reveal a cheerful young officer with a tidy little waxed moustache and brown hair parted fastidiously in the middle.

"It's good to see you, Miss Fox, Judge." He pulled off his gloves and rubbed his hands together energetically. "I don't suppose you've a drop of spirits around somewhere, do you? I'm half frozen to death, and we've got to be getting aloft again quickly."

"Of course, dear boy, of course," said Judge Fox, bustling away to get a decanter and a glass as Becky turned towards Ubaldo anxiously. She lowered her voice as she spoke to him:

"Is there some special hurry now? I thought we were well inside our schedule."

Ubaldo grimaced. "It seems the Department of Public Safety has increased its aerial patrols since we spoke last—if we don't leave here quickly we're liable to be caught by one of their Black Deltas, and you know what that might mean . . ."

Becky nodded, echoing his grimace as she looked towards the kitchen clock. *11:03 . . . For Heaven's sake, Liam, hurry!*

Liam gave Boylan a stare as flat and cold as a lake of ice, watching his grinning opponent for the slightest twitch, the most fractional movement of the eyes. He had to be in motion a split second before Boylan could send the nerve impulse to his trigger finger, and it was worrying that his arms and hands felt dead and heavy from holding them over his head for so long.

"Where shall I begin, Liam me darlin'," smirked Boylan, savoring the moment, "with a slug in yer bollocks? Or maybe one in the elbow, I reckon that should tear the arm clean off your body . . ."

Before Boylan could say more, Lukas' dynamite charge exploded like a thunderclap, knocking bricks out of the wall around them and blasting a tidal wave of hot air and sand down the tunnel. It was the split second Liam had been praying for, and as Boylan started back involuntarily, Liam was already crouching and spinning on one foot, the other leg cocked for a bonebreaking kick that landed on Boylan's knee an instant later. The big man screamed and fired in the same moment, the slug just creasing Liam's shoulder and knocking him to the ground.

"*Me knee,*" Boylan bellowed in agony, "*ye've smashed me fookin' knee!*"

Liam scrambled to his feet, snatching his Colt up off the floor as he went. "You can thank the birdbrains you're using for cracksmen," he said, "they used enough dynamite to bring down St. Pat's."

Liam turned and sprinted away in the direction of the Bleecker Street manhole, leaving Boylan howling and cursing behind him.

○—☐

As Liam edged the manhole cover up cautiously, crossing his fingers that no curfew Acmes or coppers on foot patrol were anywhere beyond his line of vision, he heard Mike's voice:

"*It's clear,*" he hissed urgently, "*hurry up out of there, will you?*"

Liam pushed the manhole cover hard and winced as his shoulder protested. Mike was squatting on his heels next to the manhole, and as Liam held up a hand he grabbed hold of it and pulled him the rest of the way out.

"Took you long enough," Mike grinned, "and you didn't have to blow up Broadway, one of our neighbors told me the corner of Gotham Savings collapsed into a big hole in the street."

Liam laughed in spite of himself. "What the hell," he said, "I figured a few drops of soup couldn't hurt." He patted his tummy: "I've got the goods right here but I can't take time to go back to your place to hand them over, I'm running too late."

"Don't worry about it," Mike said, "I figured you'd need all the speed you could get to make it uptown on time, so I borrowed some transportation. Come on."

He trotted down Bleecker Street a short way with Liam right on his heels, and then he disappeared into an alley between his townhouse and a piano factory. Halfway down the alley, a stripped down Stanley racing machine sat chugging quietly in neutral, its lights turned off. Mike jumped in behind the steering bar and Liam jumped in beside him.

"All right, cabby," Liam grinned, "there's a million-dollar tip in it if you can get this thing to Gramercy Park in ten minutes!"

Liam was grinding his teeth hard enough for Mike to punch him on the shoulder. "Take it easy on the grinding," Mike yelled, "we'll have to buy you new choppers!"

"Just *look* at that," Liam yelled bitterly, waving his hand towards the stretch of Fifth Avenue in front of them. A mob of strikers had spilled out of the upper end of Union Square along 17th Street and was battling police and militia as far uptown as the eye could see. Shots, screams, police whistles and the bloodcurdling shrieks of the Police Acmes' steam whistles made conversation impossible, so Mike just pointed right along 14th Street and held up four fingers. Liam nodded grimly. If they could get onto Fourth Avenue it would only be a few more blocks to the corner of Gramercy Park.

Mike jerked the steering bar around hard and the little Stanley spun around so sharply that it almost turned over. Liam gripped the side of the car hard and cursed the pain in his shoulder, but a moment later they were tearing down 14th and repeating the terrifying turn, this time onto Fourth. Good! Only a few stragglers running across the Avenue ahead of them and Mike pushing the Stanley so hard Liam could hear its gears whining like a band saw. 16th . . . , 17th . . . , 18th . . . . Suddenly there was a terrifying shriek from inside the machine somewhere, followed by the sounds of self-destructing machinery.

"OUT!" yelled Mike, suiting the action to the word, and sprinting up Fourth with Liam right behind him. They had just reached the corner of 19th when there was an appalling blast behind them and bits and pieces of the valiant racing machine flew threw the air. Liam grabbed Mike by the arm.

"We're almost there," he said breathlessly, "you have to take the stuff now!"

He tore open his shirt, undid the money belt and thrust it on Mike. "Get out of here," Liam said, "get that home safely, I need you to get the boys out of chokey and find Gran while I'm gone!"

Mike nodded wordlessly, embraced Liam Russian-style with a kiss on each cheek, and then tore back down the street the way they'd come, hurriedly stuffing the money belt under his own shirt as he ran. Liam pulled out his watch. 11:36!

"Be there, Becky," he said out loud, "wait for me!" He took off again, turning right on 20th and finding himself at the lower end of Gramercy Park. As he sprinted right down 20th, planning to head towards Third Avenue before turning left for the last block between there and Becky's house, his blood froze at the shriek of a steam whistle from behind him, followed by the heavy clank of running steel feet. Damn it! A curfew Acme! Dodging left, he vaulted the fence into the Park itself, running diagonally towards 21st and waiting for the second shriek. There it was, followed by the clank of feet as the Acme ran alongside the fence, unable or unwilling to jump the fence itself. Two shrieks is all you get, Liam reflected furiously, then the thing starts shooting. He hit the ground behind a boulder with some kind of plaque on it just as a stream of mini-Gatling fire roared thinly behind him and chopped through the trees and bushes overhead.

Only one thing for it, and it was a hell of a gamble. He waited for the pause as the Acme switched to a second belt, then got up to his knees behind the boulder, thumbed back the hammer on his Colt and aimed with life-or-death care at one of the thing's glowing red eyes. *Blam!* Yes! The automaton rocked back on its heels and then started to raise its Gatling arm again with grinding mechanical jerkiness. This time Liam aimed with twice the care, uncertain how many shots were left in the pistol. *Blam!* Yes, *yes!* He'd hit the thing in its other eye and now it started clanking around in circles, its steam whistle shrieking hysterically as it fired its remaining rounds into the air.

Liam took off like a race horse, vaulted the remaining fence between himself and Becky's house and then tore up the stairs two at a time till he was on the landing, grabbing the brass knocker and hammering crazily with it until suddenly the door burst open and Becky appeared.

"Thank God, you're here!" Liam gasped, collapsing through the doorway onto the hall carpet as Becky knelt over him, pulling at his bloody jacket sleeve feverishly.

"You've been shot!" she cried.

"Never mind that," Liam said, staggering to his feet, "am I in *time?*"

She glared at him, speechless with tension and exasperation, then abruptly took his face between her hands and kissed him firmly on the lips. After a moment she let go, her exasperation replaced by a cryptic smile.

"Come on," she said, "the Flyer's about to leave!" And, grabbing Liam's hand, she dragged the befuddled man along behind her towards the back of the house.

Washington, D.C.
June 28–June 29, 1877

Chapter Nineteen

iam was walking on tiptoe and breathing through his mouth to keep out the stink of old bones, or whatever it was. A dismantled brontosaurus? Something at least that big, the smell was too revolting for anything less. The last time he'd been in this place was back in '65, fresh out of the Union Army and killing time till the next troop train for New York and a blessed deliverance from the South, from hick towns of all descriptions, and especially from hominy grits—which could surely have defeated the Yanks without any outside help given another year or so of company cooks serving the things when rations were short.

He'd spent the night before celebrating his discharge drinking white lightning in every pot-house in Blacktown, then the whole morning in Willard's Hotel drinking coffee and eyeballing the respectable women, and then a couple of hours walking around the Mall trying to keep from gagging on the summer cocktail of Potomac River humidity and ripe stinks from the City Canal, until finally he escaped indoors at a red sandstone building with turrets and battlements that looked like it had escaped from his dog-eared old copy of Grimm's Fairy Tales.

The Smithsonian Institution, or the Castle as people called it. There had been a fire there not so long before and it still smelled of old smoke. But it was interesting enough, and Liam had decided that they could blow up the rest of the city, starting with all the politicians, but that they'd probably better keep the Smithsonian. And now, a dozen years later, here he was again—only not upstairs, in the daytime, but downstairs in the basement, at night and definitely not as a tourist.

He stopped abruptly, frozen by the sound of a distant door closing. Five would get you ten that was the Museum's one night watchman, roused briefly from his slumbers to have a pee . . . yup, there it was, the faint whispery rustle of the Castle's luxurious indoor plumbing, and a moment later . . . another click as another door closed. Probably the old codger had made himself comfortable in some pharaoh's sarcophagus and Liam could forget about him for the rest of the job. The guarding was of a piece with the locks and the rest of the security apparatus, which Liam was certain could be jimmied by any self-respecting ten-year-old with a bent pin.

Some contrast to the security out in the streets! Liam and Becky had had their hearts in their throats all the way from the Duchamp estate in Alexandria to the stretch of B Street, NW (the former City Canal) that ran behind the Smithsonian. Becky had been dressed (with some help from the Duchamp girls, one of whom had lost a husband in the Confederate cavalry) in fashionable widow's weeds and a heavy black veil that hid her famous face. Liam had had to make do with a slightly operatic bandage (decorated with chicken blood by the younger Miss Duchamp) that hid most of the lower part of his face and went nicely with the smoked spectacles he'd picked up in Pottsville. But even with the disguises their uneasiness had mounted steadily from the moment they hit the outskirts of Washington City.

"I haven't seen anything like it since the War," Becky had said as she peered through the curtains of their elegant steam carriage. "They must have a couple of regiments walking foot patrols, and everywhere they don't have soldiers they have Acmes or Stanton's Eyes."

"They must have heard we were coming," Liam said with a grin.

"I wish that were funny," Becky answered, "but I expect our faces are on various watch lists by now. Willie Pilkington has had my father and me under surveillance for days, and he warned me quite sternly about consorting with a villain like you. If you'll remember, your arrival at our front door was a bit on the noisy side."

She smiled at the memory and then put her veil down. "We're almost there, have you got everything you need?" Liam nodded and pulled the brim of his Homburg lower. "All right then," she said, "the driver will slow as soon as I rap on his window, and he'll pull over behind the Castle as close as he can to the cellar freight entrance. One of our people has left the padlock unlocked but apparently closed, so you should be able to be out of the car and inside the basement before you can say boo! Remember, you have to be ready and waiting by 3 a.m., the steam pantechnicon will only stop for a moment before it goes on to the next stop on the Underground Railroad."

Liam had taken her hand and held it tight until the carriage glided to a stop. "See you at three," he said, and moments later he was making his way cautiously through the graveyard gloom of the Smithsonian's basement . . .

Which must have been designed by some mad troglodyte, with more twists and turns and blind corridors than the tunnel system he'd been in a few hours ago. Thank God he'd had a set of plans to study at Duchamp's, because without them he'd probably have ended up as one more Smithsonian skeleton: *"Late nineteenth-century cracksman, New York metropolitan area."* As it was it made him promise himself twice over that he would never, but *never* take on another job where he hadn't had time for his usual preliminary reconnaissance. Now . . . the storage area was supposed to be at the end of this hallway, across from the boiler rooms.

And there it was! Liam did a double take and groaned under his breath: and there *also* were two absolutely massive Chubb locks, recently installed, as the brilliant, shop-fresh brass of the fixtures attested. Just wonderful. Every other door in this endless pile of stone equipped with a lock he could have opened by shaking his finger at it, but this one with enough lockwork to guard the Mint. With a sigh, he reached inside his jacket and got out his picks.

The one good thing about the Chubbs was that he'd just had a refresher lesson with the ones at Gotham Savings, so this time he could work pretty much by feel, leaving his mind free to roam. Of course, the only *bad* thing about that was that every time he let it off its tether his mind seemed to roam right back to Becky Fox.

It wasn't the thought of Maggie that bothered him; he had nothing but happy memories of his time with Maggie and he knew that Becky respected that and respected Maggie herself. And he wasn't worried about bringing Maggie's killer to account either. Even if it wasn't Lukas—and he'd felt something oddly genuine about what the man had said back in the tunnel—he had a feeling deep down in his guts that the thing would be sorted before this whole mess with Stanton and Pilkington was finished. No, if there was anything bad about throwing in with Becky Fox it was that the usual tidy clarity of his thinking had gotten more than a little discombobulated.

For instance: what he should be thinking about right now was what on earth these two Chubbs were doing on this one door out of all the others. As far as he knew, there was nothing in here except a lot of old junk from various Indian tribes, both the ones that Andrew Jackson had tossed out of the eastern states and exiled across the Mississippi in the Indian Removal Act of 1830, and the ones that had already been living over there before the Russians set up housekeeping and tried to turn them into slaves. As Becky had said with a touch of angry scorn, now that all our Indians were gone we found ourselves getting sentimental about them and sending American anthropologists into Little Russia to buy souvenirs of the dear old Noble Savages. Just why Liam was recovering this one particular souvenir was something Becky promised to explain once they had the thing in hand, but meanwhile he was left to scratch his head over the great big locks on the penny-ante door.

Or maybe to just let his mind skip sideways onto that kiss back on Becky's front stoop . . . Liam stayed there for a good long chunk of time after that, enjoying where he was and thinking about not much else, until he absent-mindedly started patting the door and fumbling around after a third lock, having opened the first two and willing to stay there happily opening locks until he'd squeezed the last drop of juice from Becky's kiss. *Dimwit!* He shook himself like a wet dog, dragged his mind back to business and opened the door.

On the other side of the door was a cavernous storage hall, barely lit by two or three gas jets high up on the wall and filled as far as the eye could see with row upon row of glass-fronted cabinets stuffed with dusty-looking gimcracks. Fortunately, these science birds were nice and orderly, every row had a number, and Liam had the number and the rest of the information to identify what he wanted, so he set out confidently, found his row right away, and—flicking on his pocket electric torch—moved quickly and unerringly to the exhibit he wanted.

Liam smiled, relieved at having it all go so smoothly, and shone his light on #40312, a buckskin pouch like a small saddle bag, with long fringes of buckskin around the edges and a handsome painted and beaded pattern of zig-zag stripes. The bag was bulging with mysterious lumpy objects and the printed label said: *"Medicine Bundle of Crazy Horse, Oglala*

193

Sioux chieftan, lost at the Battle of Bol'shoi Rog *(U.S.: Little Bighorn). June 17, 1876."*

Interesting. Liam had read a lot about Crazy Horse, a thinker and a warrior who seemed to be more than the equal of most of the white men he'd been up against. Taken from his village as a youngster by the head of the Tsar's *Okhrana*, a Machiavellian Grand Duke who planned to turn him against his own people, Crazy Horse had been sent to the Imperial University in St. Petersburg, where he excelled in languages and modern history. Graduating with the highest honors, Crazy Horse published a book of Byronic poetry in Russian, impregnated the Grand Duke's wife, fought a duel with the Grand Duke himself (contemptuously firing into the dirt when the Grand Duke missed his shot), and then vanished abruptly, only to turn up again in Little Russia, leading the Sioux against the Russians.

And the Americans, thought Liam as he worked on the cabinet's lock. It had raised an almighty stink the year before when Crazy Horse not only beat the cream of the Imperial Russian cavalry at the Battle of the Little Bighorn, but also a handpicked detachment of U.S. Cavalry who had been riding with the Russians under the auspices of the U.S. Military Attaché in New Petersburg. Most of them had been killed, but Crazy Horse himself had taken General Custer prisoner, and Custer's current whereabouts remained a mystery despite repeated search expeditions . . .

There! The door of the cabinet swung open and Liam lifted out the bag, turning it over in his hands and examining it curiously. So Crazy Horse lost his bag, so what? Why were Becky and her colleagues in the Freedom Party willing to go to this much trouble to return it to him?

"Young man!"

The voice—loud, deep, weirdly resonant yet somehow familiar—almost made Liam jump out of his skin. He spun around on one foot, dropping into a fighting crouch, and then slowly stood upright again, more deeply mystified than ever by the sight in front of him. From somewhere behind him in the shadows, a . . . *creature* in a wheelchair had rolled forward into the light. It looked like an Acme of some kind, but heavily modified, the covering plates on its legs and part of its chest removed to expose its works, and the usual unconvincing porcelain doll face skipped altogether in favor of a steel egg with holes for its glowing eyes and an unusual mouth and chin which seemed to be hinged and capable of movement. And speech. The weird, not-quite-natural voice continued its bass-viol thrum:

"I do hope you're not planning to steal that, son, I expect Chief Crazy Horse would reckon it insult upon injury to be robbed twice of the same treasure."

A little uncertainly, Liam cleared his throat. "I can assure you that's not my intention! In fact, I've been sent here on a mission to recover it for its owner, so you may lay your anxieties to rest, Mr. . . . ."

The automaton fixed its glowing eyes on him and then inclined its head slightly, so that Liam could almost have sworn it was overwhelmed with sadness.

"You might as well call me Mr. Nobody," the automaton said in a low rumble that seemed to throb with misery, "—indeed, my so-called friends have done their level best for some years now to make that come true."

Something had started bubbling in the back of Liam's mind as the automaton spoke and with the last few words it suddenly boiled over:

"Gettysburg!" Liam cried. "I heard you speak at Gettysburg! November, 1863, I had leave because my Gran was sick and I stopped there on the way home to see the new cemetery."

The automaton lifted its hands to its face with a clank of metal against metal and groaned hollowly, an eerie sound like an organ's pedal tone.

Liam spoke earnestly: "I'll never forget it, sir. Mr. Everett droned on and on till I thought he'd turned me to stone, like the Medusa. Then you got up and spoke for just a few minutes, and for the first time since I ran down the hill with the 20th Maine and stuck my bayonet in some poor hayseed's eye it seemed like there might have been some good in all that evil. Thank you, sir, I've always wanted to thank you for your speech!"

Liam stepped forward, the tears filling his eyes in spite of himself, and gently pulled the automaton's hands away from its face.

"What have they done to you, Mr. Lincoln? How could this *happen*?"

The automaton drew a shuddering breath and shook its head. "The day you saw me at Gettysburg, my boy, I was actually ill with the small pox. I recovered after a while, but the disease left me weak, and when Booth tried to kill me at Ford's Theatre the shock very nearly did me in."

The automaton cocked its head as if it were remembering, and its red eyes glowed in the dim light of the gas jets.

"I was barely sitting up in bed again when Stanton started haranguing me about declaring a national state of emergency. He swore up and down that the Confederate armies would be marching down Pennsylvania Avenue before the month was out if we didn't move to suppress all the plotters. I swore right back and argued till I was blue in the face to make him see how important it was to keep our hands clean and observe the law, but Stanton is as stubborn as an ox and I finally ended up in the grip of a brain fever that didn't leave me for weeks."

The Lincoln automaton shook its head despairingly, unnerving Liam with the rhythmic squeaking of its neck joint.

"When I woke up this time," Lincoln continued, "Stanton had gone ahead on his own and declared the state of emergency and he and his cronies had everything sewed up pretty much the way they liked it. I don't know if it was the aftereffects of the brain fever or just my natural melancholy, but as Stanton and his cohort waxed stronger I seemed to get weaker and weaker. Then one day a White House servant I trusted whispered a terrible bit of news into my ear: *I had been seen taking the air on the Mall,* in an open carriage . . . all while I was lying flat on my back in my bedroom, swilling iron tonic and praying for the strength to get up and fight."

Liam was baffled: "Sir? I do remember when the papers all said you'd been seen out and about again, and I remember how relieved everybody was . . ."

"That was the idea, the cheering effect on the public," Lincoln said in his gloomy basso. "But when I tell you how they did it I expect you'll think it just as crazy as I did. After Booth's attempt, Stanton had put it about that Booth had been found and killed by one of the soldiers who had pursued him. The truth was, he'd been captured, and Stanton had sealed him up in an oubliette in the old Navy building, where Stanton's new Department of Public Safety grilled him night and day for clues to the other plotters. But Booth was a little loony to begin with, and soon he went over the edge . . ."

The Lincoln automaton laughed sardonically, a sound so macabre from its artificial voice box that it sent chills up Liam's spine.

"It seems Booth had become convinced he was me, and—great actor that he was—his impersonation became (or so I've been told) letter-perfect. And if Mr. Edward Stanton knows anything at all, it's how to seize the main chance."

Liam's jaw dropped. "No! You can't mean . . ."

"But I do, son. The Lincoln you and the rest of the public have seen since late in 1867 has been none other than my failed assassin John Wilkes Booth. He is apparently so deluded and by now has read so deeply among my books and papers that he could play the part of Abraham Lincoln to any audience in the world and never be suspected as an impostor. Meanwhile he is guarded day and night and made much of by Stanton and his security officers, and kept from the public sedulously except when he must be trotted out for the occasional bit of official color. "

Liam shook his head helplessly. "But how . . ." he gestured towards the automaton and his wheelchair, at a loss for words.

"It was a foreign brain doctor," the automaton said, "Stanton promised that the man was a wonder-worker, that he knew a way to restore my old health and make me capable of prodigies of new strength."

A terrible suspicion was forming in Liam's mind. "A foreign doctor, you say? Would he have been from . . ."

"He was a Russian," the Lincoln automaton said, "a Professor Lukas . . ."

Liam was too stunned for speech, but before he could pull his thoughts together enough to reply, the Lincoln automaton abruptly wheeled his chair forward and grasped Liam by the wrist.

"What's your name, young man?" the automaton asked.

"Liam, sir, Liam McCool." The feel of those steel fingers gripping his wrist made him shiver involuntarily, but the automaton just pressed on, his tone heart-rendingly earnest:

"This has been my life ever since, Liam, what you see here. I am no longer human, my voice is not even my own but some strange confection of electric currents and vibrating rubber strings. My legs have been disabled, I assume to keep me from escaping. I am nothing at all but but a few bits of tin and the miserably tired old brain of Abraham Lincoln kept alive in some sort of China tea-pot and sustained by a handful of calorium."

The automaton's head fell forward again into its hands, and the rubber vocal chords produced a horrible sobbing sound. After a moment, it looked up again and fixed its glowing eyes on Liam:

"My memory of men tells me infallibly that you have a good heart, Liam McCool. For the love of God, please open the

198

panel in my back and disconnect the wires and steam valves that are keeping me alive so I may die the death I have surely earned by now!"

Liam jerked his hands back and shook his head violently, stricken to the heart by Lincoln's awful pain.

"My God, sir, *no!* You can't! You can't let it all go now, we *need* you!"

"*We?* Are you mad, McCool? What "we" is that?"

"Some . . . some people I know, sir!"

The automaton snorted, clearly running out of patience. "Some *people* you know? What sort of humbug . . ."

Liam bent forward and took hold of one of the cold steel hands again, his self assurance flooding back as his mind jumped from one connection to the next.

"You said your instincts told you I had a good heart, Mr. Lincoln. *Trust* your instincts then and promise me you'll wait for another twenty-four hours just as you've been waiting for years. I promise you, sir, you'll be glad that you did."

The automaton stared at him for a long moment, then sighed heavily as Liam pulled out his watch. 2:40! He had to get moving.

"Please stay here, Mr. Lincoln, don't do anything to harm yourself, and wait for my return tomorrow at the same time. Will you do that, sir?"

"Very well, Liam," the Lincoln automaton said, "though I'm not sure that twenty-four hours of hope won't be even more painful than a decade of hopelessness."

"Thank you, sir," Liam said, shaking the steel hand emphatically. "And believe me, you *will* see me tomorrow."

Almost running, he headed for the door as the automaton stared after him, its eyes glowing cryptically in the semi-darkness.

Chapter Twenty

dwin M. Stanton stood at the windows of his spacious suite in the Senate wing of the Capitol Building, staring westwards along the sunlit expanse of the National Mall towards the partly completed Washington Monument, hands clasped behind him under the tails of his black frock coat, chest puffed up aggressively, shoulders drawn back to pull in the comfortable little paunch under the black silk waistcoat with its heavy gold watch chain, head cocked with just a touch of haughtiness and his long, wispy beard jutting out from his pudgy chin like the prow of a warship, thinking: *By Gad, Stanton, the New America begins right here!*

What better symbol for a renascent Union than the network of scaffolding surrounding the Washington Monument and the resumption of the work halted nearly a quarter of a century earlier by the idiotic Know-Nothing party, supposedly because of a block of granite donated by Pope Pius IX?

Stanton snorted contemptuously and shook his head; once he had put all the genuinely important affairs of Government in order, he would see to it that anyone making a public display of his religious sentiments would be horsewhipped with equally public display. Well-bred people *never* discussed religion in front of strangers, and this small contribution to public order would be greeted by all except the Great Unwashed.

It would take a while for the remaining 300 feet of the Monument to be completed, but when it was done it would be the tallest structure in the world, and so a fitting expression of the spirit of the United States of America—the greatest nation in the world! No thanks to that loathsome vulgarian and bully Andrew Jackson, who had done his level best to elevate all the low riff-raff of the nation to the seats of power, not to mention his disastrous sale to Russia of everything west of the Mississipi simply in order to balance the 1835 budget.

Well, all that would be changed soon enough. For too long now the American people had been sidetracked from following the beacon of their Manifest Destiny, of the unique American mission to promote and defend democracy throughout the world. And not the *soi-disant* "democracy" which elevated ignorance and coarseness as values representative of the "real" America, but the true, original Democracy of the Founding Fathers—a leadership of the people by a high-minded, self-sacrificing élite, devoted not to crass self-enrichment but to the high goals which would finally make Washington the New Jerusalem.

A knock came at his outer door, bringing a frown as his vision of the Millennium shimmered away.

"Yes, Elsie," he snapped, "what in Tophet is so all-fired important?"

The door opened slightly and a mousy young woman with gold-rimmed pince-nez and her hair in a bun peeped in and cleared her throat timidly:

"So sorry to disturb you, Secretary Stanton, but you did ask me to let you know as soon as Director Pilkington arrived."

Stanton sighed as reality flooded back. "Yes, yes, quite right. Send him in, please."

The door opened wider and the dandyish Director of the Department of Public Safety entered, resplendent in a gray cashmere business suit with a faint darker stripe, a waistcoat so artfully cut that he almost looked slim despite the considerable length of gold watch chain draped across his middle, and a dark crimson tie patterned with tiny Harvard "Veritas" shields. He smiled widely (a sure sign that he was uneasy) and extended his hand.

"Good morning, sir, it's a pleasure to see you again."

"Hmph, yes," Stanton sniffed. "You're late."

"I'm truly sorry, sir," Pilkington said with a slight quaver. He was one of those men fated to regard every older man as a surrogate for his own stern and somewhat hypercritical father. "All of our Flyers are busy chasing down security threats and the trains are in total disarray, what with the strikes and sabotage. I'm sure you've heard about them burning down the Lebanon Valley Bridge, the one that crosses the Schuylkill at Reading?"

Stanton nodded sourly. Pilkington winced but bore on gamely:

"Well, I've just been told of the latest from Pittsburgh, and it seems the strikers and rioters are in control of the city. They've burned down two hotels, a grain elevator, the Union Depot, the Pittsburgh & St. Louis freight depot with 125 locomotives and hundreds of tons of coal . . ."

"Great Heavens, Willie," Stanton groaned, dropping heavily into his desk chair and waving Pilkington to a chair across from him. "It sounds like the Apocalypse."

Pilkington nodded gloomily. "Yes, sir . . ." he hesitated, swallowing painfully and longing for a large brandy and soda . . . "I'm just worried about what will happen if we unleash the *first* two Horsemen in the midst of all this unrest . . ."

Any good churchgoer knew that the Four Horsemen of the Apocalypse were Conquest, War, Famine and Death, and Stanton's expression darkened as his subordinate's fearful words sank in. He leaned across his desk and wagged a reproving finger at Pilkington, who pulled out his crimson pocket square and dabbed sweat off his forehead.

"This is no time for the faint of heart, Willie. Come Horsemen, Hell or high water, we *will* go to war with Little Russia on the Fourth of July, and if you have to use the DPS' airborne Gatlings to secure order, then so be it!"

Pilkington swallowed again, barely managing it this time. "Yes, sir," he said with a faint croak, "uh, do you suppose I might ask for a glass of water?"

Stanton peered at Pilkington appraisingly. After a moment he got up and went to the bookcase, pulled back a row of false encyclopedia spines and brought out a bottle of Old Oscar Pepper bourbon and a couple of glasses. Then he returned to his desk, filled the glasses to the brim and shoved one of them wordlessly towards Willie, who took it as if were the keys to the Pearly Gates.

"Thank you, sir," Willie said fervently, and drained half the glass at a gulp.

"Now, then, Willie," Stanton said. "Since you choose to refer to Holy Scripture in this hour of need, allow me to refer you with equal seriousness to Profane Scripture and recommend it to your memory."

He raised his right hand, parodying a favorite gesture of Reverend Moody's, and intoned:

"Here beginneth the lesson according to Stanton: *Calorium!*

Here *endeth* the lesson according to Stanton: *Calorium!*"

He lowered his hand to pick up his glass, took a swallow of Old Oscar Pepper, and resumed in a conversational tone:

"Please disregard all other scripture until such time as our troops are bivouacked in New Petersburg, our Military Governor-General is declaring the restoration of the city's *American* name, Minneapolis, and all working-class Little Russians have been put to work under American overseers at useful public works like clearing forests and building dams. And, of course, digging for pitchblende ore so that we may put

203

our savants to work learning how to refine an *all-American* supply of calorium."

"Yes, sir," Pilkington said earnestly, "you know you can count on me, sir."

"I know I can, Willie, I just want to make quite certain that you are keeping your eye firmly fixed on the brass ring. Because however many arduous passages we may have to traverse to get there, be it ensuring obedience to the July 4th Declaration of a State of Emergency among *all* classes of Americans (Virginia plantation owners or drunken 'bhoys' from the shebeens of Five Points), or making it clear once for all to the leaders of Imperial Britain and Russia and Germany that their days of Empire have ended while America's have just begun, the fact remains that the brass ring *itself*, the *summum bonum* for us as leaders of the American people, will be to set our New Jersulem on so high and impregnable a hill that no petty human contender can ever challenge us again."

Whether it was the Old Oscar Pepper or the oratory, Pilkington was staring at Stanton so raptly that the older man hated to bring the discourse down to business.

"Right, then," Stanton said with a brisk little smile, "keeping all that firmly in mind, how soon can you guarantee good order in New York City?"

Pilkington snapped back quickly. "With the Gatling guns and enough troops, maybe two more days. Even the Draft Riots only lasted three days, and the aerial gunfire will speed things up considerably."

He frowned, his uneasiness abruptly flooding back. "But you know that Papa has sent a spy to New Petersburg to find the operative you had me give up to the Little Russian Okhrana. Papa's hoping against hope to avert this war, and I'm more than a little troubled about keeping him in the dark regarding our real . . ."

Stanton sighed and spread his hands to quiet Willie. "Your father is a grand old man, for me a beloved and respected comrade-in-arms from the earliest days of our War against the Rebellion and deserving of the deepest respect despite his advanced years. But his vision is turned firmly backwards, he can't understand that we must have this war against Little Russia, a war to the knives, if we are to clear away the barriers that are interfering with our progress as the *first* among nations. And I'm afraid that your father's ideas of democracy are equally old-fashioned, formed—I'm sorry to say—by his struggles as an illegal union worker back in the old days in England." Stanton shook his head sadly. "He can see the need for extraordinary measures in extraordinary times, he can see the need for suspending habeas corpus as a measure for survival, but I'm afraid he still thinks in terms of its eventual return. Dear old fuddy-duddy, he still adheres to the antiquated notion of 'one man one vote,' and all the rest of that tired liberal rigamarole. We must cherish your dear old pa as the apple of our eyes, Willie, but he mustn't be allowed to succeed, and indeed if he keeps interfering I may have to insist on his retirement. Who was it that he sent to Little Russia?"

Willie's face darkened: "Liam McCool, the criminal he recruited as an operative amongst the Mollies. McCool is a New York gangster, and I'm afraid that Becky Fox has fallen under his spell."

Stanton recoiled sharply and his voice took on a shrill, almost panicky edge: "Are you serious, Pilkington? If that dreadful woman finds out *anything* about the plans that are under way, she could be more dangerous than a division of Little Russian troops! Where is she now? Where is *McCool* now?"

Suddenly Willie was sweating again, enough so that he could feel it running down his back in a torrent.

"Well, sir . . . I'm not exactly . . ." he spread his hands helplessly: "She disappeared last night from the house in Gramercy Square. And I'm afraid that McCool disappeared with her, after destroying one of our special Acmes. As to where they are right now . . ."

Pilkington threw decorum to the four winds and wiped his face with his coat sleeve. "It's . . . ah . . . *possible* that she's come here, an emergency all-night interrogation of her editor at *Harper's* revealed that she means to work all of her old Washington contacts for any hint at all about the circumstances surrounding the magic-lantern announcements we arranged in New York."

Stanton had sunk his face in his hands, groaning.

"Willie, Willie, Willie," he said, his voice muffled by his hands. Then he snapped erect and snarled at his terrified subordinate: "You will report at *once* to Lt. Col. Cheney, the Commander of my security forces, and between you, you will institute a search of this city that makes the ordinary fine-tooth comb look like a garden rake! Bring me McCool and Becky Fox, do . . . you . . . *understand* me?"

"Yes, *sir*!" cried Pilkington, and unconsciously giving Secretary Stanton a sharp military salute he spun on his heel and escaped.

⊙━┱

"What I can't figure out," Liam said, "is how people can just keep on swallowing Stanton's guff about the terrible dangers threatening them on every side, when all the time the only real dangers threatening them are his army of secret police and curfew Acmes and Black Deltas and God knows what all."

Liam and Becky were strolling along the manicured garden paths of the Duchamp estate, enjoying a few moments of peace and quiet before jumping back into the fray. The cooling air of the early evening was distilling the scents of the roses and the honeysuckles into a fragrance of almost narcotic sweetness, and Liam couldn't help watching Becky out of the corner of his eye and daydreaming about her even as he scolded himself for losing focus.

She was wearing what she jokingly called her "working costume," which seemed to be a castoff boy's suit of light brown tweed over a loose, collarless shirt of white linen that concealed Becky's figure from any casual inspection. Liam—unfortunately for his focus—could have imagined it even if she were rolled in a carpet.

"Believe it or not, I once heard Secretary Stanton say over juleps in Willard's Hotel that if the Government wished to have people believe a flatly preposterous lie, all they needed was for some official to repeat it in public over and over again, with an air of fervent sincerity. After a while people would believe the moon was made of green cheese." Becky smiled ruefully and shook her head. "He's been working at it since the War, after all. From chimerical Confederate balloonists to bogus anarchist tramps, he's been perfecting his craft relentlessly, and as dear old Phineas T. Barnum so succinctly put it . . ."

"There's a sucker born every minute," Liam finished with a grin.

Becky laughed. "And who knows?" she said, doing her best to sound fair and balanced, "he may even believe a lot of it." Then her jaw set and her eyes flashed as the burden of saying something nice about Stanton overwhelmed her: "But that *still* doesn't make it right for him to do what he's done to President Lincoln, or to be planning the wholesale enslavement of masses of people for the benefit of the financiers and the industrial nabobs, or to be preparing to make war on Little Russia. God knows I don't like what the Russians have done on what used to be American soil, but it doesn't justify a treacherous attack!"

Before Liam could answer, there was a flurry of activity in a rosebush ahead of them and a half-dozen sparrow-sized yellowjackets burst into sight and zoomed past Liam and

Becky with a keening whine like a band-saw cutting a heavy board, making both of them duck.

Liam crossed himself involuntarily and muttered under his breath: "*Holy Mary!*" He shook himself and turned to Becky: "I'm not afraid of much," he said with a wry smile, "but bees the size of guinea-hens are right up at the top of my list. We had some queer creatures up in the coalfields these past few months, but I thought it must be some sort of freakish local epidemic . . ."

Becky shook her head. "You weren't back in the city long enough to see what's become of the cockroaches—it doesn't bear thinking about. And one night a few weeks ago when I was walking in Gramercy Park, I saw a rat attack a dray horse and take a chunk the size of a pot roast out of its flank."

Liam grimaced as he imagined it. Mike and the boys think all that insanity is down to Stanton somehow, but I can't believe he pulled off a trick that big unless he's in league with Old Nick. Anyway, what on earth would anyone do it *for?*"

"It's not Stanton," Becky said. "As for what it's about, I have a shrewd suspicion, but it will have to wait until we meet up with Crazy Horse."

Liam gave her an appraising look and a little half-smile. "I've had a suspicion or two myself, come to that. Though I can't say I'd thought of Crazy Horse."

Becky smiled cryptically. "I promised I'd tell you more after you retrieved his medicine bundle, but the most I can say without his permission is that he's going to play a very important part in striking back against Stanton *and* the Little Russians and our returning his medicine bundle will make it possible for him to begin." She reached into the neck of her shirt and pulled out a miniature watch on a lavaliere.

"I hate to say it, but it looks like we're going to have to get moving."

"Wait a minute!" Liam held up his hands warningly: "I thought we agreed that *I* was going to be the one that went back to Washington and got President Lincoln ready for the escape, and *you* would be the one that guided the Half-Delta back to the pickup point."

Becky grinned at him. "No," she said teasingly, "*you* agreed to that, I was just listening." As he started to protest she shook her head firmly. "You can fuss and fume all you like, but I'm not going to budge. I've gotten into and out of scrapes that would make your hair stand on end, just to get a story. I'm certainly not going to sit at home knitting when I could be helping a President I admire and a man I quite like."

She smiled just a little and gave him a look so level and unwavering that he felt himself slipping again into the bottomless blue of her eyes. Much as he wanted to just let himself go he wasn't quite sure how she would feel about that, so he pulled himself back before he went over the edge.

"Very well," he said, "but you'll have to oblige me in one thing, then . . ." He reached into the pocket of his jacket and took out Maggie's nickeled Webley. "Keep this with you from now on. Do you know how to shoot?"

She nodded. "This was Miss O'Shea's, wasn't it?"

Liam nodded.

"Good," she said with a smile, "let's go."

Chapter Twenty-One

illie Pilkington was doing his best to look inconspicuous, but since he had never felt like undergoing the rigorous apprenticeship his father expected from aspiring detectives, he attracted a lot more attention being unnoticeable than he would have if he'd just sat on one of the Station's wooden benches and pretended to read a newspaper.

It was covert attention, of course—everybody else in the big brick-and-stone Pennsy station on the corner of 6th Street and B Street NW either recognized Willie from pictures in the press, or sensed immediately that he was some kind of Eye, which was enough to make them drift off forthwith to more remote parts of the Station's waiting room. Willie, meanwhile, with a dark brown bowler pulled down almost to his nose, his dark brown greatcoat swirling around him like a canvas bathing machine, and a deeply sinister pair of brownish smoked glasses, felt sure that he cut a rather dashing, anarchist-flavored figure, while remaining rigorously incognito.

Still, it was going to be July in another couple of days and the Washington heat and humidity were nearly as bad tonight as they had been in the daytime, so Willie was praying fervently for the New York train to open its doors and disgorge its passengers so he could get back to the DPS steamer and shuck off this damned coat before he melted. Ah, there! Thank God the passengers were starting to pour into the waiting room. He inclined his head and pretended to scratch his nose as he peered surreptitiously at the newcomers. Surely Becky and McCool wouldn't have dared to travel openly by train, but it wouldn't do to miss the obvious . . .

"*Sir?*"

The familiar voice came from Willie's blind side and startled him so badly that he nearly cried out. Furious at having his disguise pierced, he spun around, teeth bared in a snarl . . .

"Just what the Devil do you mean by . . ."

. . . and deflated just as quickly when he saw that it was Agent McPherson, whom he had taken for some sort of small-time drummer when he'd passed in the crowd a moment ago, and who now stood examining him with an uncertain smile.

"Sorry, sir," McPherson said, "I didn't mean to startle you."

"Ah . . . hmph . . . yes, of course I knew you were there, McPherson, I just wanted to see if you were on your toes!"

And, beckoning to McPherson to accompany him, he turned and headed towards the exit.

"Any sign of McCool here yet?" the detective asked with a barely suppressed eagerness that put Willie in mind of a big, mean cat closing in on a mouse.

"Not so far," Willie said, "but if they've come to Washington to make mischief it won't be long till we have them. Secretary Stanton has mobilized every able-bodied man from here to Annapolis, and he's printed thousands of handbills with Miss Fox's and McCool's likenesses."

McPherson grinned without a hint of mirth and narrowed his eyes hungrily as he stared at some interior vision; Willie imagined it a bit queasily—whatever the details, it surely involved severe and even gory discomfort for Liam McCool.

"Just remember," he said sharply as they exited onto 6th Street, "McCool is yours, as I promised. But no one may

211

lay a hand on Miss Fox and she must be given directly into my charge. The only reason I didn't have McCool up for murder over those two plug-uglies you hired in Five Points was because they had the temerity to assault her and he acted in her defense."

"Ah, Mr. Pilkington, dear," said McPherson, lapsing into a brogue as he continued to savor his vision of revenge, "nivver you mind yer worriting, I'm that grateful to you for calling me in at the finish, I'll be *certain* sure to see you right."

As they stepped onto the sidewalk a horde of black cabbies swarmed around them offering their services, but Pilkington just cursed and shooed them away as a big black steam pantechnicon with the Department of Public Safety's All-Seeing Eye and its motto *"Per Aspera ad Securitas"* picked out in gold leaf on its doors pulled up to the curb and its driver jumped out to hold the door open for Willie.

"Where to, sir?" the driver asked.

"I want to check out all the DPS observation posts," Willie said. "And drive slowly, we're on the lookout for a couple of fugitives."

Their helpers in the Underground Railroad had supplied Becky and Liam with a battered old steam caravan that met all their requirements handsomely. First, it had to be too old and decrepit to excite police interest while being large enough to offer a secure hiding place for President Lincoln and his wheelchair. Second, it had to be a vehicle that would offer both Liam and Becky some logical excuse for traveling in it together if explanations were demanded, and finally it had to be one the Underground Railroad wouldn't miss if for any reason Liam and Becky needed to ditch it.

Becky hesitated to ask her Alexandria hosts how they had managed to come up with the one they found, but it certainly seemed to her to fit the bill perfectly, being an ante-diluvian Confederate ambulance that had been skillfully converted into a traveling country store packed with all sorts of goods from nails to bolts of calico to a cheap rye whiskey that Liam guessed might do in a pinch for removing paint.

As for the fugitives themselves, the challenge to the younger Miss Duchamp (a prominent player in local amateur theatricals) was irresistible. Despite Liam's misgivings she trimmed his hair still shorter and fitted him with a gray wig that—according to a giggling Becky—made him look positively venerable, and then dusted his moustache with some sort of theatrical powder that matched the wig nicely. With a suitably distressed-looking suit of the sort fashionable in the days of President Jackson and his dark glasses, Liam had to admit he looked decrepit enough to make an undertaker reach for his tape-measure.

Becky, who had enacted quite a few roles in dead earnest as she traveled to far corners pretending to be anybody but a reporter, entered into the spirit of the thing happily. By the time Miss Duchamp had finished with her, her honey-blonde hair was concealed under a school-marmish wig of gray curls, while wire-rimmed spectacles, a shiny old bombazine dress with yellowed lace cuffs and some discreet India rubber padding created a total effect that made Liam break into helpless laughter and call Becky "Mother Fox" until she threatened to hit him with her cane.

But later on, after a few miles on the road back to Washington, Becky and Liam had pretty well lost the urge to laugh.

"This is bad," Liam muttered, "we haven't quite hit the outskirts of the city and we've already had to go through two checkpoints. I haven't seen this many troops around here since the end of the War."

"What worries me most," Becky said, "is whether our half-Delta will be able to land and take off again without being seen. It's been re-set now for four o'clock tomorrow morning, because that's when you can usually expect most people to be sound asleep. That's why we picked the Duchamps' tobacco fields for a landing, because they're on bottomland below the line of sight of most of the buildings in Alexandria, and we figured that would reduce the chances of a sighting to near zero. But with all these troops galumphing around . . ." She fell silent, biting her lip worriedly.

Unable to think of anything reassuring that wouldn't sound irritatingly trite, Liam just shook his head in silent agreement and kept on driving and watching mounted and steam-driven soldiers come and go. He still had his Colt and Becky had the Bulldog, and he'd managed to fill his jacket pockets with cartridges for both in the gun room at the Duchamp estate, but anything involving gunplay at this point would probably be suicidal. Still, better to go down fighting than to give Stanton a chance at putting them in cages so he could play with them.

Becky broke into his thoughts: "Do we need to check with Mike to make sure everything's in order?"

Liam smiled and shook his head, recognizing the question as the kind of worrying away at a loose tooth you always tend to do when everything's been planned to the last dot on the i's and cross on the t's. He'd been able to talk to Mike on the Duchamp's voicewire machine last night and he had it all covered. Mike would collect on an old IOU from the Grogan clan, river pirates who'd been involved in the New York area's river and ocean crimes since the days of smuggling tea and rum under the British.

Becky and Liam and the President would fly directly from the Duchamp estate to the beach just south of Barnegat Light on Jersey's Atlantic coast, less than an hour in a half-Delta. There were expensive summer homes not far away, but Liam knew from experience that these people were the kind of nobs who didn't like to get involved with anything outside their own tight little world and even the DPS wouldn't take a chance on bothering them without being invited.

The Grogans would be waiting there with the steam launch they'd used for running the blockade during the War, and in no time at all they would have Lincoln and his wheelchair off the beach and on his way to Freedom Party HQ on Shelter Island, another rich folks' hideaway at the tip of Long Island and as secure from DPS nosiness as the far side of the moon. Maybe fifty or sixty nautical miles from pickup to dropoff, a piece of cake for the Grogans, and the President himself safe and sound so fast after leaving Washington that even Stanton would be left scratching his head.

"I wouldn't go so far as to say there's *honor* among thieves," Liam said with a grin, "but there's a cast-iron code of correct behavior, and the Grogans will discharge their debt to the Butcher Boys down to the last jot and tittle. I'd rather make a deal with a crook than, say, the Rev. Henry Ward Beecher any day in the week."

Becky laughed merrily, glad of a chance for some humor. "I was catching up on some of the old news while we were killing time at the Duchamps' and I came across an account of Beecher's sermon at the Plymouth Church on the significance of the railwaymen's strike. The best part was where he said that 'while it was true that wages of $1 a day were not enough to support a man and five children if a man would insist on drinking beer and smoking, a *prudent* family could live on good bread and water in the morning, water and bread at mid-day, and good water and bread at night.' According to the report at that point there was general applause and laughter among the congregation."

"It's been a while since I read Dante," Liam said, "but I'm sure he had a circle for the Plymouth Church down there somewhere in The Inferno."

No sooner had he gotten off his little quip than a soldier stepped out into the road ahead of them and waved his arms back and forth to signal a stop.

"Damn!" muttered Liam. Things had been going too well, for sure—they weren't more than twenty minutes' drive from the Smithsonian and they'd had clear sailing all the way from the second checkpoint to here. He braked to a stop with a loud and painful screeching from the ancient machinery and turned to Becky: "Time for Mother Fox," he murmured. He leaned his head out the window and quavered in his best doddering-old-timer voice:

"What can I do for you, young fella?"

The soldier was a tow-headed infantryman with a baby face and a friendly grin. "Sorry, Dad, but we're under orders to have a look in the back of your caravan."

"Why sure, youngster, always happy to oblige a Union soldier!" He turned to Becky: "Now then, Mother, you keep a weather eye on the steam gauge, we don't want Old Betsy to blow us all to smithereens!"

The young soldier looked uneasy: "Say, Pop, is this contraption safe?"

"Safe?" chuckled Liam. "Safe? Say, is a basketful of rattlesnakes safe if you keep the lid on?" He cackled gleefully and then felt a little contrite at the hint of panic in the soldier's expression. "Aw, sonny, don't you pay me no mind, I'm just an old fool pulling your leg! Old Betsy will be just fine long's we don't keep her standing still but a couple of minutes!"

He walked around the back of the caravan and threw open the door, revealing a treasure trove of useful junk spooled, stacked and hung from the ceiling. The crate of cheap rye whiskey was right by the door and it caught the soldier's eye as he flashed his lantern around the interior.

"Say, mister, is that whiskey?"

"That's what the label says, young fella! One dollar a bottle and worth every penny."

The soldier pulled out a bottle and examined the label by the light of his lamp. "It says 'Made in China,'" he said dubiously.

"Why, sure enough," said Liam with a touch of indignation, "that's why it's a dollar, you got to pay a premium for

216

the imported stuff!" Noting that the soldier's frown was deepening Liam said, "I tell you what I'll do, you buy one bottle for a dollar and you can have another one for free, and that's just because I fought with the Union at Chapultepec in the Mexican War."

The soldier grinned: "Now that's more like it!" He fished a silver dollar out of his uniform pocket and Liam handed over two bottles with a silent prayer that Chinese hooch wouldn't do the kids any harm.

"Anything else?" Liam asked.

"That's all, Dad, you can go ahead and let Old Betsy rip!" He waved and took off to join his pals as Liam trotted back to Becky and climbed in. He handed her the soldier's coin:

"Hang on to that, Mother," he said in his normal voice, "that's our first dollar!" As Becky collapsed laughing, he let off the brakes with another tortured scream, engaged the engine and chugged briskly away towards the Smithsonian.

○──ㅠ

Blessedly, as they chugged down B Street NW towards their goal they could see that the service area behind the Smithsonian was still dimly lit, despite the sudden proliferation of carbon arc spotlights around the Mall and the Capitol Building. Less welcome was the fact that they'd had to stop two more times, and although Liam managed to oil their way through both checkpoints with liberal applications of Chinese firewater, the process had taken so much time that by this point they had eaten up all their margin for delay and then some.

Now, as if to rub it in, they saw a wink of light as the door by which Liam had entered the night before opened briefly to allow the exit of two burly DPS agents in the standardized black gabardine suits and curly-brimmed bowlers that said *"Eye!"* to everyone but the blind.

"Oh, oh," said Becky. "Should we run them down?"

"Certainly not," said Liam with a grin, "first of all it's illegal, and second of all when you run down an Eye you have to wash your whole steamer with tomato juice to get rid of the smell. I've got a better idea . . ." He reached forward and played with the steam valve until the engine started gasping and banging alarmingly. "Dear me, Mother," he said in his codger voice, "we seem to have engine trouble. I expect those clever men over there can help us fix it!"

"Ah!" Becky said. She smiled and adjusted her wire-framed spectacles as Liam pulled off the road and onto the paved area behind the Smithsonian. Immediately the two DPS men hulked towards them warningly.

"Say," said the first one in a surprisingly high, reedy voice. "This here area is off limits to the public, Grandpa, you better sling your hook before we have to haul you in!"

Liam gave the Eyes a pleading look: "Land sakes, young fella, can't you hear my poor old Betsy a-gaspin' and a-coughin'? I was hoping one of you smart youngsters was savvy enough to figure out how to help her." As the DPS man's lips tightened with impatience Liam added hastily: "I've got some mighty fine imported whiskey in the back, you can have all of it you can carry away if you'll help me out!"

The Eyes exchanged an avid look. "Show us the booze, old-timer," the First Eye said sharply, "and make it snappy."

Liam got out and did his creaky-old-bones turn as he hobbled around to the back, where he threw open the doors and gestured grandly at the remaining bottles of whiskey: "There you go, boys," he said coaxingly, "if that ain't the finest drop of whiskey you ever put down your throat I'm a monkey's uncle!"

The DPS agent pulled out a bottle and examined the label suspiciously. "China? *Chinese* rye?"

Liam gave him a hurt look. "Say, if you think I'm just funnin', you go ahead try a slug of that on me!"

The agent gave a why-not shrug, worked out the cork and tipped his head back for a healthy swallow. An instant later his eyebrows shot up nearly to his hairline and he broke off his drink, laughing and coughing:

"Whooo-*ee!* Them Celestials can brew up a mean batch of red-eye! This stuff'd take the enamel clean off a stove!"

The other agent stuck out a big paw impatiently: "All right, then, Murph, don't go hoggin' it!"

The first agent handed the bottle over and the second one tipped his head back and finished the bottle in one long, gurgling pull, determined to manage it without coughing. As the last swallow went down he straightened up, tossed the bottle to Liam and grinned happily:

"By Jingo, old man, that's some good stuff," he said when he finished. "How many of those you willing to part with if we can get your heap running right?"

Liam gestured at the case: "You fix old Betsy for me and you can have the rest of them!"

As the two half-drunk and totally delighted agents leaned forward to pull out the case, Liam moved up next to them, grabbed their heads by the sides and banged them together; then, as the stunned DPS men reeled backwards Liam did his jiu-jitsu nerve pinch on their necks, dropping them where they stood. They started snoring loudly and Liam called out to Becky:

"OK, Mother, let's tie up Mr. Stanton's birthday presents!"

As Becky jumped out and ran to join him, Liam pulled one of the big coils of rope down off the caravan's walls and cut it in half with his pocket knife. "Hands behind his back," he instructed, pulling the agent's hands behind him as if for handcuffs, "then do them up good, four or five turns of rope before you pull his heels up behind him and do the same thing with his ankles. You good with knots?"

"*Mister* McCool!" she exclaimed with an arch lift of the eyebrows.

"Why do I even ask?" he said with a laugh and the two of them went to work with a will. A couple of minutes later they were done, and Liam took out two more bottles and handed one to Becky. "Give him a good bath," he said, "just in case whoever finds them might have missed the message." Becky grinned and baptized her victim liberally while Liam did the same with his. Then they dragged the two snoring DPS men over to the deep shadows next to the coal chute and sat them against the wall to sleep it off with the empties on the ground next to them.

"They'll be good for a couple of hours now," Liam said, "and we'd better get a move on!" He trotted over to the door, tried the knob prayerfully and heaved a powerful sigh as it swung open. A moment later they had both disappeared inside, closing the door and locking it behind them.

0—ⲧ

This time Liam was used to all the twists and turns that would take them to the door of the Chubb-locked store-room, so he set off at a trot with Becky keeping up easily at his side. Despite all the extra security outside, there didn't seem to be anything different inside, and Liam was willing to bet that Stanton's Prisoner in the Iron Mask was the last thing that had occurred to anybody when they were tightening the network of guards. One final turn, and a moment later they found themselves outside the storeroom.

Liam was slightly winded, but Becky didn't seem to be the least bit bothered. "You've got a fair turn of speed for an old lady," he said to Becky with just a touch of asperity.

She smiled and laid a soothing hand on his arm: "I'm sorry, Grandpa, but those few extra years of yours were bound to take their toll sooner or later."

Liam rolled his eyes and got out the picks, hoping that this time he wouldn't have to take so long at it. But he'd only been working at the first lock for a minute or so when he heard the unmistakable eerie thrum of the Lincoln automaton's rubber vocal cords from the other side of the door:

"*Mr. McCool? Liam?*"

"Yes, sir!" said Liam excitedly. "Is there any chance you can open it from the inside?"

For answer, Liam and Becky heard first the one set of tumblers clicking and then the second, followed by the clank of Lincoln's steel fingers on the doorknob and a moment later by the door swinging open to reveal the President himself.

"Thank God for your constancy!" Lincoln said, and turning his head towards Becky with the distinctive squeak of his neck joint: "And Miss Fox, well met! I'd recognize America's most intrepid lady journalist anywhere, wig and spectacles or no!"

Impulsively she took the cold steel hand and grasped it between her two hands: "Mr. President, it breaks my heart to see you brought to this pass, and I swear to you that my friends and I will do every last thing in our power to set things right again."

Liam had pulled out his watch and examined it with a grimace. "Mr. President, Miss Fox, we are running dangerously behind our schedule and we're going to have to catch up however we can. Sir, can you get a tight grip on the arms of that chair?"

Lincoln nodded and grabbed hold of the wheelchair's arms.

"Let's go, then, folks!" Liam said, and grabbing the handles of the wheelchair he took off down the hall at a half-run, Becky keeping pace right at his side.

Outside, the two DPS men were still snoring sonorously away as the door opened a crack, and then all the way as Liam pushed Lincoln's chair out the door and Becky followed.

"We're going to have a job getting President Lincoln into the back of the caravan," Liam muttered. "Maybe we can use the rope . . ."

But before he could finish, Becky grabbed his arm and held up a finger to her lips. A moment later and he heard it too: a powerful and well-silenced steam engine was approaching the Smithsonian. Another moment or two and the vehicle had stopped at the front of the building, idling for a moment before it was turned off, the hum of its turbine purring away to nothing with the polite smoothness of very expensive machinery. A moment later there was the slam of a door, and then the rapid footsteps of two men, plainly audible in the dead stillness of the early morning. One of the men called out:

"*Murphy? Beckermann?*"

"Good lord," whispered Becky, "it's Willie!"

"Pilkington?" whispered Liam urgently.

Becky nodded, frowning. Liam pointed to the President and then made a sweeping half circle towards the van. Becky nodded emphatically, grabbed the handles of the wheelchair and took off rapidly around the van and out of sight, leaving Liam on his own to trot towards the sound of the approaching footsteps.

Pilkington was talking again as he approached the corner on the other side of which Liam stood hidden in the shadows:

"*Are you absolutely certain that you've done everything in your own and the Pilkington Agency's power to retrieve Maggie O'Shea's diary?*"

"*I swear it, sir! I had to make a run for it the minute I heard the explosion that destroyed Mr. Henderson's house, but before then I had searched every nook and cranny in her quarters!*"

Liam felt as if the breath had been knocked out of him. Pilkington's companion was *McPherson!*

Willie's answer came back in a plaintive, accusing tone: "*You* knew *how important finding that diary was to me! That bitch threatened to* ruin *me if I didn't . . .*"

As Pilkington spoke these last few words he was within a split second of turning the corner, seeing the caravan and discovering his trussed-up agents, not to mention Liam, Becky, and President Lincoln. But if Liam acted now, as he must the moment the two men came into view, he would never hear the end of Pilkington's speech and most likely the final clue to the secret of Maggie's murder.

Later he wondered if it had been a real decision or a reflex. At the moment, it seemed as if all thought flew away the moment he saw the men turn the corner and start past him. Leaping out of the shadows with the speed of a jungle predator, Liam smacked their heads together—perhaps with just a touch more enthusiasm than the move required—and then knocked them out with nerve pinches. As they crumpled to the ground, Liam called out to Becky in a low, urgent voice:

"Bring me some more rope and a couple of bottles of whiskey!"

Without waiting for her to arrive, he quickly set about stripping the two of them, leaving them in their long underwear.

"Liam McCool!" she said from behind him. "What on earth are you up to?"

"I'll tell you when we're on the road," he said grimly, pulling the two men up into sitting positions and placing them back to back before he took the rope from Becky and ran it under their arms and around their middles a couple of good stout turns. "Would you mind finishing them up?" he asked with as much deference as he could muster. "I'm going to run around front and get their steamer."

"The *DPS wagon*?" she asked incredulously.

"I promise," Liam said earnestly, "I *promise* I'll . . ."

"Yes, yes," Becky said a little testily, "you'll explain when we're on the road." As he nodded emphatically she shooed him away with a whisk of her fingers: "Go *on*, for pity's sake, hurry up!"

As Liam sprinted away, Becky set to tying Willie and McPherson up with all the rope in the coil, stifling a slightly hysterical urge to giggle as she went along. By the time she had tied the last set of knots, the two of them were encased in a good twenty-five feet of stout hemp, and there was nothing left to do but drag them over to join the two DPS agents against the wall. Becky returned for the whiskey and picked up their bowlers while she was at it, bathing each of them liberally in a stream of Chinese moonshine before jamming their hats down on top of their heads.

"A very artistic job," Lincoln rumbled from behind her and she jumped so hard she almost dropped the empty bottles.

"Thank you, Mr. President," she said, and then gave in completely to her giggles as Liam turned the corner in the DPS van.

A moment later, Liam had jumped out, gone around to the back and let down a ramp that rolled into position with the pleasing *snick!* of nicely machined metal. As he turned back he saw Becky standing there with her arms folded intransigently across her chest and Lincoln staring towards him with what he took to be equal expectancy.

"Sorry," Liam said as contritely as he could. "It's just that we've been through all the checkpoints once with the General Store caravan, and we absolutely don't have a moment to spare on the way back. If *one* checkpoint has a new set of soldiers standing guard they'll put us through the whole thing again and that will be that—the half-Delta will have to keep to its schedule and we'll be done for!"

"And they won't stop the DPS van?" she asked crossly.

"Are you serious?" Liam said, spreading his hands entreatingly. "I'm willing to bet you our first silver dollar that every single human being between here and Alexandria will melt into the distance the second our DPS chariot rolls towards them."

"Good thinking, young Liam," rumbled the Lincoln automaton, "as far as most folks are concerned a DPS van might as well be a truckload of Black Plague."

"I rest my case," Liam said.

"Oh, for Heaven's sake!" Becky muttered. As Liam pushed Lincoln up the ramp she gathered up Willie's and McPherson's clothes, tossed them into the shadows and ran for the front of the van. A moment later, they were rolling briskly down B Street NW towards Alexandria and the next leg in their journeys.

Little Russia
June 30–July 1, 1877

Chapter Twenty-Two

here it is!"

Capt. Ubaldo shouted over the noise of the steam turbines, pointing downwards through the port-side windows towards a vast cleared space in the middle of the forest, at one end of which a cross made of whitewashed boulders had been laid out as a marker.

It seemed to Liam that they had been flying forever, and that the arctic temperature inside the half-Delta had long ago frozen him nearly as solid as those woolly mammoths the Russians were always chopping out of the Siberian permafrost.

Like most people who'd never been inside one, Liam had reckoned a "half-Delta must have the same basic amenities found in a full-size Delta, the warship of the U.S. Aerial Navy. Shaped like a wedge in the form of an enormous isosceles triangle, lifted by revolutionary hydrogen "cells" held rigid by a graceful framework of aluminum struts, the standard Delta was big enough to mount multiple steam-driven Gatlings and carry a company of heavily armed aeronauts in reasonable comfort.

But as it turned out, the only thing the half-Delta shared with its namesake was its triangular shape. Designed purely for speed, it was nowhere near even half the size of the big Deltas, and anything that wasn't absolutely necessary had been stripped out of it. As far as Liam could see that included everything connected with warmth, quiet, and basic creature comforts, and at high altitudes it seemed that his time was divided between trying to get a deep breath and uncontrollable shivering. Fortunately, Becky had flown on these things before and had dragged along a life-saving armload of fur coats and blankets.

The odd thing was that although they were already into the second week of summer, there seemed to be flakes of snow swirling around them as the big controlled-descent fans drove them closer and closer to the clearing below. Not only that, but the night skies had been clear on the St. Paul side of the Mississippi, while here the moonlight was broken by heavy, wind-driven clouds that had given Ubaldo some bad moments as he crossed into Little Russia and flew over the countryside north of New Petersburg.

"Not bad enough, though," thought Liam with a flash of irritation. Ubaldo had been grating on his nerves ever since the flight from New York to Alexandria, with his showy nonchalant-aeronaut swagger and his dandyish blue flying-suit and sealskin boots. Not to mention the patent-leather hair and that damned little moustache, whose tips Ubaldo was perpetually twisting until Liam expected them to unwind all at once, possibly (if Lady Luck was any sort of pal at all) whipping off his ostentatiously patrician nose and whirling away with it.

Not that he could really blame Ubaldo for posturing, Liam thought, forcing himself against all his inclinations to be fair for a moment. Becky Fox was a ridiculously beautiful woman as well as being a world-famous reporter and as staunch a comrade as any of his pals among the Butcher Boys. But damn it all, anyway, why did she have to simper when Ubaldo oiled her up with extravagant flatteries, and what was all that folderol about his profile reminding her of Maurice Barrymore, whom she'd just seen in *Under the Gaslight* ?

"*Hang on tight!*" shouted Ubaldo as the roar of the fans rose to a shriek. A moment later there was a thump as the bottom of the airship bounced against the ground, followed by a half-dozen rapid *fwomp!-thud!s* as steam guns fired anchoring stanchions into the dirt. A moment later Ubaldo cut the engines and stood.

"*Nous sommes arrivés!*" he announced with a grin.

"*Why can't he speak bloody English?*" thought Liam crossly. He stood up and helped Becky to unfasten the safety belt that had kept her in her seat.

"Thank you, Mr. McCool," she said as she got to her feet.

"*Nichevo,*" he said gruffly. "If we're to be speaking in tongues, that's Russian for think nothing of it . . ."

"I know what it means," she said with a quizzical look.

More to hide his embarrassment than for any other reason, Liam gave her an elaborate bow and gestured towards the hatch which Ubaldo had just opened to the outside.

"After you, Miss Fox," he said with stiff formality.

Becky gave him another inquisitive look, shook her head almost imperceptibly and then turned to go out the hatch and down the steps that Ubaldo had just set up. Liam closed his eyes and counted to ten before he followed her out the hatch.

○—╍

Outside, it appeared that the snow had started falling in earnest. Ubaldo pulled out his watch and checked it, then tucked it away again and turned to Becky and Liam.

Eleven hours, twenty-three minutes. Not bad at all for a run from Shelter Island to Little Russia. I must applaud Mr. Clemens' choice of a location for the Party's clandestine headquarters, there's no aerial traffic except for seagulls, yet it's scarcely a hundred miles from Manhattan!"

Becky smiled reminiscently: "And I must say President Lincoln seemed thrilled to be at the seashore, even if he must negotiate the waterfront in a wheelchair."

Ubaldo cleared his throat apologetically and looked at his watch again: "Miss Fox, Mr. McCool, I'm afraid I've got to turn around right away and head back to Shelter Island to start my next assignment. Are you two going to be all right out here in the middle of nowhere?"

"Of course we are, Captain," said Becky firmly. "We've got our furs and our blankets, and if our contacts here are as good about keeping to their schedule as you have been about yours, we shouldn't be waiting more than a half hour."

"I don't like leaving you here in the middle of a snow storm," Ubaldo said dubiously. "There's something freakish about this weather that's got me a bit spooked. Sure, I've heard of late snows in New Petersburg and St. Paul both, but I've never *ever* heard of snow falling on one side of the Mississipi while it's a nice, clear summer evening on the other."

"Really," Becky said, taking Ubaldo's hand. "You need to go as far as you can before sunrise, and we're going to be equally busy with our missions here. I'm sure we shall all meet again in New York before long."

Ubaldo smiled at her in a way that Liam found insufferably smarmy. "I'll go peacefully if you promise to let me take you to dinner at Delmonico's when you've come back."

Becky gave him a warm smile in return. "That would be very nice indeed, Captain."

"In that case," he said, and bending over her hand he kissed it with a warmth that Liam was sure went beyond the bounds of propriety; in fact, if he kept it up much longer Liam was going to give him a good sharp rap on the bean with the brass knucks he carried for special . . .

"*Au revoir*, then, Miss Fox," Ubaldo said, standing up again. "Mr. McCool," he said with a courteous nod to Liam. A moment later he had pulled the steps back into the ship, slammed the hatch shut, cast off the lines to the anchoring stanchions and begun an eerily silent climb into the moonlit clouds.

Liam looked after the departing airship with an exasperated frown. "I just wish they'd given the OK for Ubaldo to come back for us instead of leaving us to fend for ourselves. Three days to take care of old Pilkington's assignment and make our way back to Shelter Island seems a bit of a stretch."

"I expect Mr. Clemens and the others have confidence in our resourcefulness," Becky said tartly. "And as for Capt. Ubaldo, he's already taken an uncommon lot of risks in order to help President Lincoln escape."

Liam knew he should keep his mouth shut, but it was as if his infantile self had taken over the reins and was driving him hard towards a smashup:

"Well," he said in a sniffish tone, "we certainly wouldn't want to put your darling Capt. Ubaldo in harm's way!"

Becky's eyes flared and Liam could sense a thunderbolt coming: "Liam McCool," she snapped, "I've a good mind to . . . !"

Before she could finish she was interrupted by a sound more chilling than the blizzard wind—from just beyond the edge of the forest behind them, first on one side and then on the other, came the plaintive, hungry howling of a pack of wolves.

"Oh, oh," muttered Liam, "that's torn it!"

He snatched his Colt out of an inside pocket and thumbed back the hammer. Then he reached into his jacket pocket and pulled out a big handful of the bullets for Maggie's Webley.

"You'd better keep these handy," he said to Becky, "with any luck we'll have enough bullets between us to stop them."

Becky already had the pistol out and the hammer back. "I've never shot a wolf," she said uneasily.

"I've heard it can take a couple of shots to bring one down," he said, "just keep shooting till it keels over."

As if his words had been a signal, one wolf after another moved forth out of the screening trees and formed a menacing crescent around Becky and Liam, their jaws hanging open and their tongues lolling out in what looked like hungry grins, while the intermittent moonlight made their eyes glint with cold fire.

"I never could abide dogs," Liam said grimly, "too many big teeth." He opened the front of his coat to free the handle of his sword cane.

At that, the wolf that seemed to be in the center of the crescent stepped towards Liam and snarled furiously, wrinkling up its muzzle and baring its front teeth.

"If it takes another step I'm going to shoot," Liam said.

"Try a warning shot," said Becky, "maybe it will scare them off."

The wolf took another step towards Liam and he fired into the ground a foot in front of it, throwing up a big spout of dirt and stones.

Unnervingly, none of the wolves so much as flinched. Instead, the lead wolf stepped forward again and let loose an ear-splitting howl. For a moment the creature just stood there, baring its teeth. Then it seemed to waver like a reflection in a puddle and when it solidified again it was *twice* as big—a good five feet high at the shoulder—and, Liam thought, considerably more than twice as nasty. It growled ominously, the sound as deep and hair-raising as the lions Liam had heard in the Central Park Zoo.

"Hold this a minute," Liam said, handing his Colt to Becky.

Then, with the same impossible-to-follow whirling move she had seen on the sidewalk in Five Points, Liam swept the katana out of its scabbard and flashed it through the giant wolf's middle, so that the two halves of the huge animal simply fell to either side with a thud, gushing blood onto the fresh snow.

For a moment, the tableau froze in place. Then, all the wolves started howling at once until the heaped mess of blood and guts started to stir as if something were trying to emerge from it, slowly drawing together again into a vaguely wolf-like shape until finally the creature stood before them again, its eyes glowing and its tongue lolling hungrily.

"Aw, hell!" Liam muttered, "How are we supposed to kill one of those werewolf things?""

He was interrupted by a loud and insistent *yip-yip-yip!* from behind them, the sounds wolflike but with a commanding human overtone, and no sooner did they hear it than the wolves melted back into the forest, leaving the snow behind them as smooth and unmarked as if they'd never been there.

"What on earth did we just . . . ?" Becky began, but before she could finish she was interrupted by the sound of sleigh bells and shouts:

"Miss Fox! Mr. McCool!"

As they turned to look they saw a *troika*—a sleigh drawn by three horses—whizzing towards them through the snow. There were two men in it wearing *shubk i*, heavy, hide-outside, wool-inside sheepskin coats, and tall, black sheepskin hats called *shapki*, and as the sleigh slid to a halt next to Becky and Liam, the men leapt out and advanced with their hands outstretched in a mixture of greeting and apology.

"How you can forgive for being such late?" said the sleigh's driver, a stocky man with a deeply tanned complexion, broad cheekbones and an aquiline nose. "And this when you go to such many trouble for us?"

Liam listened with fascination to the man's Russian accent, as heavy as any he'd heard back in Five Points, but overlaid with London vowels and a bizarre, French-sounding "r" borrowed from some British teacher who had tried to conquer the Russian burr.

"Chief Crazy Horse?" he asked.

"*Vash pokornyi slugá*, sir," the stocky man said, grasping the hand proffered by Liam and shaking it warmly. "Serving you humbly and also you, Miss Fox, be welcome in ancestor land of Dakota Sioux. As Russian invader calls," he added with an ironic smile, "outer skirt of New Petersburg."

Becky smiled radiantly and took Crazy Horse's hand. "I'm delighted to meet you at last," she said, "as well as your friend Mr. . . ."

She turned an inquiring eye towards the other occupant of the sleigh, a tall, slender, blue-eyed man with a very prominent nose and a slightly receding chin. He gave Becky a gallant bow and swept off the sheepskin *shapka* to reveal a dense mass of curly blonde hair:

"Laughing Wolf, Miss, very much at your service and praying that you will forgive us for your . . . ah, rude reception by my namesakes. At least I was able to scold them and send them away before they got rambunctious, though I doubt they would have done more than make a nuisance of themselves."

"I will happily forgive you both, your lateness and your—ah—*pets*," Becky said, "if you will be so kind as to *explain* the wolves and their curious metamorphoses, uh . . . *General*. Ah . . ."

The blonde-haired man replaced his *shapka* and grinned at Becky: "Yes, Miss Fox, you have caught me out. In a previous life I was George Armstrong Custer of the U.S. Army, now proudly Laughing Wolf of the Oglala Lakota Sioux and . . ."

" . . . to me blood brother and comrade," said Crazy Horse. "But please, we are explaining that and all other back in Petersburg, where is also the hot drinks and food."

"*S glubochaishim udovol'stviem,*" concurred Liam with a big grin, then, catching himself and turning to Becky: "Ah, that's to say . . ."

"Yes, Mr. McCool," she said with mild irony, "I know it means 'with the greatest pleasure,' I do believe you're inclined to underestimate me!"

And with that she led the way to the sleigh, followed closely by Crazy Horse, Custer, and a much chagrined Liam McCool.

Chapter Twenty-Three

n hour later, though the freak snowstorm continued to rage outside, the new acquaintances were snugly ensconced in Crazy Horse's rooms near the Cathedral of Saints Boris and Gleb in the center of New Petersburg, toasting their feet at the fire and sipping Armagnac. The suite was in the most fashionable quarter of the Little Russian capital, at one side of a vast cobbled square modeled on Moscow's Red Square, and the muffled *tramp! tramp!* of booted feet outside as sentries marched back and forth through the snow was a reminder that paranoia was as much in the air here as it was back in Washington.

"So," said Crazy Horse, who was clutching the medicine bundle as if he never meant to let go of it again. "If all snow flakes outside window can be thanks, still they are not enough." He grinned and shook his head, still incredulous at having his treasure back again. "You are asking: 'What? Dirty little skin bag with beads, what *is*?'" He turned to Custer.

"You have better English, Georgie, explain!"

"Gladly, Zhenya," Custer said. He turned to Becky and Liam: "If you'd been the Russian who found it on the battlefield at *Bol'shoi Rog*—that's the same as we used to call the Little Bighorn before Jackson sold it—and you'd of opened the bag up to have a look inside you'd be scratching your head.

'Well, if that don't beat all,' you'd say, 'then I ain't a white man!' Because there's nothing in there to speak of but all kinds of little odds and ends like seeds and arrowheads and snake rattles and suchlike, each one wrapped up all special in its own little pouch. But every single one of them has a story behind it that means something in this man's life as big as the Gospel is to any Baptist. And if you add on to that the fact that he was keeping it not just for himself but for his tribe, you'll have some idea why it was such a hurtful loss."

Becky leaned forward intently. "But it has a special importance *now*, sir, I sense that clearly. Can you tell me why?"

Custer looked towards Crazy Horse who nodded and picked up the thread: "You know what is Ghost Dance?"

Becky nodded slowly—"A very old ritual among many tribes in many places, one at which whites have never been welcome."

"*Sushchaia pravda!*" Crazy Horse agreed. "So, I need this bundle to make dance for Oglala as others already dance for their tribes. So that one day, ghosts and living will be together, Great Spirit will come, earth will be new again and white man will go away."

He waved his hand helplessly and turned to Custer.

"I'll do my best," Custer said, "just stop me if I get it wrong." He looked up at the ceiling for a moment, marshalling his thoughts, then shrugged and plunged in. "Crazy Horse saved my life, you know? I had more arrows in me than a pincushion has pins, and I was leaking blood like a sieve. He tells me he saw something that made him know I had to be saved and somehow he *did* it, what we would call magic, I reckon." Custer shook his head, remembering. "There'll be white men say I'm a dirty traitor, taking up with Indians, but I have to tell you it's the first time I've felt at home. And I've learned this much—the Indians, the People as they call themselves, can talk to the world around them like you talk to your mama or your pa and the world will *answer* them. Crazy Horse showed me how to begin, how to talk in baby talk, and after that I learned more on my own. And I know now that all the dancing and praying for the land to belong to the People again are being answered by the Great Spirit—that's what the snow and the wolves are about, and the big bugs and animals and plenty more that's to come yet, as the Great Spirit wills it. Just think about it for a minute: one fine day the white man just strolls in here where the People are living in harmony with Nature and the Great Spirit and he tears everything up by the roots and destroys anything they can't use. If you don't happen to like it, *bang!*, just like having a gang of outlaws come into your house and burn it down and set fire to your crops and send your family off to be slaves in some place you never heard of and all the rest of it."

Custer grinned ironically and spread his hands. "Why, shucks, I'd say the People are being mighty forebearing just making life uncomfortable for the white man. Now if you left it up to me, there's a big, unregenerate chunk of that old white George Armstrong Custer that would say: 'Hey, enough jokes, let's just kill 'em all!'" Custer shrugged: "So far, getting the white man to understand all this is like trying to explain something to a drunk in the middle of a windstorm, but we'll keep at it till we start getting through to them."

"All that sure enough sounds like magic to me," said Liam doubtfully.

Custer smiled. "It's not magic like you telling that bottle of brandy there to get up and float over here and pour you another drink and it does it, that's *against* Nature, and that's what us white men are always trying to bring off. So say I'm your regular white man studying on that bottle of brandy and it won't come over here on its own, what I do is I keep brooding over it and worrying at it and and plotting about it and the first thing you know I'm building me a steam man to pick the bottle up and bring it over and pour me a drink. You get what I mean?"

Liam burst out laughing. "Some," he said. "Only I don't have any problem getting up and grabbing the bottle myself."

He suited the action to the word, then took a thoughtful sip and grinned: "Of course, the Brits never have thought us Irish *are* white men."

Grinning, Crazy Horse got to his feet, put his arms around Liam and gave him a bear hug. "*Bratushka*, little brother!" he chuckled, "come with, I show you and Miss Fox your rooms. Tomorrow will be busy day!"

○━┳

The next morning bright and early, the four of them were seated around the dining table drinking coffee and putting away a big breakfast of eggs and fried potatoes and ham while snow flurries continued to fall outside. Becky was speaking:

"It seems to me that our best bet would be split up into two groups and divide our tasks. Mr. McCool must be in New York again no later than July 3rd, and today is already the 1st. Not only that, everything points to Stanton using the patriotic hoopla of the Fourth of July as a screen to cover his declaration of war against Little Russia. So first we must discover anything we can that puts a spoke in the wheel of Stanton's plans, at the same time as we're trying to get answers to the three questions Mr. McCool was charged with: (1) Where is Pilkington's spy, Lt. Col. Chuikov, and what information does he have for us, (2) What is the war-readiness of the Little Russian Aerial Navy, and (3) Is it true that pitchblende has been found in the lands of the Apache, and if so, where?"

Crazy Horse snorted irritably. "Three is easy. Yes, Russians have found in Chiricahua Mountains of Arizona *Guberniia*, already Apache slaves dig this filth, die from it. The People *will* free them, I swear this, and sure, Stanton can have if he comes, wears loincloth like Apache, digs with pick and shovel." He grinned wolfishly: "All he can take home such way, he can have, free gift from the People. But why? What *good*?"

"I expect that's all happened since you left Russia and came out here to the sticks," Liam said. "The Brits have a scientist that can take pitchblende and turn it into something called calorium, and just a pinch of that will run a steam engine forever and amen. And that's nice for the Brits because between their colony in Saskatchewan and their protectorate in the Congo they own just about all the pitchblende there is—" he gave Crazy Horse a wry smile, "—except for those mines in Arizona."

Crazy Horse nodded thoughtfully. "So. Very simple picture for Stanton. Buy calorium scientist, steal mines from Russians and Apaches, kick Brits downstairs."

Liam grinned. "Pretty much."

"*Kakoi svoloch!*" He shook his head disgustedly and turned to Becky: "I may speak Russian?"

"Of course," Becky said, "and I couldn't agree more, Stanton is a monumental swine."

"Ah, what a relief," Crazy Horse smiled, continuing in Russian,"for me speaking English is like running on one leg. Here's what I want to know: how can Stanton get away with all this? Why doesn't your President Lincoln put him in irons? Why don't your Congressmen impeach him?"

Liam looked towards Becky with a mute question and she nodded. "Believe it or not, we just succeeded in freeing Lincoln from a prison Stanton put him in and getting him to a safe place. The man you and the rest of the world have believed to be Lincoln is actually John Wilkes Booth, the man who tried to murder him. Instead, he now impersonates Lincoln on command, like a marionette with Stanton pulling his strings."

Both Crazy Horse and Custer looked stunned. After a moment Custer spoke:

"I've known Eddie Stanton since he took over the War Department and he is without a doubt the meanest, cruelest and coldest-hearted son of a bitch . . . ah, pardon me Miss Fox . . ."

Becky shook her head: "Who could protest such perfect taxonomical precision, General? Please continue."

"Well, then, I'll have to tell you, Zhenya, that your question about Congress is miles wide of the mark in two directions. Going one way, every man Jack of those miserable pettifoggers is crookeder'n a dog's hind leg, and the thought of them rising up in indignation against Stanton's crimes is enough to reduce a cast-iron hitching post to hysterical laughter. And looked at the other way, even if every one of those scoundrels experienced a sudden, Damascene conversion and started railing against Stanton like St. Paul, Eddie loves himself with a passion so pure and perfect that it would all go right over his head."

"Well, then," said Crazy Horse grimly, "since it looks like the People will be in his gunsights sooner or later, I have to ask Liam and Miss Fox what they're planning to *do* about him."

"That's Miss Fox's department," Liam said with a small smile, "I'm just the muscle."

Becky raised her eyebrows at him and then turned to Crazy Horse: "I certainly won't pretend it's going to be easy," she said. "Over the last few years, he has expanded his Department of Public Safety so relentlessly that there isn't a townlet in the U.S. too small to have its complement of DPS 'Eyes.' These are people from a variety of rough backgrounds whose entire raison d'être is to serve Secretary Stanton without question, since he has given them equally unquestioned power over the rest of their fellow citizens."

Crazy Horse shook his head, appalled. "Where is your famous freedom? Your democracy? The People are used to being treated like that by white men, but it's hard to believe that white men will accept it."

"Stanton has spent fifteen years—since the beginning of the Civil War—frightening Americans with ogres under the bed—now all he has to do is say 'Boo!' and everybody starts weeping and rending their garments. That means our first task is to expose his scarecrows as frauds and keep on doing it until people begin to wake up and see the truth on their own.

And that's why it's so important to us to expose Little Russia's 'war preparations' as an empty threat."

"That's a good start," Custer said, "and if I may advise you as an old cavalry hand I believe you need to go after an enemy as powerful as Eddie Stanton the way the Sioux go after the white man—hit and run, hit and run, keep nibbling away at the edges until you make him so wild he does something infernally stupid and lets you roll him up like a saddle blanket."

"I like the sound of that," grinned Liam, "that's the way my boys and I like to operate."

"Which reminds me," Custer said, "we need to address your questions about Chuikov and the Aerial Navy. Question number one sounds to me like it's for you and Crazy Horse. It'll take speaking good Russian and walking around Army headquarters like you own the place, which you fellows ought to have just about enough brass-bound gall to do handsome at. Number two," he turned to Becky with a smile, "should suit you and me just fine, being more a matter for brains and brilliant Thespian talent. I've heard you're a regular old trouper when you're on the trail of a story. How would you like to play a nice, meek Mennonite sister, come to spread the Good Word and hand out tracts while I preach and thump the Bible?"

"Say, General," laughed Liam, "if you can get Miss Fox to be meek, I'll believe every word I ever read about you being a great leader."

Becky gave Liam a prim look and folded her hands in her lap: "Goodness gracious, Brother McCool, surely it's an *awful* sin for a man to be so pig-headedly certain he knows just what a lady's thinking!"

Was there some kind of undertone there? Liam peered hard at Becky's little Mona Lisa smile, trying to divine what was going on behind it. After a moment he gave up—it would probably be a lot easier figuring out how to find Lt. Col. Chuikov, no matter where he was.

Chapter Twenty-Four

iam and Crazy Horse were strolling along the *Mississipskii Prospekt*, (what had been—"before Jackson"—Hennepin Avenue), Crazy Horse in the full regalia of a Captain in His Majesty's Imperial Little Russian Hussars, Liam in what he considered a pretty spiffy turnout as a Lieutenant in His Imperial Majesty's Own Preobrazhensky Guards. The snow had stopped and the sun was sparkling on the low rooftops of the 1850's—vintage architecture and the gilded onion domes of Little Petersburg's famed three hundred cathedrals.

"Pretty, isn't it?" Crazy Horse said in Russian (no English would be allowed till they got back to the privacy of his rooms). "St. Petersburg is even prettier—older and grander, anyway, and in some ways I'm glad I've seen both. But to be honest there are times when it feels like a curse to have seen either—that's when I'm missing my young self and feeling homesick for the sight of a dozen tipis on a cold morning like this with the smoke rising from their fires and warriors feeding their horses."

He smiled and shook his head. "At least the Russians haven't managed to do much with their American lands. New Petersburg is the only real city in Little Russia and you can see what it amounts to. As for the other cities that had started to grow up on this side of the Mississippi, they're still pretty much as they were when Jackson sold them forty years ago. To be honest, it's the Americans I worry about—with their machines and their passion for changing everything they touch it wouldn't take them long to destroy our world and make the People orphans."

"I expect Stanton would like to do just that," Liam agreed. "He talks a lot about America's Manifest Destiny, which seems to mean that God wants us to push on all the way to the Pacific and kick out anybody that gets in our way."

Crazy Horse nodded grimly. "I just hope Miss Fox's articles will make Queen Victoria and the Tsar and the Kaiser rattle their swords loudly enough to force Stanton to back down this time. Even six more months of peace will give the People the chance we need to be ready."

They walked on for a while in silence, Liam kicking chunks of ice and watching them skate down the sparsely populated street, Crazy Horse with his chin sunk on his chest, lost in thought. Finally Liam got tired of the silence:

"Well, Zhenya," he said, "I have two personal questions to which my nosiness absolutely insists on answers."

"Please," invited Crazy Horse, shaking off his morose mood.

"Very well, then, how does a gentleman whose birth name was Cha-O-Ha end up with a nickname like Zhenya?"

Crazy Horse gave him a sly smile. "Probably the same way an Irishman whose father's birth name was Francis Leonard McCool ended up with the nickname Lyovushka."

Liam raised his hands in surrender: "*Touché*. My best friend back home is a Russian named Misha. He couldn't get anywhere with 'Liam' in Russian and he got tired of calling me 'Leonardo Frentsisovich.' So he just took the 'Leonardo' and jumped up and down on it a little and came up with Lyovushka."

"Ah. Well, my secret is much more embarrassing. In my student years in Petersburg I was a slavish imitator of Pushkin's moody romantic hero Evgenii Onegin, even to the seductions and fighting a duel with my foster father." He sighed and spread his hands: "Evgenii, *ergo* Zhenya."

Liam grinned. "I won't tell if you won't. But that brings up my other question, and it's a serious one—how is that you, with all your history as a Sioux warrior, are here right in the middle of New Petersburg walking around in a Russian uniform while your foster father isn't more than half a mile from here, running the Little Russian section of the Tsar's secret police? That's crazy enough, and the *Okhrana* are frightening enough, to have me a little worried."

"Let me set your mind at rest, then. After Bol'shoi Rog I began to re-think the problem of the Little Russians. In European terms they're incredibly backwards—I don't think the entire Empire from St. Petersburg to New Petersburg has more than half a dozen modern factories, and you can see by looking around you that Little Russia won't actually get as far as 1877 until the rest of the world is making daily trips to the moon. On the other hand, Russians fight like devils, and the Empire is rich enough to buy them all the armaments they need, which will be very bad for the People if it goes on much longer. So I realized our first need was to study their weak points close up, and my assistance on that question came from one of the white man's greatest weaknesses."

"Greed?"

Crazy Horse laughed. "The only thing the People have that the white man wants is our homeland, and we can't let him have that. No, what I was thinking of is *vanity*. The white man can't believe that a poor benighted Indian would throw away the chance to be like a white man if only he could, so even though my foster father had sworn to kill me if he ever saw me again, when I sent him a message saying that I had repented my ways, that I missed Russian life and culture unbearably and wanted more than anything for him to forgive me and let me come back, he welcomed me with open arms." He smiled wryly and spread his hands. "Grand Duke Oleg Rodionovich Sheremetev is one of the wickedest men on the face of this planet, but in some ways he's so naive I can't help feeling sorry for him."

"Do you think he can help us find Chuikov?"

"Of course! Russian industry may not have gotten beyond the Middle Ages, but their secret police are the finest in the world. So before we drop in on Oleg Rodionovich you'll have to let me tell you about the years you and I spent as boon companions at the Imperial University in St. Petersburg— that way you'll have convincing answers for his inevitable questions . . ."

⊙━

At that same moment, the two kingpins of America's secret police were enjoying the mellow spring breezes wafting through the open windows of Stanton's office as they lunched at a small table set for them by Stanton's freedman valet Pompey. Willie Pilkington was resting his pudgy nose on the rim of a crystal goblet half full of Château Mouton Rothschild '65 and smiling beatifically as he inhaled the aroma.

"I must say, sir," he said with a depth of feeling he reserved solely for food and drink, "this claret is absolutely the most exquisite wine I've ever tasted. I must compliment you on your choice."

Stanton gave Willie a tolerant smile, making it clear by his nonchalance that while he appreciated fine things, at heart he was above mere sensuality.

"Willie, my boy," Stanton said, "I have to say I'm a bit disappointed in you."

Jolted, Pilkington almost poured the last gulp of wine down his starched shirtfront. Instantly, his eyes took on that hunted, flicking-from-side-to-side look that told Stanton his subordinate would gladly jump out the window if ordered to.

Excellent. Stanton wanted to be sure that what he said was engraved on the very top of Willie Pilkington's memory.

"Sir?" Pilkington asked with just the hint of a quaver.

"You know perfectly well what I mean, Willie." Stanton said. He gestured out the window towards the Mall. "It's been a good forty-eight hours since that treacherous, villainous sneak attack behind the Smithsonian Building. Do you have the culprits in hand? Indeed, are you so much as an *inch* closer to discovering who they might have been? Here we are, beyond doubt the two most powerful men in the United States of America, and it was only because those two idiots I had sent there earlier to guard Lincoln woke up first and managed to free us that we were spared being made laughing-stocks! I want you to understand, Willie, that as soon as I declare a National State of Emergency I mean to restore public hangings . . ."

"Really, sir?" Willie asked tremulously. "I mean, every other country in the civilized world has ended public hangings and if we . . ."

"I was just speaking with Frank Gowen on the voice-wire," interrupted Stanton. "He made a great point of letting me know that the hanging of the ten Molly Magees in Potts-ville has had a most salutary effect on unrest in the coalfields, and *that* was with the hangings viewed only by the elite of local society. Believe me, if we hang villains like those who attacked us and make a *public spectacle* of it, right out in the middle of the Mall for all the word to see, it will send a message that no seditionist can possibly misunderstand." He paused porten-tously and laid his hand on Willie's arm: "So for Heaven's sake, boy, *find* them for me and stop wasting time!"

Pilkington's face darkened angrily as he remembered the agony of waking up in his whisky-soaked Long Johns with his Derby crammed down over his eyes.

"I tell you, sir," he growled furiously, "it was that filthy Mick jailbird McCool who was behind it, I have no proof but

I'm just as sure as God made little green apples—I believe that low scum is behind more villainy than any man alive in the U.S. today!

Stanton pounded on the table, rattling their silverware: "Well damn it all, then, Willie, what are you going to *do* about it?"

Willie set his jaw firmly and looked as resolute as a pudgy, cowardly, boyish-looking man could manage: "If you will let me use your personal terminal, sir, I will send an official telegram to my friend at the New Petersburg office of the Okhrana, Grand Duke Sheremetev, and request his fullest possible assistance. And I'll make sure to include a complete description of McCool, so that there can be no mistake about who he is. Then, if I have your further approval, I will send copies of the circulars we printed the other night to every major city in the United States and especially to all the Mississippi River crossings, to make sure that they are aware of the possible presence of this criminal—in fact, we will offer a reward for his capture, dead or alive. A thousand dollars in gold?" Stanton nodded approvingly and Willie concluded with a catch of emotion that Moody and Sankey would have applauded: "I swear to you, sir, we will capture him and make him pay the *full price* for his villainy."

Stanton stood up and as Willie followed his lead, he put his arm around the younger man's shoulders and steered him over to the window, thinking that Pygmalion had probably felt very much like this when he had created the perfect helpmeet and brought her to life.

"Willie, my boy," he said, gesturing out the window towards the Mall and its buildings and monuments, "that's *our* America out there, ours to re-build and perfect, to raise to moral and material standards above anything dreamt of by the Founding Fathers. I won't last forever, much as I might like to, and I want to be sure when I go that I am turning over the reins to someone I can trust as fully as I would myself. You're still young and unseasoned, but already you're a magnificent adjutant."

He laid his right hand on Willie's shoulder and fixed him hypnotically with what he liked to think of as his "all-seeing eye."

"That's why I gave you the post in New York," Stanton continued, "a job which is second only to my own in national importance. That's why I've poured every dollar I could milk out of my Department's budget and every scientific and architectural resource I could muster into re-working that building on Union Square into a fitting home for America's first true political police—the Department of Public Safety that I expect you to lead to heights beyond anything dreamt of in the halls of the *Okhrana* or the *Deuxième Bureau*. Behind that drab, familiar, old–New York exterior my workmen have turned your headquarters into an armored fortress, with every refinement of modern electrical and mechanical science that Secretary Tesla has been able to devise, some of them totally exclusive to the Department of Public Safety HQ on Union Square."

Stanton beamed at Willie with the indulgent smile of a proud papa springing his best birthday treat:

"And finally, I'm told that the Spanish Inquisitors you requested from Madrid arrived in New York this morning and will be ready for service at your headquarters no later than the Fourth of July. Taken together, these are truly superlative tools for any forward-looking public safety officer to have at his disposal, and I trust and believe that you will use them to make our country a happier and more secure place."

He clapped Willie on the back and beamed at him: "My personal telegraph terminal is at your disposal, my boy, go use it in good health . . . and say hello to Grand Duke Sheremetev for me!"

Willie grabbed Stanton's hand and squeezed it fervently. "Thank you, sir," he said with a hint of tears in his eyes. "I promise I shall justify your faith in me!"

He hastened away to the telegraph room, almost at a run, as Stanton poured himself the rest of the Château Mouton Rothschild and sipped it with undisguised appreciation. A good day, he thought with a satisfied smile, a very good day indeed!

Chapter Twenty-Five

N o thank you, Miss, I'm Orthodox."

The young man—a plump, rosy-cheeked Flügel-Lieutenant in Little Russia's Aerial Navy—tipped his sky-blue and gold-braided uniform cap to Becky and dropped a silver ten-kopek piece into her collection box. She shook the box ruefully, listening to the thin rattle of a dozen or so small coins as the Russian officer strolled away.

"You were right about one thing, General . . ."

"Pastor Karl, please," Custer said with a smile. They were both speaking German, a language Becky had perfected as *Harper's* correspondent during the Franco-Prussian War and Custer had learned from his family.

"Sorry. In any event, Karl, you were right about them not bothering us as Plain Folk, but I'm afraid it's put a bit of a cramp in my *femme fatale* style as well."

Custer himself was dressed completely in sober black, including a flat-brimmed black hat and a long black overcoat that reached to the tops of his boots, while Becky was dressed almost identically except for the addition of a black poke bonnet which covered her auburn hair and threw a shadow over a face that could have launched a thousand airships if only the Russian aeronauts had been able to see it.

"I'm sure that has more than a little to do with our lackluster audience," he said with a worried frown, "but I have a feeling there's something else going on as well. I've been here a dozen times collecting intelligence as 'Pastor Karl,' and all the lads know me and stop for a chat in broken German or English or Russian. Today, though, they're all suddenly Orthodox, and they look distracted, like something troubling is on their minds."

"Look at their airfield," he continued, gesturing at the vast, snowy plain on the other side of the tall wrought-iron fence that extended for a mile in either direction from the sentry gate outside which Custer had built their small keeping-warm fire, a brazier-full of charcoal. "These Russians have no more notion of military security than a suckling pig, you can see everything they've got from here, and it consists entirely of a half-dozen barrage balloons in those sheds there, plus those two huge rigid airships over there on the west side of the field, which have been on loan from Imperial Russia since we got here and whose engines have been undergoing a refit for long enough now that American aeronauts could have built an entire squadron of new airships from the ground up. These fellows like wearing their pretty blue uniforms and drinking vodka while a gypsy orchestra keeps them amused and frankly I don't think they're in any shape to attack anything more threatening than a half-dozen stampeding buffalo. So why all the long faces? Why all the 'Orthodoxy' and bad nerves?"

As if they were bringing them an answer, a small detachment of soldiers led by an Ensign barely old enough to shave marched around the Guard House and towards the gate.

"I'm not sure I like the look of that," Becky murmured.

"Nor I," answered Custer. "But we'd better just stand our ground and offer them our blessings."

A moment later the little detachment marched through the gate and up to Becky and Custer, where the Ensign abruptly sang out:

"*Squad, halt!*"

The soldiers came to a halt with much stamping of their feet and smacking their rifles. Then the young Ensign stepped forward apologetically and addressed them in good German:

"Good morning, Pastor Karl, Miss. I'm sorry to have to trouble you, but I'm afraid I must ask you to accompany me to the Guard House for an interview with the adjutant."

"What, really?" asked Custer with mild indignation. "You fellows know me, you've stopped and chatted with me time and time again!"

"Once more, sir," the Ensign said, reddening with embarrassment, "I really do apologize, but I must ask you to come with me. And Miss, if I may, I'd like to ask you to bring your leaflets, the Adjustant asked to see them most particularly."

Becky and Custer exchanged a quick glance, then Custer picked up the stack of tracts and held out his arm for Becky to take hold of. A moment later, surrounded by Russian aeronauts, they were marching anxiously towards the Guard House.

0—┱

Crazy Horse stopped to light a long, dark brown Russian cigarette, and gestured towards the colonnaded building ahead of them:

"You see the number 16 chiseled into the stone there?"

"With all that gold leaf you couldn't really miss it," Liam said, a little puzzled.

"Well, believe it or not, my foster father actually had this whole stretch of the Boulevard renamed 'Fontanka' so that the address of this building could be 'Fontanka 16.'"

"Good Lord," Liam muttered. He got it now, that address—Fontanka 16—was the one that belonged to *Okhrana*

HQ in St. Petersburg, possibly the most feared street address throughout the Russian Empire.

"Mmm hm," Crazy Horse said, puffing on his *papirosa.* "I thought you'd like that. You see all the soldiers and plainclothes agents streaming in and out? I must tell you that this is a very strange and not very welcome sight. On a normal day you might see a half-dozen or so men going and coming. Taking this in connection with the rumors I've been hearing, I'm starting to get a bit of a *frisson.*"

"What rumors?" Liam was starting to feel the same *frisson* himself.

"Do you know anything about the Viceroy of Little Russia?

Liam grinned a little sheepishly and shrugged. "To tell the truth I've never cared a hoot about Little Russia. Now every time I turn around it seems to be jumping out of the shadows going *'Boo!'*"

"Well, as it happens our revered leader is none other then Aleksandr Aleksandrovich, the Tsar's eldest son. The old Tsar isn't so bad, you probably remember he set Russia's serfs free before Lincoln freed the blacks. True, the Industrial Party finally pressured him into *un*-freeing the serfs a couple of years ago so Russia could compete with the English factory owners and their factory serfs." Crazy Horse smiled mirthlessly. "Still, His Imperial Majesty *did* say he regretted enormously having to do it."

"Zhenya, please—the *rumors* . . ." Liam said with a touch of impatience.

"Right, sorry. Well our Viceroy doesn't even have his father's tender heart, as far as he's concerned Indians aren't any more human than horses or hunting dogs, so one might as well put them to work. He's a huge man, the size of a bear— they say he can bend horseshoes with his bare hands. And his brains are about what you'd expect from a big, sullen bear. He likes to play the trombone, sits alone in the palace tootling on the thing while he leaves running Little Russia to my foster father. And as concerns my foster father . . ." Crazy Horse shrugged. "Well, why don't I just introduce you to him, then you'll see why the rumors say that Populist terrorists from St. Petersburg are planning to blow him up quite soon, along with the Viceroy himself and all their little helpers."

"What terrorists? You mean Land and Freedom? The ones who assassinated the Chief of the Imperial Gendarmes?"

"The very same," said Crazy Horse. "*Now* of course the police and the Gendarmes and the Okhrana back in Russia are madly arresting anything that breathes in order to make up for the blunder of letting poor old General Mezentsov get stabbed to death in the streets of St. Petersburg, with the result that members of Land and Freedom are escaping and popping up here and there all over the world ready for more mischief."

He tossed the *papirosa* onto the pavement, ground it out under his heel and clapped Liam on the back:

"But I shouldn't think they've reached this backwater yet, Lev Frentsisovich, so let's go beard Papa in his den and see if we can find out about your missing Chuikov."

As Grand Duke Sheremetev's aide-de-camp held the door open for Crazy Horse and Liam, Little Russia's éminence *grise* got up from his desk and came around it to greet them. Liam wasn't sure just what he had been expecting, but almost certainly not the small, fussy, tired-looking gray-haired man who embraced Crazy Horse with the traditional kiss on both cheeks and smiled wanly as he held out his hand to Liam:

"Oleg Rodionovich Sheremetev, at your service, sir."

"Very kind of you to receive us, Excellency." Liam bowed slightly, hoping that was the right move.

"This is one of my dearest old school chums, Papa," Crazy Horse said, "Lev Frentsisovich Mikulin."

This time Sheremetev bowed: "I am honored to meet any friend of my son's," he said with surprising warmth. "I know I must seem a dusty old bore, a bit like one of Turgenev's *Fathers*, I expect, but I believe even a foster parent must care for every aspect of a son's well-being whether it be how well he eats or what sort of company he keeps."

Liam—who had been expecting an Inquisitor out of Poe's "The Pit and the Pendulum"—was a bit taken aback by this careworn paterfamilias.

"Ah . . . I think that's highly commendable, Excellency, I'm sure Zhenya is most appreciative." This last with a sly glance at Crazy Horse, who answered with a steely glare. "Yes, well," Sheremetev said fussily, "of course the boy gets a bit restive from time to time, but that's to be expected. I'm sure you experience much the same sort of scrutiny from your father, Lev Fretsisovich, back home in . . . let me see, shall I try to guess?"

Liam grinned a little weakly, in spite of himself feeling the hair stand up on the backs of his arms. One thing at least was clear, the old boy wasn't fooled for a moment into thinking that Liam was the son of some landowner in the countryside around St. Petersburg. What had been his mistake? Was he going to finish this whole crazy Little Russian adventure in front of a firing squad out behind 16 Fontanka? He darted a glance at Crazy Horse, but his companion's face betrayed nothing.

Sheremetev took the pair of pince-nez that hung around his neck on a black silk ribbon and settled them on his nose, scrutinizing Liam the way a lepidopterist examines a rare moth before sticking a pin through it. He chuckled slyly, making Liam wonder just what form getting transfixed with a pin was going to take: getting run through with a *yataghan* taken off some dead Turk during Russia's southern war?

"Come now," Shermetev said cheerfully, "you wouldn't deny an old man the practice of his favorite hobby, would you?"

Liam shook his head queasily, wondering if Sheremetev was one of those torturers who had to play with their captives first, like a cat with a mouse. "Of course not, Excellency," he said, alarmed to find that his throat had dried enough to make him hoarse.

"I thought not," said the Okhrana chief with a smile. "As it happens, I am rather accomplished as a dialectologist, I've even written various papers on the subject for the Philological Faculty at the Imperial University."

He steepled his fingers in front of his nose and pursed his lips judiciously. "Let us see now . . ." His eyes twinkled behind the pince-nez—clearly a man about to indulge in a favorite hobby. "*Khersonskaia Guberniia*, am I right? Perhaps I might even hazard a guess at . . . the city of Odessa?"

A wave of almost giddy relief swept over Liam as he tried to smile and look impressed. He had been tutored endlessly in Russian by every member of Mike's huge family, which had escaped to New York from an internecine gang war in Odessa's underworld. The Vysotskys—originally Polish—had felt right at home in that vast criminal melting pot, peopled by Ukrainians, Russians, Chechens, Jews, Armenians, Greeks, Turks, Arabs, Serbians and a motley of other peoples whose languages had all left their traces on the speech of Odessa.

"You have a very keen ear, Excellency," Liam said. "My father is indeed a banker in Odessa,"—which was only a slight exaggeration, Mike's father had been a renowned bank robber—"and I must admit I know Deribasovskaia Street better than I know the Nevskii Prospekt."

"Splendid, splendid, we shall make you just as comfortable on the Mississipskii Prospekt. Do come and sit down, let us smoke a cigar."

He gestured to a collection of comfortable-looking chairs around a low, circular table with decanters, glasses, and a large cedar humidor covered in malachite and amber which turned out to contain everything from thin Dutch cheroots dipped in powdered sugar to short, fragrant Havana Punches. After a few moments, when everybody had taken a drink and a cigar, they were interrupted by a timid knock at the door.

"Yes, yes," snapped Sheremetev, "I'm busy! What is it?"

The door opened slightly to admit just a sliver of Sheremetev's aide-de-camp, who was obviously trying to present as small a target as possible for his master's wrath. He waved a couple of pages of telegraph forms and said with an odd mixture of timidity and insistence:

"I pray you will forgive me, Excellency, but you've just had an urgent telegram from the American Public Safety chief, Pilkington."

Now Liam's blood did run cold and it was all he could do to imitate Crazy Horse's impassivity without breaking into a muck sweat. Fortunately, the young officer seemed to have pushed his chief's patience too far:

"Damn it, man!" shouted Sheremetev. "How many times do I have to tell you not to interrupt me with rubbish? I don't don't care how urgent that fool in New York may think his problem is, I *will . . . not . . . be . . . interrupted* when I have guests, do you understand me?"

The aide-de-camp's face turned a bright red and it seemed to Liam that he threw a brief, resentful look in his direction. However, the officer was too cautious to push it any further.

"Yes sir, of course, sir!" he gulped. "I'll come back later." The door closed and Liam started breathing again.

Prince Sheremetev resumed, his urbanity firmly back in place: "Now then, Lev Frentsisovich, how can I be of service to you?"

"I hate to trouble such a busy man with something so trivial," Liam said, "but I'm looking for an old friend from *gymnazium* days who I had heard was serving here as a cavalry officer—Vasilii Ilarionovich Chuikov."

Prince Sheremetev's face fell: "Oh, dear!" Obviously upset, he considered for a moment and then reached out and laid his hand on Liam's arm: "I very much regret to be the bearer of such bad news," he said, "but there's no point beating around the bush—I'm afraid Col. Chuikov was arrested, tried by a military court and executed as a spy some months ago."

Liam didn't have to put on an act to look dumfounded: his mind was racing as he tried to figure out how this would affect his agreement with Pilkington and the fate of his grandmother. Crazy Horse, seeing how badly rocked Liam was, took up the thread:

"I hadn't heard about it, Papa. May I ask who he was spying for?"

"Of course, Zhenya, I have no secrets from you. He was given up to us by the U.S. intelligence people, who had identified him as an agent of the St. Petersburg terrorist group Land and Freedom during a visit he made to New York." He spread his hands and produced his wan smile: "I have a sort of fraternal agreement with the head of their Department of Public Safety, Colonel Willard Pilkington, and we help each other out from time to time."

He made a face: "Of course that means I have to appear to take his hysterical telegrams seriously when I'm in the mood for it."

"*Colonel* Pilkington," said Liam hollowly.

"That's right," said Prince Sheremetev, "I believe he distinguished himself in the American Civil War, at Little Round Top."

"Little Round Top," Liam said in a slightly strangled tone.

"I'm sorry to have had to upset you so, Lev Frentsisovich," Prince Sheremetev said, "if there's anything at all that I can . . ."

He was interrupted by a brisk knock at the door, followed without the customary wait by the eerie re-appearance of the aide-de-camp, or rather his head, which seemed—as he stuck it into the room—to be suspended in mid-air halfway down the edge of the door. This time he seemed quite sure of himself:

"My profound apologies for interrupting again, Excellency, but it's a bit of an emergency. Just a while earlier we had a telegram from St. Petersurg saying that interrogation of a member of Land and Freedom has revealed that their leader, the terrorist Georgii Plekhanov, left Russia over a week ago bound for New Petersburg. In other words, Excllency, he could appear here at any moment, so all of the appropriate security establishments have been notified. Less than an hour ago we apprehended two foreign spies at the Naval Aerodrome—a Pastor Karl, and a Sister Isolde. They're outside now, under guard, if you would care to accompany them to the interrogation chambers?"

Liam had started sweating in earnest at this last piece of news, but fortunately Sheremetev missed Liam's expression as he turned to Crazy Horse with a mixture of affection and exasperation:

"By Jove, Zhenya, I *told* you you shouldn't be keeping company with that sausage-eating bible-thumper! If you're in the grip of some overwhelming religious enthusiasm, for goodness' sake let me find you a decent Orthodox monk to chat with!"

He sighed, clearly a man shouldering burdens almost too numerous to bear. "I hope you will excuse me, gentlemen," he continued, getting to his feet, "but duty calls."

Giving them a little half-bow, he turned and headed for the door, which opened wider to reveal the aide-de-camp—and just beyond him, in the hallway, Becky and Custer, manacled together and supervised by two heavily armed Okhrana thugs. As Liam and Crazy Horse jumped to their feet, Becky and Custer looked towards them sharply, then looked down to avoid giving themselves away.

Herding the prisoners down the hall ahead of him, Sheremetev turned back for a moment towards Liam and Crazy Horse:

"Do finish your cigars and brandy, gentlemen, I'm afraid I shall be a while."

○—ᴛ

For a moment or two, Liam and Crazy Horse stood there in a daze, oblivious as sleepwalkers. Then Liam snapped out of it abruptly and turned to Crazy Horse with a desperate mutter: "What the Devil are we going to *do*? If they think Becky and Custer know something about terrorist plots, we're never going to see them again."

Crazy Horse shook his head grimly.

"I was a secret member of Land and Freedom when I was at the University," he said in a flat, quiet voice. "Plekhanov and I were friends—he was a great figure in the revolutionary underground, loved to argue about socialist theory, thought terrorism was for morons." He shook his head slowly and spat on the floor. "Then my foster father got tired of looking for Plekhanov and arrested his whole family and sent them to dig coal in Karaganda. It was January, the temperature was -20 in the daytime, and all of them—two sisters, his mother and his father—died in the mines. Now Plekhanov believes in terror."

Liam waited, sure that Crazy Horse was heading somewhere with this. After another couple of moments, the Sioux chieftain smiled sardonically. "I remember his favorite dictum after he became a convert to terror: '*There's no problem so complicated that it can't be solved by a couple of pounds of dynamite.*'"

"I don't suppose you'd happen to know where we might find some?"

"Lev Frentsisovich, what do you take me for? Of course I do, Georgie and I have been saving some up for a party!"

With that, Crazy Horse headed out the doorway and into the hall with Liam right behind him. But before they managed to get as far as the exit, Sheremetev's aide-de-camp suddenly stepped into view from the guardroom just ahead of them, calmly covering them with a revolver and holding the sheaf of telegrams in his other hand

"I'm sorry to have to detain you, gentlemen, but we really must wait a bit until the Grand Duke can find the time to read this telegram. It appears," he continued, staring hard at Liam, "that Lt. Mikulin may not be quite what he seems. Indeed, according to Colonel Pilkington, it seems that a vicious New York criminal named McCool who speaks fluent Russian is known to be headed towards us, bent on treason and violence." He gave Liam a bogus little smile of apology. "I'm afraid, Lieutenant, you'll have to explain to the Grand Duke just how it is that you came to resemble so closely the man described by Colonel Pilkington."

Seeing Liam's ominous expression, the officer thumbed back the hammer of his revolver. "I wouldn't advise that, sir, I've just been posted here after a year on the Russo-Turkish front and my nerves are not quite what they should be."

Both Liam and Crazy Horse knew serious business when they saw it and they consented glumly to being herded into the little guardroom ahead of the aide-de-camp's pistol.

"I'll take your weapons, gentlemen, and please don't be silly."

A moment later, their pistols tucked into his white dress belt, the aide-de-camp backed towards the door.

"Please make yourselves comfortable, gentlemen, I will return with the Grand Duke as soon as it becomes possible."

With that, he closed the door gently behind him and locked it from the outside.

Liam was nearly beside himself. "Of all the filthy, stupid, *rotten* luck," he ranted, "and for it to come from that lowlife dimwit *Willie*, if I live to be a thousand years old I'll never . . ."

"Be quiet!" said Crazy Horse sharply, his voice sobering Liam like a pail of freezing water on his head. Wondering if it had all just gotten to be too much for the veteran warrior, Liam watched as he sat down in the middle of the little room's floor with his legs crossed and his arms folded on his chest, his eyes closing as he began to keen something under his breath . . . was that the Sioux language? Oblivious to Liam's presence and indeed to everything around him, Crazy Horse just sat there chanting incomprehensibly in a barely audible voice, rocking back and forth so slowly that the movement was almost imperceptible . . .

As the chanting continued, Liam began to feel increasingly uncomfortable, overcome by an incipient nausea mixed with a feeling of vertigo and a persistent sense that his eyes were going out of focus. Suddenly, for one totally unhinged second the world just seemed to *stop* . . . then Crazy Horse winked out like a candle, vanishing completely. No, wait, not completely—now, on the spot where he had been sitting, there was a small, dark scorpion, its tail curling and straightening over its back as if it were flexing the thing. Then, as abruptly as it had appeared, it ran through the gap under the guard-room door and disappeared.

Liam sat down hard on the chair behind the guard's desk, shaking his head and wondering if something inside it had just blown out and left him in the grip of some sort of brain fever. More worried by that thought than anything that had happened so far, Liam laid his head down on his arms and closed his eyes. Perhaps when he opened them again it would all have gone away . . .

A brief interval passed, he had no real idea how long. Then the door was unlocked from the outside and Crazy Horse entered hastily, holding their two pistols and the sheaf of telegrams in his hand.

"*Bozhe moi!*" he said incredulously. "Are you trying to become some sort of monster of *sang froid*, sitting there napping while I run around taking care of things?"

Liam stood up, shaking his head stupidly and opening and closing his mouth like a beached fish.

"By God, you'd better explain all this to me," he said finally.

Crazy Horse just rolled his eyes, grabbed Liam by the arm and dragged him into the hall, where the aide-de-camp was lying on the floor with his hand clutching the side of his neck, his eyes staring into nothingness with an expression of stark terror.

"Poor man seems to be suffering from a scorpion bite," Crazy Horse said. "Come on, we're going to have to leg it."

As the two of them ran out the front door Crazy Horse whistled sharply between his teeth and immediately a *troika* jingled towards them out of the snow. Liam and Crazy Horse jumped in.

"Boris and Gleb Square!" Crazy Horse shouted to the driver. "A gold ruble if you make it in less than ten minutes!"

The driver grinned at them out of his mound of furs and *shubki*: "For a gold ruble, Your Honor, I will put you there in less than *five* minutes!"

With a crack of the whip and a din of sleigh bells, the *troika* whizzed away through the thickening snow.

Chapter Twenty-Six

'm a skinwalker, that's all," Crazy Horse said. He was busily pulling open drawers and grabbing things out of the hall closet as he stuffed a large carpetbag with his and Custer's belongings. Crazy Horse had shed the hated Russian uniform and changed into an anonymous dark suit under which he wore a Sioux warrior's hair pipe breastplate and a red bandana.

"No it's not all," Liam said warningly, "speak to me!"

"*Bozhe moi!*" Crazy Horse said, waving his hand in exasperation. "The Navajo say they began it, but I say the Oglala Lakota were first and the Navajo got it from us. Whichever it may be, it just means that one who has studied the Way can learn to take the form of an animal. I chose the scorpion because it's easy and it seemed useful right then."

"I guess," said Liam wryly. "Anyway, thanks." He scooped up Becky's notebooks and writing supplies and Maggie's pistol (which Becky had regretfully decided didn't fit her Sister Isolde identity) and dumped them into the valise along with the spare ammunition.

"Think nothing of it," Crazy Horse said with a grin. "Sometime when we aren't in a hurry maybe I'll do a grizzly bear for you."

He snapped the carpetbag shut and then gestured to Liam: "Give me a hand with this, will you?"

He had pulled a floorboard up part way, but there were still lots of nails and Liam lent his back to the effort; a moment later, with a protesting shriek of wood and nails, the board ripped loose, revealing a cache with a half-dozen small packages of grease paper–wrapped dynamite, a couple of lever-action Winchesters, and a sawed-off pump-action shotgun with a rawhide sling and a canvas bag full of shells.

"Looks like enough for a first-rate goodbye party," Liam said.

"Couldn't have put it better myself," Crazy Horse with a tight grin. "Grab a handful and let's go!"

Liam took half the dynamite and the shotgun and shells, stuffed all but the gun (which he slung inside his overcoat) into Becky's valise and was just in the process of wrapping a long strip of woolen blanket around his neck for a scarf when there was a distant but clearly gigantic explosion and all the windows facing Boris and Gleb Square imploded into the room.

Crazy Horse instantly dropped into a crouch, ready for an attack; Liam just as instantly (conditioned forever by Gettysburg) flattened himself on the floor with his arms over his head. One second, two . . . then as both men realized that was all for the moment they jumped back up and ran to the windows, through which the snow was now whirling thickly.

"That came from the direction of the Viceroy's palace," Crazy Horse said. In the distance, beyond the spires of the Boris and Gleb cathedral, they could see a thick cloud of white smoke rising through the snow, illuminated by rapidly spreading flames.

"Do you think that might have been your friend Plekhanov?" Liam asked.

"Whoever it was, they used a lot more than a couple of pounds of dynamite and I think we'd better get going while we can still move freely."

Outside, a small crowd had collected near where their *troika* stood waiting. They were babbling excitedly and pointing across the Square towards the flames and smoke.

"*There* you are, Your Honors," cried the driver. "They're saying somebody's blown up the Tsarevich!" Then, collecting himself a bit, he looked more closely at his passengers' changed appearance. "Are you still planning to go back to the Fontanka?"

Crazy Horse nodded and grinned: "Wouldn't miss it for the world!" he said. "Lyovushka?"

Liam gestured politely towards the sleigh "After you, Zhenyushka!"

A moment later the *troika* tore away at full gallop, the sleigh's runners keening with speed and throwing up a double fountain of snow behind them.

By the time their sleigh entered the Fontanka, Liam could hear steady small-arms fire in the distance, interspersed with occasional muffled booms that sounded like dynamite. Crazy Horse stood up and slapped the driver on the back:

"Hey!" he shouted, "slow down! Pull over as soon as you can!"

As they hissed to a stop at the curb, the driver turned and looked at them inquisitively. Crazy Horse looked around, saw that there was nobody within hearing distance and leaned closer to the driver:

"We'd like you to be our driver for the rest of the day— you can count on being well paid, but I want to warn you that we're about to become fugitives."

The driver grinned widely, revealing a shiny gold tooth right in the middle of his smile.

"Why, bless you, Your Honors, I haven't done anything illegal since I got up this morning and a man has to keep in practice, doesn't he?" He held out his hand and shook firmly with Crazy Horse and Liam. "Now then, where are we off to?"

Liam leaned forward: "I saw the mouth of an alleyway right across the street from Fontanka 16—if you wait for us there could you cut straight through to next street when we return and get us out of here before they manage to gather their wits?"

The driver laid a finger alongside his nose and winked.

"Let's go, then," said Crazy Horse.

This time the sleigh moved off at a sedate pace, bells jingling rhythmically, and less than a minute later they were turning the corner into the alleyway Liam had spotted earlier. About halfway down the alley, the driver pulled his rig over next to a warehouse and halted his horses as Liam and Crazy Horse climbed out, their overcoat pockets stuffed with dynamite. They walked up closer to the mouth of the alleyway and stared across the street at Okhrana HQ.

"Did your foster father ever say anything that could help us find the interrogation chambers?"

"Not in so many words," Crazy horse said, "but I know they're in the basement, and probably beyond where the back of the building is, to keep screams from bothering visitors upstairs."

Liam looked at him sharply, but Crazy Horse shrugged. "Sorry, Lyovushka, but we have to expect the worst."

Liam let out a pent-up breath and nodded. "What kind of fuse do you have on this stuff?"

"Fast. It's bundled for throwing."

"Good. I'm guessing that your foster father took most of his people with him when the Palace blew, so maybe our best bet would be to walk right up to the front door and say hello."

"For a white man," Crazy Horse said, "you're pretty smart." He took a couple of his foster father's cheroots out of his pocket, gave one to Liam and lit them both up with a Lucifer he scratched on the wall next to them. "Good for lighting fuses," he said.

"Stand by for a bit of noise," he called to the driver, "I expect we'll be back pretty quickly."

Crazy Horse and Liam strode across the street and took the steps two at a time. Liam cracked the massive front door slightly and peered inside. "Better than I expected," he said, "not a soul in sight." He took out one of his bundles of dynamite, lit the fuse from the cheeroot and then pulled the doors open and tossed the bundle in as far as he could lob it before pulling the door closed and plastering himself against the wall next to it.

"Tally ho," said Crazy Horse, stuffing his fingers in his ears. An instant later there was a huge explosion inside and the bronze front doors with their bas-relief Imperial eagles blew across the street as if they were made of cardboard.

"Good stuff," Liam said, "maybe we should keep some for later."

He pumped a shell into his shotgun's chamber and charged forward into the smoke-and-dust-filled interior where a dazed-looking *Okhrannik* sat on the floor with his jaw gaping.

"You!" Liam shouted at the man. "Quick! Show us the interrogation rooms!"

Liam could see awareness and stubborn resistance both flooding back into the man's eyes.

"You'll be in big trouble . . ." the guard said in a threatening tone.

"And you'll be *dead* if you don't get going!" Liam bellowed, raising the shotgun and firing a load of buckshot at the crystal chandelier that swayed above the rotunda. With an appalling crash the chandelier tore loose from the ceiling and smashed to the floor a few feet away. Liam jammed the barrel of the gun into the man's cheek and this time he leapt up like a gazelle.

"Yes, sir, Your Honor," he shrieked. "Follow me!"

He scurried down the ruined hallway towards a big oak door with iron straps as Liam followed and Crazy Horse covered him, moving backwards and holding one of the Winchesters at the ready.

"Down here, Your Worship," the man babbled, throwing the door open.

"Stay on the door, pick off anybody coming this way," Liam said to Crazy Horse, pushing the man ahead of him down the stairs. At the bottom they found themselves at the beginning of a long hallway crossed by another about midway to its end. From this second hallway two more *okhranniki* jumped out shouting for them to halt, but they were still raising their weapons when Liam's shotgun simply blew them down the hall like dry leaves.

"Where are the German preachers?" he shouted at his guide. The man was blubbering now, expecting that he'd be next.

"Oh, Your Radiance," he quavered, "please spare my life for the sake of my old mother and my little ones . . ."

"I swear to you," Liam gritted between his teeth, "I will tear you into little strips and make your old mother *eat* them if you don't show me the Germans at *once!*"

The man gave a demented little scream and took off down the hall at a trot with Liam close behind, finally stopping outside the last door on the left.

"They're in there, Holiness," the man stuttered, "*please spare me!*"

"OPEN THE DOOR!" Liam yelled and the man leapt to obey, almost dropping the keys in his terror. As soon as the door swung open, Liam pinched the man's neck and put him to sleep, dreading what he would see inside as he stepped across the threshhold into the darkness.

"Becky?" he said hesitantly, uncertain just where she might be. A moment later a pair of strong arms suddenly encircled him and pulled him close while an unmistakable feminine form pressed urgently against him:

"What on *earth* took you so long?" she asked, and for once Liam just forgot about words and put everything he had into what he thought of ever after as The Kiss of the Ages . . .

After what seemed like nowhere near enough time, a Lucifer flared in the darkness next to Liam and he saw Custer's grinning face, sporting a split lip and a black eye.

"I hate like the Dickens to interrupt you, Hoss," Custer said, "but I'm guessing we'd better hit the trail."

"Right!" Liam managed to get out, and—taking Becky's hand firmly with one hand and and his shotgun with the other—he led them back towards the stairs at a run.

Chapter Twenty-Seven

t was a relief to leave the town behind them, especially as the continuing obligato of gunfire and explosions made it seem likely their reception would be too warm for comfort if they were seen again. Fortunately, the driver and his horses had made this drive so often that the snow and the darkness made absolutely no difference to their progress—the sleighbells jingled merrily, the runners sang against the snow, and all four of the passengers finally managed to draw a peaceful breath.

"We've had so much fun I hate to see you go," said Custer with a laugh.

"At least you'll have the shiner to remember us by," Liam said, "where are you two bound for from here?"

"Like you we've really found out all we could from being in New Petersburg," Crazy Horse said, deciding to stick to Russian since the others understood it better than his English. "Now we're going back to join the rest of the Oglala. We need to begin our Ghost Dance, and Georgie and I need to plan a grand strategy for driving the Russians out once and for all."

"What about the other whites?" Becky asked, genuinely curious. "Is there any chance of peace between you and the U.S.?"

"I expect you know the answer as well as I do," Crazy Horse answered. "If they deal with us honestly and respect our sovereignty we will welcome peace with them."

Everybody fell silent, thinking about that. Then Custer spoke up:

"How about you two? Where are you bound for from here?"

Becky and Liam exchanged a surprised look, realizing that the question had caught them in a suspended moment, the two of them levitating on a cloud of buoyant emotions between one moment of severely practical decisions and the next. Becky smiled pensively.

"Well, I know what I am obliged to do, which is report to Mr. Clemens and the other leaders of the Freedom Party and take counsel about how we should proceed with the information we discovered here. And I'm eager to discover what they have arrived at with President Lincoln—surely his situation has been kept in the darkness for far too long, but the question will be just how to put it before the American public." She looked towards Liam with an unspoken question in her eyes.

Glad of the darkness, Liam smiled back at her and took her hand between both of his. "I can tell you fellows this much—I've barely known Miss Fox a couple of weeks, but they've been pretty busy ones and I've learned a thing or two. One of them for sure is that we'd all better put our thinking caps on and figure out how to put an end to the mess we're in before it puts an end to us."

"By the Lord Harry I'll drink to that!" said Custer.

For a few minutes they were all busy with their own thoughts, though Liam didn't let go of Becky's hand. Then at last the driver's voice broke into their reveries:

"You asked me to let you know when we were five minutes away, Your Honors," he said. He gestured towards the horizon with his whip: "You see that line of light along there? That'll be the aerodrome, on the other side of that stand of woods. There's a road through the woods and we can get pretty close that way. But then you're going to have to decide what you want to do."

Liam turned to Becky and Custer. "Do you think maybe we can steal one of those barrage balloons?"

Custer nodded. "If we stage a diversion on this side of the field it's bound to draw all the aeronauts and security troops. Then you can make your move."

"The real question," Becky said dubiously, "is whether or not we'll be better off once we go up in the thing."

Custer smiled wryly. "Supposedly these are a big improvement on the ones we used in the War. Those pretty much just tugged at the end of their guide ropes, but these have tail fins of a sort, and some rudimentary steering for flying untethered. Anyway," he added, spreading his hands, "once you're up there you won't be on Russian soil any longer."

They all fell silent again as the sleigh headed down the narrow road among the trees. It suddenly seemed terribly dark and lonely after the intermittent flashes of moonlight that broke through the clouds; here, they were enclosed in a dense tunnel and Liam involuntarily found himself thinking of that huge wolf again. He looked towards Becky and saw the flash of her teeth as she smiled:

"Mmm hm. Me too. Only this time we've got Laughing Wolf with us!"

The driver gave a low whistle and held his whip up to signal his passengers as the sleigh glided to a stop.

"Here we are, Your Honors. I'll stay with you until you decide you don't need me any more, but it wouldn't be wise to take the sleigh out into the open beyond these trees."

They all got out and crept up to the edge of the tree-line, Custer taking a pocket spyglass out of his overcoat and scanning the aerodrome.

"Well, I'll be switched!" he muttered.

"What is it?" Becky asked.

Custer pointed towards the airfield. "That wasn't there this morning when they took us away. And *they* weren't either."

He handed her the glass to forestall more questions and as she looked the others heard her draw her breath sharply. Liam could barely stand the suspense:

"Hey, Miss, no hogging the glass!"

She reluctantly handed him the little telescope and the minute he looked into it he saw what the others had been reacting to: just beyond the edge of the pool of illumination cast by one of the scattered calcium arc lights there hunched an enormous, baleful triangular wedge, painted a flat black that seemed to eat the light:

"Holy Hannah!" Liam muttered. "That's the biggest Black Delta I ever saw in my life."

Becky looked apprehensive. "There was a rumor Stanton had commissioned a battleship Delta," she said, "but we all thought it was the usual Department of Public Safety propaganda. And take a closer look at the men at the gate, Liam."

Liam swung the scope across the field towards the gate and gasped as he saw what she had meant: there, unconcernedly chatting about something or other, was "Boyo" Boylan—on a crutch, thanks to Liam's work in the gas company tunnel— and a couple of his lads.

"I don't believe it," he said, and handed the glass to Crazy Horse, who looked at the men first.

"You know them?" he asked Liam and Becky.

"*Oh*, yes," they chorused.

"In fact it was me that put that bird there on a crutch," Liam said to Crazy Horse, "and I'm just wondering whether it was actually your friend Plekhanov who blew up the Palace or if it was those lads there."

"And if Boylan and his people are the ones who dyna-mited the Palace," Becky added, "that means the mysterious

Lukas will be somewhere in the wings waiting for his cue. Though just how he'll receive it with only Government wires between here and the U.S., I don't know—I suppose they're planning some sort of insurrection and they'll signal him once they succeed and take over the telegraph."

Crazy Horse looked startled. "*Lukas?*" he said. "From what I've heard here and among my old comrades in Land and Freedom, 'Lukas' is simply a *nom de guerre* for the Tsar's morganatic son Nikolai Aleksandrovich. Those who know him say he hates our beloved Viceroy beyond all the ordinary bounds of virulence."

They chewed on that for a minute before Liam broke in: "I'll tell you this much—if Lukas is aiming to come to Little Petersburg and head up a new Government there's no guessing how bad things can get. I've gone up against him and I'm not in a hurry to do it again. In fact, I'm not sure he thinks of any of us as being more interesting than the mice a scientist studies in his lab. We'd better get to New York as fast as we can and stop him before he goes any farther." He paused for a moment, then hit the punch line: "How fast do you think that monster over there will fly?"

"You're crazy, McCool," Custer blurted out. "You press the wrong button on a contraption like that and you're going to end up on the moon!"

But Becky was already thinking: "Hmmm," she said. "Any reason why our diversionary action shouldn't work just as well with that Delta as it would with a barrage balloon?"

There was a pause as Crazy Horse and Custer looked at each other and then shrugged. Crazy Horse turned to Becky:

"We'll give you five minutes to get as close to the gate as you can, crawling on your stomachs. Then when you're in position we'll throw the first bundle of dynamite, and from there on . . ." he spread his hands and smiled thinly. "It will be in the hands of the Great Spirit."

Custer was peering through his spyglass again. "By Jupiter," he said, "I think that big building over there by the barracks is what they were calling the hydrogen reservoir."

"That ought to ginger them up," Liam said with a grin. He took Custer's hand and then Crazy Horse's. "It's been an honor," he said, "not to mention a lot of good clean fun."

They all embraced and then Liam gave Becky a jocular half-bow: "After you, Miss." She nodded and headed out of the tree line into the snow, trying to blend in with the bushes as long as she could. When there was nothing left but open snow Liam pulled Becky close and held her for a long moment. Then, blessedly, the clouds closed up again and Liam whispered: "Let's get moving while it's dark. This time I'm going first." Becky didn't argue and they flopped onto the snow and started crawling as fast as they could, pulling themselves forward with their elbows and trying to keep their faces down.

It seemed to Liam that this process was lasting pretty close to forever, his knees and elbows first getting colder than he'd ever felt them, then hurting furiously, then going totally numb. Just as he started wondering if they were going to end up like those woolly mammoths, there was a shattering double explosion followed by a brilliant fireball that climbed high into the sky, lighting everything up like the sun before it winked out abruptly and gave way to a raging fire spreading among the aerodrome's buildings.

"That's our signal," Becky said excitedly.

"And there go Boylan and his playmates," Liam announced, jumping to his feet and helping Becky to hers. "If you aren't frozen solid we need to make our run for it now!"

Becky nodded solemnly, then leaned forward on an impulse and kissed him on the lips. He returned the kiss hard, then shook off the moment of foreboding:

"Come on," he said, "we aren't going to let those bums beat us."

He took off running at full speed and Becky, getting the most out of her costume's flat boots, kept right up with him. As they approached the gate, one of Boylan's men appeared around the corner of a shed and jumped back in alarm, fumbling for a gun in his belt.

"Hey! What's the big idea?"

Liam put on his thickest brogue: "Sure, it's a message I have for yez from Boyo himself!"

"Go on with yez," cried the other, approaching them suspiciously. "What is it?"

"This," Liam said with a grin, striking like a cobra and knocking the man cold with one punch. "Come on," he shouted to Becky, "we're almost there!"

There was another huge explosion—probably two bundles of dynamite at once, Liam guessed, then they were across the last patch of snow and up the little flight of metal stairs into the belly of the giant aircraft, pulling up the stairs instantly and slamming the hatch shut after them.

The inside of the giant airship was breathtaking, like the illustrations to Liam's beloved first edition of Verne's *Vingt Mille Lieues sous Les Mers* brought improbably to life. The interior of Captain Nemo's submarine Nautilus was no more luxuriously paneled in oak nor ornately trimmed with curlicues of brass or impressively packed with mysterious machinery than this nameless behemoth of Stanton's, softly lit by rows of tiny electric bulbs concealed within frosted glass globes.

On the far side of the main cabin, spread in a semicircle beneath a sort of bay window with three thick panes of glass, was a curved panel studded with dials and switches beneath which a hanging jungle growth of wires and cables could be seen. Liam and Becky headed towards it hastily, listening to the gunfire outside and watching the scurrying figures of armed men through the thick glass windows.

"We have to find a way to get this thing off the ground fast," Liam muttered.

Becky leaned forward to read the brass labels with their embossed and painted lettering. "At least it seems to have been laid out with a care for ordinary people's engineering skills," she said. "I suppose the rank-and-file aeronaut needs to be able to run it if all the officers are down."

"Thank Heaven for that," Liam said, "my engineering skills never got beyond the study of lock mechanisms." He examined the panel for a moment, then pointed to a dial labeled "Power Resources" which was divided into three arcs—the first black, the second green and the third red. "Looks like we've got plenty of power," he said. The needle of the gauge pointed straight up and down through the green arc, which was labeled "Steam Up."

"There," said Becky sharply, "throw that switch!"

In a neighboring quadrant of the panel were various knobs and knife switches, including the big one that Becky was pointing to. Above it, in large red-enamel letters, were the words "Engage Engines."

"Sounds reasonable to me," said Liam in a bemused tone.

The minute he pulled the switch down the lights dimmed momentarily, then flared as the entire enormous vessel began to quiver like a hunting dog on point and a deep, sonorous thrum of steam turbines sounded beneath their feet.

At almost the same instant they heard a furious pounding and shouting at the hatch they had slammed shut earlier, followed by a series of shots that *pinged!* off whatever the ship was armored with.

"Bloody hell!" exclaimed Liam, then: "Sorry, Becky!"

"No, no," she said, "bloody hell indeed! If one shot gets to the hydrogen in these cells we'll know just how the cockroaches in the hydrogen reservoir felt!" She looked around urgently. "There must be guns on this thing!"

In the quadrant of the panel to Liam's left there was a series of small knife switches with red handles, all in the up position and labeled "Rapid Fire." Without a second thought

Liam reached across and slammed them all down, and abruptly the ship was filled with the overwhelming racket of an unknown number of Gatling guns firing on all sides of them, with a tinkling obligatto of empty brass flying into collecting bins.

"Dear Heaven!" murmured Becky. As Liam turned towards her and followed her gaze he could see everything visible outside the windows shredding and falling to pieces in the way he remembered too well from Gettysburg. "*Enough!*" Becky added in an appalled voice. Then her glance caught something on the next quadrant of the panel and she leaned towards it curiously.

At the same moment, Liam reached across to the left and slapped the gun switches back into the up position, then lost his balance for a moment as the ship shuddered and lurched. Becky laughed helplessly and pointed to a large brass wheel with a rosewood handle fixed to it at right angles. At the left of the wheel were two-inch-high green letters spelling "ASCEND" and a green arrow sweeping around the circumference of the wheel to the right, where the rosewood handle now rested against a stop peg.

"Going up?" she quipped a little shakily.

It was a queer and overwhelming feeling: as if they really were standing in one of the new Otis steam elevators heading upwards at full speed with no top floor to stop them. Outside, the snow flurried thicker and thicker around the windows, illuminated by the lights from the cabin and the occasional shaft of moonlight. Becky turned back towards Liam and gave him a quizzical smile.

"Now what?" she said.

In the Air
July 1–July 2, 1877

Chapter Twenty-Eight

he view was definitely the most spectacular thing either of them had ever seen. Far below them, like a rolling field of snow stretching away to all four points of the compass were the clouds, illuminated by the clear, cold, unwavering light of a quarter moon. Above them and seemingly all around them were more stars than either of them knew existed, unobscured by clouds, steam-engine smoke, dust, and all the myriad things that came between earthbound humans and the heavens.

Becky and Liam were seated where they imagined the Captain and the First Mate (or something of the sort) must ordinarily sit—two very comfortable kidney-buttoned chairs of dark green leather on shiny brass pedestals that let them swivel in any direction they pleased. At the moment, they pleased to be facing forward, drinking in the stars. Finally Liam spoke:

"Becky Fox, will you marry me?"

She laughed her deep, unrestrained, joyous laugh—just hearing it made Liam smile.

"Perhaps," she said. "Liam McCool, if I marry you will you give up being King of the Cracksmen so I needn't worry every day about somebody or other clapping you in the jug?"

Liam thought that over for a bit and then grinned: "Perhaps."

"Well, then," she said with a smile, "let's just wait and see and meantime enjoy every minute we can."

"That sounds like a good plan to me."

They sat there for a little while longer, each of them playing with daydreams of the future, until finally Liam tore himself away from Becky and the view and got up. "All right," he said, "maybe we'd better figure out how to set a course and get this thing flying properly on its way home."

With a little sigh of regret Becky pushed herself free of the armchair's embrace and joined Liam at the control panel. At the top of the first bank of instruments was an enormous convex glass magnifier, perhaps three feet square, above which was a brass plaque with inch-high enamel letters reading "Mapping." It was illuminated by electric bulbs that had been recessed into its frame all the way around the edges, and was currently showing the area around New Petersburg. In the center, below the bottom edge of the magnifier, were dials labeled "Country," "City," and "Environs."

"See if you can find New York," Liam suggested. Becky bent over and turned the first knob to "U.S." which came up on the dial alphabetically (after tedious knob twirling through a gazetteer of other countries) following "Little Russia." Fascinated, Liam watched as the map of Little Russia slid out of view, only to be replaced with one of the U.S. showing the area more or less across the Mississippi from where they had just been.

"I don't think that's what we want right now," Liam said, "let's try this."

He gestured to a bank of dials and switches on the other side of the Mapping device that surrounded a steering bar pretty much like the one in any ordinary steam car. Liam pointed:

"There's the compass that shows how we're heading, which right now is due east. And there next to it is the Course Selection Compass—it looks like you move the needle the way

288

you'd set the hands of a clock and then lock it onto your course with that green switch there that says 'Set Course.' The big question is, what's the best route to get us home?"

Becky thought about it for a few moments. "The first thing we need to consider is what time we want to arrive. The main chronometer says it's 10:20 p.m., July 1st, and we need to cover something like a thousand miles at what that air speed indicator says is 200 miles per hour, so allowing for unfavorable winds and the general cussedness of things if we head directly there we would probably be arriving in or near New York uncomfortably close to dawn."

Liam nodded thoughtfully. "Hard to make a clandestine landing in broad daylight in an aerial battleship the size of Staten Island."

"It could be a bit sticky," Becky agreed.

"Another thought is Stanton's aerial patrols, you know . . . " (he made a simpering face) " . . . the ones your handsome beau Ubaldo told us about."

"I'm much stronger than you realize," Becky said with a pleasant smile, "if I hit you might be quite sorry."

"Hmph," Liam said. "Anyway, now that we've crossed the Mississippi into the U.S. we're obviously in greater danger of discovery. So what do you think about heading directly north until we cross the Canadian border and then more or less following it until we get to Lake Ontario? From there to the city is only about three hundred miles, so if we can figure out someplace remote on the Canadian side of Lake Ontario where we can lay low in the daytime tomorrow, we should be able to time our arrival late enough on the 2nd to avoid putting on a show."

Liam could see that Becky was turning the idea over thoroughly and finding it satisfactory.

"I think I know a good place," she said, "I once did a story on the Mississauga Ojibway who moved north to escape land-hungry New Yorkers. All along the Canadian side of

Lake Ontario there are huge grassy stretches of prairie where we can set this thing down for as long as we like without a soul to see us or care if they do."

"Perfect," said Liam, "let's set the course compass for due north—we should be in Canada in less than half an hour."

As Becky set the course selection compass and locked down the "Set Course" dial, Liam investigated some of the other controls on the panels in front of what they assumed to be the Captain's chair. Directly to the right on the panel facing the Captain was a red button the size of a silver dollar with an enameled label reading "TeslaBolt."

"What the Dickens do you suppose that is?" he mused, resting his thumb on it as Becky joined him. Becky looked at the button dubiously and was about to pull Liam's arm back when he gave in to temptation and pushed. Instantly a red light began flashing behind a brass label with cut-out letters reading "Capacitor Charging," at the same time as a weird, groaning whine arose somewhere behind the control panels, moving rapidly up the scale till it reached an almost unbearable pitch. Involuntarily, Becky and Liam moved closer together, but before either of them could think what to do or where to go, a lightning bolt of blinding intensity shot out into the night from somewhere below the front of the Delta, filling the air in the control area with a sharp scent of ozone followed simultaneously by a thunderclap so loud that they both scrunched their eyes tight shut and threw their hands over their ears.

When they finally opened their eyes again the serene vista of moonlit clouds was stretching in front of them once more, the only clue to what had happened a moment before being the jagged after-images that still burned in their vision.

"Holy Mary!" Liam said hollowly.

Becky looked around at the cavernous space behind them, with its cheerful brass fixtures and green shades, thick maroon carpeting, and endless expanses of decoratively carved wood and mahogany paneling.

"Just look at that," Becky said with a slight tremor in her voice. We might as well be in the lobby of a really lovely hotel, but we seem to be surrounded by more hideously lethal weaponry than our surface Navy has in any of its heavy battleships."

Liam nodded soberly. "I expect this thing will end up on Shelter Island at Freedom Party headquarters within the next few days, but once it's landed there you'd better tell Mr. Clemens to be ready to blow it to smithereens if either Stanton's or Lukas' people come after it. No politician any-where has the brains and the goodness to be trusted with a gadget like this."

Sunk in thought, Becky and Liam went back to their armchairs and watched the stars until finally the alarm on the control panel chimed.

"Well, Miss Fox," Liam said with a stretch and a yawn, "unless we're total dunces at mathematics, we should be about twenty miles into Canada by now. What do you say we re-set the course for Lake Ontario and catch a little shuteye before it starts to get light out?"

Becky smiled and copied Liam's stretch, then got up and walked over to the control panel. After a few minor adjust-ments she closed the "Set Course" switch again and looked around.

"Now where do you suppose the *officers' staterooms* are?"

Liam got up and joined her, looking around on every side and then making a face as he discovered where Becky was looking. A short corridor branched off the main cabin to the right and a couple of bulbs glowed behind a glass panel that announced "Officers' Quarters."

"Come on," she said with a laugh, and grabbing his hand she pulled him forward down the corridor. "Ah!," she said, pointing to the end of the hallway, where a brass panel on a large leather-covered door announced "Captain." "The

Captain's quarters for me," she announced and ran to the door, which opened to reveal a cozy, shipshape room with bookshelves, armchairs, green-shaded lamps and a big, comfortable-looking bed with a dark green coverlet.

"I'll just sit on the floor and guard your door till sunrise," Liam said with melodramatic gallantry.

"Like fun you will," she said, pulling him firmly inside and closing the door after them . . .

○━┰

Liam was sitting on the sandy bottom of a small, cool stream under a balmy spring sun, listening to the birds sing and watching the minnows chase each other while his freshly washed clothes dried on the grass. He had to admit it, even to a deep-dyed city boy this bucolic peace seemed pretty good. In fact, despite the incredible abundance of bad people and bad things in it, the world was actually a pretty terrific place. Of course, this conclusion became possible only if your initial premise was the presence of Becky Fox, but even so . . .

"*LIAM!*" She was calling from the direction of the Delta and she sounded excited. "*LIAM! COME QUICKLY!*"

Drying himself hastily with one of the nice thick dark-green towels he'd found in the Captain's bathroom, Liam hurried into his clothes and trotted back towards the airship.

Looking as fresh and rosy as one of the little pink flowers that speckled the prairie around them, Becky was waving Liam towards her, nearly dancing up and down in her eagerness to get him there faster.

"Gosh," he teased when he reached her, "I know kissing me is one of the finest things any right-thinking woman could do with her free time, but even so you could have waited until . . ."

She kissed him briskly and then laid a finger on his lips to shut him up. "You remember how you were saying you wished you knew what was waiting for us when we got back?"

He nodded, puzzled.

"Well," she said with a cat-that-ate-the-cream smile, "I went exploring and I found something very interesting!"

Taking his hand, she pulled him up the stairs into the main cabin, and across it to what looked like a double-length roll-top desk set into the wall opposite the control panel. Becky gestured towards it mysteriously:

"Pull it back!"

Intrigued, Liam walked over to the arched wooden cover, stuck his fingertips into the recess that concealed the latch and pulled the cover up and back. It rolled up into the wall with oiled smoothness, revealing an assortment of unfamiliar gadgets.

To one side was a brass viewing-port like the business end of a stereopticon, a sort of projecting shield with curved sides that prevented stray light from spoiling your view while you pressed your forehead against the straight part at the top. In bold red letters the brass plaque above it said "Bausch & Lomb ShurShot Bombing Sight," and below it were a series of large black knobs with knurled edges that Liam didn't really want to think about, especially considering the labels: "Canister Bombs," "Fire Bombs" and "Dynamite Bombs."

Next to that was another, similar viewing port with the label "TeslaLux Night Viewer," and finally, at the right of the group was the appliance that Becky was so excited about. It was nothing much to look at—a rosewood bar with brass fittings at either end, each of which held a little brass bowl about the size of a demitasse cup, resting on a sort of hooked holder on the panel and connected to the panel itself by a long insulated wire. Above this gadget was a brass plaque that announced it to be a "TeslaVox Transmitter and Receiver," and below it was a simple red knob with a brass arrow at its edge and the unambiguous legend: "ON—OFF."

"Go on," Becky urged, "pick the thing up and turn it on!"

Smiling a little uneasily, Liam picked it up and turned the red knob, at which point he heard a thin jabbering sound coming out of one of the brass cups. Liam gave it a mistrustful look, wondering what was supposed to happen next.

"For Heaven's sake," Becky said impatiently, "*listen to it!*" She pantomimed holding the thing up to her ear, and no sooner had Liam followed suit than he heard a thin, cross-sounding voice saying:

"Hello! Voicewire operator #81. Hello!?"

Without even thinking about it, Liam jammed the thing back onto its holder and stood staring at it incredulously.

"Is that what I think . . ."

"Of course it is!" Becky exclaimed. "We saw the other night how well Tesla's new electricity-transmitting towers are working. It seems plain enough that he's actually figured out how to transmit the energy that makes the voicewire work, *without* a wire!"

Liam was shaking his head wryly: "But of course only the Department of Public Safety can have these."

Becky spread her hands: "Let's not look a gift horse in the mouth! In a few minutes I want to call Mr. Clemens at Shelter Island and dictate a full story on what's happening—and for that matter what's *not* happening—in Little Russia. He'll be able to get it to every American paper that dares to print it and to *all* the *foreign* papers. By the end of the day the story will be going around the globe like wildfire: 'No war preparations in Little Russia!' 'Little Russian Aerial Navy a pitiful sham!' And finally, even if our facts are a little thin right now: 'Revolution breaks out in Little Russia! Gigantic dynamite explosion at Viceroy's palace!'" Becky grinned cheerfully. "I'm afraid Stanton will have to re-write his war plans, since France and England both have treaties with Russia that provide for military support in the case of unprovoked attack by a third party, and that would mean biting off a bigger risk than Stanton will want to chew."

Liam was shaking his head again, this time admiringly: "Becky Fox, you are a wonder! Stanton will be as wild as a bear with a sore paw! Go on, what's keeping you?"

She gave him a hug. "Silly man, I'll be talking forever—I thought you might like to call Mike first and find out if he's learned anything about your grandmother."

Liam kissed Becky. "You really are a wonder. Let's give it a try."

He picked up the TeslaVox gadget, and this time another operator answered:

"*Voicewire Operator #47, how can I help you?*"

A little gingerly, still not quite believing in it, he gave her Mike's voicewire number and waited for what seemed like forever. But finally a thin voice came from the cup at his ear:

"*Vysotsky!*"

"Misha!" Liam bellowed happily. "It's me!"

"*Hey, pipe down, durak, you're breaking my ear! Where are you? What've you been up to? They got posters out now, you're wanted dead or alive! What'd you do, anyway, pinch Stanton's watch?*"

Liam beckoned Becky over and instinctively cupped the thing in his hands to make it louder as she bent close to listen:

"*Druzhok, if I told you, you'd say I was smoking hop. I'll give you the whole story really soon, I promise. Right now I want to know how everything's going in the city. How are you and the boys? How's Gran?*"

Mike barked a tinny little laugh. Then: "*Ever since the other night with the riots this town is so bughouse I don't know where to start. First off, old Pilkington is out of the picture. That's O-U-T, out! His son Willie—his own son, would you believe?—has him under house arrest. And guess who Willie the Piglet put in charge of the New York Agency instead? None other than The Great Detective!*"

"McPherson?" Liam said incredulously.

"*I kid you not, batiushka,*" said Mike. "*So you can forget about any understandings you had with Papa Pig, they're all ancient history now. Except don't forget, the old man probably had to leave all his papers back at Union Square,*" *which means including your arrest record, the indictment, the sentencing recommendation and all the other little goodies he was holding over your head."*

"Oh, man," muttered Liam. "Well, OK, that'll have to be for later. Right now, #1 is where's Gran?"

"Yeah," Mike said, *"that's the part that isn't so good. I got inside word you can make book on, says she and our boys and most of the other people they picked up in the sweeps are right now sitting in a big shed they used to use for a warehouse . . . you ready for this?"*

"Nu podi zhe, chort voz'mi!" snapped Liam.

A tinny sigh at the other end. *"OK,"* said Mike, *"they're all at Sing Sing."*

Liam's jaw dropped. He stared at Becky and he didn't like what he saw there, either. He stood there for a long handful of seconds, his brain racing a thousand miles a minute. Then he put his hand over the TeslaVox gadget for a moment and spoke to Becky:

"Do you think once we pick a safe landing spot somewhere near Sing Sing you could ask Mr. Clemens to send Capt. Ubaldo to meet us there tomorrow night, the 3rd?"

Becky thought for a moment. "If he has enough warning I can't imagine why he'd say no."

Mike was running out of patience: *"Hey! You still there?"*

"Yeah, I'm here all right," Liam said slowly. "Listen, Misha, I'm going to stay where I am for another day—that'll give you enough time to get everything ready to go the minute I get back. So here's the shopping list: First of all, do we still have people on the inside at the Brooklyn Bridge building site?"

"Yeah, sure, but . . ."

"I'm going to need you to buy us some supplies before I get back. Don't worry, I'll tell you in a minute. Number two is, I want you to get in touch with the two Dannys, we need to get together with them and make some plans. Invite them to our Fourth of July party."

296

"Are you serious? You want to get together with the Whyos?"

"You *bet* I'm serious. The Dannys may think the Whyos are God, but we're *all* going to need to co-operate for a while here, no feuding. We need to get the Whyos on board first because every other gang in town but us has to go to the Dannys to ask if it's OK to breathe. If the two Dannys are OK with working together, then the rest of them will be OK. And believe me, there isn't a single one of us can draw a free breath again until we get rid of Stanton and his mob, so we're going to have to join forces to do it."

"Man!" Mike said heavily. *"You don't like to play for pennies, do you?"*

"Listen to me, Mishen'ka," Liam said, "I just spent the last day or so with General *Custer,* you know?"

"Yeah, sure," Mike chortled, *"and I was shooting craps with Genghis Khan!"*

"Dammit, Mike, *listen* to me. I'm not kidding, and Custer's in this game with us. The advice he gave me was solid gold: He said if you're going up against an enemy as big as Stanton, you want to do like the Sioux do with the white man: hit and run, hit and run over and over again, biting off a chunk here and a chunk there until he finally blows his stack and drops his guard. Then you can cut his gizzard out and throw him in the East River, OK?"

"OK, I'm listening," said Mike reflectively.

"So: #1, the Brooklyn Bridge. #2, the two Dannys. And number three is I think maybe I have an idea what to do about Sing Sing, thanks to Little Adam. We still have any credit with the Grogans?"

"Lyovushka, milyi moi," Mike said, *"I told you they owe us, they're gonna be our water taxi from now till they ferry us down the River Styx."*

"Good," said Liam, "then here's what we're going to do . . ."

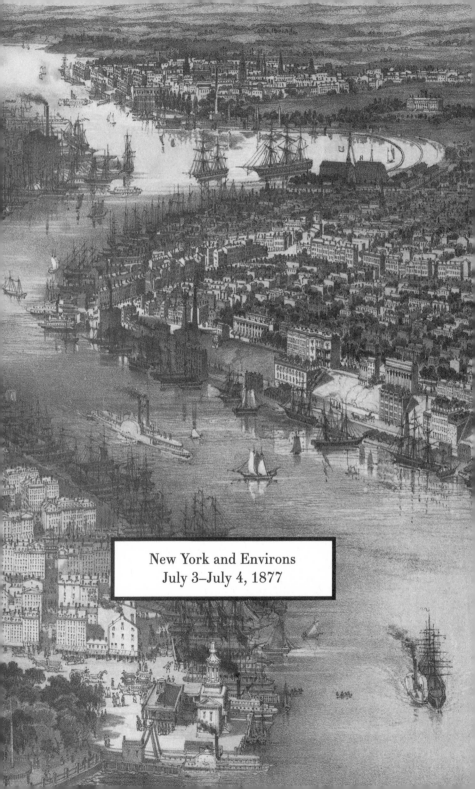

New York and Environs
July 3–July 4, 1877

Chapter Twenty-Nine

iam waded out into the chilly water and grabbed the skiff's painter as Cap'n Billy Grogan threw it to him, then turned to haul the little craft in to shore only to find the older man striding along in the water next to him, clapping him on the back and chuckling happily through his enormous Santa Claus beard.

"Aye and begorrah but you're a grand lad, Liam, I can't thank you enough for letting me horn in on your party!"

"It's me that should be thanking you, Cap'n Billy," Liam said, "our plan wouldn't be worth a plugged nickel without you and your sons."

They were speaking in low tones, acutely conscious of the grim pile hulking in the darkness behind them. Liam—like any professional cracksman—had seen Sing Sing more than once in his nightmares, but this was the first time he'd seen it with his eyes wide open and he was relieved at how dimly lit the building was both inside and out.

"Nice they're keeping it dark for us," he said to Grogan.

Grogan laughed mirthlessly. "Sure now, and why would they waste the electric? Nobody's broken out since Little Adam, and who ever heard of anybody breaking *in?*" His teeth flashed in a grin. "Besides, the electric costs good money, and they need to turn a profit for the state, that's why they call it a model prison!"

A noise in the trees nearby made them both grab for their pistols but a moment later they relaxed as Becky—in a dark enlisted-aeronaut's uniform from the Delta's supply lockers—and Ubaldo, in an equally dark officer's uniform, moved out of the shadows.

"Cap'n Billy?" Becky said. "We certainly are happy to see you!"

She took his hand and shook it firmly, and Grogan inspected her with frank admiration.

"No happier than I am to be here, Miss Fox," he said. "My son Brian was snatched in the first of Willie Pilkington's sweeps, and the Missus will be that glad to see him home again she'll be walking on air."

"Arturo Ubaldo, at your service," the Captain said, stepping forward and taking Grogan's hand with a grin. "Between us, sir, I believe you and I represent the total aerial and naval forces of this little alliance."

"Well, then, young fella," chuckled Grogan, "how can we lose?"

"If I may say so, sir," Ubaldo said respectfully, "I am a little anxious about where in town you're planning to deliver your passengers. I was in the city earlier today and I couldn't believe how many people Stanton had out in the streets. Not just Eyes and New York City police and State militia troopers, but something new. On me, anyway—hard-looking types in black uniforms with red trim and brass buttons. You know who I mean?"

"I surely do, lad," said Grogan with a grim smile. "They're our beloved Willie Pilkington's newest toys, Johndarms I think they call 'em, and from what I hear if they get their hands on you that's all she wrote, next stop Hart Island and Potter's Field. But don't you worry about my passengers tonight—this ain't Billy Grogan's first waltz, even the dock rats won't know we've landed them."

He gestured towards the Hudson: "As soon as the party starts, my boys will move in from where they're anchored offshore and come close enough to take passengers aboard. We've got four big steam launches that'll outrun anything on the River, and if we pack them tight, there's more than enough room for everyone. Liam, lad, my brother Kevin will be in our racing cruiser waiting for you and your boys. It's only thirty miles to the city, so all our passengers should be back on the streets before these yokels know what hit them."

"Perfect," said Liam. "Capt. Ubaldo, how are things on your side?"

Ubaldo grinned and twirled his little moustache, giving Liam a twinge of embarrassment as he remembered the natty pilot's narrow escape from a brass-knuckle shampoo.

"Couldn't be better, Mr. McCool. You and Miss Fox picked a fine landing spot—no nearby neighbors, but close enough to the prison that Miss Fox and I were able to cover the path through the woods in ten minutes."

Liam smiled. "My grandma can walk a harness bull right into the ground, I expect you'll find she beats your record through the woods."

"How long will it take you to fly out to Shelter Island?" Grogan asked Ubaldo.

The aeronaut laughed and shook his head—"That big Delta can get us there in no time flat. Say twenty minutes or so. Miss Fox's meeting with Mr. Clemens and President Lincoln and the others will probably last longer than it takes us to get to get there."

Grogan nodded. "Then I'll keep one of my lads waiting for you with a speedboat until you're ready to leave, Miss Fox. You just get yourself to Cedar Island Cove and we'll have you back in the City before you can say Jack Robinson!"

"Sounds like that's it, then, folks," Liam said briskly. "Let's get going, and damn the torpedoes!"

The outbuilding where the prisoners were housed was several hundred yards away through nearly pitch darkness and surrounded by a formidable fence of closely woven barbed wire supported by ten-foot-tall wooden posts, making it impossible to reach the big warehouse and a number of smaller outbuildings without going through the swinging gates—each of them another ten feet or so wide, meeting in the middle and locked with a couple of stout padlocks set into substantial steel hasps.

To one side of the gates stood a guardhouse in front of which a single blue-uniformed guard could be seen in the light of an electric bulb, sitting on an empty pickle barrel and snoring as he leaned against the wall, his rifle standing neglected on the other side of the guard booth door. The little group of rescuers was huddling behind a hay wagon parked in the shadows near the gates.

"That one guard there's as good as an army," Liam muttered, "worthless as he is. All he has to do is wake up long enough to grab that rifle and fire a single shot, and that'll be all it takes to alarm every guard in Sing Sing."

"I've got an idea," Ubaldo said. "Why don't I make you my prisoner? You cross your arms behind your back and put on your best shiftless-ruffian look, I'll be one of those mad-dog Department of Public Safety officers and I'll get him to open up so I can throw you in the hoosegow. Miss Fox and Cap'n Billy can join us as soon as the guard's subdued."

Liam grinned with relief. "You're a genius, Captain." He stood up and crossed his hands behind his back. "Your prisoner, sir!"

They moved out into the dim circle of light from the sentry box, Liam shuffling along disconsolately while Ubaldo marched stiffly behind him, every inch the martinet.

"You there! Guard!" Ubaldo snapped as they drew close. "Get up at *once!*"

The hapless guard heard Ubaldo's practiced tone of command and leapt to his feet before he was fully awake, struggling to come to attention and salute even as his brain wrestled with a dense fog of sleep and whiskey.

"*Sir!*" he cried, striking himself painfully on the nose with his saluting hand. "Corrections Officer Hasenpfeffer at your orders, sir!"

"And a good thing, too, Hasenpfeffer," Umberto growled ominously, "or I would have been forced to put you on report for dereliction of duty! Now get those gates open and help me take this terrorist scum to the DPS lockup, these are Mr. Pilkington's *express* orders!"

"Yes, sir, at once, sir, thank you for not reporting me, sir," the guard bleated, almost gibbering in his anxiety to look good for this DPS fire-eater. He pulled a big ring of keys out of his pocket and fumbled hysterically at the locks, finally getting them both open and starting to pull the gates apart . . .

A moment later, the guard was lying on the ground, once more deep asleep as Liam and Ubaldo hauled him over to the sentry box, tied him up firmly with his own belt and braces, and gagged him with his shirt. Then Liam grabbed the keyring, waved to Becky and Cap'n Billy and took off towards the warehouse. The door of the temporary prison was an enormous, barndoor sort of affair with wheels that slid along tracks, and like the main gate it was secured by two big padlocks set into heavy steel hasps.

"Aren't there any other guards?" Becky whispered tensely as Liam tried different keys.

"I'm pretty sure Cap'n Billy was right," he whispered back, "they aren't worried about people breaking in. But we'd better move fast anyway, we can't count on good luck too much longer."

Naturally it was the last two keys that opened the locks, and by the time he had them off the hasps Liam was sweating. Now, if they just had another thimbleful or two of good luck left . . . he pulled open the door slowly to keep down the noise, and as it parted to reveal the inside of the barn-like structure,

Liam heard an anxious murmur sweeping through the crowd of prisoners.

"Ssshh!" he hissed into the darkness, "keep it down in there, we're here to set you free, not hurt you—don't make a racket and wake up the guards!"

A moment later, he had the door all the way open and a sudden, involuntary cry came from the fetid, urine-and-sweat-smelling darkness:

"Liam! It's Liam, boys!"

Harry the Jap jumped out into the dim light and grabbed Liam in a fierce bear hug, followed by a dozen or so more Butcher Boys, all of them clamoring to get at Liam and whispering so loudly that Liam was sure they'd be heard by the enemy.

"Ssshh! Boys! Pipe down!!" Liam managed to get them quiet and beckoned Cap'n Billy over. "Help Cap'n Billy get everybody out of here and down the bank to the water," he hissed, "we've got boats enough to take you all back to the city. I'll be bringing up the rear guard, if something slows me down don't wait for me, we've got our own boat." He turned to Harry: "Help me find my Gran, will you?"

With a sudden sinking feeling Liam saw Harry shaking his head: "They took her away an hour ago," he said. "They said she had to go to the infirmary."

"The infirmary? What for?" Liam's voice had jumped several notches, and Harry worriedly put a finger to his lips.

"I don't know. That's the infirmary, the little building over there."

Liam followed Harry's pointing finger. A building about the size of a small stable stood nearby, its shuttered windows leaking tiny streaks of light in the darkness.

"You better be careful, though," Harry added, "it wasn't a guard that came to get her, it was an Acme. And it could talk."

Liam frowned worriedly, thinking that the only talking Acme he'd ever seen was the one Lukas had made for President Lincoln.

"OK, Harry, you go help Cap'n Billy get everybody down to the water, I'll see you in a few minutes."

Harry started back towards the inside of the barn, which was now boiling with activity, but stopped and turned back towards Liam after a few steps: "Hey! Where's Mike, anyway?"

"He's in town getting some special supplies," Liam whispered with a thin smile, "we'll tell you it about tonight when we all get home."

Harry nodded and slipped away into the darkness as Liam turned in the other direction and moved quickly and silently over to the infirmary building, stepping with exaggerated care and listening with every nerve strained for the sound of an unexpected breath or footstep. Finally he drew up next to a shuttered window and peered into the narrow crack along one side . . .

It took all the self-control he could muster to stifle the groan that rose in his throat. Gran was inside, all right, but she definitely wasn't being treated for anything: she was lying on her back, apparently out cold, strapped to some kind of padded table with wheels by a big leather strap around her chest and another around her hips.

As Liam moved to the crack on the other side of the shutters and put his eye to it, Ubaldo and Becky tiptoed up to join him and he pointed at the crack he'd just vacated, gesturing to them to take a look. Peering inside again, Liam caught his breath sharply. From here, he could see an operating table with a metal-shaded calcium arc lamp hanging over it, and on the table a patient covered with a white sheet except for his head. The head was the part they should have covered as far as Liam was concerned. Its top was missing and there didn't seem to be anything at all inside it.

"I don't believe it!" It was Becky who had hissed the words, shaking her head as she gestured Liam over to join her and Ubaldo. Liam put his eye to the crack and almost echoed

Becky at full voice. There, in the space between Gran and the operating table, a wheelchair had appeared, with an Acme seated in it. The automaton sat peacefully, its arms resting on the arms of the wheelchair and the top of its head resting on its metal lap as it looked sightlessly towards Liam and a human brain festooned with wires as thin as hairs was lowered into the cavity . . . *by Lukas!*

"*That's the limit!*" grated Liam, loudly enough that Becky dug her fingers sharply into his shoulder.

"*Sorry,*" Liam said, returning to a whisper as he took out his Colt. "*I'm going in there. You two take an extra-careful look around the outside to make sure no one else is going to be part of our little get-together and then come in and help me get Gran out of here.*"

They nodded and disappeared around the outside of the house as Liam walked over to the entrance, crossed his fingers that Lukas wouldn't have bothered to lock the door, put his hand on the knob, hesitated for another moment, then stepped sharply inside with his Colt raised.

Lukas seemed to freeze in mid-motion as he registered Liam's presence.

"What the Devil do you think you're doing, Lukas?" snapped Liam. "Why is my grandmother here?" Now that Liam didn't have to whisper any more he was almost shouting, and Lukas recovered enough from his astonishment to snarl at Liam:

"Of all the intolerable effrontery! You have the *gall*, McCool, to burst into *my* operating room in the middle of an extremely important operation, at its most crucial juncture, and ask me what *I'm* doing? I'm being interrupted by a *moron*, and if you don't stop the racket at once I will have you seized and taken across the yard to a place where they'll know what to do with you!"

Liam was so angry by now that he could barely trust himself to speak, and yet he was collected enough to be amazed at the Russian's oblivious self-confidence.

"I tell you what," Liam said a little hoarsely, "I think I'll just make things simpler by blowing a nice big hole in you and interrupting you *forever.*"

Lukas made an impatient face and looked beyond Liam. "Number Four!" he said sharply. "Guard the woman!"

There was a crash behind him and an Acme which must have been standing against the wall next to the shutter suddenly sprang forward next to the rolling table on which Liam's grandmother lay asleep, laying its massive steel fingers gently but ominously on her chest above her heart. Liam's breath caught in his throat as he thought of the brute destructive power of an Acme and Lukas registered his reaction with a grim smile.

"I believe it's checkmate, Mr. McCool," said Lukas.

"Maybe," grated Liam, "but whatever you're planning for my Gran I'm sure she'd rather be dead, so either you back that machine off her and swear on your honor to leave her completely alone or I will pull this trigger. Gran will be dead and I'm sure I'll be dead, but you will be too, and somehow I think that *that* at least is a thought that might give you pause."

Lukas looked at him for a long moment, his teeth clenched with frustration. Finally he gave Liam a curt nod. "Mr. McCool, you are the most insanely *tiresome* person I have ever met, and I have traveled the world from one end to the other. However, your proposal is accepted with the proviso that you and your friends stay *absolutely silent and do not move a muscle* until I finish this operation and take my leave. Do we understand each other completely?"

"My friends?" Liam asked innocently.

"Don't waste my time with rubbish," Lukas snapped. *"One!"* he called out, *"Three!"*

Behind Liam the heavy footsteps of Acmes sounded as two more of Lukas' creations entered, one of them firmly gripping Becky and the other Ubaldo.

"Sorry, Liam," said Becky with a grimace, "they had us before we even got around the house."

"SILENCE!" bellowed Lukas. "I have an agreement with Mr. McCool: all three of you are to remain immobile and *totally silent* until I am ready to leave, which will be in a very few minutes. So you and Mr. McCool's grandmother should be quite safe—as . . . long . . . as . . . you . . . *obey*. Do you understand?"

Glumly, the three of them nodded. Lukas looked back and forth between them, then nodded and went briskly back to work, adjusting the wires connected to the brain he had just inserted in the skull cavity of the Acme and carrying on a cheerful monologue as he worked.

"No doubt you've been told that the human brain and nervous system operate according to some quite mysterious scheme of electrical signals. I should explain at once that nothing about the brain is a mystery to me, including its electrical behavior, and so I have been at pains for some time to put my knowledge to work in combination with both the advancing technology of automaton-building and Secretary Tesla's valuable work on the wireless transmission of electrical energy and signals."

He fell silent for a few moments, humming to himself absent-mindedly as he bundled together the wires connected to the brain and led them down a channel in the automaton's neck to a point at which they disappeared into a forest of other wiring in the thing's chest. At this point the Acme's eyes suddenly started glowing with the same coldly eerie blue light as the eyes of Lukas' other Acmes and it spoke in a voice that Liam recognized as a much-improved version of President Lincoln's speaking apparatus:

"Thank you for connecting me, Father. I am pleased to be a part of your faithful servant The Brotherhood."

Lukas beamed with satisfaction and continued talking as he bolted on the top half of the Acme's head and cleaned up the remaining traces of the operation:

"You will be familiar with the word *druzhina*, Mr. McCool, 'brotherhood' is the most satisfactory translation I can come up with for the moment. The most important thing is that no matter how few or how many of them there are they all become, as soon as they are activated, part of a single limitless being, communicating their thoughts by wireless transmission. And even more useful is something that I discovered in the process of achieving this wireless communication—a procedure that allows me to overcome each brain's individual personality while retaining its native intelligence. I must admit that's why I wanted your grandmother, McCool; she proved to be far and away the most intelligent and at the same time the most stubborn of all the prisoners, and I would have been extremely interested to see if my process could overcome even her iron will."

"Careful, McCool!" he warned, holding up a finger as he saw Liam twitch towards him with barely contained fury. "Though I regret missing the chance to operate on her," he continued as Liam subsided, "there will be more than enough brains to work with in Little Russia, both Indian and European. Indeed, I expect the Indians' brains to be quite interesting experimentally."

He dusted off his hands and looked around the room the way travelers do before setting out on a trip.

"Can you imagine?" he continued, moving towards the opposite side of the room and a door which was clearly an exit. "That trumpery dictator Stanton actually thought that I was doing all this research for *him*, and that in exchange for his kindness in providing me with a laboratory and materials I would tell him the secret of refining calorium. In fact, he had intended to introduce me triumphantly to the public tomorrow at some sort of grand Fourth of July ceremony he's planning in Union Square."

He chuckled with genuine amusement and shook his head. "Silly little man—the ego of Gargantua linked to the brain of a weasel. No doubt he will be distressed to discover tomorrow that I am already in Little Petersburg, assuming the mantle of Viceroy and the leadership of a revolution that will one day sweep the world."

Lukas bowed respectfully to Becky. "Thanks to you, Miss Fox, the world now knows that our revolution has begun in Little Russia, though after today such heroic feats of reporting as yours will no longer be necessary. The moment I set foot on Little Russian soil, I will tear down the veil of silence that stretches along the borders between us—I intend to establish open communications with the rest of the world so that all will be able to see the marvels that we shall work there and treat me and my people with the respect we deserve. Meanwhile, my automaton friends will build more and more copies of themselves, and those copies will begin making multiple copies of the Battleship Delta which my helper Boylan stole from Stanton." He smiled and peered at Liam. "Did you have something to say, Mr. McCool? No? Then in that case I must take my leave of you all."

"Number Four!" he said to the Acme guarding Liam's grandmother. "Stay as you are until you hear the engine start, so that Mr. McCool will not be tempted to do anything foolish. Understood?"

"Yes, Father," the Acme said.

"Excellent." Lukas opened the door and waited as the other Acmes exited. Then he turned back to Liam: "I can only hope, Mr. McCool, that you will give up your idiotic interference with my activities if I tell you that curiosity led me to investigate the matter thoroughly and I am now quite sure that our mutual friend Maggie was killed by *McPherson*, in a fit of jealous rage when she refused his advances."

"*What?*" cried Liam in spite of himself.

"I will forgive your breaking your pledge of silence," Lukas said with a thin smile, "considering the emotional circumstances. But I know this for sure after talking to the bartender at McSorley's Ale House, where the 'Great Detective' is a regular. McPherson told the whole story to the bartender in a drunken fit of melancholy not long ago, after another woman had rejected his advances and held him up to ridicule in front of his fellow sots. And now my friends, I must beg you to excuse me!"

With that, he exited abruptly, leaving the final Acme standing guard over Liam's grandmother.

"Do not move," the Acme said stolidly. After a brief pause, Liam and the others heard the sound of a silenced Delta starting up outside, and abruptly the Acme leapt all the way across the room and crashed through the wall. Within seconds, Liam and his companions heard the muted whirring of the Delta rising over the compound and speeding away into the distance.

Liam sighed heavily; it had just about killed him to stand there like a department store dummy and let Lukas escape; but there was one solid consolation—he and Crazy Horse and the others had kicked over a great big hornet's nest as they left New Petersburg, and obviously Little Russia's brutally enforced communications barrier had kept Lukas in ignorance of what was happening there. With a little luck, Crazy Horse's foster father would soon be interrogating Lukas and then turning him over to the *okhranniki* for target practice . . . After a moment Liam shook himself free from his thoughts and turned to Becky with a tired smile:

"The noise of that Flyer will have the guards across the way up and about, that's for sure. Come on, let's undo Gran."

Becky and Liam and Ubaldo set to work with a will and before long they managed to undo the restraints. Liam's grandmother barely stirred in her deeply drugged sleep.

Liam rolled his eyes with frustration: "There's no way she'll even be able to *walk* with you, let alone hurry."

"Please, Mr. McCool, allow me!" volunteered Ubaldo, and before Liam could protest Ubaldo had hoisted his grandmother off the rolling table and onto his back in a fireman's lift. "Don't worry, Mr. McCool, we'll keep her quite safe." He turned to Becky: "And now you and I had best move *sharpish*," he said and started out the door.

Liam pulled Becky close for a split second, then pushed her towards the exit. "I'll see you tomorrow, at the party. And be careful!" He waved as she disappeared after Ubaldo, then looked around the operating theater and shook his head. "*Dosvidaniia*, Lukas," Liam muttered. "Next time." Then he pictured Lukas' arrival in New Petersburg and grinned, imagining the scene as Boylan sweated through bringing his boss up to date on the problems with their plans and laughing out loud as he imagined the Russian's frenzy over the loss of his nice new Battleship Delta.

Absolutely the biggest thing I ever stole, Liam thought. *As far as that goes, the biggest thing* anybody *ever stole.* "You maybe a Grand Duke, Lukas," Liam continued out loud, "but you still don't want to mess with the *King!*" Still chuckling, Liam turned and went out the door at a run, heading for the river and the boat to New York.

Chapter Thirty

he old codger shuffled along the Fourth Avenue side of Union Square, pausing across from the Department of Public Safety headquarters to lean on his walking stick and watch the workmen putting the finishing touches on a bank of grandstands angling towards a stage with a podium that sat in front of the DPS building, facing across the square towards the Pilkington Agency's building. All the building facades were festooned with red, white and blue bunting, and American flags of every possible size flew everywhere—from the tops of buildings, from lamp posts, from telegraph poles and from thousands of two-foot lengths of wooden doweling that were standing in fire buckets at the 14th Street corner, ready to be distributed among the crowds and waved jubilantly at the punch lines in Secretary Stanton's speech.

As the old fellow stood there smiling reflectively, a newsboy ran onto the Square from 14th Street, brandishing a folded broadsheet and shouting: "Getcher latest *Freedom*, hot off the press!!" He snatched a copy of the paper off the top of the stack he was holding under his arm and shoved it into the old man's hands, just in time for the oldster to stuff it into his pocket before a big, sweaty bluecoat ran into the scene and the boy took off again across the Square, running like a scalded cat as the copper glared after him, blowing his whistle shrilly and shouting:

"You stop right there you little bastid, before I . . . !"

But before he could even finish the sentence, the boy had lost himself in the crowd of workmen and the copper, totally winded, took off his hat and wiped his face on his sleeve.

"Tch!" croaked the old man in a querulous tenor. "Young folks! I tell you, officer, kids just don't have any respect nowadays, it's a crying shame!"

"You can say that again, Grandad!" the copper said hoarsely. "He about gave me a heart attack, that lousy little spalpeen—I've been chasing him since Second Avenue! You just wait till old Stanton declares his Emergency Regs—the troublemakers will be singing a different tune then, believe you me!"

"Emergency Regs?" quavered the old codger.

"Yeah, it ain't official yet, but I already seen the handbills back at the Precinct. Those boys in that building across the way . . ." he gestured towards the DPS HQ, "are going to be some busy little bees, stringing up seditionists."

"Well, I never!" said the old fellow, tugging nervously at his bushy gray moustache. "Is Mr. Stanton himself going to be here today?"

"You bet, old-timer," the copper said with a proprietary grin. "You come back later this afternoon and bring a folding chair, get yourself set—by the time the speeches start around seven, they're expecting fifty thousand people will be right here in this square to hear Secretary Stanton and Director Pilkington."

"My, my, that *does* beat all!" the old man said wonderingly, just as the copper clapped his hat back on and shouted furiously:

"That dirty little son of a bitch!"

The workmen across the way had finished up and were dispersing towards home, revealing the newsboy jumping up and down in front of the DPS building, thumbing his nose towards the copper and shouting across the Square: "*Flat-foot! Flaaaat-foot!*"

"We'll see about that!," the bluecoat bellowed, and took off furiously towards the newsboy, who was obviously planning to taunt the law until the last possible second.

"Attaboy!" laughed Liam in his own voice, taking the folded broadsheet out of his pocket. *FREEDOM!* it announced in huge letters, and then in smaller ones, printed in a lurid red: "*Where Is Stanton Hiding President Lincoln?*"

"Nice work, Becky," Liam murmured.

As she had told him last night on the voicewire, Stanton had boarded up all the newspapers and magazines in the country the day after they printed Becky's Little Russia exposé, and this new broadsheet had stepped into the gap, printed in huge quantities on Shelter Island and distributed by the Underground Railroad. President Lincoln himself had suggested a publicity campaign to gradually expose the secret of Stanton's betrayal, the mind-boggling story of John Wilkes Booth's imposture, and Lincoln's thrilling rescue by the Freedom Party. By the time Becky had written the final installments, the American people would be clamoring to have the real Lincoln back, Acme or no, and Lincoln would have used the pages of *Freedom* to call for a fresh slate of Presidential and Congressional candidates and fair and free national elections. If that didn't put Stanton well and truly on the skids, Liam missed his bet. True, that happy culmination was going to be down the road a ways, but it was a good plan and comforting to think about. Meanwhile, there would be plenty to keep Liam and his friends busy . . .

Liam stepped into the alleyway behind the Pilkington Agency headquarters. It was a good thing he'd been over this ground before, in the week after he'd reported to Mr. P. Having seen McPherson go through the secret door in Pilkington's bookcase, Liam decided it might be useful to know how to do it himself, and late one night he'd cased the building's entrances thoroughly. At last he'd picked a likely-looking candidate in the alley that ran behind the building on the 16th Street side, a door almost obscured by trash cans that obligingly swung away from the wall when Liam finally figured out the trick of the thing.

You had to hand it to the old boy—he had clearly paid top dollar for the construction of his secret passage, and the street-door's mechanism and the interior finish of the passageway itself were as nicely fitted and finished as a Swiss music box. When Liam got to the top, though, he found himself wishing the builder had had a moment or two of sloppiness. He was standing outside what had to be the back side of the sliding bookcase entrance and he wanted to get a look inside before he entered, but unfortunately the surface of the door on this side was as smooth as an egg.

A dim electric bulb burned above the doorway and a very obvious green button in the middle of a brass plate waited at the side of the door for Liam to press it, but he didn't feel quite ready to accept its invitation. Slowly and with as much care as he would give to the dial of a safe, he ran his fingertips back and forth across the door's glassy surface, until at last he found an area that responded to his gentle urging by sliding to one side. Once the panel had moved, it revealed a narrow slit that would have been invisible from the other side, but that was quite wide enough on this side to give Liam a view from one end of the office to the other.

Nobody home, excellent! He pressed the green button and noted with satisfaction that the sliding section of bookcase moved on rubber wheels, so smoothly and silently that there was simply nothing to hear. Then, once he was inside, he only needed to go to Pilkington's desk, check the neat brass labels along one side of the kneehole and press the necessary button for the thing to close just as silently as it had opened.

Liam pulled out his watch: 8:15 a.m. In a way, he wished he had waited to leave until Becky was back from Shelter Island—he would have enjoyed watching her reunion with her father, who had been sprung from house arrest by the boys last night. Liam looked out the window towards the DPS offices across the street, the giant gold letters spelling *"Per Aspere ad Securitas"* glittering in the early sunlight. Good old underground New York, the network of tunnels reached nicely up Manhattan to the Foxes' house in Gramercy Park, all you needed was the Butcher Boys' handy-dandy map to make it easy.

Anyway, he thought as he started a slow walk around the office prospecting for likely wall-safe locations, he had been too keyed up to hang around home waiting. First he had wanted to check the big job he and Mike had put the boys on after they brought Becky's pa safely downtown, and that had taken a while since it involved some sensitive calculations and a fair amount of friendly chit-chat with the lads as they had all been through a thing or two since Liam had left town with Becky a few days ago.

Then, after he was sure that everything was going smoothly and according to schedule, he gave in to the knowledge that his stomach was trying to digest itself and stopped at a greasy spoon he knew near the Pilkington Agency for a heaping plate of eggs and corned beef hash. After chasing that with a couple of cups of eye-popping Turkish coffee, he was ready for anything, and now . . .

. . . *Here we go*, he thought, and carefully lifted a daguerrotype of Mr. Pilkington standing on a field with President Lincoln down from the wall, revealing the dial of an aged but solid National safe. With a smile of recognition for an old acquaintance, he took out his stethoscope and started letting the dial's mechanisms speak to him. OK, *there* . . . one of the tumblers gave a tiny click, and Liam was just settling himself to search for the next one when he heard a more imperative sound behind him—someone was turning the handle of the door. Not even bothering to put the picture back, Liam leapt across the room to the stretch of wall next to the door's hinges and pulled out his Colt.

"What the divvil?" It was McPherson, and he'd frozen with surprise as he saw the safe uncovered, letting the door to the office swing slowly shut behind him. After a moment, he shook his head angrily and started towards the safe.

"Don't bother," Liam said, and this time McPherson swung around in a half-crouch, reaching towards the inside of his jacket as Liam cocked the Peacemaker. The unmistakable sound froze the Great Detective in his tracks.

"That's better," Liam said, grabbing a straight-backed chair away from a reading table and pushing it across the floor towards McPherson. "Have a seat," Liam said. McPherson obeyed grudgingly, eyeing Liam with a barely suppressed fury that turned his face red as a beet.

"Well, well," McPherson said, his voice dripping sarcasm, "sure if it isn't young Lochinvar home from the wars, all dressed up for Halloween and his thoughts turning to larceny like any young cracksman's would. Can I help you find what you're looking for, *Mister* McCool?"

"I reckon I can find it myself," Liam said. His voice had an odd edge of hoarseness to it, and he realized that he was having to fight hard against pulling the trigger, thinking about Maggie lying dead on the floor of her sitting room. "Unless maybe you moved all of Mr. P.'s papers once you'd stabbed him in the back and sold him out to Junior."

McPherson's eyes narrowed and he showed a thin line of teeth, as if he were wrestling with the urge to leap out of the chair and tear out Liam's throat. "Not that I'd ever be needing to explain meself to scum like you," he grated, "but it took Junior to see the obvious, that I was the man to head the Agency and not his old pa, so Junior took the matter up with Secretary Stanton, and he agreed that an outfit like this needed a go-ahead young fella at the helm if it was to be working hand in glove with the Secret Service."

"I carried the word to Pilkington meself, and the poor old ninny actually broke down and cried." McPherson sneered as he savored the memory: "Frankly, Mr. P. had got a bit too long in the tooth to see the obvious, whether it was the need for him to go home and write his memoirs or the fact that we needed to get all our young white men back into uniform and all the black bucks behind the machines in the factories. This is a *new* America you're trying to stand in the way of, laddie-bhoy, and if you don't get out of the way it's going to run right over you and mash you flat."

Liam shook his head wryly. "I hope you'll be as ready to run at the mouth when I find Inspector Barlow and tell him the solution to the murder of Maggie O'Shea." He smiled a little as he saw McPherson start. "That's right, McPherson, I have all the facts I need now, and as nice as it would be to shoot a hole in you, it will be a lot better fun to get a seat in the audience when they stretch your neck. Now, if you'll pull that chair around where I can keep an eye on you, I was just about to open that safe and get the stuff Mr. P. was holding over my head. After that, you can go to blazes till Barlow shows up with the coppers!"

His mouth set in a thin angry line, McPherson pushed himself and the chair towards the wall.

"That's just fine, Seamus," Liam said. "And back up a little, so I have plenty of room to shoot you in case you decide to jump out of your chair."

McPherson obeyed sullenly, eyeing Liam with a combination of suppressed anger and spiteful expectation that bothered Liam a little until he decided he hadn't time to worry about the Great Detective's state of mind—the clock was running down now, and he wanted to be well away before things got too busy. Keeping half an eye on McPherson and most of his attention on the whisper of machinery behind the safe's green-painted face, Liam heard one tumbler after another fall into place until at last there was a final, telling click.

"There we are," he said cheerfully. "Well, then, Agent McPherson, I hope you'll use your time well until the law comes for you. Start on your memoirs, it'll be a good six months before they get around to hanging you."

McPherson's only answer was a sneer, so Liam shrugged and reached for the chromed handle on the safe door, pulling it down and back to swing open, but no sooner had the door begun its movement towards Liam than he was struck by a jolt of electricity so powerful that he felt like he'd been hit by a piledriver, the galvanic jerk of his muscles flinging him backwards into the room a good six feet and stretching him out flat on the floor. His mouth had a horrible coppery, burned taste in it, and his face and fingers felt numb and dead. To add to his misery, McPherson got up and walked across to him, bending over him and grinning with venomous triumph:

"Surprised you, did we? That's a little toy Secretary Tesla made up for us, you'll be paralyzed for a few minutes, just long enough for people to come when the alarm sounds."

As if to confirm what he said, there was a knock at the office door and a moment later the door opened and Liam heard a secretary speaking:

"Is there any trouble, sir? Would you like me to summon help?"

"No thank you, Miss Willoughby," McPherson said with an unmistakably gloating tone, "I have this situation *absolutely* under control. You can turn the alarm off and notify the guards there's nothing to worry about. In fact, you can make sure I'm not disturbed for the rest of the morning, is that clear?"

"Yes sir," the secretary said, "I'll take care of it."

Liam heard the door close as McPherson walked back into his field of vision and grinned down at him. "Sure, Liam dear, I'm that fond of you I wouldn't want a soul to be interfering with our little get-together. I expect I should have told you about the shock gadget, but then we both know I'm just a naughty boy, am I right? All you have to do is reach over here on the right of the safe, you see, push up this little panel next to it and snap down that switch, and it's just as harmless as Little Miss Muffet."

Liam followed McPherson with his eyes as he swung the safe door all the way open and came out with two packets.

"I expect these are what you'd have been wanting to look at, Liam me lad. This first one has all your papers, just like Mr. P. told you. And a note he put on there saying 'Return to McCool after completion of Little Russia mission.' Truly now, could you be wanting better proof that poor old Mr. P. was ready to be put out to pasture? You don't give up a hold like that when you've got it on a useful operator. As for this other little beauty . . ."

McPherson waved the second packet at Liam and laughed out loud. "This one you'd have given your eyeteeth for, and so would Junior Pilkington if he only knew I had it, for it's none other than our darling Maggie's diary."

Liam writhed against the force of the paralysis and groaned with pure anger and frustration, but even though he could feel a tingle of sensation returning here and there, he still couldn't do more than twitch. McPherson laughed again, delighted at Liam's misery.

"Here's the thing, Liam dear. There's a long steamy story in here of Maggie's romance with Junior himself. Yes, *Junior*, complete with letters from himself and all sorts of other touching mementoes including the birth certificate of baby Mary Agnes, who was none other than Junior's love child with our Maggie. He begged her, oh how he begged, to take her 'difficulty' to a doctor he knew and trusted, who would have made it go away for good.

But you remember our stubborn Maggie, she'd have none of it. First thing you know, there was the little tyke in

Bellevue with Mama, and her ready to take her daughter home, when *ohmydeargoodness!* The little darling *disappeared!* Can you believe that? You should, for Junior wasn't inclined to become a papa and he had ample means to make his problem go away. Which it did, I discovered a while back, with the help of an agent of the DPS named Kelso who drowned the tyke in the Hudson in a burlap bag, just like a bothersome kitten. You can see why I look on that little packet as my insurance policy against all sorts of hard times, can't you?"

Laughing a thoroughly self-satisfied laugh, McPherson laid the two packets on the floor and took a pistol out of a holster in the small of his back.

"Now I think we'll have to take you across the Square to the DPS building, Liam me lad," he said with mock sigh, "much as it pains me to part with you. You'll be happy to know they've just finished renovating the holding and interrogation rooms in the cellars," he said with a chuckle, "and the very *best* part is that Junior got Secretary Stanton to request some special personnel from the Central Prison in Madrid. He'd read an article, you see—always reading, is our Junior—and it seems these fellas are carrying on a grand family tradition from their ancestors back in the bad old times. You know, those folks who winkled out the secret sinners and toasted them on the bonfires. This is supposed to be their first day on the job with us, and that should be a treat! In fact I think I'll have to come along and see how they do their questioning, it's said to be quite noisy and colorful. Does that meet with your approval, *Mister* McCool?"

He knelt down next to Liam and prodded him with the pistol, and this time Liam actually managed to get one arm up off the floor and growled so furiously that McPherson nearly collapsed with laughter.

"Ah, Liam, you're rare sport you are! Still, I guess we'd better get started, I'd say by the looks of it we'll have you moving around by the time the elevator gets you to the lobby. Now then, any last words?"

"Yes," came Becky's voice from behind him, cold as ice, "drop the gun now!"

McPherson began to turn, but Becky snapped: "I said *now*! I'm a fine shot and I'll drop *you* if you don't drop the gun."

McPherson blew out an enormous, angry sigh and set his pistol carefully on the floor. Before he could straighten up all the way, Becky hit him as hard as she could with the butt of Maggie's pistol and he keeled over with a little groan, out cold.

"Honestly," said Becky to Liam with more than a little asperity. "You *could* have waited for me, you know." She cocked her head thoughtfully for a moment and then she added, "Of course, we might have needed somebody to rescue *us*, so I suppose it's all worked out for the best." She grinned mischievously: "And I *did* get to hear the story of Maggie's diary, which sounds to me like a really sensational series for *Freedom*—we should be able to make Willie even more widely hated and despised than he is now!

She was wearing her working clothes, with a cap pulled down over her hair, and carrying a small valise into which she dumped the packets McPherson had just set on the floor, along with his pistol. Then she bent forward and kissed Liam thoroughly on the lips. Finally he succeeded in raising his other arm and pulled her down closer for a second installment. Then he started to stand up and fell over again so that Becky had to help him to his feet.

"Time!" he croaked. "The time!"

Becky pulled out her little lavalier watch and had a look at it. "Oh my goodness," she exclaimed, and pulling Liam's right arm over her shoulder she helped him cross to the window, where they stood and stared across the Square at the DPS building.

"You know about it?" he croaked in a surprised tone.

"Of course I know," she said, "I had breakfast with Papa and Mike and your grandma, and then the boys after they got back from setting things up. They told me all about about it, plus how to find the passageway into Pilkington's office, where Mike said I'd be sure to find you. By the way, the boys said you had been *way* too tough on them, so I told them you had studied the art with the Mollies and they were hard taskmasters."

Liam grinned delightedly and held up a finger. "Now!" he said. And sure enough there was a sort of premonitory tremor under their feet, then a frenzied shake as the DPS building suddenly developed a network of cracks across its facade, expelled innumerable puffs of smoke from its multitude of windows as the panes shattered, and then slowly, in an indescribably stately yet decrepit collapse, like an ancient elephant breathing its last breath, crumpled in upon itself with a vast roar of falling masonry and a cloud of smoke through which Stanton's motto glittered, askew: *"Per Aspere ad Secu-..."*

Liam pulled Becky close and gave her a thorough kiss.

"Happy Fourth of July, Miss Fox," he said.

She returned the kiss with interest and then pulled away a bit to reply:

"Happy Fourth of July, Mr. McCool."

One last satisfied look at the view from the office window, then Becky grabbed her bag and trotted back towards the secret passage. Liam took a quick look around and then waved to the gently snoring McPherson.

"Give our best to Junior," he said with a grin, and a moment later the bookshelf whispered shut behind Becky and Liam as they held hands and headed down the passage stairs towards home.